NOTHING
To lose

SCARLETT FINN

ISBN: 9781914517013

www.scarlettfinn.com

Also by Scarlett Finn

ROMANTIC SUSPENSE

GO NOVELS
GO WITH IT
GO IT ALONE
GO ALL OUT
GO ALL IN
GO FULL CIRCLE

TO DIE FOR...
TO DIE FOR TRUTH
TO DIE FOR HONOR
TO DIE FOR VIRTUE
TO DIE FOR DUTY
TO DIE FOR LOVE

KINDRED SERIES
RAVEN
SWALLOW
CUCKOO
SWIFT
FALCON
FINCH

MCDADE BROTHERS NOVELS
ALL. ONLY.
ONLY YOURS

THE EXPLICIT SERIES
EXPLICIT INSTRUCTION
EXPLICIT DETAIL
EXPLICIT MEMORY

WRECK & RUIN
RUIN ME
RUIN HIM

LOVE AGAINST THE ODDS STANDALONE COLLECTION
SWEET SEAS
HEIR'S AFFAIR
RESCUED
MAESTRO'S MUSE
GETTING TRICKY
THIRTEEN
REMEMBER WHEN...
RELUCTANT SUSPICION
XY FACTOR

HARROW DUET
FIGHTING FATE
FIGHTING BACK

THE BRANDED SERIES
BRANDED
SCARRED
MARKED

RISQUÉ SERIES
TAKE A RISK
RISK IT ALL
GAME OF RISK

EXILE
HIDE & SEEK
KISS CHASE

MISTAKE DUET
MISTAKE ME NOT
SLEIGHT MISTAKE

CONTEMPORARY ROMANCE

NOTHING TO...
NOTHING TO HIDE
NOTHING TO LOSE
NOTHING TO DECLARE
NOTHING TO US

LOST & FOUND
LOST
FOUND

ONE

THE SLEEK BLACK CAR stopped at the curb. Her address. Yep, it still existed. Roxie Kyst was officially home. Should there be a woo-hoo? It didn't feel like it.

The real world. Going strong. Good for it. Life went on regardless of her absence… why shouldn't it?

The driver opened her door to help her get out. Waiting for assistance had become habit… Wow, when had she forgotten how to open a car door? How had she become indifferent to it all? Questions would drive her insane. Time to get over the vacation and focus on home.

The building was the same, except… she didn't recognize it. Familiarity didn't visit. Joy, misery, excitement, indifference, none of those were right either. What did she feel? Numb, maybe… Like a stranger. A stranger in her own life.

After spending over three months with Zairn Lomond, touring the global Crimson nightclub network, adjusting to her old life would take time. Zairn's generosity had afforded her many incredible experiences in different countries. With him, life had been rich with people, vibrant, varied. Same old, same old would be a change of pace.

"Miss Kyst?"

The man at her side gestured toward the stoop. Another guy stood near the trunk of the Mercedes. The guy next to her was the driver, wasn't he? So who the hell was the guy at the trunk? Chauffeurs didn't work in pairs, not for a quick trip from the airport.

"I can get my own luggage," she said when guy number two popped the trunk.

"Please, Miss Kyst," the man next to her said, blocking her way. "You'll be safer inside."

Ding! Ding! His tone set off an alarm in her head.

"Oh my God," she groaned, her muscles loosening. "You're security."

"Yes, ma'am."

Well, if that wasn't just perfect. "Asshole," she muttered. The guy's startled reaction wrung a sigh from her. "Not you. What's your name?"

"Trevor," he said, just as a chunky black Escalade pulled up.

Three guys got out and headed toward guy number two at the trunk.

"Damnit," she muttered. "Who are those guys?"

Trevor glanced back. "Your team."

"Oh my God." Roxie marched over to the trunk to snatch out her purse. "Any of you get in my way, I'm not beyond calling the papers to ruin the reputation of the guy signing your paychecks."

Not that the guy who signed their paychecks had the most pristine of reputations to protect.

Don't stress about it. Take a breath and carry on.

On her walk toward the stairs, someone leaped into her path.

"Roxie! Roxie!"

Pausing, she recoiled. "Why the hell are you shouting? I'm standing right here." Short, a little smarmy, keen. Yep. This guy was familiar, and not because they'd met before. With experience, his type was easy to spot. "Got your notebook?" He held up his phone, ready and eager to type in her words. She cleared her throat and leaned in. "No comment." The guy's smile fell, which formed hers. "Get a real job."

Walking into her building had never been so eventful. She climbed the exterior stairs, digging around in her purse for the keys. When was the last time she'd unlocked a door? Stupid overstuffed, unorganized purse. Unfortunately, Zairn's diamond security pass around her neck didn't work on ye-olde-fashioned key locks. He'd spoiled her.

After turning the key and casting Trevor into the role of doorstop, she ascended the stairs. The guys would bring her luggage. Her friends were upstairs. Normality. Sanity.

If someone was home, the apartment should be unlocked... Were they home? Yes! Thank God that hadn't changed; no key required. Inside, a big "welcome back" banner hung between the windows on the far wall. Her friends, wearing party hats and blowing noisemakers, leaped from the couch to run over.

There it was. Home. Her girls were her home.

Two seconds over the threshold and already there were tears in her eyes. "You guys..." she said, dropping her purse to pull both of them into a hug. "I missed you so much."

Moisture rolled from her lashes. Her girls. Home. They were her lifeline. Her beacon of hope. Her stability. Everything would be alright again; her girls were all she needed.

"Oh no," Jane said when Roxie finally freed them. "You're crying! Why are you crying?"

Jane was quick to hug her again.

"I'd cry too if I was forced to leave Zairn Lomond in California," Toria said. "If I was forced to leave him anywhere."

Waking up with him in LA felt more like a mirage than reality. Roxie hadn't left him in the Golden State. She'd left him on his plane, in his bedroom... a million miles and a million minutes away. Maybe that was a hallucination too.

"I'm happy to see you both," Roxie said, kissing Jane and then Toria. "They're happy tears."

Her roommates helped swipe them away.

A knock at the door interrupted the trio.

"Damnit," Roxie muttered, wiping her cheeks one last time before opening the slightly ajar front door. As expected, Trevor and two of his associates stood with her luggage. "Down there…" She stepped back to point at the hallway leading off the living room. The bedrooms, bathroom, and laundry were located that way. "Last door on the right."

Moving aside, she let the men go in the indicated direction.

"Wow," Toria said. "You have a staff."

"They are not *my* staff," Roxie said. "Zairn has his panties in a bunch over this Gambatto thing. Speaking of, do you know where Porter's staying?"

"The city put him up at a hotel," Toria said. "The Grand, I think, which is funny because that's where Crimson sent us."

Roxie cringed. "I'm sorry about that. It was pure insanity."

"I didn't mind," Jane said. "It was nice not to have chores for a while."

Yeah, right. She wasn't buying it. Jane lived for chores.

"Girl, please, you brought gloves and your homemade cleaning spray. That room's never been so germ-free."

Sounded more like it. "Hey, that makes me happy. I'm glad everything's the way I left it. Everyone's just the same," Roxie said, putting an arm around each of her friends. "We're back to our same old, normal boring life."

"No! No way," Toria said, dragging her across the room. "We want every single detail. You've been jetting all over the world with like the hottest guy on the planet. We want to know everything about him."

The security guys reappeared and loitered at the mouth of the hallway as Roxie and her roommates settled themselves on the couch.

"I know you're not waiting for a tip," Roxie said. "One of you can stand outside the door. That's it."

Two of them headed that way.

Trevor came over, fishing something from his

pocket. He held up a metal cylinder on a short chain. "Mr. Lomond requires you to carry—"

"What the hell is that?" Roxie asked.

"A panic button."

She rolled her eyes upward. "Oh, for the love of…" Rising just enough to reach over, she opened her hand. "Give it to me. Just…" She snatched it to toss it onto the coffee table. Before he could say a word, she spoke. "There's a reason he didn't give it to me himself." Trevor frowned. "It wasn't because he trusted your ability to appease me. It was because he didn't want the earache." She tilted her head to the side. "Do you want the earache, Trevor? Do you?"

"No, ma'am."

She shooed him with a wave.

Something occurred to her before he got to the door. "Trevor?"

"Miss Kyst?"

Her eyes narrowed on the panic button. "Mr. Lomond didn't request I carry that. Sean Ballard did…" When there was no answer, she twisted to look at Trevor over the back of the couch. "You can tell him I was super accommodating. He'll never believe you, but you can tell him."

He nodded and left, closing the door at his back.

"Oh my God," Toria said, both she and Jane drawing in closer. "You know Sean Ballard!"

"I know him," Roxie said, wriggling out from between her friends to go around the couch and into the kitchen by the front door. "Do we have wine, tequila, anything alcoholic?"

White wine in the fridge. Score! A little liquid libation suited her mood. She grabbed the bottle and another of red from the counter. Couldn't have too much on hand. Re-entry was unsettling.

"Do you want to go out tonight?" Toria asked. "We thought we could hit the bars."

Jane laughed. "Maybe after being a VIP at Crimson, our usual haunts are beneath her."

It was good-hearted; Jane was just playing. Roxie

mustered a smile as she put the bottles on the coffee table and headed back to the kitchen.

"We can go out if you want," she said, grabbing glasses and a corkscrew. "Not sure what my new henchmen will think of that. And there's a reporter outside."

"Yeah, it was him who told us you were on your way home," Jane said. "How do they know stuff like that?"

Roxie put down the glasses and kneeled on the floor at the coffee table opposite her girls on the couch. "It's amazing the things they find out," she said, twisting the corkscrew into the bottle of red. "They pay for it... or blackmail for it... Or they wait until you're stupid enough to leave your computer streaming for the entire planet to see."

"Were you just mortified?" Jane asked.

"I didn't even know about it until nine days later. Z didn't let anyone in to see me. Idiot me didn't think much about it when I was sick. He and the doctor were the only two people I saw, no one else. Astrid would've told me, that girl can't keep a secret for anything..." She thought about their conversation forever ago on the plane. "Well, she can keep a secret, just not something like that."

"Z?" Toria said, drawing it out in a tease. "You call him Z?"

"I've called him worse," Roxie said, pouring wine for Toria, then pushing it toward her. "So have a lot of other people."

"Tell us what he's like," Jane said.

Her focus stayed on opening the white wine. "I've been away from home for three months! My days have been splashed across screens all over the world. You know what I've been doing. What's been going on here? Catch me up."

"There is like nothing fun going on here," Toria said. "I started sleeping with Simon again."

"Oh, hey, he was cool."

"Well, yeah, then I went into hiding and had to stop calling."

Roxie winced. "Oops. Sorry."

"It's okay," Toria said, scooping up her glass and sinking against the back of the couch. "I wasn't that into him.

But…" She shook a finger at Jane. "But she… she's been messing with London Guy."

"I have to message Graham for work," Jane said, accepting the wine from Roxie when she rose high on her knees to hand it over the table.

"Is he the one you had webcam sex with?" Roxie asked. "If that's being professional these days, I'm definitely re-entering the workplace as soon as possible."

Toria burst out laughing as Jane blustered and blushed. Roxie had missed her girls. Being home was a comfort. Everything was as it always had been… wasn't it?

TWO

"WE'D UNDERSTAND IF YOU needed rest," Jane said. "You've been out every night for months."

"Not every night," Roxie said, descending their building's internal stairs, holding both of her girls' hands.

"She wouldn't know what to do with herself if she wasn't out partying," Toria said. "It's only right that we get to paint the town crimson too. You see what I did there?"

Roxie smiled at her friend. "Clever."

The security guy in front of them opened the communal door to check outside and gestured it was safe. Good job, guy. She didn't miss a step and wouldn't have waited regardless, but he didn't know that.

Two other agents closed in behind them as the trio of women exited. On the top stair, she stopped, forcing her girls to do the same.

Why was…?

The reporter from earlier was on the sidewalk with a few more of his kind. Hmm. There was a gaggle of women there as well, groupies, crowded together, wearing Casanova-4-Lola tee-shirts. She smiled. They reminded her of the Experience winners.

The people hadn't taken her momentum. No. The Mercedes at the curb had done that. The driver got out and went around to open the back door.

Why was it still there? She didn't need a staff. Why was no one getting this message?

The reporters shouted. "Roxie! Rox!"

The groupies were quick to follow suit and called out to her too.

When she started down the stairs, they all rushed in. Security was quick to hold them back. Reporters, fine, block their way, but the groupies were a different matter. She smiled and gestured them around the end of the goon.

"Hey," she said. "It's freezing out tonight. You'll catch cold."

"We love you, Rox."

"Yeah, you completely rock!"

"Zairn too."

"Thank you," she said. "We both appreciate it."

"Will you sign our shirts?"

"Oh, uh…" One woman thrust a Sharpie into Roxie's hand. Jane took her purse, deciding for her. Guess autographs were on. "Sure." After removing the lid with her teeth, she started signing shoulders. "Want me to sign Z's name too?" she asked, the lid still in her teeth. "I can totally forge it."

The women laughed. "You're amazing together."

"We're not together," Roxie said, wiping off the lid before putting it back on the pen.

A reporter jumped closer. "Is that an official quote, Miss Kyst?"

"You can kiss my ass," she snapped at the reporter trying to dodge security. "That's your quote."

"Oh-kay, and we're done with the meet and greet," Toria said, opening her arms to herd Roxie into the car. As the vehicle pulled away, her friends' attention zeroed in on her. "Snappy day?"

Roxie exhaled. "I know, I'm sorry," she said, sinking back, catching her hair between her fingers. "They can just… they ride him so hard and…"

"I would too if given the chance," Toria said, nudging

her. Trust her glorious friend to joke at exactly the right moment. She'd missed her girls so much. "How long do we get to keep the car?"

"No idea," Roxie said. "I didn't know about it."

"It's amazing," Jane said, stroking the door. "You lived like this for three months?"

Toria laughed. "The private jets and five-star living were probably better than the cars. Bet this kinda thing is no big deal."

"It's a big deal," Roxie said. Being honest, she took the vehicles for granted. The jets, the suites, they were flashy. The cars conveyed them from one place to another. All of them were brand new and often full of gadgets. Still, it became second nature to expect a waiting ride. "I'll call Astrid about it later."

"No!" Toria objected. "We like it. We want a piece of the lifestyle too."

"It's incredible. Living like this…" Jane said in wonder. "What was your favorite part?"

Both women leaned in. "My favorite part…" of the trip? The sex. No, that came second to the spark of excitement when he teased her. But that wasn't what they meant. "I liked the view."

"Mmm hmm," Toria said in agreement, reminding her of Zairn. "I'd stare at him all day long."

"Oh," Jane said, grabbing her hand. "Do you have pictures?"

"Excellent question," Toria said, shifting to get a better look at her. "Anything shirtless… or, you know… pantless?"

Restraining her laugh wasn't easy. "He rarely went wandering around the suite naked… There were too many damn people in there all the time."

Not all the time. In the day, yes, people popped in and out. The evening could be busy too, depending on business and documentary needs. But after hours… after the club… after the drive home in the dark, when their hands and mouths wandered…

Getting away with what they had was crazy. Sure, it

was only eleven days, but, wow, screwing in the back of his car…? The privacy screen was always up. Ha-ha, like that mattered. It wasn't soundproof. Keeping it quiet hadn't been at the forefront of her mind during certain climactic moments.

Their favorite bar was just a couple of blocks from their apartment. The Mercedes pulled up outside it.

"I love that they know everything about you," Toria said.

Huh… How did they know? Her friends thought the Crimson people knew. Obviously, they did. But how? Had she mentioned it…? To anyone other than Zairn.

Trevor and his buddies appeared in the side window before the driver. Half a step behind, security flanked him as he opened the door. Nuts. Crazy. Wasn't this supposed to be her past, not her present?

The three women got out. Security stayed close as they entered the bar. Busy. But not crazy. The corner between the bar and the front window was their favorite spot. The tall stools around the circular tables allowed them to monitor the bar's comings and goings.

They were settling at the table when a server tried to approach. Trevor got in her way.

"Geez, man," Roxie called over the background music. "Let the woman do her job." For a second, he hesitated. Idiot. If the server couldn't bring drinks, she'd have to go to the bar where there were many more people. "I don't think she was hanging here just waiting to kill me."

The overwhelming logic apparently convinced him because he stepped aside.

"What can I get you?" the blonde asked.

Drawing in a breath, Toria began their regular order. "Lime-drop—"

"Gin and Cin with a twist, or Gin and It, whatever you call it. They're both the same," Roxie said, wincing at her friend's blinking surprise. "Stupid habit I picked up in Italy."

Her bemused friend quickly switched into a laugh. "Look at you all exotic." They finished their order, and the server left. "Okay, so tell us…" Toria supported her chin with the heel of her hand. "We want the juice now, all the dirt."

"What do you mean?"

Like she didn't know.

"Did you fuck him?"

"No!" Jane exclaimed before Roxie could even inhale. "No! We don't want her to answer that."

"Why not?" Toria asked, laughing. "Because if he's been inside any part of her, he's off-limits for us? Good point, kills the fantasy."

"No," Jane droned at their witty friend. "It's not romantic. She can't kiss and tell."

"It's in the past," Roxie said, wishing the alcohol would hurry. "Done and forgotten."

"I want to know! I want details. We always share details."

"Roxie?" That question attracted their attention around. A short woman stood just at her back. "Are you Roxie? Lomond's Delight?"

Another passing woman paused to look at her twice. "Oh my God! Yeah, you're that woman from the news… Roger, get over here."

"We're just trying to have—"

"Hey!" Trevor said, stomping up to put himself between her and the women. "Back off."

"Trevor," Roxie said, laying a hand on his arm.

As she did, it became clear the two women weren't the only ones to have noticed her. A guy, she guessed Roger, was on his way over with a half dozen others. Around the bar, people glanced their way. Whispering. Gawping.

"Shit," she murmured.

In her time with Crimson, Zairn made the rules. Sometimes she complained, but he'd kept her in the VIP zones. Protected. Another thing she'd taken for granted.

People moved on from glancing and got to moving. Some pulled out cellphones and aimed them her way, others left their seats.

"Miss Kyst," Trevor said over his shoulder, still facing the bar.

"I see it," she said, hopping off the stool. "I'm going to get out of here."

"What?" Jane asked. "We just got here."

She had an eye for it. *Now* she did. Zairn had a sixth sense with women, apparently, and was practiced enough to anticipate situations like these. She hadn't given him enough credit on that score, in jest more than reality. Zairn was incredibly smart.

Watching the crowd move closer, hearing her name on so many lips… Her own limited experience was enough to recognize the calamity careening toward them.

"Miss Kyst," Trevor said again with more warning.

"I'll send the car back for you," she said, taking her purse from the table and kissing both of her friends. "Have fun. I won't wait up."

When Trevor and his guys surrounded her, some confidence returned. For bitching about what Zairn insisted on, in that moment, she was supremely grateful. Strangers with alcohol in them, spirits running high, anything could happen.

It would die down. The interest. Eventually. Soon. Society would forget about the gossip of her association with Zairn Lomond, long before she forgot her time with him.

Being bundled out of the bar and into the car, all she could think about was him. It wasn't the same without him. Without Crimson.

Exhaling, she closed her eyes and let her head drop against the backrest. If there were pictures, he'd see them… if he cared to look. She smiled. He'd have his validation. They both knew it. Yes, he'd been right: security was a good call. Thank goodness he wasn't close by to torment her about that.

Although… naughty thoughts dialed her smile to saucy… It wouldn't be such a bad thing to be teased by him… again. That part of her life might be over, but she could still fantasize. Nothing wrong with that. Harmless.

Like she'd once told Astrid, people all over the world dreamed of Zairn Lomond. Having some real-life memories to call on put her in prime position to wake her senses. Him above her… inside her. With mental images like those, maybe it wasn't such a bad thing to have the apartment to herself for a while.

THREE

THE EASIEST WAY to find her ex was to visit his workplace. Sometimes his being a workaholic paid dividends. Not when she wanted to go places while they were together, no; but tracking him down was always easy.

His high-profile case kept him busy. While she'd love to distract him from the trial-that-could-get-him-killed, talking on the phone hadn't gotten her anywhere. Face-to-face was next on the list, so she texted him to arrange dinner, giving him no option to refuse.

The throng of reporters outside her building had increased overnight. Not all of them were official reporters. Some were citizens with blogs. Others, influencers.

The real surprise was the number of fans congregating. People who'd watched her streams. The determined autograph hunters mentioned Zairn as often as possible. Coming up with non-answer answers grew difficult. In the end, it was easier to depart with apologies. Thank God she had a date. Not a date, date, but somewhere to be.

Despite the delays, Roxie was on time and waiting on the sidewalk when Porter finally emerged from the side exit he always used. Arms folded, her brow crooked, Roxie wasn't in the mood to give him a break.

"Hey! You look good, RoRo," Porter said, putting a hand on her arm as he bowed to kiss the corner of her mouth.

"You really have the balls to smile at me?"

"I can tell you haven't had a drink yet." Porter pulled her into a hug. "I've missed you."

"I'm surprised you noticed I wasn't around," Roxie said, just looking at his hand when he offered it. "Do you think I want to socialize with a hitman's target?"

He opened his arms. "I'm fine. Do I look worried?"

Unfortunately, he was smiling, which increased her concern. "You're a complacent idiot."

Porter glanced at the car a few feet away and the goons loitering nearby. "These yours?"

"We can walk," she said. "They'll keep up. Don't change the subject."

"What was the subject?"

"You being a complacent idiot."

"We know it was Joey," Porter said, putting an arm around her to guide her along the street. "We've got him. We know it."

"Won't make much difference if you're dead."

"You tried that line already," Porter said. "This is a make or break case for my career."

"Yeah, and why the hell are you thinking about running for office? You're planning to steal Tim's job? He's always been good to us."

"I have great respect for SA Tim Unst."

"You're thirty-five. That's practically a teenager in SA terms."

"Yeah, I'm a kid," he scoffed.

"You are. Why would you—"

"The idea of congress has been floated."

"Jesus, Porter." She stopped to look at him, amazed he was the same man who'd shared her bed. "Since when do you care about politics?"

"It's something I always thought about, you know, in the back of my mind," he said, taking her hand when they started walking again. "I didn't think it would be a possibility, not for another few years. This case has accelerated plans, that's all."

"Then you didn't think through dating me," she said. "Do you think I could be a congressman's wife? I don't like kissing babies… Okay, well, kissing them is fine, but it's a downer listening to everyone's problems all day long, cutting ribbons, giving speeches, yawn."

"Wasn't the reason we broke up that you didn't want to be anyone's wife?"

She inhaled, ready to object, but his point was valid. "I could be a mistress. I'd be an excellent mistress."

"I'll call you if I get voted in… Though your recent notoriety would be helpful, you know, in a campaign… if we were together."

"*If* we were together," she said, emphasizing the first word, "there's no way my flying around the world touring nightclubs would be a plus for any political campaign."

"I've heard a lot about Lomond. That he has connections in Washington."

The way Porter let that hang implied he expected a response. Roxie waited a few extra beats before speaking. "He never mentioned anyone to me."

"Did you part on good terms? The video suggested you were friendly."

As people loved to speculate about out loud. "I'm moving forward with my life, Porter. Onward and upward."

"He's influential. He could sponsor an event, invite his contacts to—"

"The closest Crimson is in Manhattan. Why would a New Yorker care about Chicago politics?"

"He must know people in Chicago."

"Why are we talking about him?" she asked. "You're deflecting. I came down to find out when you're giving up the Gambatto thing. Because until you do, I'm stuck with my shadows."

She nodded backward to Trevor and his colleague tailing them.

Porter glanced back. "I won't give it up," he said. "I'm going to talk you through it. When you hear about the relationship Gambatto had with the victim, how he treated her, you'll be behind me. I guarantee it."

"I thought you were taking me out for dinner."

"We're going back to the hotel."

She groaned. "If we were going to eat in somewhere, you could've come over to mine. I'm hungry. I want to eat."

"We'll order room service. Toria and Jane don't know how to butt out when you're entertaining."

"It's their apartment too," she said. "They're social. Sue them."

"They don't give you privacy. Anyway, your luggage will drive me crazy."

"My luggage?" she asked.

He glanced her way. "You got in yesterday and haven't unpacked yet."

"How do you know?"

He smiled at her. "Have you?" Roxie didn't respond. "I know you, RoRo."

"Okay, you're so clever. Maybe law wasn't your calling, you should be a detective."

He laughed. "You're my specialist subject. I take comfort in your predictability… Have you got your phone?"

"The battery's dead…" Roxie's words trailed off. "Fine, okay, I'm predictable. Let's get inside and be predictable there. I want food."

Porter could try to convince her, but Roxie wasn't ready to change her mind. Gambatto was dangerous. Details of his violence wouldn't better her opinion of him. Porter could talk all night. It wouldn't erase the trouble looming on the horizon.

FOUR

"WHERE HAVE YOU BEEN?" Jane screeched the moment Roxie walked into their apartment.

"Dinner with Porter. I told you I was—"

"We were calling and calling," Toria said from the couch.

Jane hurried over and put an arm around her to rush her across the room.

"My phone died," Roxie said. "What's going…?"

The television. Talk at Sunset. The audience going wild. Oh, this was familiar. Zairn. Damn, he appeared through the curtain hot as ever. Some things would never change. The man was delicious. Even after a day of business, a night at the club, and screwing her a couple of times, he always managed to remain deliciously hot. Oh so hot.

He raised a hand in greeting, sending the rapture of those present through the roof. Drew Harvey went to meet him. The two men shook hands and exchanged a few quiet words on their walk to the couch.

With much less decorum, Jane pushed her onto the middle seat of *their* couch and sat down next to her. Toria waved the end of a phone charger in her face. Without taking her attention from the screen, Roxie dumped her purse and connected the phone to the charger.

"Zairn! Zairn!" Drew Harvey called over the audience, though that only got them cheering louder.

The host laughed. Zairn, by contrast, sat there wearing the smoldering smug expression that betrayed his confidence. He was getting exactly the reaction he expected; exactly the one he adored.

"Asshole," she whispered, pulling her feet onto the couch to fold her legs in front of her.

"Why the hell didn't we think about getting tickets?" Toria asked. "You could've gotten tickets!"

Maybe. No. Roxie couldn't be anywhere near that studio.

"My friend," Drew said, reaching over to pat Zairn's knee as the audience calmed. "Geez, how are you not deaf already?"

"I live my life at this volume," Zairn called over the audience and held up a flat hand to them. "Thank you. Thank you, that's enough."

The audience accepted his instruction and quieted. No surprise. He was like the people whisperer when he used that low, soothing voice.

"Wow," Drew Harvey said. "That's some superpower."

Zairn raised a shoulder and sank back to relax on the couch. "Years of practice."

"Controlling hordes of people in your clubs," Harvey said. "Talking of controlling people, there's supposed to be someone there next to you." Both men looked at the vacant seat. The comedian at the other end of the couch fixated on it too. "You couldn't persuade Miss Kyst to join you?"

As he turned back to the host, one side of Zairn's mouth rose, but he licked his lips to hide the reaction. Something he frequently did, though it wasn't often successful. Especially when she was the root of his amusement.

"No one persuades Miss Kyst to do anything she doesn't want to do."

He straightened his tie over his shirt buttons, which made her look at it for the first time. "The tie," she murmured.

It was the same one she'd tied for him on the day they met Greg and his colleagues in Boston.

"She didn't want to come?" Drew Harvey asked.

"Miss Kyst has done plenty for Crimson," Zairn said. "She prefers to deliver her messages through her stream."

"Present tense?" the host asked. "Will she be continuing her streams? She was extremely popular and drove record numbers of users to your website."

"I think she's eager to return to life as normal."

"You think? Have you discussed it with her?"

"Personally? No," Zairn said. No, because who had time to talk when the alternative was crazy, hot sex? "The Crimson Tour was taxing for all of us."

"But you're not getting a break. You're on your way back to New York, to get the club ready for its New Year's Eve opening, aren't you?"

"Not yet," Zairn said. "We have to check out a few potential sites for the next Crimson location, and there's unfinished business in Tokyo."

"That's right. You missed Tokyo, Miss Kyst was ill."

"That's correct."

"Calling her 'Miss Kyst' feels too formal. She's been in our living rooms, our bedrooms. She became a friend to all of us. Do you think she'd object to us calling her Roxanne?"

"She wouldn't. Though it's not her name," Zairn said. "She goes by Roxie."

"Roxie, okay," Harvey said. "Sorry, Roxie…" He glanced at the camera for the apology and then returned his focus to the guest. "There's so much we have to get through that blurting this out is—"

"Roxie and I have dealt with many direct and insensitive questions about our relationship. We were friends. We had good fun. She's an easy woman to get along with… most of the time."

"And did you…" Drew raised his brows and bobbed his head, suggesting something more intimate.

"If I had, do you think I'd talk about it here on

national television, Drew?" Zairn asked, easy and relaxed as he teased the host.

"She's an attractive woman."

"Gorgeous," Zairn said. "Any man would be lucky to have her affection."

"But you didn't…"

Zairn laughed. "Let's talk about your social life… when was the last time—"

"Okay," Harvey said, holding up his hands in surrender. "Just doing my job here, man."

The two of them laughed off the interaction, but Roxie noticed the twitch of tension in Zairn's shoulder.

"Relax," she whispered. "It's not personal."

Drew Harvey turned to the camera. "We have to take a quick break now, but there will be plenty more from Zairn next, don't go anywhere."

As the show went to break, her phone vibrated in her lap, indicating it was turning on again.

"Okay, now you have to dish the dirt," Toria said.

"He got offended when Drew Harvey got her name wrong," Jane said. "Did you notice that?"

Scrolling through her phone, Roxie found a certain woman's name and pressed call.

It rang just four times before Astrid picked up. "Roxie?"

"Who chose the tie?" she asked with a smile on her face.

"I, uh… I don't know. Are you watching?"

"Yes," Roxie said. "He needs to relax. They'll move on to Kesley and Vegas next."

"I think he's doing great," Astrid said. "We worried he'd blow the whole interview. He's been snappy all day."

"Tired," Roxie said, closing her eyes. That was no excuse; Zairn was used to operating on little sleep. "Are you flying out tonight?"

"In the morning," Astrid said. "Kesley's waiting at the club for him." Of course she was. Kesley needed support and leaned on Zairn. Roxie understood. He was a capable guy and excelled at taking care of people. "Have you seen the pictures?"

"Pictures?" Roxie asked, frowning. "What pictures?"

"Of you and your ex going into his hotel earlier."

"Oh my God," she gasped. "Those people need to get a life."

"Mr. Lomond wanted me to call you about additional security. If you're going to be socializing with the man prosecuting the case, he thinks you should have close quarter protection."

"I don't care what he thinks," Roxie said. "I won't live my life in fear. Someone should take Joseph Gambatto down. What he did to that woman… what she lived through was horrific."

"I don't know what… Maybe you should talk to Mr. Lomond about it."

"If Z wanted to talk to me, he wouldn't have asked you to make the call," Roxie said. Why was such a fury heating her blood? "I don't want his security. I don't want his help. I got on just fine before him and plan to do the same after him."

She hung up and stood, extricating herself from the charger cord to march toward her room.

"Roxie!" Toria called after her.

"I don't give a damn," Roxie said without slowing down. "Watch, don't watch. I've had my fill of Crimson and Zairn Lomond. I'm done. I'm through."

There was no reason for her to be angry about Zairn's words or him farming her out to Astrid. They needed space. On the day they'd parted, she'd declared there would be no calls from her to him. She had no intention of going back on her word. That was it. Over.

FIVE

WAS IT MORTIFYING? Yes. Did it have to be done? Yes.

After snapping at Astrid during Talk at Sunset, Roxie had little choice except to call the assistant and prostrate herself. A couple of days had gone by, but it still plagued her mind.

With the apartment to herself, there wouldn't be a better time. On the floor between the couch and the coffee table, the ring of the phone droned in her ear.

The seconds dragged.

"Come on," she murmured. "Pick up… Please…"

Another few days without talking to Astrid might drive her nuts.

"Roxie?"

Surprise jerked her. "You picked up."

"Yes. Are you okay?"

"Am I…" Trust the young woman to be concerned rather than mad. "Astrid," Roxie moaned. "I was horrible to you. Be pissed at me."

"I'm not, I…" Astrid said. "It can't be easy for you, what you're going through."

"What I'm going through?"

There was a pause. "You were close to him… A part of everything here and now you're not. If it was taken away from me, I'd be devastated."

Having tried to focus on happier things, she moved the conversation along. "You're in Tokyo?"

"Yes," Astrid said. "Right now, but… Something happened, I don't know what. Miss Walsh was emotional and… We're flying to Perth in a few hours."

"Perth, Australia?"

"Yes."

Weird. There was no Crimson in Perth. Maybe it was one of the potential sites for the next club. With all of Zairn's various business interests, the possibilities were endless. Kesley's involvement tossed in a hoard of variables too. Were they going for Zairn or for Kesley?

It was sweet of Astrid to trust her with new information. Flattering even. Still, a smidge of concern crept in. Astrid was too trusting. That could get all of them in trouble sometime.

"He'll be in New York for Thanksgiving… Sean said we might get home."

Thanksgiving was over two weeks away. They wouldn't be in the country for a while. Zairn's lifestyle wasn't conducive to sticking around in one place for long. It was a wonder he bothered with apartments anywhere. Maybe it was just convenience. Everyone needed a mailing address, even billionaires.

"That's good."

"Sean won't leave Mr. Lomond if he's alone, he never does over the holidays, ever," Astrid said. "Kesley talked about hosting in New York. There's a professional kitchen at their disposal."

"Makes sense," Roxie said.

A nibble of discomfort tickled her shoulders. It wasn't jealousy, but it was something. Being on the outside was strange.

"Sean said Mr. Lomond would fly in everyone's families. There are a few hotel room floors in the flagship building… I could ask Sean if you could—"

"No! No, God, no," Roxie said, laughing off the suggestion. "I have to go to my crazy folks' and I wouldn't wish them on anyone… I was a contest winner. We're not family. I don't expect to see him again… ever."

Why was the confidence fading from her words? Nothing she said was false. They hadn't become family just because they spent a few weeks together. Stone's prediction rang true. With her back in her natural habitat, all lives were returning to normal.

"I don't think he's sleeping with her," Astrid said into the lingering silence. "Sean said he needs some time. His mood's been off… in case you were… wondering."

Most people would've thought she and Zairn weren't sleeping together during their eleven days. An outsider may have said Zairn's mood was off during that time too. He'd shut everyone out, said little, and seized on every opportunity they had to be alone.

Not that it mattered. Eleven days was eleven days, and it was over.

"I called to apologize for my behavior. You didn't deserve what I said to you. I appreciate everything you and Crimson did for me."

"Rox—"

"My invitation stands. If you're ever in Chicago, looking for a good time, drop by. I'd love to see you."

"We're not often by that way," Astrid said. "You could still call."

"You're busy, God knows you are. If you need tips on givin' 'em hell, call me. You have a big life to live, Astrid Ballard. Live it well and to the max. Anything is possible. You're a badass, don't forget that."

"You're an amazing person, Rox."

"Yeah, yeah," she said, shrugging it off. "I'm an A-plus badass. Make me proud."

"I'll try… bye."

The phone stayed at her ear until the line died. Only then did her hand sink to her lap. An A-plus badass? More like a world class fool. There was no tomorrow with Astrid. Their connection dwindled to nothing the moment she'd stepped off Zairn's plane.

Life would be as it always was... Except she wasn't the same. Who was she? What had changed? More to the point, how did she go back to the way things used to be? Who was Roxie Kyst post-Zairn Lomond? Post-Crimson? Post-eleven days and incredible mile-high sex? It didn't matter. Even if she didn't feel normal, she'd fake it. Eventually, it would become real... right?

SIX

THANKSGIVING LANDED EXACTLY three weeks after she stepped off the Zee-Jet. As usual, her family was crazy. Their consistency was a comfort. Without knowing it, they offered some distraction from lingering thoughts of him. Christmas was about the same. The holidays kept her busy.

Almost eight weeks had passed since she'd seen or had direct contact with Zairn. Not that she was counting the days or anything. Gradually, time was doing its work. Reporters didn't crowd outside her building anymore. Sometimes a fan might be out there, and people recognized her on the street once in a while. Hence her continued avoidance of crowds.

Ditching security altogether wasn't an option. Trevor told her that all the time... He wasn't as good as Ballard. Giving security the slip was easier after they stopped standing outside her front door. They'd walk the block or wander the building. Personally, she believed Trevor had his eye on another tenant. No doubt the hottie on the fourth floor.

Relinquishing the Mercedes had been a no-brainer. At first, the driver didn't take the hint. She'd gone two whole weeks ignoring the car on her curb before it vanished.

Life was returning to how it should be. Normality would be waiting just around the corner.

On the twenty-ninth of December, her girls decided a shopping spree was in order. Yeah, not a good idea. Her credit card had seen enough action, so she sent them on their way alone.

Lying on the couch, reading, her roommates came barreling back into the apartment.

"It's way too short," Jane was saying, her vibrant voice brimming with excitement.

"You have to be daring! It's Crimson," Toria said. They dumped their bags at the back of the couch and noticed her spread out on it. "Rox, will you tell her she has to dress sexy for Crimson?"

"It's not a requirement," Roxie said, turning the page of her book.

Though there may be spot underwear checks… She subdued her smile. Her friends wouldn't get the joke. In fact, it would get her into trouble.

"What are you going to wear, Rox?" Jane asked. "Can we see your dress?"

"She has the most amazing dresses paid for by the Crimson King himself," Toria said. "She's spoiled for choice."

"You can raid my closet," Roxie said, preferring to think of him as the Crimson Emperor. "There are a few sexy, slinky numbers."

"Which one are you planning to wear?"

"For what?"

"New York," Toria said, propping a hip on the back of the couch.

"New York?"

"Yeah, New Year's Eve," Toria said. "You do remember that New Year comes like a week after Christmas." Actually, she'd been trying to forget about the next major event in the calendar. "According to the email I got from the Talk at Sunset people, the train takes like an entire day. We have to show up at the station tomorrow. Our tickets will be waiting there for us."

That mental picture put a smile on her face. "Zairn

Lomond never took a train a day in his life."

"Well, we wouldn't know," Toria said, coming around the couch to sit on the edge of the coffee table facing her. "Since you refuse to talk about him."

"I know I keep saying you shouldn't kiss and tell…" Jane said, skirting the couch to sit by her feet. "But there's a chance we'll meet him at the party."

"Yeah, if we have to cover for you, it would be good to know why," Toria said. "Was he an asshole? Did he get drunk and feel you up?"

"That's in the past, guys."

Toria growled in frustration. "That's what you always say!"

Jane scooted up the couch to sit at her hip. "Did you get drunk and feel him up?"

"Yeah," Toria said. "Because if you did, I wouldn't worry about it. Women probably grope him all the time. I would."

Not inaccurate; not something it was fun to dwell on either.

"If it's something like that, you could always use the New Year's party to apologize. He didn't seem mad at you that time on Talk at Sunset."

"He's not mad at me, and I'm not mad at him," Roxie said. "No one has to apologize for anything, which is why there's no need for me to go to the party."

"What?" her friends hollered.

Sitting up, she slipped a bookmark in between the pages.

"You have to go," Jane pleaded. "Why didn't you tell us this when we talked about it before?"

The party had come up about fifty times in the last month.

"What are you hiding?" Toria asked.

"You can't party here; people won't leave you alone," Jane said. "You can relax in New York if they let us into the VIP area… Oh, or maybe we'll get into the Ruby Room!"

"There's no way you'd pass up a chance at a party like this without a major reason."

"I have a reason," Roxie said. "I don't want to go. I've done enough traveling this year."

"This is *the* club," Jane said. "*The* Crimson. Why wouldn't you want to go? You've been everywhere else."

Except Tokyo, but that wasn't the point.

"I've been to the New York club," Roxie said. "I toured it when it was being refurbed."

"Now it's done," Jane said, taking her hand. "It will be open. Music. Dancing. People. You love nightclubs."

"There's something she's not telling us," Toria said. "She doesn't trust us."

"I trust you," Roxie said. "I just don't wanna go."

"Okay," Jane said and sighed. "Do you think we have time to return all our stuff before closing?"

"Maybe," Toria said, standing up in time with Jane. "We'll have to hustle."

"No!" Roxie said, reaching out to grab both of them. "I want you to go. Go and have a great time. Crimson is amazing. You were right, you shouldn't pass up this chance."

"If you're not going, we're not going," Toria said. "If he's an asshole, then he's an asshole. We take your word for it."

"I didn't say that," Roxie said. "You should go. Meet him. Send my regards."

Toria's brows rose. "Your regards?" she asked. "What is this? Like the fifties? Either you come or none of us go. It's as simple as that. We're not leaving you here alone on New Year." She looked at Jane. "We won't get tickets for anything else this late. We'll stay home, invite a few people over… You know, loser people who don't have plans already."

"No," Roxie said, adamant and amused. "You're going. Both of you."

"Then you're coming."

"I couldn't even if I wanted to," Roxie said, shrugging without letting go of her friends. "I told Porter he could have my tickets… Which reminds me, I should find out if I need physical tickets."

Because she wouldn't give her diamond to anyone.

Even a potential future congressman.

Leaving the couch and her friends, Roxie went to her bedroom. Toria had mentioned an email. One hadn't come to her… had it? The leather binder gifted to her on the last day in LA was the only place tickets or instructions might be. She'd never unzipped it… or been tempted.

Retrieving it from the lowest drawer of her nightstand, she sat on her bed to unzip it and flicked open the cover expecting to recognize what was inside. Most of the contents were familiar. Everything except…

The box. A jewelry box… Where had that come from? It hadn't been there before… had it? Smaller than the one for the diamond pendant she still wore every day, the style of both boxes was the same. On this one, above the space for her thumbprint, two words were engraved: "*Wear me.*"

"Wear me," she whispered, aligning her thumbprint to unlock the box.

The gem inside took her breath. A huge, deep red ruby sparkled up at her. Set in what appeared to be a platinum ring, the oval cut gem was complemented by small diamonds in its four corners.

Writing on the inside of the lid caught her eye. "*Empress—for when you're ready. Casanova.*" She didn't want to be a Crimson Queen. Trust him to grant that wish while simultaneously disregarding it. The man had talent; no one could deny that.

"Asshole," she whispered through her smile.

With shaking fingers, she took the ring out. If it was in a locked box like the diamond, it must have some security significance… or be super expensive. It didn't matter. Something so gorgeous should be protected.

Sliding it onto her middle finger, she still wasn't breathing right when moisture dripped onto her knuckles. Damn him. Walking away was necessary. Whenever he invaded her thoughts, she reminded herself of that. Their fling was fun. Just fun. She'd asserted that over and over. He'd given her what she wanted.

"*I'm embarrassed by my response to your honesty.*"

His words in the Vegas office. What did it mean? She

hadn't thought twice about it… not until after they were apart. Every time her mind replayed that conversation, she'd wondered…

"I'm used to getting my own way. Used to getting whatever I want."

What had he meant? Why hadn't she asked him what he wanted? He'd admitted his petulance, his immaturity, but she hadn't done the same. They'd never had a real conversation. Not about them. Reminding him they couldn't have anything more than fun was her way of maintaining control. Of protecting herself. At the time, she hadn't known it. Her subconscious convinced her she was as easy and go with the flow as always. That everything was business as usual.

Roxie didn't want Zairn to be different. Hadn't wanted to admit that he was. But was he?

None of the lies or half-truths she told herself explained the pain that had struck almost every day since leaving the Zee-Jet. Clutching her hand to her chest, she closed her eyes. She missed him. Every minute of every day. Whenever something happened, she still longed to talk to him about it. She missed playing with him. Teasing. Talking. She missed her playmate.

"Rox?"

Startled out of her reflection, she kept her hand over the ring, hiding it from her friends loitering in the doorway.

"Are you okay?" Jane asked.

Both of them were curious. Did they know she was on edge? Probably.

As Roxie smiled at them, she slipped the ring from her finger to hide it in her fist. "Yeah," she said. "Everything I have is here."

Although she couldn't be sure there weren't things they shouldn't see.

"You didn't show us this," Toria said, approaching.

Roxie tucked the ring under her knee and snapped the box shut to toss it toward her pillow.

"What is that?" Jane asked.

"It's the box for the bling," Toria said, hardly paying attention to anything other than the binder as she turned it toward her. "What is the…" Peeking out from behind the presentation certificate was a slip of paper. Toria took it out first and held it up to their roommate. "This is the check."

Roxie slid further back onto the bed, ensuring to keep the ring hidden as she did.

Jane gasped and grabbed the check. "This is for fifty thousand dollars!"

"You didn't cash it," Toria said, then set a frown on her. "Why didn't you cash it?"

Roxie shrugged. "It didn't feel right. I had an amazing time on the tour. A lot of time and expense was lavished on me. I didn't want to take their money too."

When Toria took the check back, Jane folded her hands on her upper chest. "That's so sweet."

"And so stupid," Toria said. "You should cash it."

"No," Roxie said.

"I'll cash it," Toria said.

Roxie slipped the check from Toria and tore it up, throwing the pieces into the air. "We don't want Crimson money."

It hadn't occurred to her to so much as look at the check.

"You know his autograph was on that," Toria said. "I always wanted his autograph."

"*I wasn't talking to you. I know better than to ask for anything from the woman who can't charge a cellphone…*"

Why couldn't she get him out of her head? For weeks, every little thing reminded her of him. The way he smiled. That mischievous look in his eye when she said something he found sexy. He found everything sexy. That he got through a day without getting himself tangled up with some woman, any woman, was amazing.

Her friends were talking about the check. About whether they could get another issued. All Roxie wanted to do was go back to that room. Any room with him in it.

Rome came to mind. The way he'd kissed her neck and talked of Paris and running away together. Not long later, he'd run away from her. He'd always leave. It was the nature of what he did. Zairn didn't stay in one place for any longer than necessary. His docket was always full, and she yearned too much.

For three months, she'd been spoiled with his time and attention. It wasn't realistic to expect that could ever translate to a normal, stable relationship.

A gasp joined a screech.

Roxie jumped. "Geez, you two!"

Toria was holding something else, she guessed from the binder, and waved it her way. "You have a plane!"

"I have a plane?" Roxie asked, snatching the piece of paper to see what her friend was talking about. "Oh my God."

Toria was right. According to the itinerary, there would be a private jet waiting, ready to take her and her passengers to New York on New Year's Eve.

"It says you have a room reserved inside the Crimson building too," Jane said. "They have like five floors of hotel rooms in the same building as the club."

"Everything Rouge is run from the flagship site," Roxie murmured, scrutinizing the sheet.

It talked of a champagne reception and a seven-course meal. Too much? No, it was exactly Zairn's style. Though planning would've been Tibbs's responsibility… also Zairn's style.

Jane and Toria were talking again, getting themselves excited about the notion of a private jet and a fine dining meal.

"Come on," Toria said, grabbing Roxie's wrist. "You can't say no to this. We have to go."

Both of her friends' expressions pleaded with her.

Roxie just smiled. "Crimson prides itself on showing guests a good time. How can I say no to that?"

Her friends screamed and hugged her and started talking at a zillion miles an hour.

Refusing to go was another protection mechanism. Seeing him again… how would she react? What if he ignored her? What if he didn't? Being out of the loop in Barcelona had been difficult to handle. Going to Manhattan, possibly seeing the faces of people who'd been her world for a short while… it wouldn't be easy. Still, if she didn't take advantage of this one last chance, how would she ever forgive herself?

SEVEN

THE JET WAS AS SUMPTUOUS as Roxie would expect from Rouge. It wasn't either of Zairn's, but that wasn't a surprise. He owned a company that specialized in private planes. Sending a jet meant nothing. As the premium prizewinner, the excess made sense.

Toria and Jane hammered the champagne. Their spirits were high. So much so that Roxie could disguise her own wariness. Her friends were right that she loved nightclubs. Crimson always showed her a good time. Nothing to worry about. Everything would be just fine.

Job offers from entertainment companies, media conglomerates, and random scam artists still hit her email. When that didn't work, they called. Unrecognized numbers got diverted to voicemail. She emptied her mailbox without listening to the messages. The email folders she'd created on the Triple Seven came in useful too.

The most important step in getting back to how things used to be was her return to Lomond ignorance. Dampening the frequent urge to Google him, Roxie turned the other way any time her friends mentioned Zairn or Crimson. Of course, they noticed, but it was easy to shrug off.

She hadn't shown interest before the tour; there was no need to force it on her afterward.

Her friends weren't stupid. They knew she was avoiding talking about her time on the tour. Whatever her reasons, they'd given her the respect of not probing too deep. Being back in the thick of Crimson again, that luxury may not last.

Other than her friends playing with the touchscreen music system on the jet, the flight and landing were uneventful.

Like stepping back in time, the Bentley and driver waiting on the tarmac put a smile on her face. It was validation that she hadn't dreamed up the decadence of Zairn's lifestyle. It really was as lavish as she remembered.

In Manhattan, the Bentley drove past the entrance of Rouge HQ. The impressive glass frontage revealed the wine bar and restaurant inside, both of which appeared to be already open. Not that it was easy to see. Barriers held back the masses of people on either side of the entrance canopy.

"Oh my God," Toria said, jumping closer to the window. "Look at all those people out there."

"What do you think they're waiting for?" Jane asked.

The scene was familiar from days gone by. Crowds waiting. Eager. For what? Anything. Acknowledgement. A sighting. A reward.

As she admired the winter sunshine reflecting the red sparkle of the building, the car turned into the next alleyway. It paused while the fifteen-foot-high metal gates opened, then continued on into the wide alley.

The moment they stopped, Toria reached for the door handle. Roxie stalled her. She said nothing, just waited until the driver came to open the door. Toria got out with Roxie right behind her.

A gorgeous young blonde came rushing over. "Miss Kyst," the blonde said. "Miss Kyst, hi. I'm Jenna, your personal hostess."

"Yeah, I don't need one of those," Roxie said, helping Jane out of the car.

"Wow, look at this place," Jane said, staggering to the

side to crane her neck. "I can't even see the top."

"Over a thousand feet," Jenna said. "Seventy-seven floors. You should see the view from the top."

The top was Zairn's residence. As per what she'd been told, not personal experience.

"It's incredible," Toria said, rushing over to hug her. "I can't believe you've been here and don't gush about it constantly. Are all the Crimson venues this incredible? I've seen pictures online, but—"

"Okay, breathe," Roxie said, taking both of Toria's hands.

"Do you think he's in the building?" Jane asked, leaping closer.

"Yeah," Toria flipped around to zero in on Jenna. "Where is Zairn Lomond right now?"

Roxie almost laughed. "She won't know that. Ballard doesn't know where he is most of the time and that guy's trained to spot him."

"Do you know where he is?" Jane asked.

Jenna squirmed. "Not exactly," she said, then perked up. "But he will be in residence before midnight."

"Yeah, 'cause it's New Year's Eve, and he's hosting the party," Toria said, unimpressed. "Even I knew that."

"Will he be at the champagne reception?" Jane asked, always the optimist. "At the dinner?"

"No, those are just for winners. You'll also have your own VIP area tonight, so we encourage winners to mingle." Jenna ushered them inside, her practiced spiel and plastic smile striking in their insincerity. "The top five will, of course, have their private audience with Mr. Lomond at the beginning of the evening. Before that, there's a tour of the city planned and the chance to avail yourselves of our spa."

Jane and Toria bounced with excitement. "Spa?"

They went along a glass corridor that showcased the busy restaurant to one side and a dark space to the other. Part of the club, Roxie knew that from her tour. At the head of the corridor, Jenna flashed a red security badge at a scanner and the glass doors opened, taking them to a central location.

"Where do we check-in? We'll need our luggage."

Jenna opened her arm toward the reception by a bank of elevators. "If you just give your names to the woman seated over there, we'll have your things brought in." Toria and Jane went to the reception. Roxie intended to follow, except Jenna stalled her. "Miss Kyst, you're only down as a plus one. The rules are very strict about—"

"I don't have a plus one," Roxie said, pointing at Toria. "Toria won the tickets, Jane is her plus one."

"Oh," Jenna said, taken aback. "I see." She smiled. "Perfect!"

Telling Porter he wasn't getting to use her tickets wasn't fun. He suggested coming as her plus one. Way too complicated. One ex was already on her worry list, two would push her luck to its limits.

"Do I need to check-in?" Roxie asked.

Jenna shook her head. "No. There is a very specific set of rules for you, Miss Kyst."

That didn't inspire confidence. The glass building allowed her attention to drift toward the crowds on the sidewalk. Zairn lived a glamorous life, she got it, people were interested.

The view brought back memories. Once upon a time, those crowds called her name. Bypassing that gauntlet was a relief. Getting into the Lomond's Delight persona required a dose of alcohol.

"Ah, but, um…" Jenna again. Geez, spit it out, woman. "It may not be a good idea for you to join the city tour. Security is a little worried about… The people outside are Crimson fans. The type of people who…"

"Might know who I am… or who I was."

Smile refreshed, Perfect Jenna's hair glittered under the gleaming interior lights. "I'm sure you've forgotten what it's like to be so close to Mr. Lomond… what it's like when he's around." No. Not really. If only… "Security thinks it may not be safe. We don't want anything to happen to such a valued member of the Crimson team."

"Not a member," Roxie said. "A veteran."

"Right," Jenna said with a laugh, though Roxie wasn't really sure the woman heard her. "Excitement about the re-opening, the reveal of the new club, it's at a high right now. People are coming from far away to be here, just to be close. Mr. Lomond is very popular."

"Except he isn't here right now. All those people out there want him. They're hungry… my familiar face may cause problems. Security problems."

Or media problems. There was always the chance of her opening her big mouth and dropping them all in it. Zairn wasn't the only one with talents.

"If you really want to go—"

"No," Roxie said, relieved to have the out. "My girls will love it. I'm happy to take it easy."

As was becoming her new normal.

Spending nights in wasn't so bad. When nights turned to days and she became a hermit, then she'd worry. That was a problem for another day.

EIGHT

EACH OF THE THREE WOMEN'S hotel rooms contained gifts, food, champagne, jewelry. Her friends lapped it up. For her, it was too much. Over the top. Odd.

Since a certain argument in an LA hotel suite, she hadn't been this close to his world without being a part of it.

Did they get special treatment because she used to fuck the guy who owned the building? If so, the lavish gifts were tawdry. If not, then she was just any other person staying in his hotel. Did she want to be different? Given that their intimacy had been a secret, it wasn't like Zairn could request exclusive extras without raising suspicion. The idea of Ballard sneaking around to leave diamonds on behalf of his boss was outright hilarious. Too much to process, her exhausted mind needed a break.

Skipping the city tour was easy to explain to her girls. The crowds outside had renewed fervor. Interest may have waned at home, somewhat, but the club opening, New Year, the media was hyped. Fans were never far behind… yadda, yadda, yadda.

Without Zairn around, she would be a prime target for attention. The world knew about her win on Talk at

Sunset. That she'd spent time with Zairn and his people. And they'd seen the now infamous Sydney viral stream. Being gawked at for her association with Zairn, when they no longer had one, didn't seem right.

After Jenna left, her girls tried to change her mind with promises to protect her. Security had been absent since Trevor and his guys stayed behind at the airport in Chicago. Maybe freedom was a possibility in Crimson Palace.

A bus tour around the city was more than she wanted to handle. Nothing would've stopped her if she really wanted to go on the excursion. Why hadn't she considered the potency of Crimson interest in the famous city? Anyone who came from far and wide to queue and crowd outside Rouge HQ would know her. Some of them may have watched her streams or asked questions live.

Her nerves jangled. Excitement quaked her too. Crimson was in her life again. The club. The fun. The security. Proximity was enough to remind her of the life she'd lived on tour. He was in her head. Maybe potential proximity to him was a factor too. Insane. She was no one to him anymore. A stranger. One of dozens of Talk at Sunset prizewinners. Lost in the crowd.

Her suitcase was on a stand next to the window. The first thing she'd do was find her dress. There, yeah, Porter could spin on it. Unpacking less than an hour after arrival, a miracle. Maybe not so predictable after all, huh? She put the dress on a hanger and left it in the bathroom, ready to be steamed when she took her shower later.

Going back to her case, she retrieved the two jewelry boxes from the zipped section inside the lid. One housed her diamond pendant. The other her ruby ring. Opening the latter, she admired the beautiful gem. More too much. Extravagant. Keeping it as a memento would be wrong. No way. She'd never be able to show it to anyone. Never be able to insure it.

Returning it was the right thing to do. The only thing to do. And it just so happened that was the perfect moment. Downstairs, Jenna said Zairn wasn't in the building. His apartment, penthouse, whatever it was called, was within reach—and empty.

What about security? Her diamond wouldn't be authorized anymore. Unless… maybe no one thought to take it from the system. It wasn't like she was close enough to any place sensitive to abuse it.

Would it hurt to check? Obviously, Roxie didn't think so because she ended up in the elevator, ring box in hand. Seventy-seven floors. Except the options didn't go anywhere near that high.

What to do? How to get close? Oh! The elevator bank by the main reception might offer more options. Down she went. Good try, but the directory in the lobby only had listings up to floor seventy. Guess that was closer than any other choice.

Pressing the call button for that elevator, to her surprise, it opened straight away. Great. Floor seventy, please, and… nothing happened. Drawing attention to herself would negate avoiding the masses. What to do? What to do? That square above the numbers was familiar… What did it look like? Her jewelry boxes. Ah-ha! Her thumbprint gave relieved triumph. One quick scan, the doors closed, and the elevator moved.

Seventy.

It better not open on some fancy business floor. If people saw her, it wouldn't be a big deal, right? She had done nothing wrong. The doors opened to another lobby area. No one was around. The glass walls showed various desks and computers, but no one was working. At the far end of the corridor, the incredible view from her elevated position tempted her closer. How was the glass red on the outside without impugning the natural light with any rosy hue on the inside? Hmm.

Amazing as the vista was, loitering wasn't a good idea. Her mission was to return the ruby. That was it. There wouldn't be other apartments by his, so leaving it on the doorstep should be fine. No one could steal it.

Now, how did she get to seventy-seven?

Two of the elevators opposite had numbers above them that went to seventy-five. The elevator in the middle was different. The doors were a warmer color and engraved with beautiful, intricate patterns. No numbers above. The plate behind the call button displayed the same engravings. Beautiful.

She pressed the button. Nothing happened. Maybe it was the same as the last one. Yep. Her thumb granted access inside. Easy. Someone should update security once in a while. Zairn wouldn't want strangers partying on his floor, of course not. But, geez, paranoid much? Even just finding the right elevator was a nightmare.

Inside there were three choices: lobby, seventy-six, or seventy-seven. Progress. Another thumbprint scan closed the doors. Seventy-seven. Uh… Nothing happened. Selecting it and scanning her fingerprint again… still nothing.

Hmm.

The doors were closed. Maybe that was the setup. The elevator imprisoned any unauthorized persons who tried to use it. Scan again. Seventy-seven. Nothing. Again. Nothing. Ahh! So infuriating!

Plucking her diamond from her cleavage, she waved it around, recalling Zairn's spiel on smart sensors. Problem was, she didn't know where to aim or what it wanted her to do. Stupid rules.

So her assumption about security was wrong. Her diamond wasn't authorized any longer. Had it ever been authorized for the top floor? For Zairn's apartment? No. Probably not.

Stuck inside the damn metal box, Roxie couldn't give up if she wanted to. Maybe after a fifth failed attempt, the elevator would send her hurtling to the lobby, executing the security threat. Efficient.

Her diamond had found its limit. She touched the gem. Maybe mailing it back would work.

Why had she kept the diamond anyway? He'd said she could, but why hadn't she insisted on giving it back? Now the ring too. He'd think she kept that. It wouldn't occur to him she'd only just found it.

Opening the box to marvel at the jewel again, she said a last goodbye. The elevator moved. What in the hell? Just like that. For no reason whatso—the ring. Her focus jumped to the gem. She'd thought that it might have held some security sway. Bingo.

The doors opened. On instinct, she walked on out and… oh.

An impressive, open living space… it took a minute to catch on. No front door. No doormat. She was in his apartment. Shit.

The beautiful space was warm, decorated in neutral shades of greys and off-whites with a few black accents. It was Zairn to a tee. Two separate seating areas, grand high ceilings, vast amounts of space. Snooping would be wrong, wouldn't it? She was there anyway… and couldn't leave the jewelry lying just anywhere. It would have to be somewhere that only Zairn would find it.

Opening doors, she peeked in on an internal pool room and a movie theatre. Neither of which allowed in any light. The next door opened into the master suite. Wow… the size and epic view beyond the floor-to-ceiling windows, it had to be the most magnificent bedroom in the world. Not just the building, the world.

How many of his intimate spaces had she visited? London, sure, she'd slept there. The Triple Seven. The Zee-Jet. Okay, so she hadn't slept there, but they'd definitely used the bed. Being in his New York place felt different. Because it had been so long since they'd seen each other? In London, it was normal to be in Zairn's space. Even if he had been mad at her while she was there.

Just like in London, there was a seating area to the left. She only explored one way, but it didn't look like there were designated his and hers zones. In the huge bathroom, she discovered a freestanding tub next to the window. Amazing.

Deeper than a standard tub, the white oval was tempting. Bathing right in front of an immense window that overlooked the most famous park in the world: who wouldn't want that experience? In any other place, she'd fill it up and strip off. That wasn't really appropriate. Wasn't appropriate at all. Just the fact that she noted it would be inappropriate was a sign of personal growth. Mental high five.

That achievement deserved a reward. Proud of herself, she put the ruby in its box on the vanity and slipped off her shoes. No one would care if she hopped in to get a better perspective, right? She'd imagine the being naked part. Stepping over the side of the tub, she lowered herself down, holding each of the sides, and rested her head against the back edge. It could do with a few adjustments, but it wasn't bad.

Peeking at the view, she slid lower, smiling at the thought of doing something so daring. Being naked so close to the world... Closing her eyes, she dreamed of being submerged in pure luxury.

NINE

IN ROXIE'S MIND, the fantasy could last forever. The warmth of the water seeping into every crevice. The light of the glorious sky shining down to sparkle off the bubbles. What a picture…

"I'm no expert…" Shit. "But I think you're doing it wrong."

One of her eyes opened to confirm, yeah, that was Zairn, standing just inside the bathroom smirking at her. At least one thing hadn't changed.

"I was just…" Sitting up, she drummed her nails on either side of the tub. "Playing make-believe." As he went to the vanity, Roxie jumped out of the tub. "I didn't know you were a bathtub fan."

"I'm not," he said, putting his phone and a big stack of small paper squares down.

"I always wanted one of those claw-foot roll-top types… you know, the ones that are higher at the end. They're called slipper tubs, which I always thought was cool. Bathing in a slipper. Sounds like something out of a nursery rhyme." Silence. Was he listening or ignoring her? Despite the massive mirror in front of him, he couldn't even bring himself to peek her way. He picked up the ruby box. Oh… "I came by to return that… I thought you'd have a front door. I didn't realize the elevator opened right into your living room. That's dangerous, by the way. I'm surprised Ballard agreed to it."

He twisted to look at her over his shoulder. "Why are you nervous?"

"I'm not nervous. Why would you think I—" In such haste to get the words out, she proved his point. She exhaled and smiled. "Maybe 'cause I just got caught fantasizing in your tub."

"I've caught you doing worse," he said, taking off his jacket. He tossed it to the seat behind him, near the door, then loosened his tie. "Your journey okay?"

"In a private jet? Chauffeured around? My every whim attended to? It was a nightmare." His attention jumped to hers in the mirror. Roxie laughed. "Now who's acting out of character? I'm kidding. It was fine. Fun."

"Fun," he said.

Well, she wasn't totally sure if he said it or if his lips just moved that way. Maybe using that word was insensitive. The sensation of being unbalanced wasn't fun. Not unbalanced in a mental patient kind of way. More in a "the-floor-wouldn't-stop-lurching-beneath-her-feet" type way.

He finished taking off his tie and dropped it onto the vanity before undoing a couple of his shirt buttons.

"You look good." The focus of his reflection slid up to hers. She was moving toward him. Was that a good idea? Maybe… maybe not. Figuring out sense was harder than acting on instinct. "You've been working out."

"Hitting on me, Roxanna?" he asked, turning his back to the mirror to observe her tiptoeing closer.

"Paying you a compliment," she said, sure he noticed the playful angle of her lips that just wouldn't behave. "That's a nice thing to do when you get caught breaking and entering."

"What did you break?"

She raised one shoulder in a half-shrug. "Nothing… yet. It's still early."

"And you reserve the right?"

"Always," she murmured, tipping her chin higher

when she stopped in his personal space. No doubt about it, she was definitely closer than was polite. "I reserve the right to do anything I want, any time I want."

"And I reserve the right to support you in whatever you choose to do."

"Might be expensive."

"Who cares about money?"

"Not me."

"I noticed," he said, examining her face. "Damn, you're gorgeous. How did I forget what it feels like to be this close to you?"

"You didn't," Roxie said, her eyes trained to his even as she picked up his hand to press it against her cheek. "There's just nothing like living it."

Closing her eyes, she tilted her face and let him take control of the caress.

"You didn't like the ruby?" he asked, his thumb brushing across her lower lip. " 'Cause I will keep trying until I get it right."

"The ruby is beautiful," she said, her heavy eyes opening just a sliver. "It's too much."

"No, it's not," he said, the back of his fingers drifting down the front of her throat. Pushing her shoulders back, she arched into the advance. "It's not even close to enough."

"I only found it this week. I didn't open the binder until Toria and Jane were persuading me to come."

"You didn't want to come?" Her lips curled higher, encouraging his smile. "You are going to get us into trouble, Roxanna." On a quiet laugh, his hand dropped from her throat, leaving her cold. Her own petulance rose. "Tibbs said something about you not cashing the check. That was a couple of weeks after you left; I assumed the issue was fixed." And he hadn't been interested enough to follow-up. "We can write you another one, or I can transfer money directly into—"

"I don't want your money."

Why had his hand stopped at her neck? He hadn't touched her any lower than that… like Kesley said he was with other women. *Other* women.

"It's company money and you're entitled to it," he

said, taking out his cufflinks to fold his sleeves up his forearms. "That was the prize. So was tonight. If you had to be persuaded to attend, we didn't do our job on the tour very well."

"It wasn't the club I worried about seeing."

He paused in his folding. "Me?"

"I couldn't decide which would be worse," she admitted, resting a hip on the vanity, folding her arms. "If you treated me the same as every other prizewinner or if you didn't."

His short exhale came at the same time his head went back. "Jesus…"

"What?" she asked, offended by his tone. "You don't want me to be honest?"

"Honesty has never been a problem for you, Roxanna."

She didn't appreciate the bass of those curt words. "Was for you."

"Yeah, and then I gave you everything. You walked away anyway."

"Wait a second," she said, standing straight. "Are we really arguing about this?"

"How do you want me to treat you? Do you want me to ignore you? Pretend you're not there? Like you've been doing with me for the past two months?"

How dare he? Why was he talking to her this way? "I told you I wouldn't use you like everyone else!"

"How is picking up the damn phone using me? How is having a conversation using me? What the hell, Rox? I gave you more than any other woman ever got."

"I don't want your stupid ruby."

"You don't get it," he snapped. "You don't get it at all."

"Apparently," she said. "Because I'm not bowled over by your wealth, what? I'm stupid? There are other ways to connect with people that don't involve money, Z!"

"What other ways?" he asked, stepping back to open his arms. "I'm here, Roxanna. Right here. Fucking teach me if you know so damn well." She didn't know how to respond.

"Maybe it's just that you're a coward. You were definitely right about one thing, you don't have a damn clue what you want."

"Oh, and you're Mr. Put Yourself Out There?"

"I put myself out there for you, and you couldn't give an inch. Not one fucking inch. I always thought the joking around was a game, foreplay, but damnit, you just need to win, don't you? You always have to come out on top."

"What the hell are you talking about?" she screeched, exasperated.

He drove his fingers into his hair. "How can one woman be so fucking blind? You are so switched on, Roxie, so switched on. How can you be so fucking tone-deaf to what's going on here?"

"I know exactly what's going on," she said, looking around for her shoes. "Because I didn't fall over myself for your attention, because I didn't beg and whimper and plead, you're pissed off." She swiped her shoes up from the floor. "I'm so sorry that I didn't throw myself on the pyre of our relationship."

"If we had a relationship, I'd concede," he said, following her from the bathroom. "But we didn't. What we had was sordid and cheap. Bullshit in the face of what it could've been. You're so damn scared to let yourself trust someone, anyone."

"I trust plenty of people," she called back over her shoulder. "I trust my girls, my family—"

"You dictate the terms of every relationship in your life," he said, hurrying to get past and in her way. "You push people away with jokes and act like you're impervious, but you're terrified. Just like every other person when they let themselves feel for someone else."

When he tried to touch her face, she swatted his hand away. "Don't talk to me about fear. That's how you want me to live my life, in fear. Why? Because then I'll have to rely on you? I'll need your security and your money for protection, so I'll be beholden to you? You know, what Porter's doing is right—"

"Oh, here we go," he said, throwing up his arms.

"Yes! Here we go," she said, increasing her volume as

he turned to take a few steps. "You had security on me from the minute I got back to my apartment. From the minute I got off that plane, and you didn't even have the balls to tell me!"

With his momentum, he pivoted to look at her again. "Maybe I didn't want to go ten rounds about how dangerous the Gambattos are. Maybe I didn't want to beg you to be smart about your life."

"It's my life, Z. If I want to—"

"But it's not your decision. It's Clement's decision. His case. His career. His future. You're just letting him drag you down with him."

"Porter and I aren't together, so I don't know how—"

"You've spent a lot of time with him the last two months," Zairn said. "I'd ask if you were sure you weren't together, but I know how good you are at stringing a guy along with sex without it ever meaning anything to you."

Stunned, Roxie couldn't believe how they'd digressed. She hadn't intended to see him and yet there they were, arguing like they hadn't missed a second. Except, they'd never argued, not really, not like they were arguing now.

"Is that what I did?" she asked. "String you along with sex? What exactly was I stringing you along for?"

"Entertainment."

"Oh, is that what it was? So it meant nothing to me, that's what you think?"

"That's precisely what I think."

Her eyes burned, though she couldn't tell if it was out of anger or grief. "Now who has no idea," she asked, her voice calm.

"Tell me," he beseeched with the same thread of anger as before. "If I'm so in the goddamn dark, tell me, Roxanna. Enlighten me."

"No," she said, shaking her head once as her arms folded again.

"That," he said, pointing at her. "That there is your default. We get right there, right to the precipice." He came a step closer again, measuring an inch with his thumb and forefinger. "And you shut down. You stick your chin in the air, fold your arms, and it's matter closed. You put up your goddamn walls, and you're done. You will never have something spectacular if you don't let someone behind those walls."

"At least I don't run," she said, countering her hurt by provoking his. "If it gets tough, you bolt. You said you were used to getting your own way. When someone else dares to have an opinion different to yours, dares to have their own thoughts, their own opinion, you turn your back."

"I have never turned my back on you," he growled.

"No? What the hell was abandoning me in Rome? Disappearing without a word? Then I find out later, you were in communication with Tibbs the whole time. What was that? You just wanted to hurt me?" She showed him her palm. "No, wait, sorry, that came later, didn't it? When you showed up at a wedding chapel with your ex-girlfriend. Your ex-girlfriend who was clearly still in love with you. That was patently obvious to me when I hardly knew either of you, so there's no way Mr. Astute missed it."

"You know what that was," he said, his voice growing deeper again. "She needed my help with—"

"And you talk about picking up the phone like I did something so offensive to you?" she asked, hot with frustration at all the things she'd never known she wanted to say. "You fucked me, walked out on me, and the next time I see you, you've shacked up with the next victim!"

"Don't say it like I treated you bad," he said, sneering at her. "You knew what you were getting into when you kissed me. And don't forget that, Little Miss Perfect, you kissed me."

"Because it had been how long? How long had we been dancing around it and you just wouldn't step up. Who's the coward here again?"

"Getting involved with you was so off-limits—so beyond off-limits—"

"Didn't stop you spending the night with me once, twice, how many times? You wanted me, don't even deny that you did."

"Yeah, I fucking did. I wanted you." Marching over, he didn't stop until he was right up close. "Giving in to that was the dumbest fucking thing I ever did because it destroyed me. You destroyed me, Roxanna."

"Then why the hell would you give me the ruby?"

He stepped back to take her hand and slapped the box into her palm. "Because I am not afraid of it. You're afraid of it."

"Sometimes it's like you don't know me at all."

"I don't, Roxanna," he said, holding up his hands and backing off. "No one does. That's exactly how you want it."

"Then you'll have no problem treating me like any other prizewinner."

"No," he said, slipping his hands into his pockets. "You want to be a stranger? I will grant that wish."

"Good," she said, returning to her path to the elevator.

It opened the moment she called it, which was a reprieve for her tormented, exhausted heart. Using her thumbprint seemed to take an age, but at least it closed the doors. She pressed for the lobby, but the elevator didn't move. It took her a second to remember what had worked before. The ruby. That explained why Zairn returned it. He wanted her out of there. Far away from his life. He always made a point of granting her wishes, so it was her turn to do the same for him.

TEN

IT WAS TOO LOUD. The champagne reception. The dinner. Everything was just too loud. Her head ached, her thoughts rattled. Too quick or too slow, her life had lost its rhythm. The food was awful. Maybe not the food, but her experience of it. She didn't want to eat and didn't want to socialize. She wanted to scream at the world. At herself. At the past and everything in the future.

Their argument replayed over and over. Swinging from extreme to extreme wasn't good for her health or her sanity. Sometimes she was so mad, it felt as though her blood was boiling. Other times, it was like being deep underwater, struggling for air.

Her friends were jubilant. Ecstatic and happy about every little thing. She couldn't do it. Couldn't pretend that the flatware was fascinating or the centerpieces exquisite. She just didn't care.

"Come on!" Toria exclaimed. "Bree and Jill will be here any second."

Somehow, they'd settled on getting ready for the New Year party in her room. The details of how that happened were fuzzy. His words mired her mind.

"*...it destroyed me. You destroyed me, Roxanna.*"

How could he say that unless he wanted to hurt her? She hadn't wanted to hurt him, let alone destroy him. He'd owned those words and their sentiment. He wasn't afraid or ashamed. He was so together. So much more mature and knowing than she was close to being. He didn't worry about anyone judging him, not anyone real.

"*Because I am not afraid of it. You're afraid of it.*"

What was she afraid of? Admitting to herself that she was a mess was a big step and a revelation. No one could hope she'd fix herself on the same night as that epiphany. Except that night may be the only chance she'd have to fix whatever was broken between her and Zairn. Though, looking back, had it ever been unbroken?

"I am so jealous," Toria said, spraying her hairspray again. "You get to go hang out with him."

"Maybe we could switch out," Jane said, giggling with Toria. "He wouldn't notice, right?"

He'd notice if one of her friends showed up instead of her, but would probably be grateful.

"We're going to the winner's VIP area. Zairn has his own super-secret room, the Ruby Room," Toria said. "We'll wait in our zone while you're there. How long do you think you'll be alone with him?"

Roxie wouldn't be alone with him ever again.

The pendulum swung back to infuriation. So smooth, he'd used such decorum in kicking her out that she'd almost missed it. Yep, no denying it, he'd kicked her out of his apartment. He was finished.

For two months, Roxie had consoled herself to the idea that her experience with Zairn Lomond was in the past. But, on that day, it felt different. A chance of seeing him at the New Year's party always existed. Some part of her subconscious knew that. Maybe her strength to walk away had come from there.

A knock at the door saved her from pondering that conundrum. Jane went hurrying over to play hostess and opened it to welcome their friends. Rather than just Jill and Bree, the guys from the final five, Ron and Dale, were there too.

"Ready to get going?"

Everyone grabbed their things and bundled out of the room.

From memory, the club took up the rear half of the first floor. There was an internal entrance around the corner from the wine bar. Turned out they didn't have to worry about finding the right route. When the elevator doors opened, an employee leaped forward to show them the way. A few other employees loitered around, presumably for the other winners to show up. Someone had to guide the ordinary people to the VIP area.

They went around and through an internal door. It wasn't far. After ascending a set of stairs to get an incredible view across the massive public dance space, they turned ninety degrees and went up another half flight. Ushered into a VIP area with its own private bar, the glazed walls provided an extended view of the masses down below. Impressive. More impressive than some of the other Crimson clubs. Its modern, almost futuristic, décor offered an all-encompassing atmosphere.

The bar at the back of the space was next to a flight of stairs. At the top, elevator doors to the left, another VIP entrance straight ahead. Despite it being glass-fronted, seeing inside was difficult from their inferior position. That area hadn't been part of her original tour.

"We'll ask you to wait here while we organize your drinks order," their escort said. "Once everyone's settled, the final five can come with me to the Ruby Room."

"Oh my God, the Ruby Room," Jill said.

"That's only open when Zairn is here in New York," Bree squeed.

"The glass distorts cameras, so cellphones can't film through it," Ron said, slipping his hands into his pockets. "I know things."

Yeah, like how to be an ass. Though that information was useful… or it would be if she had any intention of ever going to the Ruby Room.

"We should find a table," Jane said.

Every table had individual armchairs around it. Some two, others up to twelve. At the opposite end of the room, where perpendicular panes of glass met, was a dancefloor. With its own dedicated sound system, if she wasn't wrong. Had that been there during her first tour? No. The whole space had been tables and chairs; she'd have noticed a dancefloor for sure.

"Yeah, a table," Toria agreed with Jane. "Before they fill up."

"There's a ten over there," Roxie said and started that way.

Toria grabbed her arm. "We'll get it," she said. "You don't want to miss the private audience thing."

Yes, she did. How did she tell them that without piquing their suspicion? Roxie licked her lips to buy some time to think of what to say, but there was no discreet way to say it.

She shrugged. "I do," she said, narrowing her eyes when Toria frowned. "I do want to miss it."

Taken aback, Toria seemed bewildered. "What the hell happened?" She slid an arm around Roxie's waist. "Whatever it was, you have to talk about it."

"I can't," Roxie said, shaking her head. Pain was heavy in her chest. She didn't understand why the idea of Zairn pretending to be a stranger hurt like it did. He stirred up so much within her. Hoping her friend would take the hint, she breathed in and widened her smile. "Let's get really drunk and dance until we can't stand up."

"You got it, babe," Toria said, smacking a long kiss on her cheek. They held eye contact for just a moment. Her friend's acceptance meant the world to her. Especially now, her shredded emotions needed the support. "Go grab the table, I'll get the drinks."

Her friend did more than offer acceptance. Jill, Bree, Ron, and Dale were ushered into the Ruby Room above the bar. Whenever anyone approached to remind her that the private audience was in progress, Toria would slide in and chase the person away.

Other winners came to join their table. It was full by

the time the foursome returned from the Ruby Room. Revelers, begging for every detail, swamped them. Roxie didn't blame them for the excitement; it was common for people to react that way regarding proximity to Zairn.

Another drink went by… Time ticked on… She wasn't feeling any of it.

"Rox?" Toria's voice startled her. Both she and Jane crouched next to her. How had she missed their approach? "Do you want to go home?"

"No," she said, widening her fake smile. "No, this is great."

"You're not yourself," Jane called over the music. "I'm sorry we made you come."

"It's great, really," Roxie said, trying to convince them and herself. "You haven't danced yet. You should dance."

"Do you want to dance with us? It's only a few minutes to midnight."

New Year's Eve. Wow. She'd forgotten they were there for New Year's Eve.

"No, you guys go," Roxie said.

"That's it! Now we know you've gone crazy," Toria said and took her hand. "We're taking you home."

She kissed Toria's knuckles. "No, I want to stay. I want you to stay… You go dance, I just need to splash some water on my face. I'll come join you after."

"You promise?" Toria asked.

Roxie nodded. Her friends stood up, pulling her to her feet. Restroom access was next to the dancefloor. The three of them hugged before Roxie went through the door and up a short flight of stairs. She weaved through the group of women leaving the restroom at the same time she was entering.

A couple of women were fixing their makeup at a distant vanity. Before they could get a look at her, she went into the privacy of a stall. What to do? She needed to snap out of it. Fast. How could she be herself? She couldn't figure out who the hell inhabited her. Someone else was in her body. She didn't belong to it; she wasn't Roxie. Not as Roxie had been.

If she could get away with sneaking home to hide under her covers, she would do it. Roxie Kyst didn't sneak away or hide. Didn't refuse a chance to dance and drink. Claustrophobia clawed at her. Another unfamiliar sensation. The minute the makeup-fixing women's voices receded from the room, she threw open the stall door to leap out.

Alone. All the stalls were open and vacant. Okay. Good.

Agitation hyped her up. Stop. Stop pacing. Take a breath. Wash hands. Not face, or she'd lose her makeup. Be normal. She touched her cheeks with wet hands and then dried them off.

The dryer was by the vanity area at the far end of the narrow restroom.

Roxie planted her hands on the counter to lean in close and look herself in the eye. "Get it together," she whispered. Blinking at her own reflection again, she took a deep breath. "You can do this, Roxanna."

Using the full version of her name reminded her of the only other person who used it. Closing her eyes, her head sank down. Her friends could see right through her. Why shouldn't they? She didn't know what was real and what was fake anymore. Whatever she was experiencing, it wasn't like heartache as she'd ever known it.

The quiet sound of the door falling back into its frame didn't stir her. The click of what sounded like a lock straight after did. She opened her eyes. Who would...? Zairn. There he stood at the other end of the long space, just looking at her.

What was there to say?

When he started walking, his pace growing as he got closer, she turned around. He caught her face and hauled her up as he came down to join their mouths. Oh, his kiss. It erased all the BS. What was it? What did he feel? She couldn't tell anything about herself, but was sure she'd never been more grateful. The balm she needed to salve her hurt was there in his kiss. She tasted it on his slick tongue as it smudged against hers. She felt it in the sure cradle of his hands on her cheeks.

"I'm sorry," he murmured, allowing his lips to leave hers for just a second. "I'm sorry. I was an asshole—"

"No," she gasped, stealing another kiss as her hands clambered to hold his clothes and stroke his body. "I'm sorry. It was me. You were right. I'm sorry, baby."

He let go of her face to boost her up onto the vanity. They were kissing again. Like they never had or not like she could remember. There had always been urgency, always desperation in their need, but that moment wasn't the same.

What was in her soul? It didn't matter. All she needed was what he could give. Fighting to prove the resolve of her kiss outmatched his, she caught his hips with her legs and pulled him closer. Close enough that her fingers could loosen his belt and curl around his shaft.

There was no permission, didn't need to be. She was handling what was hers, in that moment at least. The glide of his hands on her thighs told her his thoughts were the same. He squeezed her ass to pull her closer. Roxie took on the task of moving her underwear aside and guiding him back to his home.

Doing it there, in a public restroom, regardless of the locked door, was a bad idea. Anyone with a key could walk in and catch them. But there were no worries. None that could interrupt their unity.

She knew then what he'd meant about forgetting what it was like to be close to each other. They were close in the most intimate way. Their hands searched bodies they'd once shared at their liberties.

He kept one hand on the mirror as the other held her in prime position. The demand of his need brought his hips to and from hers at such a pace, it was difficult to breathe fast enough to fuel the union. She begged for him, pleaded for more as the perfect angle of their bodies stimulated her in just the right places.

Just thinking about being with him was almost enough to take her to climax. There she was, spoiled by all of him. What else was there in the world? What else was life about?

The sharp injection of endorphins wrought a scream

from her throat. It burned in its decisive pitch. The only thing able to reduce her sorrow was exactly what he granted: him. All of him. Even if only for a moment.

Her ears were still ringing when the vague chant of a countdown wheedled its way in.

"Happy New Year," he panted, sweeping her hair from her face as he bowed to kiss her again.

The world was celebrating a new dawn as Roxie realized a new self.

"We brought it in with a bang," she said on a whimpering laugh.

Zairn just smiled and rested his forehead on hers, stroking her hair back from the side of her head over and over. "Yes, we did."

She appreciated his acceptance of her light humor so much. "Maybe we should've done that earlier instead of fighting."

"It's good, baby," he said, his hand skimming down her back. "We said what should've been said months ago."

A few seconds into the new year, it was clear the one ahead would be very different from the previous.

"My girls will be looking for me," she whispered. When he rose to peer down at her, she curved a hand around the back of his neck. "I'm not putting up walls. I just don't think being caught going at it in the bathroom would deliver the best message on your opening night."

He kissed her. With a hand on the back of her head, he coaxed her mouth to his and kissed her hard. As her nails dug into his shirt, he parted their lips just enough to breathe in.

"I needed this," he said, his breathing ragged. "To be with you again."

"Helluva way to bring in the New Year," she said, smiling at him. "If I can get away later, you want more?"

"Your ruby grants you access to wherever I am… whatever I have."

They kissed again. When he fastened his pants, Roxie slid forward, urging him back so she could slip off the vanity. Their disparate heights meant their lips separated before her feet hit the floor.

"There might be people out there."

He pointed to a door she'd barely noticed at the end of the vanity. "Employee access."

"Wow, and you still chose to do the dramatic entrance?" Catching his collar, she pulled him down to kiss him again. "I like it."

"I knew you would."

"Cocky," she teased like it was a warning.

"Just the way you like me."

"I like you every way," she said, loosening her smile to let him see something more real within her. "Every way, Zairn Lomond."

As her hand slid onto his cheek, he dipped lower to join their lips for a quick second. "Are you getting romantic on me?"

She shrugged. "Ah, I blame it on the alcohol."

"You've only had two and a half drinks."

Roxie laughed. "How can you possibly know I'm halfway through a drink?"

"Because I told Tibbs to get rid of it. You don't leave your drink in a club and then go back to it. Rookie mistake. I expected more from a pro like you."

"It's your VIP area, Casanova. Your club."

"And I know how alluring you are, Miss Kyst. Stronger men than me have failed to resist."

"You resisted for a long time," she whispered, looping her arms around his neck.

"No more. Never again," he said, nuzzling her mouth. "Now are you going to see your girls or am I taking you upstairs to bed?"

"You have a party to host."

"I prefer the private variety with you in my bed."

"I slept in your bed in London."

"I know, I refuse to let them change the sheets," he said, making her laugh as he hooked an arm around her waist to sit her on the vanity again.

The moment cool granite touched her thighs, she pushed him to hop down again. "No. No. See, now you're distracting me all with sex again. I just got laid, I need to go get drunk now… I'm doing tonight in reverse."

Smoothing her skirt, she couldn't help the happy sway of her hips. It was just as impossible to ignore the glimpses she got of him in the mirror above the sinks as she sashayed past.

"I missed you, Lola Bunny," he called out to her.

Spinning around, she blew him a kiss and watched him linger before disappearing through the employee door.

In the club, she'd said splashing water on her face would be revitalizing. With the grin and glow Zairn had delivered, her friends were going to think the water had magical powers.

ELEVEN

LYING IN THE MIDDLE of Zairn's bed, still warmed by their latest union, Roxie had never been more relaxed. "What did you tell everyone?"

"Everyone?" he asked, on his side next to her, teasing her with the light sweep of his fingertips.

"The party was still going when I said goodnight," she said. "There's no way your secret corner was abandoned. Everyone wants tea with the Emperor."

"I came upstairs around one. Good thing about being in charge, I don't owe anyone any explanations."

"Does Ballard know?"

"That we had sex in the ladies' room?"

"I feel sort of privileged," she said, wiggling her shoulders in a strutting shrug. "Being the first woman you nailed in your remodeled club." She frowned. "You didn't nail anyone else in the club tonight, did you?"

"No," he said on an exhaled laugh and bowed to kiss her forehead. "I really missed you."

Although it wasn't her natural state to reach deep down inside herself to pull out her most intimate thoughts, Roxie wanted to show trust. At the start of their association, she'd been cool with him not trusting her. Then he'd gone above and beyond to show that he did. Never anywhere along the way had she faced or accepted her own trust issues.

"I liked your tie choice on Talk at Sunset."

"Mm hmm," he said in a way that implied he knew more. She blinked innocent eyes at him. "And you went postal at Astrid because I suggested you needed better security."

"I didn't go postal," she said, tracing her fingernails across his chest. "I was mad that you farmed me out to staff."

"Is that why you were mad?" he asked, unconvinced. "You weren't maybe looking for a reason to put space between us?"

Hmm, peering deeper, her powers of deduction weren't at their peak. "Astrid would never have told you that. How did—"

"Tibbs told me," he said.

Yeah, that made more sense. Astrid wasn't confident with the personal and Zairn Lomond, but she was more relaxed with Tibbs.

"I didn't enjoy being out of the loop. In Rome, when you left, things changed. Our eleven days were great. You know I had an incredible time, but I think…" Taking a deep breath, she was grateful for that last drink in the club. "I was just aware that you could disappear any time; cut me off whenever you pleased."

"I'm sorry, babe," he said, still caressing her. "It won't happen again."

"You left because of me though, didn't you? Because I was so blasé about us having sex." He didn't answer with words; the twitch of his brow did it for him. "It was fun. The sex was incredible."

"And it was all you wanted."

Roxie sighed. "Don't take it personally. I don't think about a future with a guy I like," she said. "Too many things come up. No one can predict what's coming. People have different views too, different values. What's the point of getting sucked into a fantasy that can never play out? I've seen it happen over and over, not just with me, but with friends, women everywhere. They build a guy up to be something he never was and will never be. They think about houses and white dresses and kids, and when it all falls apart, they're stunned. Devastated. It's crazy because the only place the fantasy ever existed was in their heads. No one let those women down except themselves."

"Is that what you want? Houses, white dresses, and kids?"

"Hmm," she breathed out the murmur of a laugh. "Porter has designs on running for office. He said it was something that had always been in the back of his mind. Who knows if that's true…? I said he didn't think through dating me if that was his aspiration. I'd make a terrible congressman's wife."

"You're compassionate. You're smart and gregarious," he said. "Don't sell yourself short." A moment passed, then he drew in an exaggerated breath. "That said, I don't think you should be a congressman's wife."

"I'm the woman who jetted around the world with a renowned lothario and streamed her private life to the world. I don't have to worry about anyone hanging their hat on my moral coat hook any time soon."

"What about the lothario?" he asked. "Can he hang his hat on your moral coat hook?"

Her gaze drifted up to his, her lips quirking. "That sounds so dirty," she said, laughing.

"You make everything dirty," he said, rearing back to scoop her body up on top of his.

Still laughing, she kissed his jaw, his mouth, his chin. Staying the night might not be a good idea. The elevator opened into the apartment and his people came and went as they pleased.

If there was a possibility of interruptions, she needed to know. "What are the chances of company?"

"You want company?" he asked, gathering her hair away from her face, becoming more discerning. "Is this about the woman you like? I can't remember her name."

"You remember everyone's names," she said, opening her teeth on his stubble. "I love it when you don't shave."

"I make a point of forgetting the names of people you want to sleep with."

"*I* want to sleep with?" she asked, sitting up, straddling him. "What woman do I want to sleep with?"

"From the final five."

It only took her a second to figure out who he meant. "Bree? I didn't want to sleep with her. I said you wanted to sleep with her."

"I hadn't met her."

"I saw the way you checked her out on Talk at Sunset that first night. You and Drew Harvey and every other guy with eyes in his head."

He smiled. "You know what I remember about that night? The woman who drew her unimpressed eyes off me the minute I thought to look at her."

Opening her hands on his chest, she laughed. "I did not. God, you make me sound like such a bitch."

"Not a bitch. It intrigued me… I looked at you and read challenge."

Sitting up, he threw his arms around her and flipped her onto her back, putting himself on top.

"I knew it was the chase," she said, her cheeks aching with the width of her grin. "It's all you men are interested in."

"I told myself that night, that minute, to stay the hell away from you. I knew if I got mixed up with you, I'd be sunk."

"And then I started spouting truth to the world…" Stretching both arms straight out at either side of his head, she tested her muscles before draping her arms around him. "You're welcome."

"I was so pissed."

"I know, I was there."

"All of a sudden we're getting news alerts about the contest being a con. News outlets were requesting comment. When Knox called to find out what the hell was going on, I was at my limit."

"There was something sexy about you storming in the way you did. That, '*I own the world*' thing you do? That's sexy."

"You didn't blink. You matched me barb for barb.

God…" He groaned, showing her the tension in his tight jaw. "I wanted to fuck you right there."

"Well…" Roxie rolled her eyes to their top corners and continued very matter of fact. "There were a lot of other people in the room, so that would've been inappropriate. I learn a lot about inappropriate when I spend time with you."

"And then you walked out in those pajamas…"

She lost some of her faux starch when the memory put another smile on her face. "It didn't occur to me to seduce you."

"Which was probably exactly why I wanted you. You're not like any other woman, Roxanna Kyst."

"I suppose if I'd wanted into your wallet, I could've given head or something…" She sighed, returning to her aloof state. "Next time, don't pay for everything up-front. Add some caveat in the small print that the contest winner has to submit to regular internal examination by your cock… or something."

"You think we'll have a next time?" he asked, brushing his lips across hers.

"Yes, the next time your reputation takes a hit."

"How about you take our next winner on tour?"

"Uh, duh," she said, playing again. "I don't have a plane. Or, you know, millions of dollars to pay for hotels and meals and drinks and whatever. Some people whatever a lot."

"I'll give you a credit card," he murmured before kissing her again.

"Could I take someone on a Crimson tour?" Roxie pondered the point. "That would be a long time without sex. When did we first have sex?" she asked, running her fingers into his hair when he descended to kiss her neck and shoulder. "Rome. We knew each other like what? Six, seven weeks? I don't think I could tour Crimson for a full three months without sex… Though maybe it wouldn't be so bad if you weren't around… could be your bad influence corrupted me. You kept flirting with me. Makes me horny when you do that." She smiled when his response was to flick her nipple with his tongue. "That too. You know, for being an ass man, you sure spend a lot of time with my breasts."

"You like it when I spend time with them."

She smiled because it was nice to know he'd noticed. "See, you're doing it now, just like on tour. All the time, everywhere we went, you just kept talking about sex on and on… I guess it's the lifestyle. You must have access to all kinds of elite pussy."

"Elite pussy?" he asked, his mouth on the underside of her breast. "You have such a way with words, Lola."

"A guy like you doesn't have to go six weeks without sex. You don't have to go six minutes." Which put a thought in her head. She scooped both hands on his face to pull his mouth from her body to look him in the eye. "Were you having sex on the tour? Before me?"

"No," he said, nothing but truth shining from him— truth and desire.

"We've never been exclusive."

"I wasn't sleeping with anyone else. I haven't slept with anyone else since you won the tour."

"Okay," she said, letting him go back to his kissing. "Just had to confirm there was no chance of you passing on a gross venereal disease or something. Still crossing my fingers on the chance of a lawsuit."

"Boy, this is sexy talk," he said, circling her navel with the tip of his tongue.

"Wait a minute…"

"And she caught up," he muttered to himself, his lips on her belly.

"Since I won means you haven't been with anyone these last two months," she said. "You meant while we were together, on the tour… right?" He didn't respond, just kissed her lower abdomen. Before he got to the real sweet spot, she grabbed his head again and pulled his mouth away from its expedition. "Casanova?"

He cleared his throat, suggesting he was reaching his limit of humoring her. "Are you going to tell me you've been rolling in the hay with other guys since the last time we saw each other?"

"I don't live on a farm, so no. No hay," she said, stroking his hair away from his forehead. "But that's different."

"How is that different?"

"I am not a party god," she said. "Or subjected to hundreds of thousands of men rubbing up against me all day long."

He was smirking again. "Hundreds of thousands?" Rising, he kissed her lips quick. "Ballard's got your back, women don't get that close."

"This is not about my back. You could sleep with them if you wanted to. It's allowed, we didn't ever... We haven't even spoken to each other for two months."

"Doesn't mean I wasn't paying attention. Do you think I enjoyed watching you walk into Clement's hotel every day?"

The media sure liked keeping track of people. "I didn't walk in there every day."

"Twenty-four hours after you left my bed, you were in his hotel."

"I went to meet him to talk about the case. To talk him out of taking the job of First Chair. You wanted me to do that, you thought it put me at risk."

"It does put you at risk."

"So then talking him out of it is a coup for you. And you can save your cents on Trevor and his gang."

"My cents are not the issue. Your life and you keeping it are the issues."

"Okay, so, yeah, if Porter steps back..."

"Did he step back?" Roxie pushed out her lips, accepting his point even though it irked her. "So he said no, why did you keep going back?"

"He's my friend. I'm usually friendly with my exes. Look at me, right now, naked under you, isn't that friendly?"

Shifting away, he fixed the covers and lay down with his head on his pillow. Roxie didn't like the foot of space he left between them.

They lay there. In the dark. Quietly... for a minute.

"Porter wanted to get married," Roxie said, thinking of Zairn's confession about Dayah. That hadn't been easy, but the truth had brought them closer. "He wanted to get married.

I didn't."

"You don't want to get married?"

"Not any time soon," she said, rolling onto her side, tucking her arm between her head and the pillow. "I didn't want the kind of life he wanted. I guess his proposal was just a way of putting that in perspective."

"What kind of life do you want?"

"I don't know," she said. "I told you I didn't know what I wanted."

"But you knew you didn't want him."

"Porter's too sensible for me. He thinks he's playing with me, but he doesn't really get it. I've never been with a man who got me…" Beneath the covers, she slipped a hand onto his abs. "I should've been so turned off, you were so goddamn arrogant… But it got me off. Your confidence. The way you talked to me, to other people…" She paused, replaying their early interactions and her initial impressions of him. "Then you knew how to mix my drink." His head moved in the pillow and she caught the glint of his eyes fixating on her. "You didn't just have the goods to back it up. You were so thorough; nothing was left to chance. I didn't have to be careful with you… Kesley was right, it's the respect. Even when we were teasing each other, I never worried, I felt nothing except the utmost respect from you."

For a score of seconds, they considered each other. Until the words came out of her mouth, they were new to her. She hadn't put language to any of it before.

"Slide that hand a little lower. I've got a lot of hot, hard respect for you over here."

On a laugh, she moved closer and lowered her hand to wrap it around his cock, but it was his lips that she kissed. "You get me, Z," she whispered. "You get me and I should've told you that before. I guess I just couldn't… I couldn't picture what that looked like if we weren't traveling and clubbing together every day."

"You said it yourself," he said. "You don't have to be careful with me."

"You say that now and then leave me standing in Rome alone and fucked. What would I do if next time your people just leave me there?"

"I told you that won't happen again."

"Usually, when I argue with a guy, the worst he'll do is storm out to a bar or mouth off to his buddies. When you and I argue, I have to worry about the media cluing me in on where you are after you have a ring on your finger."

"I didn't marry her."

"I know that," she said, flopping onto her back, pushing her hair up away from her forehead. "And it shouldn't matter to me if you did." Roxie had never been so frustrated with herself. "Why do I keep obsessing about it?"

"Do you think if I had married her…" he said, appearing on his side next to her again, "that a piece of paper would change things between us?"

She made eye contact. "I can't sleep with you if you're married, Z. I'm laid back about most things, but I can't be with another woman's man. I told you that in Vegas when we said hello in that office."

His brows rose. "Said hello by going at it like we'd been celibate for ten years."

"I had been celibate since Rome," she said, and gestured at herself. "And, hello, you call me a rabbit for a reason."

"That your way of telling me you were going at it with Clement?" he murmured, stroking her.

"I haven't slept with Porter since before you and I met. Before he and I broke up. Porter doesn't do sex like that. I mean, he doesn't care about sex. It's not something that drives him. I don't think he thinks about it that much. The case gets him off. If he wins a case or has a good day, he has happy sex. If he loses or has a bad day, it's frustrated sex." She sighed. "The latter was better."

"Because…?"

Surprised that he'd ask, she angled to get a better look at him. "Is that a real question?" His half-nod-shrug seemed to suggest it was. "You want to talk about me having sex with other men?"

"I want you to talk about everything," he said. "Even if it does make me want to follow through on that hit I threatened before." He smiled to show he was kidding. "Things have always been innate between us. There's something instinctual about this, whatever this is. But…" He raised his brows and came a little lower. "Haven't you noticed it gets easier, and the sex gets better, the more we tell each other things?"

The sex got progressively better every time. Until he pointed it out, Roxie hadn't thought about the correlation. Each time they were intimate, it seemed they hit a high impossible to beat. Every time she was proved wrong.

Her gaze flicked back and forth between his eyes. "I like the way you want me. How you know I want sex without us exchanging a word. You knew we needed it tonight. The last time we saw each other, we were screaming in anger. But you knew… You touch me with the same arrogant entitlement that you show everything else. No…" A frown tensed her forehead as she fought to figure it out. "It's more than that… I don't feel like I'm the same as anything else, as any other woman, when we're together."

"You're not," he said, combing his fingers through her bangs and into the length of her hair draped over her shoulder.

"When Kesley first told me about you…" Her head shook just a little. "It was like she was talking about a stranger. She talked about how careful you are with women. How you don't touch them in certain ways or do things that could be misconstrued. It was just… strange. You were never like that with me. But I've seen it. After she pointed it out, I've noticed it a lot. She's totally right. But… you were never like that with me."

"Because it always felt right," he said. "Men. In general, the world over, have to be aware of these things, hyperaware, especially now. It's right that they should be. No one should ever be uncomfortable or feel pressured… So, yeah, I ensure my interactions with women are neutral. With you, I didn't think about it. I wanted to touch you, so I did. It was automatic. My mind and body were conditioned to do it, required to do it… And you always responded. It felt right, Rox."

"I didn't bring it up so you could apologize. I don't want that… I like being different," she said, wriggling further under the covers, tucking herself closer. "We never spoke like this before. It's goofy. I don't think I like it."

"Hey," he said, curling a finger around the edge of the covers she was attempting to hide under. "No walls… I like that you don't correct me and say there's no us."

Comments she hadn't thought twice about plagued him. Hearing them back demonstrated why. She wouldn't appreciate being shrugged off and dismissed all the time. Hell, sometimes she'd actually laughed. Maybe she was a bitch.

Roxie drew in a breath. "My mom was a mom. A mom and a wife. That was it. She volunteered but didn't have any friends not connected to me and my brother and sister. I never wanted that life. To identify myself by what I was to others… I don't know what I want. That's the honest truth. I know I still want to be me. That's it."

"I'd never ask you to change, Roxanna. All I want is the complete, unfiltered you. That's it."

"Come here," she murmured, coiling her arms around his neck to tempt him down for a kiss.

Arching her body, she rubbed her chest against him.

When he tried to break the kiss, she just tightened her hold and whined. "This you seducing me to change the subject?" he asked, their lips still connected.

"Turn it on, Party Boy," she mumbled against his kiss. "Show me a good time."

Sneaking into his bed might have felt naughty after telling her friends it was her bedtime, but it wasn't wrong. Being alone with him, wrapped in the intimacy of night, Roxie was adjusting to their new dynamic. Even if it meant nothing in the light of day, she wanted to live in the moment with him. Life had never been so good.

TWELVE

ROXIE DIDN'T LIKE WAKING UP. Rather, waking up was fine. It was the getting out of bed that wasn't appealing.

"...emergency. Tibbs sent me the report an hour ago."

"Opening night going off without a hitch? Zero drama or intrigue. It's a fucking miracle."

Two male voices. The first was the man she'd spent the night with. The second she recognized as a man she hadn't seen since California. Both men were coming closer.

"You should have more faith," Zairn said, an obvious smile in his voice.

"The only negative we got, and it came up a lot, was your refusal to do a sit down."

"For the duration of our contract, we have exclusivity with Hatfield for anything that happens in the clubs," Zairn said. It sounded like he was in the room. "And we have a press conference later."

"After you interview with Hatfield."

Raising one arm in an exaggerated stretch, Roxie whined in a yawn.

"What the—are you fucking kidding me that—" Her

arm flopped down, flattening the covers, thus revealing her identity to the cynical Ballard. His mouth closed, and he turned a deadpan look to Zairn. "It's on me that I didn't anticipate this."

"You did anticipate it, bud," Zairn said, going over to slap his friend's arm. "That's why you told me not to contact her while she was in the building."

He sauntered toward the bed.

"So you heard the advice," Ballard said, "you just ignored it."

"It's my fault," Roxie said, scooching closer to Zairn when he sat on the bed. "I broke—"

"And I entered," Zairn interrupted, tipping up her chin to kiss her. "Are you hungry? I can have something sent up."

"No, you can't," Ballard said. "You have brunch with the final five."

"He already fed me today," Roxie teased. "That counts for something."

"Too much information," Ballard said. "I don't need the details."

"I didn't know you were squeamish," Roxie said. Flopping onto her back, Zairn's pillow caught her head. "He wasn't squeamish like this about us before, was he?"

"He never had to see you naked in my bed. We were discreet, at your request, before."

"I guess this isn't really discreet." She sighed and closed her eyes to appreciate the comfort one last time. "Okay, I guess I better walk of shame it back to my own room."

"Walk of shame?" Zairn said. "You weren't ashamed last night."

When his lips touched hers, it was too easy to wind her arms around him and force him closer.

"If you want me to cancel the breakfast, give me a reason," Ballard said. "One the winners will buy… and something Og won't question."

Loathed to let him go, Roxie only did it out of necessity. "He's not canceling." She feathered her fingers across his stubble. "You didn't shave."

"No, I did not," he said, his lips slanting.

Damn, he was a tease. "Curse your responsibilities," she whispered to his frustrating delight. "Can you grab my dress, so I don't have to *show* Ballard too much information?"

"I'm out," Ballard declared. "I'll wait in the other room."

Roxie didn't take her smiling eyes from Zairn's. "I'm going to skip the group breakfast."

"Because…"

"Because I think it would be inappropriate to jump you in a public restaurant."

He laughed and flicked her hair from her brow. "I own it."

"Doesn't make it not illegal," she said, then realized something. "I don't think we've ever appeared together for anything other than the documentary."

Which meant at the Crimson clubs and that footage hadn't aired yet.

"There was that time in Sydney."

When she streamed them to the world. "Yeah," she groaned, "and that ended so well."

"Ended with us in bed, can't say I'm sorry about it."

"I just don't think we'll do well at a table with other people. People still stop me in the street to ask about us. Like not even just you, but us. As if I'm going to spill my secrets to a stranger on the street."

"People don't think of us as strangers. They think they know us." Her from her streams and him from the media's insatiable appetite for him. "Do you want to go public?"

"Oh, yeah, and Ballard's perfect, drama-free event suddenly becomes a feeding frenzy. No. I don't want that. What we are is not their business, remember?"

"It's on the table," he said, kissing her.

"Outing us?" she asked. "We can't do that. Not until we know if there is an us."

He stopped kissing to frown at her. "You think this was a one-night thing?"

"I think I go back to Chicago tonight and you don't."

"You want me in Chicago, I'll come to Chicago," he said. "Or you can stay here. As long as you want. Move in."

A jolt of alarm shot through her. "Do you ask all your one-night stands to live with you?" His scowl was enough to betray his displeasure. "Okay," she said, patting his shoulders before easing him up.

Leaving the bed, Roxie crossed the broad space to go into the bathroom. The idea of taking a shower in the large glass stall appealed, but she had to put last night's dress back on, which would negate the being clean thing. She ran her fingers into her tangled hair and bent over to splash water on her face, cleaning off remnants of the previous night's makeup.

"This was not a one-night thing."

She raised her head to see his reflection in the mirror behind hers. "We spent one night together. You don't move in with someone after one night."

"It's more than one night, we had—"

"Eleven days together. In secret," she said, crooking a brow. "You're moving fling and subsequent one-night stand into serious commitment literally overnight." She intended to grab a towel from the shelf next to the sink. Except there were so many of them, she didn't know where to begin. "Which do I use?"

Without looking, he grabbed one and thrust it into her hands. "You can work anywhere," he said. "Why not New York? The most coveted city in the world."

"Yeah," she said, putting the towel down. "Where's your toothbrush?" He pressed the panel under the vanity and out popped a drawer containing a toothbrush, toothpaste, and a bunch of other things. "Who keeps their toothbrush in a drawer?" Although she asked, Roxie didn't expect an answer. "I can work anywhere." She picked up his toothbrush and paste. "But I live with my friends, my family are in Chicago. I have a life in Chicago."

"One which includes your ex-boyfriend's trial," he said. "Staying here would mean being safe."

"How often are you even in New York anyway?" she asked, putting toothpaste on the brush. "You don't live here ninety percent of the time. What would I do here by myself?"

"You'd be safe here," he said as she began to brush. "In Rome, I told you I wanted the right to hash everything out with you. I have that right now, this is more than a one-night thing. We're figuring this out. I won't wait another two months to see you again. New York is an incredible city. You could do whatever you want. There's office space downstairs, plenty of it, pick an office, hell, pick a floor, work from there. Or spend your days melting plastic and getting manicures, if that's what makes you happy."

She bowed to spit and then tipped higher to make eye contact with his reflection. "That would never make me happy. If you don't know me well enough to understand I couldn't be that kind of woman, then we're putting the brakes on right here."

"I'm not saying you're about the money—"

"And in Rome, you said I'd fight the chains any man tried to put on me. That was the woman you had sex with. That same woman was in your bed last night. You think I'll suddenly simper and defer? Not a chance."

She continued to brush.

"Roxanna, I don't want you to change anything about yourself. Not one damn thing. Ever. But you have to understand there are two people in this relationship. You can't decide unilaterally."

She spat again and rinsed the brush. "I decide about me. Especially about where I lay my head and where I call home. I have never been the type of woman to uproot herself chasing after a guy."

"So you'd rather I uproot myself chasing after you?"

"No one has to uproot themselves," she said, swerving around him to go back into the bedroom, winding through the seating area. "You can't just say 'relationship' and it automatically becomes real."

"So that's it," he asked, on her trail again. "One night and we're done... again."

"I'm not saying we're done," she said, stepping into her dress and picking up the straps to loop them onto her shoulders. "We just don't have to make all the decisions right this minute… do we?"

Though he was frowning when she turned, Roxie felt him acquiesce just a little. "No, we don't."

Going to him, she locked her fingers at the back of his neck. "Because if we're not just a one-night thing, then we have time to figure it out."

"I'm used to being decisive," he grumbled, his tone suggesting he was calming.

"Yes, but I'm not business," she said. "And I'm not a woman asking you for something or in need of your help. You don't have to save me, Z. I'm just fine."

"You're more than fine," he said, sliding his hands onto her hips. "We have time."

"Yeah," she said, smiling. "Did you change your number?" His head shook a little. "Me either. Maybe if you have a day off sometime, we can hook up in Chicago… I could come here to visit when you're in town."

"Sounds more like an affair than a relationship."

Pulling him down, she brought their lips to within an inch of each other. "What's so wrong with that?"

Slipping her tongue between his lips, Roxie relished being in his life again. There were a lot of unknowns in front of them. A lot of possibilities too. Rushing in libido-first rarely ended well. Taking their time, figuring it out one step at a time was a smarter choice; especially given their public exposure. The media might be more interested in him as an individual than her, but speculation about them had been rife after her streaming mishap.

If they were ever going to be together, they'd have to build a strong foundation. Once the media found out, it would be madness and mayhem. Zairn had experience of that. Roxie had some too. But she didn't want the people she cared about to suffer as they had the last time. They'd have to be sure. Ready. Prepared.

THIRTEEN

"ROXIE! ROXIE! ROXIE!"

Why was Jane screaming?

Rushing out of her bedroom into the living room, Roxie arrived just in time to see Toria switch on the TV and begin flipping through channels.

"What is it?" she asked. "What's going on?"

No answer came. Her girls were glued to the TV. When Toria got to the entertainment news, both roommates shook fingers at the screen, though it wasn't necessary.

Zairn. Again. When else did they get so animated?

"I've told you," Roxie said on a sigh. "I don't give a damn. Don't call me through for this shit."

Going back to her bedroom, she returned to her mirror and breathed out. If it was something important, Zairn would call her. He would.

Just a week ago, she'd left him in his New York apartment. An affair, at the time, sounded sexy and exciting. Having Zairn in her life meant expecting scandalous news every once in a while. Some story on the news didn't necessarily translate to fact. Whatever it was—

Jane appeared in her doorway. "Rox," she said. "You

need to come out here and see this."

Makeup gave her a focus. "I really don't."

"It's about his assistant. Your friend."

She paused. "My friend?"

Nodding, Jane reached for her hand. "Astrid."

"What the hell did she do?"

Dropping the makeup brush, she took Jane's hand and followed her back into the living room. Having encouraged Astrid to be more adventurous, a whisper of excitement curled in her belly. Here was hoping she'd jumped in with both feet.

"It's unclear how long the two have been involved in a relationship…" the anchor on TV said. "If it is indeed a relationship. It may, perhaps, have been a one-night stand."

"Who are they talking about?" Roxie asked.

Maybe Astrid got herself mixed up with her own rock star. Happy speculation froze when a picture appeared on the screen. One followed another. Astrid and Zairn together. Outside, somewhere, talking… Darkness shrouded them, light came from further away. The street, maybe? If they were outside a club… The next one showed them in a different position. Astrid against the wall, Zairn up close. Super close. Then he was touching her face. Raising her chin… Their faces were in profile, slightly angled away. She couldn't make out their expressions. Another shot, them getting into a car together.

"Sources close to the pair have verified their extended time together. It was also reported that Zairn left his own grand re-opening at New Year early. Could the couple have had a private celebration?"

"Oh God," Roxie groaned. "Switch it off."

"This is huge!" Toria said, glued to the screen. "He's never been with an employee, never. Like ever."

"I get it," she said, marching over to snatch the remote from Toria. With one decisive move, she turned off the TV and dropped the remote onto the couch. Her girls screeched in protest. "He's not with an employee now. Can we get ready, please?"

"How do you know?" Toria called after her as she

started back to her bedroom.

"If he wanted to fuck her, he'd have done it by now!"

In her bedroom, she closed the door and exhaled. Laying a hand on the dresser by the door, irritation and exhaustion warred. For living life like this, Zairn deserved a medal. Talk about resilient. But that didn't matter now. Astrid was the first concern. Zairn took this kind of thing in his stride. Astrid, on the other hand…

No doubt the young woman was tearing herself apart. She hadn't wanted to admit her attraction to him. Now the world was speculating on the likelihood of them having a sexual relationship. Having been in that position, Roxie was qualified to talk it out.

She and her girls were supposed to be hitting the town; the call would have to be quick. No, it would be as long as it had to be. If Toria and Jane wanted to go without her, that was just fine.

Her phone was in her purse, ready for the night. The moment she took it out, it rang. A number… not a name. Unfamiliar numbers should be diverted to voicemail. Except, if it was the media, she needed to know they had her number. Damnit.

Pressing "accept" she took a chance. "Yeah?"

"Little Rox?"

"Ballard," she said, her tense shoulders dropped. "It's bullshit."

He breathed out a single laugh. "That's what I was calling to tell you."

Wandering to the bed, she needed to sit and find her calm again. "It's okay. You don't have to call me every time some overeager reporter recounts his fantasy as fact."

"He wanted me to say, he's not farming you out." She smiled. "He's in a room with—"

"I know the players," she said. "Crisis management."

"Yeah, 'cept he's more worried about you. This kinda shit never used to be part of my job."

"You're welcome. How is Astrid?"

"Quiet, tense… freaking out. She's my cousin. If I thought for a second he'd—"

"I know, geez," she said. "I know the story is bullshit. But Z is free to be with whoever he wants." No reply. "Long-distance relationships never work. Even if we want them to. So, yeah, we'll hook up if we can, but that doesn't make me his girlfriend or him accountable to me. His life is his own."

"Have you talked this week?"

"Yeah. He called to check we got home safe after New Year and… maybe a couple of other times." Phone sex was another of his fortes. Made sense, the guy lived his life on the road, but, wow. It hadn't been a Porter thing; she was rusty. "He doesn't have to call every minute."

"You know… you two talk about this thing completely differently."

"You called to make sure I knew he and Astrid weren't screwing," she said, tucking her heels against the frame of her bed by the mattress. "You're not going to turn it into a lecture, are you?"

"Remember Rome?" he asked. Oh, yes, she sure did. "The guy who stormed out after you told him it was just fun?"

Licking her lips, it was difficult to forget the guy who'd abandoned her. "I've told him I won't apologize for who I am. He went from one-night thing to asking me to live with him. I know his life differs from most. That he's used to being decisive, but what the hell? I live in the real world where people date, people have fuck buddies, friends with benefits. People don't relocate their lives after one night of incredible sex."

"I get it. You're not from the same world." Right. Why was he getting on her case if he knew that? "Why did you get together again in New York?"

Why? Because it hadn't been within her power to refuse him after their mouths met. Hell, it wasn't in her power to ever refuse him.

"What happened to your habit of never getting involved in his relationships with women?"

"Usually when he's with a woman, she's with us… She expects updates… and the press know about the relationship. This secret thing…"

"Doesn't answer my question, Ballard. Why get

involved with this?"

"He's my friend, Rox. And this means something to him. You mean something… You're the only one who doesn't get it."

"I get it. He wants to turn my life upside down, so he can get his rocks off whenever he feels like it."

"You really think he's like that?"

Her next exhale became a groan as she sank onto her back. "My life is in Chicago. I know what that life looks like. What my life looks like… The life he lives isn't real… It's a fantasy."

"It is real. You lived it for three months."

"A relationship can't be sustained like that. In each other's faces every minute. Together twenty-four-seven. And what happens next time we fight? What? We're forced to stay together because we're due on a flight or I get dumped somewhere until… what? If New York hadn't been next on the agenda, how long would I have stayed in London alone? If we're halfway across the world, I can't walk out for some air or take some space without the paparazzi mobbing me."

"You have access to the media, your own voice. If he fucks you over—"

"What? I should cause another crisis?" She laughed, though it wasn't in humor. "Can't you see how crazy that is? I can't hold him to ransom? He has to be with me, to be nice to me, in case I threaten to spill secrets to the press? I would never do that. No matter the circumstances. I have no interest in hurting him."

"But you have the power to do it."

"He's a grown man, Ballard. He can tell me this himself, if he wants to."

"I'm talking to you as his friend. I don't know what you two talk about, it's not whatever's going on between you. Neither of you have a goddamn clue… You're gonna hurt him again, Rox. He's responsible for thousands of jobs, thousands of lives rely on his network."

"This your way of telling me to walk away?"

"There's a reason I told him to stay away from you. Maybe it's 'cause I'm on the outside, but… you're coming at this from two different places. There's a decade between you, he's used to young but—"

"Oh, so now I'm just immature?"

"Inexperienced," he said. "He's never gone this long without a relationship. Since Dayah he…"

"I don't want to talk about that," she said.

It didn't feel right to talk about his personal life, his private life, even with his best friend.

"It's been almost two years, the media are clutching at straws. For a long time, this guy and those connected to him were their bread and butter. They could take one tip or another and run with it. Showing up outside Crimson was usually a ticket to headlines… But he's changed."

"Since Dayah."

"If you're gonna hurt him, Rox… if this isn't it for you, walk away before you destroy him."

Too late. According to Zairn, she'd already done that. "Did you tell him this? He had a chance to walk away in New York, he didn't take it."

If he hadn't come to the restroom to make up, there would've been a big, bold period at the end of whatever they'd been.

"I told him to stay away from you," Ballard said. "He didn't listen."

"And you think I will?"

Would she? Was he right? His friend should look out for him. Hers would if they knew about any of it. Not having anyone to talk things out with was a first for her. No one could tell her what she felt, but saying words out loud, it made a difference.

If there was a chance this was the Porter proposal all over again…

"Give me it." The bass of his voice snapped her from her thoughts. "Lola—"

"Don't," she said, "Ballard's in the room with you, don't grovel in front of an audience."

A second passed. "Babe, I was going to—"

"I know what you were going to and I'm saying don't."

"You mad?"

"No," she said. "It's hilarious, actually. How could anyone think a woman as beautiful and smart as Astrid would get it together with a second-rate player?"

His exhale was a disbelieving laugh. "Maybe I took advantage of her."

"Yeah, you'd have to," she said, her lips curling. "You'd never be so lucky. Ballard said nothing about his cousin losing her mind."

"Was good enough for you," he teased in return, warmth and seduction in his honeyed words.

"I'm an experimenter," she said. "Sometimes I go crazy. I'm into charity too, I've told you that plenty."

"Gives me a break."

"Don't you forget it. Astrid deserves at least a nine. You've gotta start pitching in your own league, honey."

"You're breaking the bad news? Someone has to be honest, right?"

"Yep… you're lucky I'm so generous."

He laughed. "Want me to send something sparkly?"

"No," she said, boosting herself off the bed to wander to her dresser. In the top drawer, under all the clothes, she slipped out the box containing her ruby. "I'm going out tonight." Hooking the phone between her head and shoulder, she slipped the ring on her finger. "I might drunk call you later, what time zone are you in?"

"Doesn't matter," he said. "I'll make myself available. But…" His hesitant tone was more serious than before. "It's not a good idea for you to go out tonight."

Always worried, always cautious. He could be such a buzzkill. "We'll take Trevor and his—"

"Let me call around," he said. "Get you something private… Chicago isn't known for—"

"Don't talk smack about my city," she warned, hiding her tease behind outrage.

"You wouldn't consider a ride to Boston or New York?"

"A ride," she said, holding up her hand to admire the ring that didn't grace her hand as often as it should. "You mean a plane."

"I can have a plane on the tarmac in twenty minutes."

"Then it's two hours before I get my first drink," she said. "How do I explain that to Toria and Jane?" Shaking her head at no one, she put the ring away. "No. No way."

"I can keep you safe in Crimson. You love the club…" Her lack of response provided her opinion. "Rouge own bars in Chicago. Pick one and we'll close it for you."

"Z," she said, tucking an arm under her breasts. "Is it the point to change the story? Give the reporters something else to chase down? I'll do it if you want to take the heat from Astrid, but—"

"Damnit, baby, why won't you let me keep you safe?"

"We're not going to fight about this," she sang.

Going out after the tour had been impossible. New York and the grand re-opening had refreshed fan interest. Going out with her girls in Chicago was supposed to be their test balloon. Would it be possible to have an anonymous night on the town? Sort of typical that Zairn would be the top story again.

"Lola—"

"Okay," she conceded. "I'll stay home."

"You know I don't want to restrict you," he said, frustrated, though not as much as her. "If the world knew—"

"I said I would stay home. I've gotta go break it to the girls."

"Baby, if you just let me… Go to New York, stay in my place. I'll send a car for—"

"Zairn," she said, cool and calm. "This is not your fault. And I am not mad. Just promise me you'll take care of Astrid, she'll be mortified about this."

"You want me to take care of her but won't let me take care of you."

"I can look after me, Skippy. I've got booze in the kitchen and great tunes. I can party anywhere."

"I know you can."

"Oh, but if I call later and ask for transport to one of your clubs, say no."

"My clubs are your playground. You have

unrestricted access, twenty-four-seven, three hundred and sixty-five days a year. Your security clearance is higher than mine."

It wouldn't be true, but was a nice idea. "Say no," she said, adamant in her playfulness.

"I can still have sex with you though, right?"

"Phone sex, yes. I wouldn't be able to explain your random appearance to my roommates."

"We could meet at a hotel."

"Thought I wasn't allowed out," she said. "Showing up with your entourage is a little less discreet than me going out with my girls."

"You know I'll randomly appear at your apartment sometime, right? Best thing about affairs is the spontaneity."

She fought to subdue her smile. "Now I know why the press love you so much," she said. "You do their job for them. Go untangle your current mess before tying up the next one."

"Okay, baby. Call later. Don't go out."

"Go break some hearts, Casanova," she said and hung up.

Stumbling from one drama to the next was no way to live. No one could claim life with Zairn Lomond was ever close to boring.

FOURTEEN

THEIR NIGHT OUT became a love in. From party tunes to romantic ballads and impromptu karaoke explosions, they'd run the musical gauntlet... and made a serious dent in their alcohol stores.

Approaching the end of the night, melancholy slipped in. "I just... need for it to stop," Roxie said to the liquid in her glass. "For people to let me go back to who I was before."

Even if she wasn't the same person on the inside.

"Because you hated it?" Toria asked from the armchair at the end of the coffee table. "The streaming and the interacting?"

Her attention flew up. "No! No, it's not that. Streaming was fun and the people who commented were incredible. It was amazing talking to such a passionate group. Communicating with people like that. With the world. It was a privilege and an honor."

"So go on your stream and say that. Ask people to leave you alone. But if you loved it so much, why would you want it to stop?"

"Because it's not mine," she said. "Crimson doesn't

belong to me." He doesn't belong to me. Crazy thought. Keeping it easy saved them both a lot of aggravation. "They invited me there for a specific period, and now that period is over. It's finished."

"Have they shut you out? Can you still login?"

Roxie shrugged, reaching for the liquor. "I don't know."

"Try it. If you're not authorized, we'll know they've shut you out. If you are, you're still allowed to use it."

"Yeah, come on."

"No, I don't—people might wonder what's going on. Why I think I have the right—"

"They don't," Toria said, taking her hand. "Trust me, we are those people…" she gestured between herself and the nodding Jane. "We never had anyone engage like you did. There's a reason you're adored online. You're personable and fun. And we want the updates."

"Don't do that," Roxie said, squirming. "Don't talk to me like I'm famous."

Jane smiled at Toria. "Don't look now, honey, but you are." Her girls were amused. Lucky them. "Famous and adored. Now, we don't know Zairn like you do…"

"Lucky bitch," Toria mumbled behind her glass, following the words with a smile.

"But I don't think he'd be mad at you for talking to people… would he?"

"He owns the website," she said, thinking back to Boston.

"Wouldn't he cancel your access if he didn't want you on there?"

"He'd tell Tibbs to have the credentials revoked."

"There you go."

Toria leaned back to look across the room at Roxie's laptop. "Only one way to find out."

Did she want to know if her access endured? Maybe… Okay, so the honest answer was yes. Hmm. If she didn't, what else would she do? Drunk calling Zairn for sex was a bad idea. It wasn't like he'd ever accused her of being too reserved. The girls would want to know who she was talking to if they heard…

"Okay," she said, gulping the last of her drink and putting the glass down. "Let's find out."

Her girls leaped up in time with her, eeking and screeching in excitement.

Next to the hallway, her desk faced the kitchen. Opening her laptop to switch it on, she glanced around.

"What happened to my drink?" Her girls headed for the hallway, bottles and glasses aplenty. "Uh, where are you going?"

"To login," Jane declared.

"Our favorite streamer is about to transmit," Toria said, scampering over to kiss her cheek before returning to Jane.

"You can…" she called after them. "Stay with me to…" A bedroom door closed. Exhaling, she sat down and logged into her computer. "This is a bad idea."

Saying the words didn't change her actions. The Crimson web address flew off her fingers, as did her user credentials. Wow, everything worked. She was still authorized… She hadn't expected that.

"Lomond's Delight," she murmured while navigating to the streaming section. Clicking the button put a smile on her face. "Okay… Usually, I wait… I know, I should wait until we have more viewers… Maybe I shouldn't wait." More viewers meant more eyes on the car crash. Why did she think that and carry on anyway? Pushing her shoulders back, she adjusted the tilt of the screen so the camera would capture all of her. "It's been a while. I know it's been a while… I'm not a part of the Crimson machine anymore. Nope. Not me. I'm a free, free agent…" The comments were stacking up. "Anyone who frequents this site knows Zairn Lomond was in the news tonight… Not a surprise, it feels like when is he not." She sighed. "You've heard the stories, and it's not my place to offer commentary… Nope. No siree… It's not my place…" But she was going to do it anyway. "The interest, people covet it. Fame, I guess you'd call it. I know many people wish for fame.

"The coveting people would say only those who have

it drone on about its pitfalls… But imagine it… just for a minute…" Running her fingers through her bangs, she swept them to the side. "Stuck in your apartment, afraid to go out for fear you'll be mobbed… I'll be honest…" She showed a hand. "I've never been 'afraid' out there. I'm more aware of what those who are protecting me go through. It's easy for me… it was always easy for me. Not because I wanted it, but because Crimson knows what they're doing… They're smart people, kind people. They don't deserve what they're forced to endure. It's a nightmare, never knowing when you'll walk into a crush, always being aware of…" She frowned. "I guess I wasn't aware… Everything was taken care of and then I came home after the tour and it didn't go away. It got better but… People are people, you know? Like Zairn and Astrid, Kesley Walsh, they're all human beings with feelings and rights… Most of us would say they chose that life, Zairn and Kesley anyway… But that doesn't mean they should be subjected to constant attention. It's weird, people calling your name, they want a quote or a comment… I didn't even know if my credentials would work…" Babbling, she was babbling… probably not making much sense. "I love every person who's commented, anyone who logs on to watch, I appreciate that you care. You wouldn't be here if you didn't care, maybe not about me, but Crimson and Zairn. It matters that you care. We all care… Yes, there's negativity in here sometimes, but most of the time… Each and every one of you is valuable to me. To Crimson…"

Glancing at the comments, she read a question.

Q: Are we important to Zairn?

"Yes," Roxie answered. "You are important to Zairn. He cares about people. He cares about all of you, and those in his life. That's all he wants, is to protect the people around him…" At least in her jabbering, she was getting a chance to talk out what was in her own head. "It's harder for him to see others pursued or harassed, he just wants to help. To make things better."

Q: Are you back? For good? We miss you!

The comments kept on coming. Even if her eyes weren't alcohol-crossed, she wouldn't be able to read all of them. No one could read that fast.

"This was an impulse. Logging on, I mean. I wanted to… I haven't forgotten about any of you or about Crimson. I missed you too. My friends said I should check if I was still authorized… and to ask that maybe if you see me around town, you just let me be." Dropping an elbow to the desk, her brow creased as she propped her chin on the heel of her hand. "But I don't think I want you guys to leave me be. People are great. Everyone is kind and… it's not people who are difficult to deal with… It's sensationalism in the press, you know? How they take the tiniest crumb of something and blow it up into a big mammoth deal…" While saying the words, she sank back, gesturing with her arms. "Some people are in the public eye, fair enough. They might choose it, and maybe it would be naïve not to expect scrutiny. But people like Astrid…" Scrunching her face, she shook her head. "She's the kindest, sweetest, quietest woman in the world, she's amazing. Imagine someone saying you were sleeping with your boss… now imagine it's not just watercooler chat, but your picture, a picture of a private moment, blasted all across the world. Millions of people see it. On the TV, people talk about you and your life, your intimate life… and the worst part is it's bullshit.

"What do you do? Scream innocence knowing the world will accuse you of protesting too much or say nothing and let the lie continue. It's lose-lose…"

A question caught her eye.

Q: Are you jealous of Astrid?

"Am I jealous of Astrid?" Roxie repeated, her head tilting while she pondered. "She lives a full and busy life and doesn't have much chance to slow down or reflect. She works hard. Very hard and has a position of power, I guess. I'm jealous she's so wonderful. I'm not always so wonderful. She's one of those people you can only like because they're just so dedicated. She takes her job seriously. Crimson means a lot to her."

Q: Are you going to visit Crimson again? Which is your favorite Crimson club?

"I couldn't possibly pick a favorite," she said. "Sorry, that's a question about my favorite Crimson. I have my favorite memories from certain clubs, but I have my private reasons for those."

Q: If it's bullshit, what were Zairn and Astrid doing cozied up in an alley?

"Hmm, why were they together in that alley? I have no idea, and I shouldn't. None of us should. It's not our business. They weren't doing anything illegal. Everyone is entitled to their privacy."

Q: Zairn should sue everyone who ran with the story. Would you support him?

"Would I support Zairn suing?" Swinging her chair in an arc back and forth, she tucked her heels on the edge against her ass. "I'd support whatever he wanted to do. He understands they have a job. Everyone is just trying to make their way in the world…"

Q: Are you in love with him?

Q: Were you really together?

Q: How many times did you sleep with him?

So many questions about her relationship with Zairn. The relationship they'd never confirmed or acknowledged. Logging on put her in a corner. Either she answered or got the hell out of there.

"Okay, peeps, I'm going to leave it there. I've said too much already. You're wonderful. All of you. Thank you to all of you for your support. Keep on loving Crimson."

She offered a sort of wave and ended the stream. A second later, she closed the laptop lid, folded her arms on it and dropped her face to them. What the hell did she just do?

A moment passed. "Honey…" Jane said, stroking Roxie's hair.

Standing up, she headed for her room. "I'm going to bed."

"You were allowed in," Toria called after her. "They didn't lock you out."

Her lips curled. No, he hadn't locked her out. Crimson might not be her home, but it didn't mind her visiting. Either that or it was an oversight. Would she regret what she'd said in the morning? Maybe. Probably. But going to sleep with Zairn on her mind was never a bad thing.

"ROXIE! ROXIE! WAKE UP!"

Groaning, she didn't have time to turn over before someone landed on the bed beside her. "What the—"

"Look! Look!"

Fighting with her covers, which were pinned at one side by her roommate, she twisted over onto her back. "What is going on—"

"He's talking about you," Jane said, full of that familiar excitement.

"Who's talking about me?"

"Zairn," Jane said, swiping Roxie's hair from her face. "Look. You have to look."

"Zairn's talking about me?" It took her a second to process. When the words sank in, her eyes opened as far as her frown would let them. "Why is he talking about me?" Pushing up to sit, it was a battle to get with it… and to control her giant yawn. Right up until Toria appeared in the doorway with coffee. Hope. "Ah, I love you."

Wearing a smile, Toria came over to sit on Roxie's other side, handing over the coffee. "You're used to being served, Miss Famous."

Oh God. The stream… what the hell had she been thinking? It was a blur. She hadn't been drunk enough that intoxication could hold up as a valid excuse in court… or with Ogilvie. Who wasn't a media whore? What had she said? Was it that bad? Who knew? Self-preservation was blocking out the memory.

"Are you alive yet?" Jane said, raising her tablet. "Will you watch him? Roxie? Will you watch him?"

"Will I watch him?" Roxie mumbled.

Her girls adjusted her pillows and came in close on either side, trapping her in. Focusing on the coffee, she had no choice except to watch when Jane pressed play on the paused image.

"…but you saw it?" someone behind the camera asked.

"I saw it?" Zairn asked. "Yes, I saw it."

"Will you be taking legal action?"

"Against who?" Zairn asked, glancing off to the side. Where was he? Outside somewhere… hot. It was bright. Hence why he was wearing sunglasses. Did she recognize the building behind him?

"Legal action against Roxanne Kyst…" the reporter asked, "or the media?"

He cleared his throat. "It's Roxanna Kyst not Roxanne, and only a fool would take her on in court."

"Don't you forget it, buddy," Roxie muttered behind the rim of her coffee cup.

"So the media?"

"He got offended about your name again," Jane whispered.

Toria shushed her and tracked the picture back a couple of frames. "We're missing it."

"So the media?" the off-camera guy asked again.

"All of them? Forgetting for a moment that it's a symbiotic relationship… and that I dearly love a family who owns a vast portion of your affiliates? No. I have better things to do with my time."

"What was your reaction to her comments?" another

someone asked.

"I block out a lot of what she says," he murmured, retrieving his ringing phone from his inside pocket.

He read the screen and pressed it, stopping the ringing.

"Did someone sever her access to the Crimson site?" a reporter asked. "Did Roxanna get permission before streaming again?"

"Those questions contradict each other," Zairn said, checking something on his screen. "No one severed her access, not on my order, and she doesn't require permission."

"But it's your—"

"Look," he said, his attention leaving the phone to land on the questioner. "We gave Roxanna a voice. It's not one Crimson plan to silence. She is welcome to avail herself of it anytime she chooses. The last thing I would ever do is censor Roxanna Kyst. Her audience appreciates her honesty. We all should."

"When was the last time you spoke to Miss Kyst?"

"That's all, thanks," Zairn said, turning his back to stride away from those he'd left clamoring for more.

"Aww," Jane said, hugging the tablet to her chest. "He'd never censor you."

"He knows better," Roxie said, trying to pull her blankets from under her friends. "We should put a block on that website, so I can't access it again."

"It's your voice," Toria said. "That's what Zairn said."

He should know better. Roxie spoke her mind even in tough times… even when she should keep her lips sealed. She'd been too ill to remember what happened in the Sydney stream and too drunk to pick her words the previous night. Roxanna Kyst uncensored would not work out for anyone in the long-term.

And what was his comment about blocking out what she said and calling anyone who took her on a fool? If it was just them, fine, she loved the banter. The media would notice if he played with her in public like that. She'd told him not to argue with her in front of Hatfield and his crew. Had he forgotten the world didn't know about them? Damn, both of them seemed to enjoy the quicksand. It was warm, comforting, right until the second it pulled them under for good.

FIFTEEN

KEEPING HIS NAME OUT of her mouth was the best plan, and the only one likely to save him from her catastrophes. A celeb hitting rehab replaced the Astrid scandal. Thank God for the fickle tabloids.

Staying away from the Crimson website, she'd stuck a post-it onto her laptop, reminding her not to login. The word "Crimson" with a thick black cross through it. That should do the trick.

Zairn, in his typical way, wasn't worried. He didn't berate her for the stream. In fact, the next time they'd spoken, he didn't bring it up at all. She had to broach the subject. He'd shrugged it off and started talking about how much he wanted her. Tough to stay on topic when he went that route.

Phone sex was easier than corporate-media politics. Much more fun too. They talked a lot. Like a lot, a lot. Maybe not in depth, but in frequency. Usually at least once a day or every other day. He was a busy guy, always in the middle of something or on his way somewhere. Her roommates worked during the day. Roxie didn't mind taking breaks, so time zones didn't screw too much with their opportunities to communicate. Her memory for charging her phone on the other hand…

He hadn't called that day. Hadn't even tried. Which she knew because her charged cellphone stayed next to her keyboard all day. No call. Hanging by the phone waiting for a guy to call wasn't her style. Worrying would be pointless. If anything grave had befallen him, the media would loop her in. Such close scrutiny had its positive side… odd comfort.

Any other guy might have gotten bored or moved on. Her previous blunders served Zairn multiple chances to cut her off. For some reason, he hadn't… The sex. That had to be the answer. Though, as she'd told him, he didn't have to go six minutes without it. Zairn Lomond could get laid on any continent. Even the inhospitable ones.

Although two weeks had passed since the Astrid scandal and the drunken streaming, people still approached her. Especially in bars when the alcohol flowed. Staying in had become her default. Better safe than sorry, she didn't want anyone to get hurt.

One of Toria's friends was opening a new bar. Her girls had gone along to the event in a show of support… and angling for free drinks. In advance, Roxie told Zairn that she'd have the apartment to herself. Several times. It was the perfect chance for them to do the video thing he loved so much. And, of course, it was the day he'd chosen to go dark. Typical.

Walking across the living room in her pajamas, Roxie dialed his number for like the fifth time that day. It rang until the voicemail clicked in.

She opened the freezer to retrieve ice-cream. "Three weeks into the new year and you're dodging my calls already," she said, grabbing a spoon from the drawer. "I'm into the Cherry Garcia. Just letting you know. If my ass has grown next time we get together, this is why. Oh, and, by the way, I don't chase guys. I don't wait around for them either. If I have to go out and get laid later, it'll be to wash you out of my system." She sighed. "Call me when you can, Casanova."

She was teasing. Of course. He'd know the threat was part of their game. Even though they'd never had an actual conversation about limiting their social lives for each other, Roxie had no desire to go out and pick anyone up. How would the media react? Would she get her picture in the paper? Would Mr. Whoever sell his story? A shiver went through her. What had Crimson done to her life?

Popping the lid from the ice-cream, she scooped some out and pressed it to her tongue, keeping the spoon in her mouth while grabbing the remote control and dropping onto the couch.

If he didn't call soon, she might go join her friends at the bar. It was only eight something… still time to get ready… if Trevor was ready. Should she let him know going out was a possibility?

The TV came on. Before she could switch to a streaming service, a female voice stalled her.

"…Crimson spokesperson has confirmed."

Confirmed what? Dragging the spoon from her mouth, she stabbed it into the ice-cream and leaned closer to the television. So much for the media would keep her in the loop. Maybe she should've checked the TV before calling.

"This is an unusual decision, isn't it?" a faceless anchor asked.

"Yes," the reporter said. The camera zoomed out a little, offering more background. That was Chicago. Right behind the woman was… the Grand Hotel… in Chicago. "They have confirmed that negotiations were taking place in secret. For how long, we're unsure, but the contracts are legitimate. The sale has already gone through."

"It's a coup for Chicago," the anchor said. "The word was there were no immediate plans for future Crimson venues in North America. Lomond himself had indicated that he was looking to expand in international territories. He was especially interested in strengthening ties with both Europe and Australia."

"Zairn Lomond hasn't offered comment on these developments. Eyewitness reports suggest he checked in here at the Grand early this morning, although we have no footage to verify the exact time of his arrival. His people have been seen, but we have no evidence of his specific whereabouts."

"That's going around," Roxie murmured, shoving the ice-cream onto the coffee table and prodding the remote's power button to silence the television.

Leaping up to hurry over to the door, she grabbed a hoodie and stuffed her arms into the sleeves. Yeah, she was only wearing pajamas. No one cared. If reporters saw her, they'd have more to worry about than her apparel.

The sneak was in town. An explanation from the horse's mouth was better than getting it from Debbie Newswoman. Gobbling up possibly false morsels from the media should be reserved for those people who hadn't sucked his dick… Something she'd apparently need to make clear to him. What was he doing in her city?

Jane's ballet flats were the only shoes by the door. Fine, they'd do. She grabbed the spare keys from a hook, foregoing her purse. She didn't need it; she needed to find out what was going on.

Opening the door brought her maelstrom of thoughts to a complete crashing halt. There was a man on her threshold, fist raised as if to knock.

The actual man she'd been about to track down. Convenient. It took a second to process that Zairn was there.

Grabbing hold of his jacket, she hurried backwards, yanking him inside. "What the hell?" she asked, slamming the door and dropping the keys. "I called! You're on the news."

"I know," he said, unzipping her hoodie to push it from her shoulders, continuing to walk her backwards. "You were coming to see me?"

"Yes! You know, when most men make huge business decisions related to the location of the woman they're screwing, they include such women in that decision."

"Coming to see me with Lola Bunny?"

Yes, she was wearing her pajamas, so what? "Who cares what I'm wearing?"

"Not me," he said, taking her top off to cast it aside. "I care about where your bedroom is."

"You didn't even call. You can't just come in here and expect to…" The slight curl of his lips was her reality check. "Okay, so you can, but only because you're good at it."

Snatching his hand, she stomped in the bedroom's direction. After three weeks of sex without touching, being intimate was inevitable. Besides, they'd never achieve anything if they didn't slake their thirst for each other first.

"WHY CHICAGO?" Roxie asked, still sort of amazed that Zairn was lying in her bed. "Tell me why."

"I'm surprised you have to ask," he said, stroking her hip.

"You're not moving here or anything, right?"

"Would that be so terrible?"

It hadn't occurred to her for a second that he'd ever…

"If you follow me around like a puppy dog, maybe," she said, stroking her leg up and down between his. "I have a pretty full schedule of puppy dog followers."

His smile was slow. All of him was loose and relaxed. She liked him like this. The way he took up space in the middle of her bed. The way she had no choice but to touch him… and how he wouldn't apologize for maintaining constant contact.

"Bet you do, baby," he purred, smoldering without effort. It came completely naturally to him. "Chicago means something to you. Why shouldn't I invest in a city that means so much to the woman I'm with?"

Shit. A certain city prosecutor with political aspirations would be pleased to hear that.

"Oh God," Roxie said, sinking onto her back on top of his arm, covering her eyes. "You're invested in Chicago."

"Is that a bad thing?"

"Yes," she said, dropping her arm to the bed on an exhale. "But only because it means an awkward conversation with Porter."

He frowned. "I don't—"

"Never mind," she said, reaching for his furthest hand to put it on her body, forcing him closer. "Why didn't you tell me? I thought you were on this no secrets kick."

"It wasn't a secret, it was a surprise," he said. "You don't want to live in New York, so I had to come up with a plan B."

"I didn't say I'd never, ever live in New York," she said. "It just didn't make sense to rush into anything."

"Didn't?" His brows rose a fraction. "Does it make sense now?"

No secrets wasn't always pleasant. "I don't know, Z. I just… this is the first time I've had such a long-distance fuck buddy."

"I don't even get friends with benefits status?" he asked. "Ouch."

She ran her fingertips up his torso. "You know what I mean," she said, though it pained her to admit vulnerability.

"It's not easy being apart," he said, stroking her face.

"In some ways it was easier when we didn't talk… After the tour, I could tell myself we were done… Maybe we should've left it there."

"Would that make you happy?"

The gleam in his heavy eyes betrayed his opinion and that he knew hers too. The gorgeous, cocky, incredible prick. Reading her wasn't supposed to be another of his specialties.

Roxie drew in a breath, tempting his hand to her breast. "Seems everywhere I look there's something new about the New York club," she said. "Reminds me of the night we spent there."

"The apartment's there any time you want to use it," he said. "There are Valentine's events coming up."

"Are you going to be in New York on Valentine's?"

What a stupid question? They couldn't spend time together on the one day of the year meant for committed couples.

"Your ruby grants you access whether or not I'm there," he said.

Yeah, hence how she'd ended up in his tub. "It's not the apartment I want to see."

"You're always welcome wherever I am. Just call Ballard and he'll ready a jet for you. A car will pick you up from here. You don't even have to call Ballard, you have open accounts with the transport companies. I'll get you the numbers."

Except that contradicted what they were: secret.

"You're telling me to call Ballard because he's the only one who knows about us," she said, stroking his arm. "Your people would think it was weird if I just rocked up to your hotel somewhere halfway across the world."

"I don't care about other people, Lola. If you ever need me, call and tell me to get my ass to your door and I'll always show."

That didn't sound like the kind of thing one fuck buddy would say to another. "No one in your camp thought Chicago was an odd choice?"

He smiled. "No one asked. We were never explicit about us, but they know there's something here. You don't think they picked up on it on tour?"

Roxie had thought the same thing. "Ballard's the only one who knows about New York though, right? They don't know that we're…"

"The phone rings and I disappear," he said. "They've noticed that."

"So they know there's a woman involved."

"What are you asking? If we keep doing this, we're going to be found out eventually."

He'd told her that early in their association. The night in Vegas when he thought she'd called for sex. His experience told him that secret sex didn't stay secret.

Roxie inhaled. "I know."

"And that seems to depress you."

Hooking a hand around the back of his neck, she pulled him down for a quick kiss. "It doesn't depress me. The media gauntlet doesn't scare me. I'd even take Ogilvie glowering at me."

"So what's the problem?"

She met his eye. "I have to tell my girls."

He softened with the new understanding. "They don't know anything?"

"They know I don't talk about you," she said. "And that I was weird about New York, before we went and then refused every invite into your area."

"My area is your area," he said, his voice thick with innuendo as he sank lower for another kiss.

"They thought I got drunk and felt you up."

"I should be so lucky."

She smiled. "Then they wondered if you got drunk and felt me up."

The warmth of his laugh heated her lips. "I should be so lucky."

"They know there's something I haven't talked about… I didn't talk about you after the tour."

"You didn't?"

They basked in each other, their eyes dancing while their lips hovered. The low light brought the mood even closer. Talking to him, in her bedroom, in their sex sheets… They'd never been so alone. So intimate.

"What would I have said?" she murmured. "To them, you're public property, what the media portray you to be. You're not an actual person. They'd support me through anything. Anything at all. If I told them you were scum, they'd believe me." His pleasing, subtle smile proved he understood that was a compliment to her friends, not an insult to him. "I just don't know how to explain that…"

"That what, baby?" he asked, tucking her hair behind her ear.

"If we're fuck buddies, friends with benefits, I can justify not telling them the truth."

"Are you worried about their reaction?"

Was she?

"You know I don't mean to be glib. I don't want to hurt you… or to hurt them. Why am I so bad at this?"

Whatever she was trying to communicate didn't manifest. A loud scraping buzz intruded on their moment. The communal door alarm from the intercom in the living room. Thank God for small favors.

"That's our food," she said, rolling out of bed.

"Babe—"

"I'll be back in a minute," she said, picking up his tee-shirt to put it on. "We mere mortals have to plate our own food and get our own forks."

"Philistines," he said, linking his fingers at the back of his head. "Do you want me to answer the door?"

She scoffed. "Yeah, 'cause that's not a media wet dream waiting to happen."

"I don't know if I like this guy seeing so much of your legs."

She returned to bend over and kiss him. "I have dresses shorter than this, which you should know 'cause you bought them… You've taken them off my body too."

When she rose again, his eyes were closed. "I'll just lie here and remember those times. Wait for you to serve me."

She kissed him again, taking him by surprise, and spun around to flounce out of the room. Roxie was halfway to the front door before she remembered her purse was in the bedroom. Letting the guy in was job one, paying him would come after.

Two steps later, the door opened. Startled to a stop, Roxie expected to see a presumptuous delivery guy. Instead, her two best friends came rushing in.

"There's a food guy out here," Toria said, holding the door for Jane.

"Have you seen the news?" Jane asked. "Oh my God."

No, that came a second later.

"Lo, there's cash in my—"

Yeah, okay, so he'd obviously seen her friends standing there gawking.

Roxie winced and raised a fist to first point a forefinger at her girls, then straighten her thumb toward the guy she couldn't see. "Please tell me he's wearing pants."

SIXTEEN

NO ONE SAID ANYTHING. For how long? No idea. Forever. A feeble knock on the door kicked them from pause.

"I have cash," Zairn said.

By the time Roxie turned around, he was right next to her. She planted a hand on his bare chest to halt him. Thank goodness, he had put on sweats. Nothing else, but pants were something. Better than nothing.

"No," she said, taking his wallet. "I'll pay him. You stay here."

Their eye contact communicated so much. There was an apology in his gaze, resolve too. Maybe he hadn't meant for it to happen, but it had.

Crossing the rest of the way, she squeezed between her friends to go around the door and hand cash to the delivery guy.

They exchanged money for food. "I don't have change for—"

"Keep it," Roxie said, closing the door. "Ever think of carrying something smaller than a hundred?" She took the food bag and his wallet over to put them on the kitchen counter. Now it was time to face the music. Moistening her lips, she turned back to the people in the room. All remained in their previous positions. No one even twitched. "It's sort of my urge to say this isn't what it looks like, but I'm not really sure what else it could be."

"Roxanna—"

"No, wait," she said, going over to stand equidistant between the guy and the girls. "I guess we should start the old-fashioned way. Victoria Lovell, Jane Simmons, meet Zairn Lomond. Zairn, these are my girls."

"It's a pleasure," he said to no reply. His expression morphed to a frown. "Do they speak?"

"Probably not while you're standing there half naked," she said, noting how low his sweats were slung. "God, I take it for granted how hot you are. Wanna put some more clothes on?"

"You're wearing my tee-shirt."

"Right," she said, looking down at her apparel.

"I'll grab my sweatshirt."

He went back to the bedroom, which gave her some time to breathe.

"Oh my God," Jane hissed.

Roxie went to her girls. "I'm sorry I didn't tell you, it was just… It's complicated."

"That you kicked us out to have secret sex with your secret boyfriend?" Toria asked.

"No!" Roxie said. "I had no idea he was in Chicago. He just showed up."

"On the night we happen to be out," Toria said. "What? You didn't trust us?"

"I did trust you, I do… The whole thing is… it's a long story."

"Which you could've told us fifty times," Toria said, taking a hard line that wasn't usually her style. "You're having an affair with the hottest guy on earth. How do you forget to mention that?"

From the abrupt way both women tensed, Roxie guessed Zairn had joined them again. They just stood there, wide-eyed, staring beyond her, saying nothing. Had they stopped breathing too?

Turning on the spot, Roxie sought Zairn. "You should go."

"You sure?" She nodded and went to him. He skimmed the back of his index finger down her cheek to her jaw, which he tipped up to kiss her. "I have meetings tomorrow, but nothing I can't get out of. Come over later if you—"

"There are already cameras camped outside the hotel," she said.

One side of his mouth rose. "Didn't stop you earlier when you planned to charge on in with nothing but Lola Bunny."

She shrugged. "The press are used to me acting crazy."

"Act crazy later," he said, dipping to kiss her again. "Is all I'm saying."

"Maybe," she said. "I'll call you."

"Oh, and the brush-off burns," he teased and winked before scooping an arm around her shoulders to guide her toward the door.

"You're not kissing me on the doorstep," she said, drawing the zip of his sweatshirt higher.

"Why not?" he murmured in his playboy drawl. "I've kissed you everywhere else."

Roxie bumped him with her hip. "People will talk."

"Not used to that by now?"

Her friends didn't move out of the way.

"No. No," Jane said. "No, we can't—no."

Huh, well, imagine that. She would've put good money on Toria being the first to talk. The lack of sense suited Jane given what, or rather who, she faced.

Zairn lowered his mouth to her hair. "Is she okay?"

"She's a big fan," Roxie said, patting his stomach. "He has a big enough ego, Jane, believe me. You stoke it and there's a chance he won't make it back to his people with all that extra weight."

"I am a big fan," Jane said, the words bursting out of her. Didn't she just say that? Maybe Jane wasn't capable of hearing while in her laser-precise trance. "Like a huge fan."

She grabbed Toria to haul her closer. "Toria and me bonded over our mutual love in the Zairn Lomond Crimsettes."

"I didn't know that," Roxie said. "I don't even know what that is."

"Me—I… Toria and I bonded over our mutual love," Jane said, color growing in her cheeks. "Sorry, that's what I meant to say."

"Thank you," Zairn said, in a tone she'd heard the world over.

That smooth, gentle intonation had women of every nationality soaking through their panties.

"Stop tormenting my friends," Roxie said, prodding him in the stomach. "Remember the hands off forever rule."

"I don't know your rules."

"Right," Roxie said.

"You make them up as you go along."

"No," she droned, scrunching her face in a mock sneer. "I was talking about it with Astrid, actually. Astrid knows my rules…" She relaxed. "Another reason I knew you weren't sleeping with her."

"This is why you wouldn't talk about him," Toria said, fixating on her. "Why you'd walk away any time his name came up?"

"Yes," Roxie said, owning her actions.

"Because it was going on the whole time."

"No," Roxie said, shaking her head. "Like I said, it's complicated."

"It's my fault," Zairn said. "I have strict rules about—"

"If you even *thought* about giving me rules like that, I'd bite your balls off the next time you put them in my mouth," Roxie said. "They know that about me." She took Toria's hand. "I'm sorry. I wanted to tell you, but then there was nothing to say. It was… over after the tour and I didn't want to put anyone in a position of having to lie for me."

"Roxie lived under a lot of pressure on the tour," Zairn said. "When you live under that kind of scrutiny, your perception of the world is altered. It has an effect on all of us."

"There's a part of him you know better than I do," Roxie said to her girls. "And it was that part I couldn't give you. I don't know him like you do. I don't know Zairn Lomond: The Legend. I mean I've seen it, I've witnessed it all over the world, I just… I've never connected with that part of him."

"The part that involves the private jets?" he asked, sort of skeptical. "With chauffeur driven luxury cars and endless credit limits in designer stores?"

"Oh no, that part I've connected with," Roxie said, turning a smile up to him. "I haven't connected with the part that shakes hands at rope lines. The part that sits above everyone on his personal, private, VIP couch. Mr. Untouchable. The part that sits on Talk at Sunset and smolders."

"You're nuts about that guy," he strutted.

"The guy who shakes hands with sports stars whose names I can't pronounce. The guy constantly having tits flashed at him. The guy who's careful about acting with women in a way that can't be misconstrued… The one who's mobbed the minute he walks out of the restricted VIP areas."

"My experience saved you from it. That's why I pulled the shutters around you after Sydney."

"The guy who smothers me with his paranoia," she said, rolling her eyes. "I know that guy."

"How many guys am I?"

"As many as I want you to be," she said, flashing him a grin.

"Okay. As long as I'm always the guy you want to go to bed with…"

"Beds are optional in our relationship."

"Yeah," he said, like an idea had just struck him. "Why haven't I seen your closet?"

She laughed. "I'll have to clean it out before we do it in there. My closet's standing room only."

"We'll knock through to the apartment next door."

"Uh, I think the neighbors might complain."

"No, they won't. Trevor's a laid-back guy. And he does what he's told."

She needed a second to fathom the implication of… "You rented the apartment next door for security?"

"I bought it, but, yeah…" Shocked, her arm dropped from his waist when she stepped back to gape up at him. "Where do you think the backup came from?"

"He's never needed backup, and holy hell, Z! That's like crazy stalker territory."

"Only if I moved in and drilled holes to watch you."

"Okay," she said, her head angling forward. "We're not going to talk about this anymore. I want Stone back, geez, I need him to protect me from you."

"Since I took ownership of your safety, have you been hurt?"

"This," she said, gesturing between them. "This conversation right here is hurting me." The gradual ascent of his smile was too endearing to maintain her faux affront. "I don't care…" She raised her chin. "I don't care that you're hot and smart and kind and funny… Okay, fine, you can drill holes, but if I see anything on the internet…"

He laughed and hooked an arm around her neck to pull her to him. He kissed her head. "What we are is not their business," he murmured against her.

Roxie looked up at him. "Never."

"Oh my God," Toria said, attracting everyone's attention. "It's real."

Roxie blew out a fed-up breath. "So he keeps telling me."

The Zairn her girls knew probably didn't have it in him to be serious about any woman. That guy portrayed such confidence that no relationship would matter enough to root itself deep. That guy would pick 'em up and put 'em down as he wanted them. Just like he'd said.

"Oh my God," Toria said again, more excited than before. "I have like a zillion questions."

"No!" Jane said, bouncing closer. "I get to ask first."

It was funny, but enlivening funny. "This is the part of him I don't know," Roxie said, stepping aside to present him to her roommates. "I don't know his history, his movements. No idea of his measurements, I've never even measured his cock…" She deepened her tone to flirtatious. "Though it's definitely bigger than average."

"Babe," Zairn said, though she recognized his amusement. He was enjoying her.

"What?" she asked, all exaggerated innocence. "The confidence comes from somewhere. I'm just saying, it's justified."

"I can't believe you're dating Zairn Lomond!" Jane said, following it with an excited gasp.

"I have sex with him," Roxie said, going into the kitchen. "I talk with him. We don't really do much dating."

"I took you around the world, babe."

"Yeah, but not because you wanted in my pants." She retrieved wine from the fridge. "I mean you did, you were wild for me from the beginning." Roxie poured wine into three glasses. "You did that because of the contest. How many times did we go out together?" She paused to point at her roommates. "Tell them, because they don't believe me. How much time did we really spend together in Crimson venues?"

"On tour or after?"

She glanced his way, appreciating the mischief in his words. "New York doesn't count."

"Most of the time we spent together was in hotels."

"Yeah, he didn't even hang with me on the flights."

"Brought you home, didn't I?"

"You brought me home because you wanted sex, Skippy."

"Like you wanted romance," he mock scoffed.

"I told you to stay with Ballard," she said, putting the wine back in the fridge. "I wanted the plane."

"Not much to do on the 737 alone, you should've hijacked the Triple Seven."

"Oh my God," Jane screeched, accepting a wine glass. "You flew on the Zee-Jet and didn't tell us?"

"Totally wasted on you," Toria said, taking the proffered drink.

She smiled at her friend before hooking her finger around Zairn's. "The only spirit we have is tequila."

"Need me to go out and pick something up?"

"Hmm," Roxie hummed. "Yeah, you wandering the streets in my neighborhood, that's what I want."

"I can call someone…" he trailed off when he touched his pockets. "I turned my phone off. It's in your room."

"Tequila or cheap, nasty wine. Those are your choices."

"You got water?"

"Oh, wow," she said, twirling around and leaning back on him. "Aren't you high maintenance?"

"If you were together," Toria said. "Why didn't you do the meet and greet thing at New Year?"

"She was pissed at me," Zairn said, which was good.

If he didn't inject himself into the conversation, her friends would never address him directly.

Just a shame he was totally wrong.

"I was not pissed at you," Roxie said, putting ice in a glass.

"So the screaming at each other in the afternoon was…"

Roxie tipped all the way back to look around the fridge and bobbed her brows twice. "Foreplay."

He exhaled a laugh. "Yeah, everything is with you, baby."

"Oh my God," Toria said. Those three words seemed to be the theme of the night. "You used the mobbed by the crowd thing as an excuse not to go on the city tour with us. All the time you were getting laid."

"Oh no," Roxie said, opening a bottle of water to pour it over the ice. "I definitely wasn't doing that."

"Is that why you went to bed early?" Jane asked. "Because you were depressed about arguing?"

"I think we're getting distracted," Toria said. "Zairn Lomond is in our living room!" She looped an arm through Jane's. "It's actually him."

Roxie's phone began to ring as she went to hand Zairn his glass. "Boundaries, baby," she said. "Remember those boundaries."

SEVENTEEN

ROXIE'S PHONE WAS ON LOUD in anticipation of Zairn's call, otherwise she may not have heard it. Her chattering girls ushered Zairn toward the couch as she hurried around it to get the device.

While picking up the melted ice-cream from the coffee table, she read the name of the caller.

Interesting. "Yes, I have him," she answered the call without any greeting, leaving the couch area while her girls herded Zairn closer to it. "And you can't have him. I need him for something I'm not gonna tell you about."

"Trish Gambatto sent a statement to the press," Ballard said, ignoring the quip. "She's claiming we made the Chicago decision to accommodate our support for her brother."

"Oh my God," she murmured, lowering the ice-cream to the sink.

"Rox…"

"I know," she said, already striding across the room.

"Og can't find him, he's assuming Trish has a point," Ballard said. "He's going crazy." There was a noise in the background. "Hold on."

Roxie put herself in front of Zairn before he could sit. "You need to go back to the hotel. Everyone's going nuts. Trish made a statement you won't like." She gave him her phone. "Let me go get changed."

He'd need his shirt. The zipped up sweatshirt would cover him, but unless he could convince Ogilvie he'd been at the gym, the outfit wouldn't make sense. Less so if he didn't have a tee-shirt.

She took off his tee-shirt and grabbed a hair tie to pile her hair on her head in a messy bun.

Zairn entered, phone at his ear. "Get dressed."

"Me?" she asked, immediately realizing it was a stupid question.

"You're coming with me." Porter. Shit. Trying to play the situation out, Roxie didn't see any way to handle it without her talking Porter down. Zairn checked the phone to touch the screen, then his hand dropped to his side. "There's a crisis, babe. When your guy's having a crisis, you stand with him." Hmm, interesting that he was going there, but there wasn't time to analyze it. A noise came from the phone, so he quickly touched the screen and put it to his ear. "Yeah, I'm here. We'll be ready."

He hung up the phone and put it on her dresser as he unzipped his sweatshirt to shirk it. After putting on the tee-shirt she'd dumped on the bed, he put his sweatshirt on again.

"No," Roxie said, shaking her head. "The press don't know you're here. You can't walk into the hotel with me at your side. There's enough going on without adding to the drama."

"Won't take the press long to arrive here. Trust me, they're probably on their way… or camped outside."

"Why would—"

"Babe, there's a story about me in Chicago. It was only a matter of time before they showed up at yours."

"Because they think I'm your ex-girlfriend," she said, her fingers rising to the hair by her temples. "Oh God, and Trish is your ex too. We're like warring ex-girlfriends."

"Trish and I were nothing like us. It was years ago and casual."

"But she's out there making statements about your intentions."

"While I'm in bed with you," he snapped. "Which position would you prefer?"

Edging closer, patience wasn't natural, but she held onto it anyway. "Don't get defensive with me. I'll be nice about it this once. Next time, I kick you out."

"I'm sorry, Lo," he said on a sigh. "This is not how I expected tonight to go. Three weeks I waited to see you… I thought we were going to have a night together… I'm sick of the bullshit."

"Whatever happens with Trish and the press doesn't matter," she said. "We're still us." Whatever the hell that meant. "We're not changing for the sake of other people. We can't rush this."

His disappointment was palpable. "Rox…"

"Listen," she said, going over to lay her hands on his arms. "Remember what you said to me on the plane, before we were ever together? You said we would never be forced to do anything, much less discuss what's going on between you and me. We are not a footnote to the Gambatto story and we are not giving this to them, to the world, before we're ready."

Regardless of whether he was hearing her, his expression betrayed his displeasure. "I am ready."

"I won't be forced into it, Z. Into anything. You're not thinking smart. With the Gambattos… with Trish… I have value for you. For Crimson. That value will shrink if you make us the story." Pausing, she edged into teasing. "Remember, there are two of us in this relationship. You can't decide unilaterally." That was supposed to make him smile, but he didn't. Roxie slid her arms around his waist. "You're used to getting what you want. Is this Rome all over again?"

"No. This is not that."

Her brows rose because she wasn't so sure. "Do you think your people will appreciate us being 'out' before they know about us?"

"Ogilvie?"

"Yes," she said. "Ogilvie. Tibbs… the docu guys. Salad and Elson will want to control the story."

"I don't give a shit about them."

"Stop it," she said, straightening to lay her hands on his chest. "You need a clear head. Deal with the Gambatto drama. At the other side of this, you'll realize I was right… And I expect acknowledgement of that when you come to your senses." When she smiled again, he exhaled some of his tension. "Go do your job, Casanova. Call me later."

"I should never have used that 'two of us in this relationship' line," he mumbled, bowing to kiss her.

Roxie dug her nails into his neck to hold him at her level. "The price of success," she whispered, closing her eyes to savor his lips. "Thank you for coming over. It was an amazing surprise."

He tightened the circle of his embrace to pick her off her feet when he stood up straight. "Expect more of them."

"You know I can't repay you."

Not to the same degree.

"Opening the door is payment enough," he said and kissed her again. "I'll call you later."

She nodded and welcomed another slower, deeper kiss. As he stepped away, their fingers tangled. Eventually they had to part. His hand drifted away, he put up the hood of his sweatshirt, and then he was gone.

Breathing into the silence for a few seconds, Roxie gave him a chance to get out of the apartment before grabbing clothes. It was late, but Lola was inappropriate. Ideally, she'd have a shower… there wasn't time.

"Roxie!" Toria yelled from the living room.

She grabbed her shoes from the closet and went in the shout's direction. Her friends were sitting on the couch, watching the TV as she approached. The anchor was talking again, declaring that Kesley Walsh had made a statement supporting Zairn.

"Well," Roxie murmured. "Now it's a party."

"What has she got to do with it?" Jane asked.

"I don't know," Roxie said, bending down to scoop her feet into shoes.

Toria gasped. "Oh my God, Vegas. They were in that chapel together…" She was tugging on Jane's arm. "They got married."

"They didn't get married," Roxie said, glancing around for her phone. Zairn had put it on her dresser in the— oh, man, was that his wallet on the kitchen counter? "Damnit."

She went to grab it. Her phone would be running on fumes. That wasn't exactly new.

"This is unbelievable," Toria said. "I can't believe you're a part of this."

"I'm not," Roxie said, starting toward her bedroom. "But I'm gonna be."

From a night of lounging on the couch with her ice-cream, Roxie's evening had certainly picked up. The sex was a bonus; it gave her a second wind and heightened her determination. Zairn had his PR situation to manage, she'd take care of the legalities. Good thing she used to sleep with the man in charge of them.

EIGHTEEN

A YOUNG WOMAN answered the door. Roxie didn't wait for an invitation into the hotel suite. She pushed the door aside and strode in, giving the woman no choice but to move. Just as she expected, Porter was at the head of the central table with a few of his underlings standing around him.

With a brow raise, she side-nodded in the bedroom's direction and maintained her momentum. What she had to say wasn't suitable for an audience.

Opening the door, she went inside, dumped her purse on the bed and spun around just as Porter closed the door behind him.

"Ro—"

"It's bullshit."

"I can't talk to you about this," Porter said, careful in his words as he progressed deeper into the room. "He's a material witness."

For anyone threatening Zairn, her patience was zero. "No," she said, raising a straight finger. "You absolutely cannot suck him into this."

"Coming here for his girlfriend? He put himself in it. If he wants to play hero, I have no choice but to question him about what he knows. What he's seen. What's been said in his vicinity."

She shook her head. "He won't talk to you."

"Then he'll be subpoenaed."

"He won't answer questions. He can't."

"Then he'll be held in contempt."

"Goddamnit, Porter," Roxie said, balling a fist at her side as her foot rose to stomp. "This is not a competition." Frustrated, it was laughable that Zairn once accused her of always needing to win. "Not everything is a career opportunity."

"Lomond came to my city. He put himself in my case."

Her ex was so infuriating. "This is not your city. You're not the only one who lives here."

"Yeah, the Gambattos do too."

"I live here, you idiot. I do not want my tax dollars wasted on this dead-end," Roxie said. "Zairn doesn't know what happened to Miss Illinois. He knows nothing about Joey Gambatto's crime. It wasn't even on his radar until your apartment went up in flames."

"He might not be aware of what he knows."

Oh, restraining her temper wasn't easy… Okay, so she wasn't exactly playing it cool, but she deserved a goddamn medal for maintaining any kind of calm. Buttons were being pushed all over the place.

"Don't bullshit me," she sneered. "This is me you're talking to, Porter. You drag Zairn into this and your profile skyrockets."

He exhaled in disbelief. "God, you think I'm shallow. Why did you date me if I was such a sleaze?"

Her hands went to her hips. "Maybe that's why we broke up."

"And you think you'll do better with Lomond?"

"You've never met the man," Roxie said. "Don't pass judgement on his character."

"If he wants to meet, we'll meet."

His habit of manipulating words to suit his meaning wasn't limited to his professional life. "I didn't say that. I can't think of any reason he'd want to meet with you. Especially if you're going to accuse him of something or invite the circus into his life."

"Open your eyes, RoRo, that guy brings the circus. He is the circus!"

"No," she said, shaking her head and grabbing her purse. "I'm not gonna let you do this."

"I'm not doing anything," he said, opening his arms. "Except my job."

"This is not about your job."

"That's all it's about. My career is what I have. It's what I live for."

"Yeah, I get that," she said. "I thought you'd be reasonable. I thought you were good at your job; that you could sniff out desperation. Apparently, I was wrong." Roxie walked past him but called back, "You should know that's not something I say regularly."

"Desperation," Porter said as she reached the door. Roxie knew that tone and turned slowly. "When was the last time Lomond spoke to Trish?"

"I don't know."

Her ex about-faced, more discerning when their eyes met. "I could put you on the stand."

"That would be hearsay and a conflict of interest. You can't interrogate the woman you used to fuck."

"There's no rule against it. We'd let the court and jury know about our previous relationship, just to cover our asses."

"Your ass," she said, resting her shoulder blades on the door. "I'm quite happy with my ass uncovered. That way I can yell at you just like the old days."

"If you're uncomfortable with me examining you, we can have Natalie do it."

"Who's Natalie? The little blonde who let me in?" With a tsk, she tick-tocked her finger back and forth. "Future congressmen should beware of perky blondes bearing gifts."

Porter was no good at playing with her. "Lomond is with the Gambattos or he's against them," he said, ever the professional.

"Zairn is neither. He's Switzerland. He trusts the

justice system to do its job."

"But he won't talk to me? All I can infer from that is that he's guilty of something."

Her quick wit was good for more than just teasing. "Or that he's a busy man in the public eye who doesn't have time to play games."

"He just bought a building. He'll have to stick around to do something with it."

"He can manage a remodel from thirty thousand feet. He did it with New York. Chicago won't be half as much trouble."

Though he did have more contacts in New York, more employees. As far as she knew, there was no Rouge base in Illinois.

"Have you seen inside?"

"New York, yes. Chicago, no. I found out about that on TV tonight."

"But he called and asked you to come over here to handle me. What's he afraid of?"

"No one is afraid of anything," she said. "I came here of my own volition. I do have that power, you know. To decide for myself."

"What did he say?" Damn, Porter had the bit in his teeth. "When Trish released her statement?

"I wasn't there. What the hell do—"

"Walk away," he said, softening. "RoRo, you get caught up in things and you don't always think through—"

"Don't patronize me."

"I'm trying to protect you," he snapped. "Goddamnit, Roxie, this guy could be complicit in murder. Maybe more than one. You need to think about you and if you—"

"More than one," she said, taking a step toward him. "What does that mean? More than one."

He sealed his lips like he wouldn't say anything, but his shoulders fell as she kept on looking into him, waiting for an explanation. "I got a call from the DA in California twenty minutes ago."

"So?"

"You think you know Lomond so well…"

"Don't fuck around, Porter. If you've got something to say—"

"I never told you how Ava Marilyn died." No, he hadn't. He'd talked about her abusive involvement with Joey Gambatto and events in their relationship. "Trust me that Lomond isn't who you think he is. You could be in danger and—"

"How did she die?" Roxie asked. Porter hadn't cited that omission for no reason. "Porter?"

"You won't understand the significance. There are things we choose not to release to the public."

"She was in the bathtub, wasn't she?" When Porter's curious eyes narrowed, she exhaled. "Oh my God, Porter, would you just tell me?"

"Exsanguination," Porter said. "She had bruises and injuries consistent with abuse, but ultimately… Her wrists were cut."

"And you can make murder?" Porter didn't answer. "Okay," Roxie said and turned around.

"Roxie—"

"I'll let myself out."

Leaving the bedroom, she didn't look at any of Porter's people as she exited the suite. Now what? Having an answer for everything was her thing. Being sure and resilient… Damnit, why were her wiles abandoning her when she needed them most?

Okay. Take a breath. Think.

If Porter was going to tie Zairn up in his investigation, phone records could be subpoenaed. The hotel probably had cameras too. Law enforcement would be able to see if she went straight to his suite after leaving Porter's. That could get both men into trouble. Bypassing the elevator, she went to the stairwell, fumbling around in her purse for her phone. The first thing she saw was a news alert declaring Zairn Lomond was expected to make a statement in the coming minutes.

Minutes?

Roxie dialed Astrid without really thinking. It rang and rang. "Come on," she muttered. "Come on. Come on."

The drone of the ringing in her ear was foreboding. It sent quakes of fear through her. Whatever she did, she had to own it, screw the consequences. Her feet took her up the stairs. Up and up while she listened to the ringing. She lost count; maybe it rang five times, maybe it was fifty. The only thing certain was her need to warn him of the axe overhead.

On the top floor, she yanked open the stairwell door just in time to see the perpendicular elevator doors begin to close. Sprinting toward them, she grabbed the metal just moments before it closed and used all of her might to push it back.

Ready to make her declaration, she sucked in a long breath, but was brought up short by the sight of strangers. They weren't the people she'd expected. Before there was time to regroup, someone spoke behind her.

"Roxanna?"

Spinning on the spot, she was met with a familiar sight. Zairn central between Ballard and Ogilvie. Tibbs and Astrid were behind them with press liaison Salad and head of public relations Terry Elson in the rear.

Roxie narrowed her focus on the concerned Zairn. "You can't," she said, stepping toward him, vaguely aware of the elevator doors closing behind her. "You cannot make this statement and you need to get a lawyer. The best lawyer on the whole planet. I don't care what it costs."

"What's wrong?"

She laid a hand on the center of his chest. "Trust me, Casanova," she whispered. "Please."

NINETEEN

STANDING IN THE ENCLOSED SPACE between Zairn's suite and the elevator, Roxie maintained eye contact with the man under her palm.

"We have to get this out there," Ogilvie said. Roxie held her conviction through Zairn's scrutiny. "We can't wait for—"

"Everyone back inside," Zairn said. Relief. He'd listened. Thank God. "You too, Lola."

He took her shoulder to guide her around in front of him and urged her into the suite with everyone else behind them.

What should she say? Where the hell should she begin? The gorgeous room's luxurious décor barely registered. Yeah, it was lovely. Expensive... How should she break the news? He'd be devastated. Even if he didn't show it, living through the Dayah Lynn situation again would take its toll.

"What is this about?" Ogilvie asked.

"I don't know," Zairn said. "Roxie's going to tell us."

His hand wasn't on her shoulder anymore. She turned to seek him out and found the others seating themselves on the pale couches and armchairs. All focused on her.

Waiting.

Anticipating.

Expecting answers.

Standing there in front of the vast windows, night bearing down behind her, she glanced from one face to the next. "I used to sleep with the guy prosecuting the Gambatto case," she said. Maybe wasn't the best start. "For those of you who don't know."

"Do you want to do this in private, babe?" Zairn asked, shifting to the edge of his seat.

"If it's about Gambatto, everyone needs to hear it," Ballard said. "Especially if it involves you getting a lawyer."

"I don't know exactly," she said, still searching everyone. "I mean he didn't give me specifics… Well, he did, but—"

"Lo?"

"Trust me, it would be smart to get a lawyer. Until you know what you're facing, you can't make a statement to the press. You could end up being cross-examined about anything you say now. Turn of phrase matters."

He'd said that to her on the night they met.

"You haven't told us anything," Ogilvie said. "The longer we delay, the worse it will be. They need a statement."

"They don't *need* anything," Roxie said, frustrated that Ogilvie was always so eager to talk to outsiders. She settled on Zairn. "There's a difference between what they're entitled to and what they think they're entitled to."

"Babe, give us something. There has to be a reason, something he said—"

"He talked to the DA in California."

Zairn's demeanor changed. Concern cloaked him before a much more severe defense tensed all of his muscles.

"Ackley," Ballard muttered.

"What does that mean?" Salad asked.

"It means we're done talking about this here," Ballard said and stood up. "Tibbs, call the airport, tell them we're on our way. Og—"

"I'll have Dunlap meet us in New York."

Ballard nodded. "We'll need a no comment

statement. One that doesn't sound like a no comment statement or that we back tracked from making a statement," he said, pointing to Salad and Elson. "Tibbs, stick with them, we want real-time updates."

Ogilvie and Tibbs stood up in sync with Salad and Elson. Everyone was ready to mobilize. Good. Great. Yes, this was what they needed.

"No," Zairn said, stalling his people. His attention tracked to hers. A couple of beats passed, then he stood up. "Lo. Come with me." He started walking. "Ballard, you too."

Resisting her automatic urge to play with him by refusing the order, Roxie went after him. From the corner of her eye, she noticed Ogilvie following along too. Not her place to say it, but was he invited?

They went to a curved corridor, past a couple of doors and through the open double ones at the end. The bright light in the shiny room only highlighted how immaculate it was.

Zairn strode to the end of the bed and turned around to face the door. Roxie, on the other hand, kept on going past the bottom corner of the bed to drop her purse onto the nightstand. Her shoulders ached and the back of her neck tingled. Tension wasn't good for her.

"Og, we don't need you in this," Zairn said.

"You damn well do," Ogilvie asserted, slamming the doors. Roxie curled a leg under herself to sit on the edge of the bed. "You need me to talk some sense into you. Why does she have to be here?" He tipped his chin past Zairn toward her, without going so far as to look at her. "You heard her, she's screwing the prosecutor, who's apparently coming for you. Maybe he sent her here for information."

Drawing in a deliberately audible breath, Roxie dropped her shoulders. "I haven't even showered since the last time your boss came inside me," she said on a faux yawn, sinking onto her back, parallel to the headboard. She relaxed her head Zairn's way when he swung back a quarter turn to smirk at her innocence. "What? You said you were ready. Does it matter if Ogilvie knows?"

"If you were going to do it anyway, why didn't you

ride with me?"

Roxie rolled onto her side, supporting her head with a hand. "Haven't I proved my value? If I hadn't gone to Porter, we wouldn't know what we do."

"I didn't see you on the news."

"I came in through the basement," she said and winked. "I know people."

Like Porter. Assuring an ASA could have people smuggled in unnoticed was a sort of prerequisite for the hotel sheltering him.

"I bet you do."

"In this town, you need a way in, maybe I can hook you up."

"For a price?"

One side of her smile ascended. "A hottie like you could persuade me into a mutually beneficial arrangement. Stick with me and we'll have some fun, honey."

Seeing his smile was a relief. With all the drama that was going on, it was gratifying to offer him some comfort.

"Are you two flirting?" Ogilvie said, practically spitting the words. "Now?"

"Be glad that's all they're doing," Ballard muttered.

"You knew about this? You've known about this?"

"What's the problem, Og?" she asked. "You liked me the last time we saw each other. At the end of the tour."

"When you were good for us," Ogilvie said. "This is not good for us."

"It's good for you I stopped the statement. Anything said now could end up replayed in court."

"Your ex has a vendetta against us," Ogilvie said, nodding. "Because you two had sex."

"Porter doesn't know that," she said. "And he has no vendetta. He didn't call California. California called him."

"Do we risk reaching out to Ackley?" Ballard asked.

"Who's that?" Roxie asked.

"The California DA," Zairn said, putting his back to her again. "And no, Ballard, we don't. We talk to Dunlap first."

"Who's Dunlap?" Roxie asked, laying on her back

again.

"Lawyer."

She toed her shoes off and raised her feet to the bed. "On the phone or in person?"

"We'll get him here."

"In the morning?"

"Yeah," Zairn said.

"Don't answer her questions when she hasn't offered us anything," Ogilvie barked. "I don't care how tight her pussy is, Z."

"Hey," Zairn was quick with his offense. "The only person allowed to disrespect her pussy is me."

She smiled. That was just further foreplay and would probably aggravate Ogilvie.

"If disrespect is what it will take for you to see sense…" Ogilvie said. "We have to circle the wagons until we find out what is going on. If someone is out to get you…"

"This is the wagons circled," Zairn said.

"Not with her in the room," Ogilvie said, barging forward. She rose onto her elbows when he appeared at the side of the bed beyond her knees. "What did he say to you? What is your interest in this? Why stop the statement? Has the guy got a case or is he blowing smoke?"

"Ogilvie," Zairn snapped.

Roxie held up her hand to him and rose to sit up, keeping her focus on Ogilvie. "I'm just a lay, I get it. You have no reason to trust me. I love that you care about Z enough to want to protect him. I thought he should talk to a lawyer before making the statement. If he chooses to make one, after he knows what I know, that's his call."

"Why did California call? How are they involved?"

"I'm not a detective," she said. "I don't know all the details."

"She's right," Ballard said, breaking her and Ogilvie's stare out.

"We need investigators on this."

"I'll call Stone," Ballard said, retrieving his phone from his pocket and heading out the door.

"Zairn, there's no way that—"

"Out, Ogilvie," Zairn said, slipping his hands into his pockets as he moseyed around.

"You can't—"

"Out!" Zairn yelled with such severity, Roxie jumped.

It startled Ogilvie too. He silenced, but sucked in his fury and stormed out, slamming the door again.

"Guess I'm in the bad books," Roxie said, climbing to her knees on the bed. "There goes my plan to stay the night."

He wandered around to the side of the bed where Ogilvie had just been. "You think I'm going to let you out of here after what you just pulled?"

"Your overseer doesn't like me," she said, walking on her knees to the edge of the bed to slide her hands up his torso.

"He's stressed. Scandal makes him nervous."

"And you relish it?"

He touched her hair. "How do I get this down?"

Women in his past were probably too sleek to sport the messy bun. With a quick pull and twist, she freed her hair and looped the tie around her wrist.

"Do you think the press will be out front all night?"

"Doesn't matter to you," he said. "You'll be right here." She looped her arms around him to hold her body against his, tipping up her chin to meet his eye. "Her wrists were cut?"

"In the tub," she said. "There was evidence of abuse, but the ultimate cause of death was—"

"Exsanguination. Damnit… Ackley sees this as his second chance… I don't even know where Ava lived. I remember the reports of her death… We were in Seoul the night it happened. They can make murder?"

She nodded. "He didn't take me through their evidence. I'll go back to him. Tomorrow, maybe. See if he'll give me anymore."

"You trust him to talk off the record?"

"To you? Not yet. Let me sit with it a minute. He's really wrapped up in this case. It'll take some time to ease him back to reality."

"This could get bumpy."

"The scandal?" she asked to which he nodded slowly, losing his fingers in her hair, combing it through. "Are you telling me to keep my distance?"

He smiled. "When we hit bumps like these, it's best to be squeaky clean."

"Shame I'm so dirty, huh?"

"Mm hmm," he said, scooping both hands around her jaw to angle her mouth to meet his. "I need to be with you tonight, Lola."

"I need a shower," she said, squeezing his shoulders, then feeling her way to his shirt buttons to begin undoing them. "And I didn't bring my jammies."

"What a shame for you," he said, stroking her hair from her face over and over in a slow, soothing caress. "What you did tonight means something."

"So I get to be on top?"

He eased back just an inch, one eye narrowed in a squint. "That a reward for you or for me?"

"I should call my girls. Let them know I'm alive."

"And that you're staying over."

Wearing a smile, she snagged her purse from the nightstand to rake around for her phone. "That too."

"It won't have any juice," Zairn said before she found what she was looking for. "Use the landline."

"No way."

"We can afford it, babe," he said on a sort of snicker.

Dropping her hands to the purse in her lap, Roxie couldn't believe his blasé attitude. Wasn't he supposed to be a smart forward thinker? "There's a chance your hotel records will be subpoenaed. Do you want to explain why there's a call from your hotel room to my apartment? At all, let alone at this time of night?"

"My girlfriend was calling her friends," he said. "Where's the scandal in that?"

"Humor me," she said, going back to her search. "I'll put it in your dock and go take a shower. That should juice it up enough."

"Putting my dock in your port? Yeah, baby, that

usually does it."

His smirk was so proud that it stopped her search again. "Do you get that this is serious? That you could go to jail?"

"Whoa, wait a second," he said, quickly frowning. "Are you, Miss Lola Bunny, going stale and serious on me now?"

When he sat on the bed, she sighed and pushed her purse aside to shuffle a little closer. "This is my fault," she said. "You wouldn't be here if it wasn't for me. You wouldn't have been in Chicago. Trish would have had no reason to make a statement. California wouldn't have called to share information and you wouldn't be on Porter's radar."

"You're right," he said with a straight face. "It is completely your fault." She blinked. The next thing she knew, he was laughing. "Baby, come on…" He took her hand. "I fell in love with your sense of humor, don't lose it now. Yes, I probably wouldn't be here if it wasn't for you. Probably. No one can say anything for sure. Less than twenty-four hours after I first heard your name, you were in a jail cell. I don't care about the drama. Shit happens. I deal with it." Opening his fingers, he took hers between them. "If I had the choice to be out of this Gambatto mess or be with you… it's not even a contest, baby. It's you all the way. Every time."

The door opened. Zairn twisted around to see Tibbs enter.

"Oh," Tibbs faltered. "I didn't…"

Zairn left the bed to head over to his assistant.

"Best when the Empress stays over to knock before you come in."

"I don't care if he sees my tits," Roxie said, finally plucking her phone from her bag. "I draw the line at motor-boating."

"Okay," Zairn said, throwing a glare her way, which only stirred her mischief. "So I'll be making the rules, follow my instructions. Not hers. Knock before you come into the bedroom when Rox is here."

"Knock," Tibbs said, a tentative edge in both his voice and his expression. "Will she be staying over… with you?"

"Yes," Zairn said.

She couldn't really see the look on his face, but it seemed like he didn't get it.

After putting her phone in his dock, she settled in the middle of the bed, her legs extended. "He's asking if you're screwing me and I didn't give you permission to tell people."

"You told Astrid."

Roxie gasped. "I never did! Why do you think I… because I talk to her? I didn't confirm anything. So now Tibbs, Astrid, Ballard and Ogilvie know."

"And your girls."

She bit the inside corner of her mouth. "This is getting complicated. Does Salad know?" She cringed. "I don't want Salad to know."

"Salad figured this out when you tackled him at the entrance to our bedroom on the Triple Seven," Zairn said. "Can we get back to why Tibbs interrupted us?"

She pushed herself to the edge of the bed and bounced onto her feet. "Knock yourself out. I'm going to take a shower."

Leaving, when they had the opportunity to sleep together without the entire world knowing it, would be nuts. He'd said he needed to be with her and Roxie would deliver… Chances to do that could be scarce while the mess played out.

TWENTY

WAKING UP ALONE was par for the course. Roxie would've thought sleeping with a guy known for living the nightlife might mean companionship with another late sleeper. Make no mistake, Zairn could sleep in and often did. But there wasn't a man more practiced at burning the candle at both ends.

Yawning, she pushed her hair from her face and went to the closet to grab a shirt. She finished buttoning it and rounded the curve of the hallway.

Only one person occupied the living room. A guy. Flicking through news channels on the silent TV.

The lawyer? Maybe. What was his name?

Somehow, he sensed her and turned.

Familiar… Roxie scrutinized him. "Why do I know your face?" she asked, pretty sure they'd never met. Hot like that didn't fall out a woman's brain. He smiled, and she got it. "You're Knox Collier."

"Guilty."

Her lips curled upward. "Wow, you're Knox Collier," she murmured, sure everyone who met him fell at his feet. Everyone but her. The surreal moment was kind of funny for some reason. "Your family owns like everything."

"We don't own everything."

Her chin rose. "Name one thing you don't own."

"We don't own you."

Her smile flashed higher. "Good answer."

A door closed. A few seconds later, Zairn appeared at the head of the wide hallway, heading her way.

She pointed across the room. "Knox Collier is here."

"Yeah," Zairn said, taking the side of her neck to draw her closer. "We just call him Knox."

He kissed her.

It took a second to remember they had an audience. "Uh," she said, smacking his arm. "Get off me, you crazy pervert." He just smiled, so she rocked closer to murmur from the corner of her mouth. "Knox Collier is here. You know, of the media monarchy Colliers."

"Yeah, we've met." Tightening his grip on her neck to narrow the space between them, Zairn stage whispered, "Our secret is safe. We know he's screwing the coffee cart girl."

"Ha," Knox said in a burst of unamused laughter. "And that's the last time I tell you anything."

"This what you billionaires do to amuse yourselves?" she asked, glancing from one man to the other. "Tease each other about bedding women in lower tax brackets?"

Zairn carried on like she hadn't asked anything. "It's nothing to be ashamed of." Without giving her his weight, he draped an arm across her shoulders like he was leaning on her. "She's cute. Cute suits you, Knox. Didn't think it would, but it does."

"I want to see cute," Roxie said, tugging Zairn's tee-shirt at his stomach.

"You've got to have a picture," Zairn said, earning himself another fake laugh.

"Not one I'd show the likes of you."

"Is it a naked pic?" Roxie asked, curling her fingers into the fabric. "Zairn doesn't want to end up on my bad side today, I absolutely promise he won't get a boner."

The surprise that hit Knox put another smile on his

face. "Blunt is right."

"Blunt," she said, looking up at Zairn. "That's what you told him about me. Blunt? I'll be blunt next time you want your cock sucked, Loose Lips."

"Blunt isn't a bad thing," Knox said.

Uh huh, yeah, right. "Said the man who hears dollar signs instead of words when people talk."

"I think she's going for a perfect score."

"Show us the naked picture already," she said, undoing one of her buttons. "If it's tit for tat, I'm completely naked under this shirt. I'll show you his, if you show us yours."

Knox's brows rose as he landed amusement on his friend.

Zairn pushed her hand away from her buttons. "No one's showing anyone anything."

"Party pooper," Knox said.

"He's having a bad week," Roxie said, patting Zairn's torso.

Tugging her closer, Zairn kissed her head. "You hungry?"

"I want toast… and fruit. Some kind of fruit. Where have you been anyway?"

"Gym."

"If you'd woken me up, you could've had your workout in bed."

"I like knowing you're in my bed," he said, like that explained anything.

The entry door closed again.

Putting space between them, she waited to see who would appear. Tibbs, Ballard, and someone she didn't know.

"Thanks for making the trip, Dunlap," Zairn said, crossing to shake the new guy's hand.

Dunlap! Yes, that was the lawyer's name.

"Chicago's closer than other places you've had me come."

Zairn just nodded. "Do you need anything? Food? Drink?"

"Tibbs was thorough, as always."

After getting the nod from his boss, Tibbs retreated

to depart.

Knox went over to shake Dunlap's hand too. "You up to speed?"

"Almost. I want to go over a few things."

"Fire away," Knox said, which was sort of rich given he wasn't the one in deep. "You'll get nothing but truth from the men here."

And the women? It was tough not to be offended when she was so blatantly singled out.

"The important thing to restate is no allegations have been made," Dunlap said as they gravitated to the seating area to settle themselves.

As he sat, Zairn took her hips to guide her down at his side. He wasn't so good at the secret involvement thing.

"Not publicly," Zairn said, doing his usual of resting an arm across her lap when she crossed her legs toward him.

"And prosecutors haven't been in touch?"

"The implication being…" Roxie said, having never been accused of being a shrinking violet. "I'm causing drama for no reason or making everything up?"

Zairn squeezed her knee. "We have credible information, Dunlap. We want to be prepared for whatever comes down the line."

"And you have your own investigation underway?" Dunlap asked and nodded, so she assumed he got his answer non-verbally. "Good. Information is key here. I'll speak to the prosecutor. Begin putting a team together."

"The prosecutor doesn't know we have this information yet," Ballard said. "We might get further details later."

"Or I can just make them up now," Roxie said, folding her arms. "Since that's what he's accusing me of doing."

"Babe," Zairn said, squeezing her knee again.

"Why would I come up here and stop the statement unless I thought it could harm you?"

He twisted to make eye contact. "Did I doubt you? For a second? Would you let the man do his job?"

"I'd never let anyone be rude about you."

"You walked away whenever my name was mentioned."

Damn her roommates for revealing that.

One shoulder rose just a little. "Point taken."

"You're hot when you pout," he mumbled.

Despite his smile, she grabbed his chin to refocus him on the lawyer. "Pay attention."

Though she'd relaxed a little, her arms folded again when she let him go.

Dunlap continued. "Do we have any reason to believe that Joey Gambatto was in California at the time of Dayah's death?"

Straight to the point. Though Roxie bristled a little, the men in the room were intent.

"Trish was in LA," Knox said. "At Crimson that weekend."

"You were with her?" Dunlap asked Zairn. "You didn't tell me that."

"I wasn't with her at Crimson," Zairn said. "I didn't see her until after I left Dayah's."

"I saw Trish at the club," Knox said. "After Z and Dayah left. If she was in town, there's a chance Joey was too."

"Did she mention her brother?"

"All she wanted to talk about was Zairn and Kesley breaking up."

"That was a few weeks before," Dunlap said to Zairn. "Had Trish been in touch?"

"I don't know," Zairn said on a semi-exhale. "Women call. They don't call. I don't set my watch by it."

"We can check your phone records."

"Yeah, 'cause they will," Knox said. "We need to be a step ahead of this."

"We'll pull everything on the prosecutor. Everyone's got skeletons."

First, Ballard looked at her, Knox was a few seconds behind. The man at her side didn't turn, but his fingertips began to trace circles on the outside of her knee.

What the hell? Baffling. Astonishing. "That's our go to?" she asked, almost dumbfounded. "To slander Porter? Do you know that the previous lead on the case had to be relieved after injury? Did you ever wonder why they picked Porter to be the new lead? He's not a skeleton kind of guy."

"Don't misunderstand me," Dunlap said. "There's also a good chance we can persuade this guy to work with us."

"Dirt doesn't have to be illegal," Knox said, leaning forward to rest his elbows on his knees.

"Right," Dunlap agreed. "Maybe he fudges on his taxes or has a porn habit. Hell, even something kinky in the bedroom could be enough."

The air of expectation increased. Roxie wasn't a fool and didn't have to wonder what they anticipated.

Her chin rose at an angle. "Choose your next words carefully, gentlemen," she warned, "…unless you want to see them in print tomorrow morning."

"You're threatening us?" Dunlap asked, startled.

Zairn took her hand, probably in an attempt to loosen her up. "That's Roxie's way of telling us she won't reveal intimate secrets."

"A quality we should all be grateful for," Ballard said.

Okay, so they wouldn't be sitting up late into the night sharing secrets and braiding each other's hair, but Roxie took a second to appreciate how far she and Ballard had come.

Reorienting her proverbial dish took a second. With her eyes closed, she rested three fingers on her forehead. "Porter's not an idiot," she said. "He wouldn't come after Zairn unless he had something rock solid. We know that can't exist because Zairn didn't hurt anyone." Her hand dropped to her lap; she locked eyes with the suspicious Dunlap. "What do you need to prove murder?" Despite asking, she recited the answer in time with the lawyer. "Motive, means, and opportunity."

"Yes," Dunlap said.

She smiled. "We're going to be fine."

"Glad you're so sure," Knox said. "Want to clue the rest of us in?"

"I can reason Porter out of it," she said, pulling her and Zairn's joined hands to her chest, squeezing her other hand around his knuckles.

"Geez, if we're relying on Roxie logic, we really are in trouble," Ballard muttered.

Roxie half ignored him and half told herself it was a joke. "A wall of lawyers will meet anything Porter tosses at Zairn. Good lawyers too." She pointed at Dunlap. "Don't take that as a compliment. I haven't decided if I like you yet." Her thoughts sprang back to the point. "Gambatto will want to hide behind that wall too. Zairn's lawyers will get him off, which could mean getting Gambatto off too. Say whatever you want about Porter Clement, he does want the bad guys behind bars."

"Maybe we offer the hand of friendship," Dunlap said, perking up with optimism. "Maybe we can help this Clement make his case."

Letting go of Zairn, Roxie moved closer to the edge of her seat. "He won't take a bribe, and I'm not sure how I feel about Zairn using his contacts for information. That could be dangerous. Physically and with regard to his reputation."

Zairn rubbed her back. "I know how to be discreet."

Not when it came to them, but that was a different issue. "If you knew something that would help Miss Illinois get justice, you would've shared it already," she said over her shoulder without turning around.

"Trish only got to Knox that night because of her Queen status," Ballard said. "With what's going on, we can't risk her getting near you."

"If someone hurt Dayah…" Dunlap muttered. "Why? Because she meant something to you? Kesley always believed you cheated with Dayah."

Kesley had told her that too. "Why would Kesley care about Miss Illinois?"

"I don't know, I'm simply making the connection. Crimson was the only place anyone could've got to her that night. It was the only place you were."

"And everyone saw the argument," Knox said. "Great prelude to setting you up."

"Dayah spent a lot of time at the New York club too."

"We don't know there's a Crimson connection," Zairn said.

"You're the Crimson connection," Knox said. "You knew both women."

"I met Ava once, maybe twice."

"Were you intimate with her?" Dunlap asked.

"He does not have to answer that question," Roxie said, patting his thigh as she pushed herself back a little, though she remained sitting upright. "It's not like there's a serial killer going after every woman he ever slept with."

"No, just the most recent ones," Ballard said, deadpan.

From one face to the next, all were fixated on her. "What?" she asked, bouncing around to check out Zairn only to discover the same expression on his face.

"Lo…" he said, sweeping the hair away from her shoulder.

"No, that's crazy. You know that's not what this is about."

"We don't know anything for sure and until we do…"

"Safest thing to do is pull everyone's security clearance," Knox said. "Including the Queens. Anyone we can't trust one hundred percent is on the outside from here on out."

"Agreed. That means every pre-Dayah Queen," Ballard said. "Gives us cover for pulling Trish's clearance without raising suspicion."

"How many are post?" Dunlap asked. "They'll be the only ones clear in this… unless it's a pathology they've had since before you met."

Ballard had the answer. "Rox is the only one you've had me clear in that time window."

"Yeah," Zairn said, rubbing her back again. "But she's not a Queen. She's the Empress."

His hand slid up her back to grip her neck to draw her against him.

"You're only being nice to me because I know the prosecutor."

"Of course," he said, burying his mouth in her hair.

"What other reason is there?"

She raised her head just a little. With her back against his torso, she couldn't actually see him. "Uh, 'cause you want your cock sucked later, because you want me to open my legs whenever you're at a loose end."

"Yeah, well, you do those things anyway. Soon as I switch it on, you don't stand a chance of resisting."

She smiled. When they teased and played, everything seemed much simpler.

"Your investigator should get more information," Dunlap said, examining her and Zairn. "This is a crucial time. Roxie was right about the statement. From now on, nothing goes out to the public without my say so."

"Oh, there's a new sheriff in town," Roxie cooed.

Zairn let go of her neck to loop his arm around it. "You made your choice, Roxanna. Live with it."

"You said you wanted to keep the inner circle small," Dunlap said. "Limiting the flow of information is smart. It's vital." He became more somber. "Are you certain?"

"Yes," Zairn said without hesitation.

"I'll have to liaise with your public relations team."

"I'll bring everyone else in," Ballard said, rising to stalk away.

Glancing back at Zairn, Roxie stroked his thigh. "Can we talk a minute? Alone?"

"Yeah," he said, helping her up. "We'll be back."

TWENTY-ONE

WITH A HAND on the small of her back, Zairn guided Roxie into the bedroom they'd shared last night.

"What's wrong?" he asked once the doors were closed.

Roxie folded her arms. "Where's Ogilvie?"

His jaw tightened. The ease of his gaze became so tense that it was instantly mad. "Keeping his distance, if he's smart."

"Because he's not a fan of the fabulous Roxie Kyst?" she asked. "You should be grateful he cares about you enough to be wary. Let's be honest, your cock leads you when I'm around. Ogilvie is thinking with his other head. You need someone thinking straight."

"He doesn't understand you."

She shrugged. "I don't understand me most of the time."

"This. He doesn't understand this," he said, coming over to slip his hands under her hair onto the sides of her neck. "Women in the past wanted something. They were needy or demanding. Women like that are unreliable."

She snorted out a laugh. "And you think I'm reliable?

Have you been paying attention? Hello, I'm a crisis event."

"I trust you, Lola," he said, gathering her into his arms. "We're facing a major test. There's no one I need with me more than I need you."

"You were fine about it last night," she said, tucking her arms against him. "Shit happens, I deal with it. That's what you said."

"Why are you second-guessing me? You don't want me to trust you? We were out of contact for two months; that was your chance to flip on me. If it passed you by, that's on you."

"I want you to trust me," she said. "This isn't about me, it's about you wrecking your relationship with Ogilvie out of some warped sense of chivalry. You and me don't have one mind. We don't have to think the same way about everything."

"But you're trying to change my mind on this."

"No," she said, shaking her head. "I want to understand and make clear that even though Ogilvie doesn't like me, I don't expect you to cast him out. It doesn't have to be one or the other. You can have both."

Assessing her, he took his time before breaking the silence. "You're a difficult woman to read," he said. "A difficult woman to please."

That took her aback. "I had no idea you felt that way. You think I'm high maintenance?" She considered it for a second; her arms dropped to her sides. "Am I high maintenance?"

"You're independent. You don't need anything… which gives me no way to win you back."

"Win me back?" she asked, exploring his expression. "You have no way to control me, is that what you mean? Because I don't need your money."

"And because you still don't get it," he murmured, combing his fingers through her hair.

Her smile was tight. "Wanna have sex with me? Everything will feel better when you're inside me."

"Always does," he said, his fingers still tangled in her hair when he cupped her jaw. "In New York, you said we had time. That we didn't have to decide anything in a hurry."

Her hands rested on his chest. "We still don't."

"This will get complicated. The press won't let this one go. It's sex and murder, two of their favorite things."

"I won't betray you," she said, touching his jaw.

"Didn't occur to me to doubt that," he said, flashing his suave smile. "I'm apologizing in advance."

"We traveled the world together and had the masses 'shipping' us. I lived through you before, I'll do it again."

"Cost us two months together. I can't be without you for that long again."

"We didn't come back here to talk about this. We came so I could tell you not to freeze out Ogilvie. It won't win you points with me. Now…" Roxie pushed out of his arms to lay her hands on her hips and sway left to right. "Sex or no sex?"

It took him less than a minute to peruse her figure. His growing feral smile transferred to the light in his eyes. "Why ask when you already know the answer?"

Rushing forward, he seized her waist and picked her up to toss her onto the bed. She was laughing when he appeared over her. Zairn was the perfect mix of man and playmate. Losing him to the Gambatto debacle would be more than a miscarriage of justice, it would break her heart and poison her soul. She couldn't let it happen.

SOMEONE KNOCKED on the bedroom door as Roxie sat on the edge of the bed. Given the earlier warning, she expected it to be Tibbs. Instead, Astrid peeked into the room.

"Hey," Roxie said, bundling her hair up onto her head again. "Come in. Don't just loiter there. I haven't seen you in forever! Where have you been?"

Astrid glanced left to right. "Are you sure? I wouldn't usually—"

"Yes," Roxie said, gesturing her over. "Don't worry about Lord Lomond, he's on a call."

Though Astrid crept in, she stayed by the door, still scanning the room for something. "I don't want to interrupt."

"He's in the closet," Roxie said, rolling her eyes. "I

don't know who he's talking to. I don't care that much. Maybe arranging my surprise birthday party, who knows?"

"Oh, your birthday is coming up?" Astrid produced her phone. "Any likes or dislikes that—"

"That's not why you came in here," Roxie said, springing from the bed to go over and take Astrid's elbow to drag her deeper into the room. "What do you need?"

"I don't need anything," Astrid said, almost squirming. "Everyone has gathered and… They're getting restless and eager for Mr. Lomond's input."

"So you came to drag us out of our sex den." Roxie leaned back to shout into the air, "Casanova!"

"Why do you call him that?" Astrid whispered.

"Because he's all that," Roxie said. From the way the assistant jolted, Roxie guessed Zairn had joined them. She twisted around to check and groaned at the sight of him just outside the closet, typing something into his phone. "Good God, man! I had time to blow-dry and you couldn't even put on a shirt? Didn't you learn your lesson at my place?"

"Astrid, what do you need?" he muttered, still typing, completely ignoring the woman he'd just bedded.

"Uh… just to tell you—"

"We're being rude," Roxie said. "Well, you're being rude. People came here to see you and you couldn't tear yourself away from my pussy long enough to greet them."

"You offered your pussy, Lola. It would've been rude to reject it."

Turning to the side, she put a hand on her hip. "What does that mean? Any time a woman propositions you, you have to acquiesce? Cool for them."

Astrid cleared her throat. "Are you two…?"

"Together?" Roxie asked. "Who can be that specific in the twenty-first century, right, Z?"

"Whatever you say, dear," he said, finally looking up from his phone. "We'll be out in a minute, Astrid. Phone downstairs and get them to send food up. Just a selection of whatever… and fruit salad for her ladyship."

Though he smiled at her, Roxie narrowed her eyes.

"Yes, sir," Astrid said and quickly scurried out.

"That's weird, you know," Roxie said, strolling around the bed. "That she calls you sir. You're not a sir."

"Not to you."

"Yeah, but, it's weird. She's my friend and you're screwing me." Roxie stopped a couple of yards away. "You wouldn't ask Toria and Jane to call you sir."

"They don't work for me."

"If you were screwing Astrid, you wouldn't make her call you sir… unless that's her thing."

"I don't sleep with employees."

"Just because you haven't done it yet, doesn't mean you never will."

He arched a brow at her. "Nothing wrong with my willpower."

"Ah," she said, raising a straight finger. "You wouldn't need willpower unless you were tempted."

Lunging forward, he grabbed her arm to haul her against him. "I'll send someone over to your place."

"To tempt me?"

"Nothing's more tempting than this," he said. "I meant I'll send someone to get your things."

"With me?" she asked. "I'll be more conspicuous on my own. I got in through the alley last night. No one noticed me."

"Trish has linked me to this. The press know Porter, the prosecutor, is your ex."

"I know, they'll be looking for comment. I've got two exes on opposite sides of a case," she said on a sigh. "I would like it noted that I'm not the one who caused the trouble this time. You must have a thing for women who attract drama."

"Trish is acting on behalf of her brother."

"You think he's coaching her?" she asked.

"She's supporting her family," Zairn said. "I'd expect everyone to act the same in her position."

"Damn. Do you always have to be so accommodating? I know you can get mad, you get mad at me, why not get mad about this?"

"I'm passionate about you."

"You should be passionate about your freedom," she

said. "Just so you know, I won't wait for you if you go to prison."

The way she amused him hadn't changed. Seemed he never got used to her. Roxie wasn't sorry that he still enjoyed her company… and her quirks.

"What if I give you complete control over the company?" he asked.

"Then I definitely won't wait for you. I'll be too busy jetting around the world, romancing as many young bucks as I can get my hands on."

His lips thinned as they stretched in a smile. "What happened to wanting a man who knows what he's doing?"

"I figure I should spread the knowledge. You know, give something back."

"Sex. You figure you should give sex back?"

She scoffed. "You're just jealous you didn't think of it first."

"Yeah, I gave back enough in my twenties. "

Admiring his chest, she stroked her hands down his pecs before digging her nails in. "Did we really spend eleven days together?"

"You don't remember?"

"I remember sneaking into your room at night and out again before the sun rose."

"No need to sneak anymore, baby," he said, the back of his fingers drifting over the hair beyond her temple.

Looking him in the eye, she dug her nails in a little deeper. "You utter the words 'move in' again, I'll scream until the reporters on the street hear me."

"I didn't say a word," he said, smirking.

"That look on your face," she said, squeezing his jaw. "You're too hot and rich for your own good, you know that?"

"Mm hmm," he said, still enjoying her as he backed her toward the bed.

Roxie was quick to plant her hands and feet to stall him, refusing to budge. "You've had your Roxie quota today, Skippy."

"I could convince you otherwise," he said, descending like his goal was his mouth on her neck.

She leaped aside. "Yeah, maybe you could." He could, but Roxie wouldn't give him such an easy win. Not when teasing him was so fun. "But we're in crisis right now. Crises, actually. Sex won't cure any of them."

"It'll cure something else," he said, advancing, forcing her into retreat. "If I go inside, I'll need memories of you to keep me warm at night."

"If you go inside, it'll be because of this," she said as her back hit the door. "Because you were too busy having sex to solve the problem."

He laid a hand on the door above her head. "It would be worth it, baby," he drawled.

When he began to stoop again, Roxie grabbed one of the door handles to pull it open. "Rain-check," she said, darting out the door and closing it again fast.

Zairn would have to find a shirt before he came after her. Taking advantage of the head start, Roxie grabbed her purse and hightailed it out of there, offering only a wave over her head as a farewell to the others. Serious people in the room wouldn't care about her departure. Certain parties would relish seeing the back of her. But that wasn't why she left. No. Roxie knew she could be useful and was already formulating a cunning plan.

TWENTY-TWO

FLUFFING HER HAIR, Roxie checked her appearance in her bedroom mirror.

"You look great," Toria said. "You always look amazing."

Jane squeezed her waist from behind. "If anyone can make Porter see sense, it's you."

"Sex was my fallback position when we argued... I always won with sex."

Toria pulled her dress down to reveal more of her chest. "Make sure these girls say hello," she said. "Does Zairn know your fallback?"

"Zairn doesn't even know Porter's coming over," Roxie said, adjusting her boobs in her bra. "I'm not going to have sex with Porter. He's too in his own head at the moment, it would be awful."

"That's why you're not doing it?" Toria asked. "Not because you have a gorgeous billionaire crazy for you?"

"Z and I are... complicated."

Whose expectations was she trying to temper?

"You think he'd be okay with it?" Jane asked. The vulnerability of her innocence was always difficult to ignore.

Despite her life experience, Jane still believed in fairy tales. "You'd have to tell him if you slept with someone else. You can't lie."

"This is exactly why we whisper when we're naughty," Toria said, throwing both arms around Jane. "You're all heart, honey."

"I won't sleep with Porter. Less chance of him being reasonable if I did."

He'd want to avoid the appearance of adjusting his trial strategy because his ex-girlfriend was good on her back.

The front door closed.

They all heard it and looked at each other.

"Good luck," Jane whispered, hugging her.

"We'll be right next door if you need us," Toria said, kissing her cheek.

Zairn's purchase of the apartment next door was coming in handy. Her girls could give them privacy, which would relax Porter, and could stay close for moral support. And any other kind of support as needed.

Her two roommates joined hands and scurried out. The mumbling of voices carried as she looked at her reflection again.

Convincing Porter was vital. Speaking her mind was a way of life, but it had never been more important to do it well. When the front door closed again, she bounced away from the mirror to head out to the living room.

"Guess it was a good thing I kept my key," Porter said, putting the keys on the kitchen counter. "Been a while since you called me over here so late."

He moseyed around to face her. With the width of the room between them, they tried to read each other.

"Thank you for coming," she said. "Were you seen?"

"There's a squad of reporters out front."

Nodding, Roxie walked into the kitchen, rolling her eyes as she sighed. "I know, it's a pain. That's why I told you to come in around back."

"Yeah, your bodyguard is scaring people away out there." Opening the fridge to retrieve a beer, their eyes locked when she turned, intending to hand it over. "Lomond?"

"He's been paying for security for me since the tour." She shrugged. "It's not a big deal."

"I knew it," he said. Raising his arms up, he pivoted away. "I came here against my better judgement. How do you always do this to me?"

"I do what?" she asked, slamming the beer on the counter. "What did I do wrong this time?"

He spun to look at her. "You're advocating for him. I could tell by your mood last night… Is he here?"

"No!" Roxie objected. "No, he's not here."

Whenever Porter was uncomfortable or felt cornered, he grabbed for control. "Why do you give a shit about this guy? Are you sleeping with him?"

Roxie knew her ex too well. "I didn't invite you here to have a conversation about my sex life."

"You're protecting him."

"You always know best, don't you?"

"Am I wrong? Tell me I'm wrong."

"I invited you here to do you a favor."

He reversed to prop himself against the back of the couch. "I can't wait to hear this."

"You are taking on the wrong opponent," she said, creeping closer. "If you drag Zairn into your investigation, his people will ruin you."

"You don't know if he's innocent. You don't know that at all."

"I do," she said, pushing positive shoulders back. "I know he's innocent."

He coughed out a laugh. "Because you read sincerity in his big brown eyes?"

"His eyes are blue, actually. And I know it because everyone is innocent until proven guilty. That's still the case in this country, isn't it, counselor?" He faltered. "Don't let your prejudice, your dislike of a guy who your ex may or may not be screwing, destroy the case you've built."

"Ro, I—"

"If you were any kind of professional, you would listen to what I have to say. Zairn Lomond, like him or loathe him, is a resourceful guy. He will hire lawyers. Bigger, rougher, scarier lawyers than you. And they won't stop at, 'if the glove don't fit…' They will chew you up." She showed him a palm. "And no, this is not a threat. Zairn doesn't even know you're here. He'll probably go crazy when he finds out I stepped in."

"Crazy enough to hurt you?"

She sneered. "No, counselor. Zairn Lomond cares about people. He looks after people. His whole life is dedicated to pleasing people."

"Maybe that's why he snapped. Maybe playing Mr. Nice Guy all the time drove him insane."

"No," she said, triumphant as she folded her arms. "If you did your research, you'd find out that his reputation isn't sparkling clean. He's romanced women he shouldn't and let the party get out of hand more than a few times. He isn't about living the most moral life; Zairn lives and let's live. He doesn't muscle in on other people's business."

"Does he know Trish Gambatto's business? She claims to be the whole reason Lomond is here." She sealed her lips. "RoRo, you're asking me to listen and be open, but you're holding back. Fair is fair."

"I know," she conceded on an exhale.

"You believe in this guy. You've spent a lot of time with him and I know you don't trust easy. If he's got something, if there's something going on between you…"

The point wasn't her social life. "You're the smartest guy I know," she said, edging closer. "The way you talk when you're passionate about a case…" She took his hand. "It's enchanting. Even when I didn't have a clue what you were talking about, your certainty made me certain."

"This isn't like that. I can't give up on a lead because you think you know a guy."

"California couldn't make murder because Dayah wasn't murdered."

"So says you."

"So says the DA and medical examiner in California. If Z had any idea that Dayah was so fragile, he would've helped her, not walked away. This is a guy who has the connections and the means to get someone help."

"You weren't there—"

"No, I wasn't. Neither were you. That case has been put to bed already. Do you really want to drag Dayah's family through the ordeal all over again?" Letting him go, her hands landed on her hips. "When was Ava Marilyn killed? Was Zairn in town? Have you checked? I know the answer: he wasn't. He didn't have the opportunity to kill her; he didn't even know her address." Three of her fingers shot up between them. She took her time folding one of them down. "There goes one of your trifecta. Did he have the means?" Her lower lip pushed out as she shrugged. "Yeah, he does, in the same way all of us do. What was used? A knife? A razor blade? Most people have something sharp in their homes. But you want to know where your real problem is?"

"Motivation."

She smiled and nodded. "Motivation. Ava was seeing Gambatto. They had a volatile relationship, you know that already. Zairn had no reason to want her dead. He doesn't do shady deals, even if he did, he wouldn't do them in front of random beauty queens. He's been building his business for twenty years, it means everything to him. He's dated all sorts of women and is friends with hundreds more. Why would he suddenly decide to draw blood?"

"All kinds of stories are coming out about historical incidents involving high-profile men."

"About Zairn?" He didn't reply. "No, because you could interview a thousand women and none of them would accuse him of violence or cruelty." She grabbed for Porter's hands again. "This is your case. Yours. Your big landmark, career defining case."

His eyes relaxed as his head tilted. "My ego? That's your in?"

Okay, so it wouldn't necessarily have worked with Zairn either, but he'd have teased with her for a while before calling her out.

"All I'm trying to say is that you were in charge of this, you had a handle on it. Why does one call from a guy thousands of miles away mix it up? You're running this. You call the shots. Not him."

"We have to exhaust every lead."

"It isn't your lead. I don't know what California has against Zairn…" Though she'd file that question away for later. "But he's not a piece of your puzzle. By bringing him into it, you're risking Gambatto having the chance of representation that will ruin everything."

"Ro—"

"Again, not a threat. If you accuse Zairn, he'll lawyer up. You already have Joey on remand, you have a case against him. To connect Zairn, you'll have to put him somewhere in that case. So, by default, if Zairn's lawyers rightfully defend him and win, your case against Joey falls apart and he walks. A violent criminal walks."

"Even if all that is true, it doesn't explain one thing."

Anticipating him was easy. "Why Trish made her statement? It's like I said, she's a desperate woman trying to force Zairn's hand. She wants her brother free. They can't afford representation on the same level Zairn can."

"They used to be together."

"It was casual. They weren't soulmates." Restraining a snort of cynicism was difficult. Necessary, but difficult. "If they were, Zairn would've come back to be at her side the minute her brother was arrested."

"Maybe he thought Joey would get himself out of this mess."

"He doesn't have to think that because if you bring Zairn into it, you'll be handing Joey the keys to his cell all by yourself."

He shook his head. "You're trying to psych me out."

"Tell me I'm not making sense. You must have thought all of this yourself. The smartest guy I know doesn't need me to tell him. You know I'm right."

"I don't know why he came here. The club in Chicago. It doesn't make sense. It's suspicious. I can't ignore that. I can't reason it away." They just looked at each other. "Unless you want to tell me he came here for another reason. For another woman… For you."

Roxie inhaled and held her breath. Before she was forced to say a word, a knock at the door saved her. Thank you, higher powers!

Scampering backward, Roxie turned at the last minute. She opened the door just a couple of inches to peek out with one eye. Now the real fun would begin.

"What's the password?" she asked.

His lack of reaction was amusing in itself. "You called me over to play games?"

Her hip popped to the side. Zairn couldn't see it, but her anatomy was definitely responding to him.

"I'm surprised you're surprised."

Intrigue lit him. "What you wearing?"

"Not what you're thinking," she said. "On the day we met, I told you I don't do lingerie."

"The lingerie I can do without," he said in full swagger mode.

"Did you have to sneak out?"

"I'm an adult, I don't need permission to come see my—"

"You don't answer to anyone either," she said. "No one except me."

Her wink curled his lips. "Open the door and I'll answer to you all night."

"I'm so glad you said that."

TWENTY-THREE

THROWING OPEN THE DOOR, Roxie bounded back, presenting the room for him. Zairn got one step inside, then Porter stood up straight. The men looked at each other. Neither said a word.

Pouncing closer, Roxie took Zairn's hand to guide him inside. The men remained silent as she went to close the door.

"Okay, now, I know neither of you expected—"

"Clement," Zairn said in cool acknowledgment.

"Lomond," Porter said in return. "She always gets what she wants."

"Yes, she does."

"Okay, don't bond over me," she said, shaking both hands, approaching Zairn again.

The two men fixated on each other. "You said we couldn't trust him off the record," Zairn said.

"I said you couldn't," Roxie said, raising her brows at Porter as she veered around Zairn. "He exaggerates."

"Not about this," Porter said. "If you're dirty, I'll figure it out, Lomond. And if you hurt her—"

"Okay," Roxie said, shifting to glance back and forth

between them. "I did this because I trusted both of you to cut through the bullshit. If this plays out through a dozen middlemen, neither of you will back down first. I am not staking reputations and freedoms on a game of Telephone. Show me that cooler heads can prevail. That you're both as smart as I've vouched you can be."

"No bullshit. I want the truth," Porter said. "Why Chicago? If you have an intimate relationship with Trish—"

"For Roxanna," Zairn said. Her jaw swung loose. "She doesn't want to live in New York."

"Don't tell him that," she said, hands on hips.

His gaze dropped to her. "No bullshit."

"You didn't even tell me you were coming here before you bought real estate."

"If he told you first, you'd never have let him do it."

Whirling on Porter, her affront only awarded her a shrug. "What's that supposed to mean?"

"The chase is never over with you, babe," Porter said. "You wouldn't know what to do in a relationship if you stopped running for one second."

"*If* I was in a relationship, I'd know what to do," she said. "I'm great at relationships."

"You're terrible at relationships."

"I didn't come looking for it, buddy," she said, jabbing her forefinger his way then hers. "You pursued me."

"Thus, she makes my case. Thanks, RoRo."

Reversing, she glanced back and forth between the men. "Talk to each other. Don't talk to me."

"You talked to Ackley?" Zairn asked Porter.

"Guy's got it in for you."

"Yeah, he does. Because he can't put the pieces together any other way. No one felt right about the way Dayah died."

"Can't be a coincidence," Porter said. "I assume Rox told you Ava Marilyn's cause of death."

"He deserved to know you were going to ambush him," Roxie said. "Innocent until proven guilty, remember?"

"You sense trouble and run in headfirst," Porter said, shaking his head at her. "He isn't the first guy you've been wrong about."

She folded her arms. "I could say the same thing about you. Zairn is not a killer."

"Then explain it to me," Porter said, sauntering closer. "She who always has an answer for everything. Tell me why two seemingly unconnected women die at almost opposite sides of the country in exactly the same way?"

"It wasn't the same way, Ava was beaten."

"There was a disturbance at Dayah's residence."

"Maybe she was just messy," Roxie said. "He wasn't in town when Ava died. Didn't we already cover this?"

"Lola," Zairn said, curling his fingers around the back of her neck. "Why don't you let me take this?"

Folding her arms, she set her expectation on Porter, keeping Zairn at her back. "Okay, so talk."

Zairn kissed the top of her head.

Porter was unimpressed. "Means nothing if I can't question him directly."

"You can question him."

"You keep answering for him!"

"It's okay, babe," Zairn said. "I've got this. Why don't you give us a minute?"

Being excused from her own living room left Roxie speechless. Zairn showed his smile, but she couldn't react. If they wanted to talk shop, she didn't have to be present. But she hadn't expected they wouldn't need her.

"I'm surprised you don't want her here as an independent witness," Porter said.

"Think any judge would call her independent? You're her ex."

"And you are her… what?"

"No." Roxie leaped into the fray. "You can talk all you want about the cases, but leave me out of it."

"He already said he came here for you," Porter said. "He could be lying… or he could be crazy in love with you. Doesn't mean he gets you… I know that from firsthand experience."

"Baby," Zairn said, stroking her back. "Trust me."

He nodded in the direction of her bedroom, so she

started walking. "Fine, I'll go. But no comparing notes. Find something else to bond over. You both like Scotch, try that…" Even when both men were behind her, she kept talking. "Neither of you like dancing… real dancing, not the slow stuff."

"You own nightclubs and don't like dancing?" Porter asked. "How does that work?"

"She exaggerates," Zairn said, which she had to accept, tit for tat.

Though if Zairn didn't give her a full, complete, and satisfying account of what was said between the men, it would be a long time before she'd accept his tat again.

THE FIRST THREE MINUTES in the bedroom were spent cursing it for being the farthest from the living room. After that, she paced a while and ended up flopping down on her bed. The pair of them knew her too well. They'd deliberately keep their voices low to avoid being heard.

Her ceiling needed to be painted. The weird crack in the corner above her window was growing. Not for sure, it just looked longer than she remembered… maybe it was Zairn's fault. He was pretty vigorous in screwing her the other night.

"How do you feel about pearls?"

She hadn't heard him approach, but that suave drawl was unmistakable.

"If you make some joke about giving me a pearl necklace—"

"And prove I don't know you at all?" he asked, appearing in her peripheral vision at the end of the bed. "You swallow, baby."

Rolling onto her side, she propped her head on a hand. "Makes me so happy you have that memory, Skippy. It'll be all you have to keep you warm at night."

"Because…"

"You know I set you up with him," she said, sitting up straight. "I set up this little meet and then you two… You kicked me out of my own living room."

He rounded the foot of the bed and sat on the corner. "I can't concentrate when you're around, Lola, you know that."

"Don't sweet talk me." Dropping onto her back again, Roxie sought her reassuring ceiling. "I'm sulking."

"Okay," he said. His fingertips met her knee and ascended. "You keep sulking…" She heard rather than saw him taking off his jacket. "I'll just… be down here."

Sulking wasn't effective with Zairn; he was just going to have sex with her anyway. She'd never been particularly good at giving the silent treatment. The sensation of his lips on her thigh put a chink in her resolve. If he got much higher, she'd be the one jumping him.

His mouth ascended. A shiver went through her; it snaked up her spine until even her scalp tingled.

"What happened?" she asked, opening her fingers in his hair. "I want to know… I should know… Are you going to jail? Porter's not a yeller, I wish he was a yeller. I'd have heard what was going on if he was a yeller."

Zairn eased her dress higher. Her hips moved of their own accord, letting him gather the fabric above her ass.

He kissed her inner thighs and nuzzled the panties covering his prize. The heat of his breath on the fabric aroused her inner muscles. Squeezing and squirming, she released his hair when he rose to hook the elastic of her panties to slide it down her legs.

Before he could return to his previous spot, she closed her legs, drawing them up to her chest. The question in his eyes was met with defiance in hers.

"No pussy until you tell me."

"If I'm going to jail?"

"Casanova," she whimpered in her persuasive way. "Satisfy me."

"You read my mind," he teased, but she wasn't giving it up. "I have to talk to Trish."

"That was the agreement?" Her feet dropped to the edge of the bed as he removed his tee-shirt and toed off his sneakers. "You have to talk to your ex-girlfriend… What does Porter think? That she'll confess?"

"Trish and I were casual, she wasn't a girlfriend…" He narrowed one eye. "Sure I've said that to you before."

"Casual, casual, casual," she said, raising her knees again to slide her soles onto his abs. "You're casual with all your lady friends. Doesn't make them not your girlfriends… Kesley was the exception, I guess…"

"You think Kesley was the exception?" He smirked, stroking her feet, her ankles, her shins. "Roxanna Kyst."

"Why do you have to talk to Trish? To give Joey a message?"

"To find out what she knows."

"I thought the cops and lawyers already questioned her."

The swagger of his smile showcased his arrogance. "I'm more persuasive."

"So you'll seduce it out of her," she said, her toes tracking to his ribs. "Like you seduced me out of my sulk."

"You're easy, baby," he said, guiding her legs around him as he descended to lie above her, his forearms braced on either side of her head.

"I wouldn't tell you my secrets." Roxie coiled her arms around his neck to pull him closer. "I'm keeping my mystery."

He kissed her. "I'll spend a lifetime trying to get in."

"To my pants? At what point do you say been there, done that?"

"Is that what you're waiting for? Me to get bored?" He kissed her again. "What was tonight about? For you?"

"It wasn't for me. Porter needed to see you himself. He needed to see the man, not the legend."

"You're obsessed with the legend."

"Actually…" she said, caressing his cheek. "I prefer this version of you. The guy who comes to my apartment in the middle of the night when I call. The guy who doesn't care about the cracks in my walls or my single-minded ex-boyfriend."

"Clement's dedicated to his work, I respect that."

"But he should be more discerning in who he listens to."

"You're talking about Ackley?"

"Yes! He should listen to me over a stranger. We were together for two years and he doesn't even know that guy."

"Professional experience goes a long way."

"I lived and breathed Porter's cases with him. Talking it out was his way of getting to some big important conclusions."

"You are the only reason he gave me a break. The only reason he's willing to hang back until I talk to Trish."

"Which Og and Salad and Elson and Dunlap will hate. Isn't their advice to put as much distance between you as possible?"

"This is less about public opinion and more about Ava Marilyn. If I can have a conversation that gets Clement closer to a conviction…"

"But it's dangerous, snitching like that."

"We're not talking about testifying. I have to know if Joe's guilty."

"Are you thinking about linking him to Dayah? If Trish was in town, maybe he was too. Isn't that what Knox said?"

He shrugged. "Maybe. One step at a time. I don't want to unlock doors that should stay locked."

Which reminded her…

She gasped. "Did you lock the door? Jane and Toria are next door in your little security hang out. They won't get back in if—"

"Clement said the door is left unlocked until all three of you are home. So it's unlocked."

She relaxed. "He likes to tell me how my roommates can't butt out." She licked her lips. "I'd probably be accused of the same if the shoe was on some other guy's foot, you know?"

"Hardly ever." His mouth brushed hers. "Have I given up enough for you to give it up?"

"You should sue Ackley, the California DA guy, that's what you should do. Make his life hell. He can't just go about making stuff up and spreading his lies."

He drew back to get a clearer view of her. "How do

you know it's lies?"

"How do I know it—what are you implying? That you might be guilty? Please!" The outrageous suggestion almost made her laugh. "You weren't even in town when Ava Marilyn died."

"Which you only know because I told you. Maybe I lied."

"Zairn Lomond," she said, slapping both hands onto his cheeks. "Do you think I'd be with a man capable of that?"

"Are you?"

"Am I what?"

"With me."

The billion dollar question. He had all the money in the world and still couldn't get a straight answer. He must be sick of her always holding a part of herself back. Why did he keep pushing? Keep asking for more when what they had was working.

"You talk too much, Casanova," she said, coiling her legs around him. "Why aren't you having sex with me?"

His exhale and narrowed eye betrayed he was wise to her diversion. Every time he brought up what they were, she pivoted to something else. He just wouldn't take the hint.

TWENTY-FOUR

TOSSING HER HAIR from her face, Roxie dragged her feet as she walked up the hall toward the voices in the living room. Her girls were in the kitchen. Toria on her feet, pouring coffee. Jane sitting at the breakfast bar.

As soon as the latter saw her, she spun on her stool, waving her hands.

"You're never going to believe," Jane whispered, grabbing her wrist to yank her closer. "Zairn Lomond is in our shower."

Toria laughed. "Zairn Lomond was in her last night. I don't think she cares about the shower."

"I care," Roxie said, passing her girls to pour coffee. "But his clothes are all over my bedroom, so I figured he didn't go home naked."

"You were okay that he might be out here with us, waving his tackle around?"

Smiling, she took the cup to her lips. "We have rules, girls. It doesn't matter what he waves at anyone. It belongs to me."

In that room anyway.

"It's so weird, I can't wrap my head around it," Jane

said, grinning ear to ear. "You're dating Zairn Lomond."

"We don't go on dates," she said and paused. "Déjà vu."

"You are determined to wreck this for yourself," Toria said. "You're always determined to wreck any good thing that comes into your life."

"Uh…" Roxie tilted her ear higher. "What's that I hear? Pot… are you calling the kettle black?"

She raised her brows at the smiling Toria. "Do you want to tell us what happened last night? When Porter was here, not the sex part… although I'm open to hearing—"

"Zairn Lomond got off in our apartment," Jane squealed, dumping her coffee cup to grab Toria's hand. "It's so exciting!"

The front door opened. In came Ballard with Tibbs on his heels. The assistant made a beeline for the hallway, the jump bag and a garment bag over his shoulder. No shame. They just strode on in like they owned the place. Zairn had bought the apartment next door without her knowledge. Maybe he'd got two for the price of one and bought hers out from under her too.

"What's up, Little Rox?" Ballard asked, passing them to go around the couch.

"Did the press see you coming in?"

"Give me a little credit," he said, swiping up the remote control to turn on the TV. "You've got a useful network of alleys out the back of your building. It's pretty easy to get in unseen."

Especially when his boss also owned an apartment in the building.

"What are you doing here?" she asked, retrieving another cup to half fill it with coffee. "Don't they have TVs in your hotel?"

Tibbs had disappeared. She didn't see him in the hall as she went over to offer the cup to Ballard.

"Thanks," he said, gulping some down, then handing it back.

"I'm not your table," she said, putting the cup on the coffee table. Ballard pulled the TV out while retrieving something from his pocket. "What are you doing to my TV?"

"Keeping the trains running on time," Ballard said. "You've screwed with everyone's timetable."

"I didn't screw with anyone," she said. "I'm a woman living here. You and your boss love just showing up."

"What happened with Clement?"

She tossed her hair away from her face. "How long has Z been up? Looping everyone in."

"The news doesn't stop just 'cause you're sleeping."

"I don't care about the news, I care about him sneaking around while I'm sleeping."

"You sleep a lot, Rox," Ballard said, attaching his device to some wire before pushing the TV back.

"What are you doing?" she asked, trying to peek at his phone when he took it from his pocket.

He jabbed at the screen and stepped back. Too busy trying to see what he was doing, she didn't notice anything on the screen until Jane squealed and leaped up to run away.

The TV was full of people. Ogilvie, Dunlap, Elson, Salad… in the Grand suite living room she'd last seen them in.

"You're invading my apartment," Roxie said. "What if I was naked?"

"If you were naked, I wouldn't be here," Ballard said. "I don't want to see too much information."

She smiled, even though he'd turned back to the TV. New York.

"I'm going to check on Jane," Toria said.

Her mood changed as her roommate departed. She mouthed an apology and Toria shrugged. Was she mad? Maybe. Roxie appreciated Toria giving them the room without them having to ask. If her girls were mad, she'd kick every guy out and—if she couldn't figure how to unplug Ballard's gadget—toss the TV out the window.

In almost the same second Toria disappeared, Tibbs came into the living room.

"Where is he?" Ogilvie snapped.

"I chained him to my bed," she said before anyone could get a word in. Skirting the coffee table, she sat in the middle of the couch. "I'm holding him for sexual ransom."

"What are you—"

"She's kidding," Ballard said.

From his glare, she guessed he wasn't happy. Zairn had warned her that Ogilvie couldn't detect sarcasm.

"Does she have to be present?" Ogilvie asked, grinding his teeth.

"No," Roxie said, twining a length of hair around her finger. "I'm only here to annoy you…" She set her own glare on the TV, noticing the camera attached to the top. "Oh, and because this is my apartment. You want to have meetings without me? Do it in your hotel."

"We would if you hadn't lured him to your bed."

"Lured? You think I'm an enchanting siren? Your boy came to my bed of his own accord. He could've chosen not to. He had a clear shot at a clean exit and didn't take it… Guess my pussy must be super, extra tight."

The others may be outraged by the comment, but she was talking to Ogilvie, no one else.

Elson pushed Salad, kicking him into gear. "Yes, uh…" Salad cleared his throat. "With the current situation, the uncertainty and the potential for negative press, we, uh…" He inhaled and straightened, gesturing as he spoke. "You are, technically… Your connection to Crimson is…"

"The contest," she said.

What bomb was Salad about to drop? The guy was twitchy. She didn't like it.

"Given that… the media interest and the… legal issues…"

Ah, this was the gentle let down. "It can't be like you picked the winner based on who was best suited to ride Zairn's cock."

"Yes," Dunlap said. "Exactly."

"Don't worry about me rocking the boat. I'm not a girlfriend, I'm a lay, just ask Ogilvie."

"Anyone you tell about—"

"I haven't told anyone," she said.

"Roxie isn't our enemy," Ballard said. "Didn't she prove that by alerting us to Ackley's bullshit?"

"It has to be made clear," Elson said. "The connection… No one can know about… not yet. Your roommates…"

"Don't people in public relations have to be excellent communicators?" she asked. "You're telling me to deny any personal involvement with Zairn. And to make sure my roommates won't blab either. You don't have to worry. We have no intention of going public and I have no intention of causing trouble."

"You threatened to contact the press," Dunlap said. "You can't fault us for protecting—"

"We should get out of Chicago," Ogilvie said. "Dump the club, clear out. Put some distance between ourselves and the women of this city."

Yeah, uh huh, go ahead. He could draw his eyes off her, she would take it… though not quietly. "I don't really care if you dump the club, but can I just point out to all the glarers that I wasn't the one who made a statement to the press about my brother. I wasn't the one who called Porter and stirred up the frenzy."

"We wouldn't be here if it wasn't for you. He wouldn't be here."

Touché. Okay, yeah, she had to give him that. Having thought the same thing, it would be hypocritical not to accept the point.

"Can you even do that?" she asked, appealing to Ballard. "Sell so soon after buying?"

"He won't sell," Ballard said. "Running away implies guilt."

"…yeah, babe…" Zairn. On the phone. Coming in their direction from the hallway. "I know. Don't worry about that. I'll take care of it…" He stopped between the couch and perpendicular armchair. "It's under control… Babe, you don't have to think about it anymore… I've got it… Yeah."

He hung up and put the phone in his inside pocket. Shirt, jacket, slacks, such a consummate professional. Thinking of him that way was funny when just a few hours ago, she'd been lying naked on top of him talking dirty.

"Trish?" Ballard asked.

"Yeah, where we at?"

Straight to business. If he'd been up early enough to arrange a cross-city meeting, why hadn't he returned to his hotel to do it in person?

"We emailed the statement to you," Dunlap said.

"Yeah, I read it."

He took his phone from his pocket again. That thing was in and out, in and out, and no orgasm at the end. Poor thing. What a deprivation.

His fingers moved on the screen, then he held it toward her.

"You don't have to give the statement in person," Elson said. "We'll release it. Just need your approval."

Zairn was looking at the TV. What did he want her to do with his phone? She took it, none the wiser.

"You're letting her read it?" Ogilvie asked without disguising his disapproval.

Oh, the statement. She got it and read along. Neutral, respectful, calm.

"She's in the circle, Og. Get over it."

Another opportunity for mischief. Why couldn't she resist? "Thought you said I wouldn't get in your inner circle," she said, locking his phone.

"I said winning the contest wouldn't open my inner circle to you," he said. "You did an end-around."

"I did?" she asked, handing his phone back. "How did I do that?"

"You let me into your inner circle." Of course that deserved a suave wink. Sleazy, but funny too. "What do you think of the statement?"

Roxie shrugged. "I like it. But don't go on my word, I'm not a lawyer or a PR guru, whatever."

"You're a Zairn Lomond guru."

"I am?"

The corner of his mouth rose. "You're getting there. Do we release the statement?"

"If you want… Are you in a hurry?"

He frowned. "No, why?"

"You said you had to talk to Trish," she said. "Is that

what you were setting up on the phone?"

"Yeah, we're meeting in an hour."

"Okay," she said. "As the only woman present, and viewing this through a personal lens, I have to tell you… I would be much more receptive to whatever you had to say if you weren't, in the same hour we're meeting, releasing statements to the press."

"We say nothing negative about her brother."

"The statement creates distance," she explained to the men on the TV without looking at them. "It's platitudes. '…*the justice system do its job… run its course…*' If I want your support, I want it all the way. Trish spoke to the press, didn't she? She wants it out there that you're on her side; that you believe in her brother. Your statement doesn't show pride and determination, it's fear… or apathy. If I need your support, I don't want you to be afraid of giving it… and I definitely don't want you not to care."

"We have our own interests to look after," Ogilvie said.

Zairn was listening. That was all she needed. Whatever he chose to do was up to him.

"I'm your whatever," she said. "We're sleeping together…" Waving at the screen, she silenced those who blustered, her eyes locked to Zairn's. "If my brother was in prison and I asked for your support, is that the statement you'd rush to release?"

"Baby, I've told you. You and Trish are not—"

"Does she know that?" Roxie said. "From the female perspective… The way she talks about you, talks *for* you, she thinks you had something, thinks maybe you still do… or hopes anyway. She's appealing to a man she cares about for help…"

"You didn't want me to help her," he said. "You said if I cared about what happened to Ava Marilyn—"

"I'm not telling you to help Trish now. All I'm trying to say is that you're on your way to talk to her. I don't know what she'll ask or what you plan to say. This statement boxes you in, it sends a message. Do you want to waste your time with Trish talking over your statement? Arguing about it and what it really means? What do you lose by putting off the statement's release until after you've seen her and got a better sense of what you're dealing with? You'll get a more open and honest woman if she doesn't fear your primary concern is protecting your own interests."

"She's got a point," Ballard said.

"Our stock prices are already fluctuating," Ogilvie said. "We can't put this off any longer."

Maybe the business advice was sound. Her perspective was different. "I don't know anything about stock prices," Roxie said. "But, unlike the rest of you, I've known Porter Clement for longer than twenty-four hours. He didn't agree to keep a lid on his office only for yours to pre-empt him. If he thinks you're being underhanded, he'll be underhanded right back. He's competitive. You know how important his career is, he's not winning any points by gagging his people. He's doing you a favor and one that's costing him… I know the State's Attorney too, he doesn't give a crap about your business or reputation. Right now, Tim Unst is watching Porter's profile eclipse his own. The male ego is a delicate thing. Porter's feeling the pressure, I guarantee it."

And the slightest thing could tip the balance against them.

"We can't trust him," Ogilvie interjected. Her attention stayed locked on Zairn's. "Withholding the statement would be a mistake. What are we waiting for?"

"To get a feel for the room," Zairn muttered. "Lola's right, we'll get more from Trish if she's not on the defensive. After I talk to her, I'll know which way we're going. We'll be able to release a statement with some balls rather than this weak, spineless thing."

"She's making corporate decisions now?" Ogilvie barked. "Jesus Christ, son! Grab your damn balls and snap out of it!"

Whoa, boy. Giving her opinion was just part of her. She wasn't shy or afraid of voicing her viewpoint. But if Zairn's people were questioning his ability, maybe it was a mistake to be so forthright.

"I am not your son," Zairn said, his voice all bass and

authority. "You're only in the room because she spoke for you yesterday. If you want to step out, no one will stop you."

"Zairn," she murmured. Hoping to soothe, she scooched to the end of the couch to reach for his hand. "Your advisors want what's best for you."

His attention leaped to her. "And what do you want?"

Wow, even in a room of others… Was that rhetorical? It was rhetorical, right? She wanted what was best for him. They were talking about the situation, not… them.

"We can't turn on each other now," Ballard said. "This is it, as far as the circle goes until this Gambatto thing is over."

That could be months. It would be months. Could be years. There would be a trial. A conviction, maybe an appeal. If Gambatto was acquitted, what then? Would it be over?

They were talking about some other business thing, a person she'd never met.

Her swirling thoughts put her on her feet. "Excuse me," she said.

"Babe?" Zairn asked, stalling her with an arm across her body as she passed. "What's wrong?"

"Nothing. I'm going to check on my girls and take a shower."

TWENTY-FIVE

ZAIRN DIDN'T LOOK totally convinced, but nodded and let her pass. Toria's bedroom door was open, no one in there. Roxie went to Jane's room and opened the door to sneak around it. The women sat on the bed facing each other.

"Big drama?" Toria asked.

Roxie went over to flop face first onto the bed. "Drama all over the place." Rolling over, she rose to her elbows. "He just argued with a guy he's known practically his whole life because the guy did what he's been doing for years. What is going on?"

"You don't know their politics," Toria said. "Maybe the guy is a prick."

"Which guy?" Roxie asked. "Ogilvie or Zairn?" Toria shrugged. "I'm sorry you got kicked out your own living room… I have some experience with that. It sucks."

"We weren't kicked out," Toria said. "Jane just freaked about being in her pajamas in front of people."

"You knew Zairn was here," Roxie said. "He has a thing for jammies."

"He does?" Jane asked, all blinking innocence.

"No," Roxie said, dropping onto her back and linking

her fingers under her breasts. "He likes lingerie, I don't. We're completely incompatible."

"You've done some kinky stuff in the bedroom," Toria said. "What about that guy who wanted to pee on you?"

She shuddered. "What's your point?"

"If lace is what he needs…"

"I don't see him dressing up for me," Roxie said. "How come there isn't a male equivalent to lingerie?"

"That's your problem with it? Sexual inequality?" Toria asked, laughing. "Honey, have you seen your man without a shirt? 'Cause I have and hell-oh. We throw a bra over our tits and they squirt in their pants. Ten second job. Abs like that…" She arched one brow. "That's a serious gym addiction, babe. And one you should encourage… If a G-string is what it takes to keep him happy, go with it. He has enough money, you can bury your self-loathing in retail therapy."

Just a short time with her girls and already she felt better.

"We'll get our living room back. He has a thing soon."

"Ballard is hotter in person than you led us to believe."

"I never led you to believe anything," she said, taking Toria's hand to link their fingers. "Though you already knew who he was."

"Yeah, 'cause of our Crimsettes thing. He's hotter in the flesh."

"What is this Crimsettes thing?" she asked, her brow descending. "How come I never heard about it?"

"You're not addicted to the internet like we are," Toria said. "Or as addicted to Zairn Lomond."

"I still can't believe you're…" Jane considered her words. "Seeing him, can I at least say that?"

Toria shook their joined hands. "Yeah, dish, how good is he between the sheets?" Closing her eyes, she appealed to the heavens. "Please don't shatter my entire belief system."

"He's good," Roxie said. "More than good."

"You didn't get that from the screaming last night?"

Jane asked, her cheeks pinking. "That wasn't the fragile ego thing you talked about, was it?"

"Nope, all real," Roxie said. "There is nothing wrong with his ego." Why were the two of them looking at each other like that? Something was going on. Glancing back and forth between her friends, she narrowed her eyes. "What?"

"You ask," Jane said to Toria, a grin splitting her face. "It's too soon."

"We won't know unless we ask."

"She's not ready to tell us."

Left, right, back, forth, what was going on?

"I wasn't lying when I said I hadn't measured his cock," Roxie said. "But it's definitely above average… well above average… I'll do it later… if we're alone. Obviously, I won't do it in front of people."

"No, that's not…" Jane stopped to sigh.

"Oh, what the hell," Toria said and sucked in a deep breath. "We want to see the ruby."

"The ruby?" Roxie asked.

How did her friends know about the ruby?

"Yeah, come on," Toria said. "Don't bullshit us. He gives every Crimson Queen the hair slide with the ruby… We want to see the ruby."

"I don't have a hair slide," she said. Toria's head dropped to the side. From the looks on their faces, neither of them believed her. "I don't. I really don't."

"Are you trying to say this is the first time you've heard about the Queen rubies?"

"No," Roxie said. "Kesley showed me hers. I know what you're talking about. She invited me to the dinner too."

As Toria gasped, Jane squealed… again.

"They meet in the spring. Oh my God," Jane said, snatching her other hand. "You have to go."

"If you don't, I'm so taking your space."

"I haven't heard from Kesley," Roxie said. "I doubt I'll get an invite." Even if she did, it wouldn't be smart to go while Zairn's forces were so nervous about their association. "And I don't have a hair slide, so…"

"Why wouldn't he give her a Queen ruby?"

"Maybe he's not that into her," Toria said, releasing her hand. "And the bubble bursts. He's just the same as every other guy chasing tail."

"I don't have a *Queen* ruby," Roxie said, sitting up to slide herself to the edge of the bed and onto her feet. "But he gave me *a* ruby…" Wandering to the door, she lingered as her friends leaped up to chase after her. "Wanna see?"

Both nodded, eager, grabbing for her. All three scurried to Roxie's room. Digging the ruby box from her dresser, Roxie put it on top and let them look for a second.

"Wear me," Jane said. "Wear it? What is it?"

"Open it already!"

Laughing, Roxie put her thumb on top to unlock the box. Her girls inhaled as she opened it up. Their surprise was understandable; sometimes her memory underestimated its magnificence.

"Oh my God," Jane whispered, clamping both hands over her mouth.

"That is so much more than a stupid hair slide," Toria said, her eyes wide.

"It's a ring," Jane mumbled behind her fingers. "He gave you a ring."

"Empress," Toria said. "You're the Empress!" Roxie shrugged. "For when you're ready… ready for what?"

"Are you crazy?" Jane said, snapping to it. "It's a ring!" Jane took it from the box to slide it onto her finger. "A man only gives a woman a ring for one reason."

"True," Toria said. "And you accepted it, so…"

"What did he say when he gave it to you?" Jane asked. "Was it romantic? Where were you? Italy? France?"

"There isn't a Crimson in France," Toria said.

"He didn't say anything. I found it just before New Year, in the leather binder thing, in my bedroom."

"Oh my God, and you didn't tell us? What is it doing in your underwear drawer? If I had a ring like this, I'd wear it every day."

"I can hardly wear something like that with the press hanging around outside."

"You could've told us," Jane said, trying the ring on

a different finger before Toria took it.

"Why didn't you tell us?" Toria asked, admiring the ring on her own finger. "About any of it?"

"We danced around it for a long time on the tour. When we did eventually have sex, we had a blowout like the next day and then he disappeared."

"He disappeared?" Jane asked.

"They left me in London."

"Oh my God, and he was in Vegas. That was why you were apart?"

"We were apart because he showed up with Kesley Walsh and caused an international incident." That was how the Crimson crew saw it anyway. "We didn't see each other again until I got to Vegas."

"And you made up?" Jane swooned for a second, but followed it with a frown. "Did he sleep with Kesley between you guys doing it and seeing him in Vegas?"

"No," Roxie said, letting Toria take her hand to slide the jewel onto her ring finger. The band was too big. It stayed on her middle finger every time she'd worn it. "But he could have. We weren't defined."

"Honey, a man does not give a woman a ring like that without expecting wedding bells. That's as defined as you get."

"You should get married in New York," Jane said.

"What?" Toria snapped. "No! The Bahamas, baby. He has his own island. We're going to visit it soon."

Jane gasped. "Yes! Yes! You should get married while we're there!"

Her ears rang. Was that the sound of wedding bells? They weren't optimistic and happy. They were… ominous. What the hell was he doing giving her a ring like that? The money, yeah, she understood he had it. Maybe that had obscured her view of the ruby's significance. Sometimes it was easy to take the flash for granted, like it wasn't that big a deal. Seeing it through her girls' eyes was stunning. The ring Porter tried to put on her finger was only a fraction of the size of the ruby. She'd taken one look and handed it back.

Damnit. How did Zairn do this to her? How did he relax her and lull her into thinking that she had the reins all the while… Shit. She'd held the reins. When did she hand them to him? Probably the same minute she put the ruby on her finger.

"I'm gonna take a shower," Roxie said, yanking the ring off to put it back in the box.

"Don't freak," Toria said like she was talking to a scared animal. "It'll be okay."

"It will not be okay!"

Jane was careful in closing the door, giving them some privacy of their own. "It's not a bad thing. Toria's right, you can't wreck this for yourself."

"We're not… We're not supposed to be…" Slamming her drawer, she dropped her forearms and head on the dresser. "I'm such an idiot."

"You are not an idiot," Toria said from her other side. Jane had to be the one stroking her hair. "You've caught yourself a fish. Isn't that what we're all trying to do?"

"No, I don't want a fish. Not yet," Roxie said, reversing away from her friends until her legs hit the side of her bed. "This is what he does. He rushes me and I…" She sank onto the bed. "God, why did I kiss him?"

"You kissed him?"

"You're surprised?" Toria asked Jane as the two women sat on either side of her. "Our Rox has never been shy about taking what she wants. We love that about her."

"What happened to dating?"

"You keep telling us you're not dating," Jane said.

"Which makes accepting the ring more ridiculous. It isn't a relationship. Not like a real… He's always on the other side of the planet. Even if he's with me, I never know when he'll choose to just disappear… Kesley said he couldn't maintain it. It's true… And she thought him and Dayah were sleeping together while they were still together."

"You don't trust him?" Jane asked.

"She'd be an idiot to think a guy like him doesn't get offered it all the time."

"I've seen it," Roxie said. "The way women throw themselves at him… They did it right in front of me…" Damn, was she repeating Kesley's words? How had she become this woman? Why wouldn't women proposition him in front of her? He didn't owe her anything. "I have to shower."

To wash him out of her system.

This was exactly why it was a good idea to keep her friends in the loop. Talking things out with her girls gave her the wake-up call she needed. Getting involved in a long-distance whatever, pretending it was all fun and games. She'd needed a harsh slap to snap herself out of it. Thank God for her girls.

TWENTY-SIX

ZAIRN TRIED TO TALK to her in private before he left. No dice. No. Nu-uh, she wasn't falling into another trap. It wasn't like she overtly ran away from him. No, just kept herself busy around people, ensuring he had no chance of talking to her before he was due to meet Trish.

The Crimson crew left, taking their devices with them, and Roxie breathed out. Deconstructing what this and that meant. Looking for hidden meaning. Figuring out the true implications of someone's words… It was beyond her. So rather than face the pit she'd dug for herself, she worked.

Her friends tried to coax her outside, but she couldn't go into the world. Maintaining a façade was tough enough when she knew what was behind it. That day, Roxie knew nothing about who she was or how she could've been so stupid.

Her girls sent her an online message inviting her to join them for dinner. They'd met up with some people from their social circle and were going to make a night of it. Good for them. Someone should have fun.

Work. Work. Work.

Her phone was off. This time it was no accident. She

didn't want to deal with any of it. Not the TV with its reporters and impromptu meetings. Not phone calls. Text messages. In her apartment, submerged in her work, she didn't have to think about today, tomorrow, or anything except the words on the page.

Another message flashed up. Porter.

> **PC: *Meet me in Tim's office.***

What? That was it. Meet him at… Why would she want to meet him in the State's Attorney's office? Geez, another meeting? Tim didn't even like her. If he did, he hid it well. Her initial urge was to ignore the message. But, damnit, Porter had come when she called. Not doing the same would be beyond rude and unkind.

Anyway, despite her mini-major meltdown about Zairn, she wished nothing bad for him. If Porter and his boss were cooking up something shady, she wanted to know about it.

> **RK: *Give me an hour.***

It was only upon entering her bedroom that she noticed how dark it was outside. What time was it anyway? Why would Porter be in the office so late? None of the possibilities she came up with were positive.

She changed clothes quickly, figuring the faster she did, the sooner she'd get the skinny. Curiosity had to be satisfied. That was the point of it. None of her security guys loitered outside her front door. Good. It was tough to slip by security when they blocked the only viable exit.

At the end of the rear alley, a guy gestured her into a waiting car. For real? What was going on? The same guy drove her to a side service entrance and ushered her through darkened passages. All very clandestine.

If she wasn't totally freaked, it would be sort of fun.

Maybe she was being arrested for something. What had she done recently that might fall into the category of illegal? That she wouldn't be able to talk her way out of. Hmm. Short list and, yes, she rated her ability to win an interrogation showdown.

What was Porter doing that he needed her brought there? Some reporters were in front of her building, but they'd be the backup people, the understudies. The real stars were camped outside the Grand. Where the real action was. So why not just come to her place like he had last night?

The mystery chauffeur man opened the State's Attorney's office and gestured her inside. The door closed behind her. Huh… She was alone. In the dark. Rubbing her arms, she shook off the chill in the air. Yeah, it was creepy.

The lamp on the desk would—nope, wait, was she being setup? The prospect of snooping accusations kept her away from the desk. To one side was the chesterfield furniture. At the other was a long mahogany table. During business hours, it was a room for work. In the middle of the night—

A door in the corner opened. Porter. Yeah, it was about time.

She opened her arms, tossing her purse at the couch. "What is going on?"

"Are you alone?"

"Yes, I'm alone," she said. "I haven't spoken to Zairn since this morning, but I'm telling you, whatever scheme you're—"

"It's not a scheme," he said, putting a hand on her arm to guide her closer to the desk. "Tim wanted to—"

The door opened again. When Porter turned, she got to see who was joining them. Goddamn Tim Unst, the State's Attorney.

"Miss Kyst," he said, wearing a broad smile as he came to them. "Thank you for joining us."

"Mm hmm," she said, laying the evil eye on Porter for a flash of a second before smiling at the SA.

Before he even got to them, Tim was reaching for her hand. She gave him hers, of course, but uh, exactly what the hell was going on?

"Your help is… invaluable. You've done something really spectacular here," Tim said, clasping his other hand around hers as he continued to shake. Even when he stopped, he didn't let go. "You are far more than I gave you credit for."

"Wow, what a fabulous underhanded compliment," she said, inspecting both of them.

"No! Sorry, I… You're a beautiful woman, of course—"

"And that excuses a multitude of sins, I suppose. After a positive comment about her appearance, any woman should fall in line, shouldn't she?"

"What are you doing?" Porter mumbled under his breath.

"Porter, I am not—"

"Would you excuse us a second, sir?" Porter asked, grabbing her arm to pull her away from the SA.

"I'll give you a moment," the confused SA said, departing to leave them alone.

As soon as the door was closed, she yanked her arm out of Porter's grip. "You are a snake and I can't believe I wasted two years of my twenties on you."

"Ro—"

"Don't RoRo me," she said, shoving his hand away when he tried to touch her arm again. "I trusted you!"

"You're yelling at me," he stated.

"Yes! I am yelling at you because I trusted you and you… If Zairn won't sue your ass, I will."

His lips quirked. "You're going to sue me?"

"Yes!" she said, nodding while not appreciating his badly hidden amusement. "I will. I will sue you, Porter Clement."

"For what?" he asked. "I don't think you can sue your ex-boyfriend for annoying you."

"I'll sue the office," she said, throwing her arms up as she turned to pace away. "I may not be billionaire rich, but I'll find a billionaire to ride who'll pay for the best for me."

"Are you accepting applications?"

Zairn.

Spinning around, her mouth dropped open when she

saw him by the door Porter and Unst had used. "Casanova," she exhaled.

"Yeah," he said, smiling as he approached. "The best what? What do you need?"

"Do you care?" she asked, passing Porter to meet Zairn in the middle of the room.

"No," he said, running his fingers through her hair. "You get a blank check."

And he had to go and remind her of the ruby. Stepping back, the tension that rippled through her wasn't easy to hide. After being with Porter for so long, he'd see it. And backing away from Zairn? Why not just take out a full-page ad? Damn their compulsion for intimate proximity.

"What are you doing here?" she asked, sidelining her hysteria to focus.

There was no way she could talk to Zairn about them in their current surroundings.

"He achieved the impossible," Porter said. "That's what he's doing."

"It's not that big a deal," Zairn said.

Despite his confident stance, the humble thing wasn't an act. No cameras. No fans. He was so just… him. Why did that have to be the day she severed their connection? Whatever he'd done… there was only one reason for his presence: her.

"Either you're that arrogant or that modest."

"Go with the first," Roxie said, knowing it was actually the second, but he didn't show "him" to everyone. "What did he do?"

"Trish Gambatto is testifying against her brother… against her family."

What in the actual…? The first to admit that she paid little attention to underworld news, even she understood that was a massive deal.

"How did he do that?" she asked Porter, but immediately turned to Zairn. "No, I don't want you to do that."

Zairn's ease disappeared as his brow descended. Damnit. Why did she say that? It wasn't her place to tell him what to do. That morning, or lunchtime, or whatever, hadn't she opened her big mouth in front of Ogilvie and caused aggravation? Her opinion was irrelevant. When would she learn?

"It's done," Porter said.

"Nothing's done until I say it is," Zairn said, fixated on her. "What's wrong, Lo?"

"I need to learn to keep my mouth shut," she said in a long rush.

"No, you don't. What is going on?"

"The only way this possibly…" Roxie blinked her focus to Porter. "The city wouldn't pay for the level of security she'll need. And Trish Gambatto wouldn't trust Chicago witness protection. No one would be that stupid. The Gambattos own most officials in the whole state… Am I wrong?"

"About corruption in the state? I plead the Fifth. About what it will cost to give her peace of mind? No, you're not wrong."

"Which means Zairn's paying for it," she said, resisting the urge to shake her ex. "You thought I'd be okay with this…" Except maybe not. "You knew I would hate this." Her ex didn't reply. In fact, when his eyes flitted to the side and he licked his lip, it was proof she was on the money. "It's incredibly dangerous."

"It's the right thing to do."

"To dangle a woman in front of her family? To present her to the world as a prime target."

"She trusts Lomond's assertions he'll keep her safe."

"Yeah, maybe, what about him? You think the Gambattos will be okay with him standing between them and Trish?"

"Lola—"

"No!" she said, yanking her arm from his reach. "This is insanity. Why would you get involved with…?"

Except she was the answer.

"This is about Ava Marilyn," Zairn said. "Money breeds power, it wins every time. Remember Rome?" How could she forget? "You told me it was about justice. It can only run its course if it's given all the facts. Trish has those facts."

"She puts her brother in jail and then what?" she asked. "Are you going to support her for the rest of your life?"

"What's the alternative?" he asked. "I stand up in front of a hundred cameras and slaughter his reputation? Shout out his guilt? You think that will make me a friend to the Gambattos?" No, and they'd have to deal with the scorned woman too. "I say nothing, walk away, and let Ackley dedicate his life to convicting me for a crime that never happened? Do you know why Joey Gambatto killed Ava the way he did? Because of Dayah. Might not have been him, but he saw the circus, watched me walk despite the accusations…" A copycat. "This is my mess."

"You are not responsible for what happened to Dayah Lynn," she said, gravitating his way when he came closer. "You are not." Laying a hand on his cheek, she traced her thumb back and forth. "You have too good a heart."

"Shh," he said, turning his head to kiss her thumb. "We don't want that getting out. Tell me no and I'll shut it down."

"Lomo—"

Zairn's hand rose toward Porter, silencing him.

"You have to stop this," she said. "I say things out loud and they happen. It shouldn't be this way."

"It's details, babe."

"Details that could hurt you."

He smiled. "This conversation right here is hurting me."

"Oh God," she groaned, the top of her head falling against him.

"She was never this complicated with me," Porter said. "She had no problem telling me what to do."

"This is her playing make believe," Zairn said, his hand resting on the back of her neck to stroke her hair. "Making believe I'm in charge for a minute."

"Oh, yeah, I know that game."

Great. The two of them were bonding again.

"You better not be using me as your common

denominator," she mumbled.

"What am I doing, Lola?" Zairn said, still stroking. "Pulling the plug or seeing this through?"

Joseph Gambatto was not a virtuous human being. As for his sister? Roxie had paid little attention to specifics, but if Zairn had dated her, he'd seen something good. Porter wanted the bad guys behind bars. Zairn could get sucked into it if they pulled out of the deal now.

Her head fell back, so she could meet his eye. "You're supposed to get along with everyone. You made an enemy today."

"Lomond. Clement."

That was Tim. Thank God Zairn's body was blocking hers from the view of the door. Backing away when he turned, she didn't want anyone seeing more than was necessary.

"Sir?"

"There's still work to do. Trish is asking for you."

Zairn looked her way again. "You okay in here for a while?"

"Sure," she said, shrugging and moseying in the couch's direction. "I'll just add this chapter to the memoir I'm writing. Danger and intrigue at the SA's office… how's that for a title?"

"Miss Kyst—"

"She's kidding," Zairn and Porter said at the same time.

Yeah, she didn't like that… Though it was better than the alternative. They could just as easily have despised each other.

She shook her hands at them. "Shoo, shoo, go get your work done. Who knows when the urge to stream will come upon me?"

"You okay?" Zairn asked again.

Roxie nodded, shooing him with her hands. His smile disappeared as he headed over to join Tim in the corner room.

"He made a friend too."

Taking her attention from the door, she blinked at Porter. "What?"

"You said he made an enemy and you're right. You're

right that it's a risk too. But he made a friend, in me, in Tim… in the city of Chicago."

"I don't want to see him hurt, that's all. Didn't I go nuts when I found out your apartment was burned down? I don't want people I care about to be in danger."

Shaking his head, he wandered closer. "This time last year, the ring was burning a hole in my pocket."

Dropping her shoulders to the back of the couch, she sighed. "Port, do we have to do this now?"

"I wouldn't have believed it unless I saw it with my own eyes," he said. "That's all I wanted to say."

She wasn't sure what he meant and didn't want to ask. "I really can't cope with anymore commentary on my life today, please."

"I got you something," he said, turning away to head for the desk.

"You got me something?" she asked, springing up to perch on the edge of the couch again, doing her meerkat, trying to see what he was retrieving from the drawer.

He came toward her, keeping whatever he was holding hidden in his hands. "I didn't get it exactly, I had my assistant bring it."

"Is Natalie your new assistant? I meant what I said about blondes bearing gifts."

"Natalie's an ASA. And I'm not sleeping with her… Not that I need to explain myself. You've clearly moved on."

That softened her exaggerated interest in the gift. "Porter, I—"

"It's okay," he said and smiled, sitting at her side. "I wanted to hate him, but it wasn't as easy as I thought it would be."

"I'm familiar with what that feels like… And, uh…" Damn, this was awkward. "Nobody really knows about us, I mean… I'm not saying there is an us, but if there was—"

"We don't want to make an enemy of him. The guy has influence… more than we could ever dream to have. He could just as quickly turn it against us."

Yes. She hadn't looked at it from that perspective. Not seriously. If Porter and his boss had political aspirations… Zairn would be a useful guy to have on side.

"What'd you get me?"

He held his hand out. She opened hers beneath it and he put the object in her palm. A rectangle thing. "Uh… thank you."

"It's a power bank," he said. "A portable charger."

Restraining her laugh, she showed him the twist of her smile. "My hero." He leaned in to kiss the corner of her mouth, then stood up to go back toward the corner room. "I note you didn't do this while we were together."

"If I wanted to get laid, it was better not to talk to you." She laughed. He didn't often joke. When he did, she appreciated it. "Don't tell anyone where you are or who's here."

"Are you kidding?" she asked, slipping off her shoes to cross her legs on the seat. "I have a Tetris personal best to beat."

"Try not to pull anything."

Digging in her purse, she sought her phone. "Good luck saving the world."

"One criminal at a time," he said just before going through the door.

Zairn had convinced Trish to turn on her family. That was huge. His powers of persuasion were awe-inspiring. Just another reason to make things clear. If they let this thing get away from them, it would snowball, fast.

His colleagues were right. It wasn't the best time, Rouge-wise, for news to break that the CEO was screwing a contest winner. It wasn't the right time for them either. She didn't want to hurt him, she really didn't. Accepting the ruby sent the completely wrong message. Wasn't that why she'd tried to return it in New York? Why had they never talked about it? Because serious wasn't them? Maybe.

Zairn was amazing. Too amazing. Too smart and decent. They needed to talk. Wasn't that always the way? Whenever they needed to talk, some drama happened, or they got distracted by sex. She had to be strong. It was time to talk it out.

TWENTY-SEVEN

TETRIS WASN'T THAT ENGROSSING. Modern technology was great though. Between reading the news and watching a bunch of videos, she stayed occupied. Checking her email came next. Sender: Greg Hatfield. Hmm, what did he want?

The door opened, not the corner one, the main door. Who was coming to…?

When the woman came in, surprise stunned her into silence.

"Roxie…" she said in what sounded like a rush of relief.

"Kesley," Roxie replied, struggling to get with it enough to stand when the actress came over, arms open.

"It's insane, isn't it?" Kesley pulled her into a hug. "It's fantastic, but terrifying too."

The woman smelled so expensive. What was that perfume? Maybe she just bathed in money and success. Is that what all rich, beautiful people did? How was this her life? It wasn't. Who the hell's life was it? Not hers, that was for sure.

Kesley took her shoulders to release the embrace. "How are you doing?"

"How am I doing?" Roxie asked, reading nothing but sympathy in the woman's eyes. "I'm fine. Sitting here on my ass…" Another interesting point, why the hell was she still there? "How did you…? Someone called you?"

"Yes," Kesley said, taking off her wool cape thing. Roxie took it to let Kesley remove her gloves too. "He is a power to be reckoned with, isn't he?"

Narrowing an eye, Roxie wasn't sure she followed. "Who are we talking about?"

"Zairn!" Kesley said, laughing. "He's got Trish into some mess. Don't misunderstand me, it's fantastic. She needed to be free of that family, but… He just mobilizes, snaps his fingers and, everything gets done… He takes care of his Queens. All of us."

"Mm hmm," Roxie managed, going to hang the cape on the hat stand. "He called you?"

"Trish called me."

"I didn't realize you were friends."

"Oh, we're all friends," Kesley said. "His Queens support each other. It's tradition for the most recent Queen to take care of the previous one. Ensures we don't leave anyone behind and that there's no animosity. Trish was previous to me, so we're bonded. And Dayah, well…" Roxie turned to her. "I had little chance to bond with her before… I suppose that makes it your responsibility to take care of me."

Hardly. Most of what she'd learned about the Queen thing came from Kesley. If anything, it was the other way around. Or it would be, except…

"I'm, uh, actually… I'm not a Queen."

Kesley frowned. Or at least that's what it looked like she was maybe trying to do. The woman was too perfect to be associated with any wrinkles or flaws.

"But I thought…" Yeah, a lot of people did, which was precisely the problem. "If you're not… why are you here?"

She swung a thumb in the corner door's direction. "I used to date the ASA."

"Oh!" Kesley said, a hand rising to her décolletage. "Of course. You facilitated Zairn's connection to the authorities. His network is just incredible, isn't it? He always knows someone, somewhere who can get him what he needs." The actress came over to take her hand. "Thank you, Roxie. You didn't have to help us. Him or Trish. We appreciate it. So much. Her life will be so much better now and her brother will be where he deserves to be."

"No problem."

Technically, it was true. She had facilitated Zairn meeting Porter. That meeting led to this one.

"They're in there?" Kesley asked, glancing at the corner door.

Roxie nodded and accepted Kesley's kiss on her cheek. The beauty left her to sail across the room and through the door. Just like that, not a sound. Perfection on invisible wheels.

Closing her eyes, Roxie shook her head once. What the hell was she doing there? Why was she hanging around? Because Zairn asked her to? She'd blow a big fat raspberry to that if there was anyone around to hear it.

Nope.

Grabbing her things, she headed out. Porter wanted to thank her, to let her know what was going on. He'd done both. The SA had shaken her hand. Good for him. Roxie had a life waiting for her… somewhere.

TWENTY-EIGHT

MM. GOOD DREAM. Hands on her body, his mouth on her neck… Why couldn't she feel his skin? His weight above her? The heat of them united… Dangnabit!

Opening her eyes, Roxie tried to free her arm, but the way he leaned pinned the covers down.

"Lola?" he said, sweeping her hair from her eyes.

She squinted through the darkness. "What? How did you get in here?"

"Clement gave me his key," Zairn whispered. "He said something about passing the mantle."

"Right, yeah, whatever," she said, closing her eyes, seeking her cozy place. "Have sex with me or go to sleep, stop waking me up."

"Damn, you're sexy," he said on a snicker. "Can I bribe you onto a plane? I'll have sex with you there."

"What plane?"

"The 737."

"Your love nest."

"Yep," he said.

"That's a good bed."

"Happy memories. Do you need your computer?

Where's your purse?"

"I'm not going out," she said, pulling the covers up to her chin. They didn't come as far as she wanted because he was sitting on them. "I'm in bed. I'm sleeping."

"I can carry you down to the car, if you want headlines."

"Why do we need a car? Don't be a snob. You didn't mind my bed when my legs were open."

"Hey," he said, smoothing his fingertips over her brow. "I love any bed you're in. I have an early meeting in LA."

That filtered through. Although her eyes didn't open, her chin tilted his way. "You're leaving?" She hadn't known he was coming, so it wasn't earth-shattering that she didn't know when he was departing either. Being with him wasn't... But she wasn't with him... was she? "I need to ask you a question."

"Okay," he said. "Prefacing your question with a question ratchets up the pressure. Is there a prize if I get the answer right?"

Playing was their way, and it wasn't like her to be nervous. She wanted to know; putting it out there was the only option.

"Is the ruby an engagement ring?"

Silence. No response. He was still sitting on the edge of her bed, his fist supporting him at her other side. She could feel him but didn't hear a sound.

Turning her head further, she opened her eyes, seeking his. That damn indecipherable thing again. Was he pissed because it obviously was or shocked she was way off base?

"You..." he said, his voice low and slow. "Are beautiful... the sexiest goddamn woman I've ever met..." Unlikely, but okay. "Any guy would be lucky to put a ring on your finger."

That was encouraging... maybe. "It's your ring we're talking about."

His fingers combed into her hair. "Roxanna Kyst, I am in awe of you. You surprise the hell out of me. I've never been more grateful to have a person in my life…" His fingers drifted down her cheek. "When I take a shot at making an honest woman of you, Roxanna, you'll know it."

"There's only one reason a man gives a woman a ring."

"That from your girls?" he asked. She offered a slight nod. "You think I don't know you; they think I don't. We only had eleven days together as an us, yes, but we lived together for three months. I know you, Lola Bunny."

"You know me and you gave me a ring. Why?"

"Because I already gave you a pendant, and the ruby was too big for earrings."

"Z—"

"You're building up those walls again, Lola. What changed? I knew there was something off with you tonight. I thought it was about Clement being in the room, but it was about the ruby… and your girls…"

Standing up, he took off his jacket and tossed it on the dresser.

"What are you doing?" she asked as he loosened his tie.

"I'm not leaving while your head's a mess about us. Supporting you is my priority, Ackley can wait."

"Ackley?" she asked, sitting up, folding her legs in front of herself under the covers. "The DA in California? You can't cancel a meeting with him."

He dropped his tie on the bed. "I'll reschedule," he said, undoing his shirt buttons. "With Trish and the Gambattos, I've neglected you—"

"Oh no, no," she said, throwing back the covers to leap out of bed. "You are not going to turn me into one of those women. A woman who needs propped up, a clingy delicate flower who can't function without a man at her side."

"You'll always function, baby. *I* won't function if I'm on the road wondering what the hell's going on in your head."

"This from the guy who bought a building in my city without telling me. I never know what's going on in your head."

"I won't let you pick a fight with me," he said,

retrieving his phone from his jacket.

"No," she said, rushing to pluck the phone from his hand. "You can't just decide to pause your life because I'm having a meltdown. You are going to California."

"The media shit doesn't bother me, I've dealt with it a long time. It can distract me… Sometimes I get mired… You're good for reminding me what's important."

"Now you're going to tell me I'm important and I'll freak out again. Just go to California."

"So you can push me even further away? Rox—"

"I don't know what we're doing here, Zairn. Tonight, with Porter and Kesley showing up. Your life is… you have a real impact, you make your mark everywhere. You're a force, Zairn Lomond. You're… powerful and—"

"If this is the 'you're too good for me' speech, try another one. I know you like letting me down gently, but that one won't fly."

"I don't think you're too good for me, I think… We're so different and… long-distance relationships never work and—"

"Can I have my phone?" he asked, opening his hand toward her. "Or call Tibbs, tell him to cancel Ackley."

"You're going to California. You are going to tell that S-O-B to stay out of your life. You tell him if he thinks to mention your name to anyone ever again, it better be to say what a fine, upstanding gentleman you are."

"Come with me, tell him yourself."

"Zairn…" she warned.

"I won't walk out of here until I know we're good. You knew we weren't engaged. How could we be engaged when you keep saying we're not dating?" he said, his volume rising. "You think I'd keep my fiancée a secret? What next? A clandestine wedding? A classified kid?"

"I thought we weren't fighting," she said, stepping closer to toy with one of his shirt buttons. "We get distracted by sex and drama."

"Yes, we do."

"Am I wrecking your life?"

"Why would you…?" He frowned and scooped a

hand onto her face. "No, you're not."

"You'd be smart to sell Chicago," Roxie said. "Ogilvie is right."

"Ballard told me about this morning. We're moving ahead with Chicago. And given you're the only one in this city I trust, you'll be my point person on the ground as long as you're here."

"Even if I break up with you?"

He smiled, proving his confidence. "Especially if you break up with me," he said. "Used to getting what I want, remember? I told you I'd keep on trying until I got it right." For a few seconds, he studied her. "You've never done this before. The long-distance thing. Your girls just found out, so there will be a lot of talk." True. "I get it. And your life would be much simpler if we called it a day."

"Why do I sense there's a but?"

"Are you happy?" he asked. "When we're together, you and me, are you happy?"

"It can't be that easy."

"It is that easy. I have the tee-shirt. I can recognize when something is worth the work. You are worth it, Lola. This is worth it. You make me happy. I know I'm in this. Only you can decide if you're happier with me in your life or without me. Am I worth the work?"

When he put it like that, she'd be a bitch to say no. Really listening brought her to a concession: he was right. Having him around complicated everything for both of them. But the thought of sending him away and never seeing him again…

She handed his phone back.

"Is this goodbye?" he asked, probably because she hadn't looked at him.

"You'll need it to call me when you land," she said, reaching for his neck to pull him down for a kiss. She continued to nuzzle her mouth on his. "You make me happy, Casanova. I used to be smarter than this."

"You and me both. I'll call you from the plane."

"You need to sleep," she said, relaxing when his hands slid onto her waist. "When was the last time you slept?"

"In your bed."

And he'd got up at the crack of whatever to set up his cross-town meeting.

"You need to take better care of yourself."

"Why?"

"Because I say so."

"And you have the reins."

Her lips curled as she bowed back, trusting his grip to stabilize her. "I forgot that for a second today."

"Don't forget again," he said. "You've got this. What you say goes. You haven't figured that out yet?"

"I don't mind having our reins, but in business and your private, personal life—"

"You don't think you're my private, personal life?"

"I think you don't have to make decisions based on my opinions."

"I listen to your opinion and reach my own conclusion."

"Promise?" The half-smile was so damn… "Get out of here, Lomond," she said, warming to a tingle. Pushing his hands away, she backed up. "Go on."

"What's wrong?" he teased, advancing on her.

"Switch it off, Casanova. You're on your way out." Her back hit the wall. "So go."

"Ah, and she can't resist," he said, his hands creeping onto her body again.

"Not a chance, Skippy. I'm half asleep, I didn't even notice you."

"Mm hmm."

"You have a plane to catch," she said, enraptured by the suave adoration in his gaze.

"It'll wait for me."

Toria was right, she'd be an idiot not to acknowledge how many women offered their bodies to this man. The power, the looks, the money, the lifestyle; they held appeal for a lot of people. But acknowledging that and pigeonholing him as a cheater were two different things.

"You didn't sleep with Dayah until after you broke up with Kesley."

Some of his intimate light dimmed. "Are you asking me or telling me?"

"Telling you," she said. "I know Kesley thinks the opposite."

"But you think different."

"You don't care what I think," she said. "You only want me for my body."

Sliding back into their game was a warm blanket on a cold night. Teasing him, being teased, it ignited their fire.

"Yeah, damn straight," he said, pulling her against him. "What you doing thinking about fidelity?" Seeing Kesley, the talk of Dayah and the Queens put it in her head. "Would it be so bad?"

"What?"

"Fidelity." Would it be so bad to be in a faithful relationship with Zairn? "I have no interest in being with anyone else."

"Z…" she whined.

"It's okay." He kissed her hairline. "Just letting you know."

"You love tormenting me."

"I live for it."

"I know," she said, giving him a light push. He backed off. "Wait a sec."

Going into the closet, she turned on the light to search in her purse. When she found his wallet and yanked it out, she held it out the door toward him.

"I forgot about that," he said, taking it.

She stuffed everything back into her purse and zipped it up again. "Only you could go thousands of miles without your wallet and be totally cool about it."

"Most things are on account," he said. "And I don't get carded at my own bars."

"You don't get drinks at your own bars, someone else does that for you."

"Details," he said, putting his wallet in his back pocket. "Come here." Lunging forward, he grabbed her arm to tug her out of the closet and into his arms. "I'll call you from the plane."

"I'll only be sleeping."

"Me too, but I'll call you anyway. Where's your phone?"

"In my purse." He didn't even ask before going into her closet and purse to retrieve the device. "What are you doing?" she asked when he took it over to her nightstand.

Where did the charger come from? He took it off the nightstand to plug it into the outlet and connected it to her phone.

"If you keep forgetting, I'll hire someone to ensure your phone is charged. They'll follow you around with a dock."

That was no idle threat. He absolutely would.

"You're a control freak."

"Yeah, one who doesn't want to spend his life worrying you won't be able to call for help if you need it because your phone is out of power."

"Okay," she said, tucking herself against him when he wrapped her in his arms. "You'll call me from the plane?"

"I'll call you from the plane," he murmured, crouching to kiss her.

They'd be apart. Again. Long-distance relationships never worked. In that minute, she didn't care. He made her happy and for as long as she had it, she'd cherish it.

When he withdrew, she was loathed to open her eyes. Watching him walk out was so difficult. If she asked him to stay, he would. Would it be so bad if…? Boy, was she in trouble.

"Be good," he whispered on her lips. "I'm always at the end of the phone."

After another brief kiss, the heat of his form ebbed. She stayed on pause. In her room. Eyes closed. Waiting for the moment… The front door closed. He was gone. Again.

Opening her eyes, she exhaled. "So long," she murmured to no one, laying a hand on the dresser to support herself. Wait, what was…? The dark metal rectangle on the wood hadn't been there before…

Turning it over, she recognized her own name embossed on the matte surface. She recognized the logo too.

Damn him. Her lips curled. He always had to be looking after her. A credit card. One without a limit she'd bet. Typical that he didn't tell her. He just did what he believed to be best and snuck it in under the radar. Asshole… Man, yes, she was in trouble.

TWENTY-NINE

"HELLO?"

A woman. Huh. "Hello?"

"He's just wrapping up a meeting."

"Astrid!" Roxie exclaimed, delighted that her friend had answered Zairn's phone. "How are you, honey? I called you a couple of days ago."

"I'm sorry, I missed the call."

In her kitchen, she gathered her relaxation tools. "That's fine. I don't always pick up either. I wanted to check-in. We haven't talked since… I don't think Lord Lomond's room counts." Silence. "Astrid, you're not getting weird on me, are you?"

"No. No, I—"

"My screwing him doesn't change our friendship. We should talk more."

"I just thought… you know… since the pictures."

She smiled and poured sugar onto a plate. "Honey, you worry too much. Whatever was going on, I care about both of you. You're out there together, I hope you do look out for each other. Besides…" Retrieving a glass from the freezer, she used a lime wedge to wet the rim. "I made the first move on him. You're an amazing person, Astrid, but if your plan was to jump him, you'd have done it before I came into the picture… And out in the street? That's not your style."

"It was just…"

"Mortifying? I'm sorry, honey. I know what it's like to have the whole world speculating on your sex life."

"Is that why you aren't with us?"

"Why? No, I live in Chicago," she said, the wedge gliding around and around. "I'm at home."

"Shouldn't you be here?"

"That's your life, Astrid."

Oh, and the world couldn't know about her and Zairn. Another reason it wouldn't be a good idea to jump on a plane. Sometimes being strong wasn't easy, especially in particularly horny moments.

"Sir, I—"

"Lola?"

Roxie paused. "Did you just snatch the phone from Astrid?" she asked, inverting the glass in the sugar. "You're so rude."

"It go okay?"

Zairn freight-trained right on with whatever was in his head. His day must've been demanding.

"Did you get the plans?" she asked, trying to steady him by slowing her words.

"I got your email but haven't looked at it yet. I just got out of a meeting."

Yes, Astrid filled her in. Even without the warning, she could interpret him by his pace and urgency. Boardroom Lomond needed to chill out; he wasn't talking to his suits anymore.

"You're a brave man, you know," she said, ready to ease him back into the guy she wanted to talk with. "Confident."

"You've met me, babe, those are not revelations. Why are we pointing that out today?"

Ah, was that him? A hint, maybe. Yoo-hoo, don't be shy, playmate.

"Sending me to your club to meet contractors…"

Roxie said. "It's brave or really stupid."

"Because you have terrible taste in decor?"

She coughed in disbelief. "I am way more amazing than any project manager you could hire," she said, pouring liquor into the cocktail shaker. "I have experience of clubs all over the world… We should talk salary, how many zeros am I getting for running your errands?"

"There's the self-assured sasspot I know."

She licked her damp fingers. "I never went anywhere. You're the one who's all starched today."

"Starched?"

"Is this 'cause I woke you up at four a.m.? You tell me to call when I wake up, I do, and then you're grumpy about it… You know I suck with time zones."

"Hence why my watch is set to Roxie time," he said, putting a smile on her face. "I wasn't grumpy, I was horny and you wouldn't deliver."

So much for just out of the boardroom… And now she was wondering if he'd ever do her in a boardroom. Damn her rascally mind.

"I had a video call with a client at twelve thirty and I had to get ready… I brought you into the shower with me, didn't I?"

"Yeah," he said. "To flaunt what I can't touch."

She laughed. God, she missed him. "It's been over two weeks since you touched me. That's our sex life, unfortunately, baby. You don't mind so much when we're under the covers together and you're talking to me."

Her stomach flipped just thinking about some of the arousing scenarios he put in her head.

"I like having your full attention," he murmured, the deep vibration reminding her of their late nights.

"And I'm used to sharing you with the world," she said. "Though if these contractors you keep sending me to call the press, I guess I'd be hot property again too. How do you explain your ex-bed-buddy attending Crimson meetings?"

"If they call the press, they don't get the job. We'll know they have no integrity."

"And I'll be a hostage in my own home again. I guess

sending me to the meetings is some kind of honor test. Oh, Casanova, you're using me!"

"You're smiling." Yeah, she was. Damn him for knowing her voice so well. "You're safe. Security is right on your doorstep."

"And my driver's back too."

"You've been running my errands. Which contractor did you pick for your club?"

"You keep calling it my club."

"I bought Chicago for you, baby. You need somewhere safe to party… If you won't come to Crimson, Crimson will come to you."

"You started planning Chicago's Crimson before you tried to tempt me to your clubs."

"How do you know that?"

"Because I know you, baby. You're used to getting what you want."

"Yeah, and what I want right now is for you to pick a contractor."

"I met with three different guys. Three different plans. You're a busy, busy guy, but you have to review them and pick."

"Which one do you love the most?"

"If I had a favorite, I'd only send one."

"Like you did with the exterior patio."

"Exactly. I know my mind."

Putting the lid on the shaker, she caught the phone between her shoulder and head to mix it.

"You're drinking?"

"Been a long day," she said. "I guess being in your club put me in the mood."

"Gin and Cin?"

"Couldn't get Cin, so I'm on the lime-drops tonight."

"Do you want me to come mix it for you?"

"Too late, Casanova," she said, turning her glass to pour her drink. "Never tastes as good as when you do it."

"That's true about a lot of things."

"It is," she said, sipping her drink as she sashayed toward the couch. "You should know, I've got the place to myself. I'm all alone…"

"I'm in Sydney with six other guys."

"So…" she said, drawing out the word, "you don't want me to take off my clothes and video call?"

"I want you to give me six minutes to get out the building and back to my hotel."

With her arm up to steady her drink, she laughed and dropped onto the couch. "Guess I'll have to hope my driver or security guys are more available."

"I pay them to serve you, not to service you. They follow my instructions."

"Like Tibbs?"

"Yeah, I'm clear about their limits."

Something else he shouldn't voice. The rife speculation about them erased the need to be explicit. Most of his associates would assume there was an uncrossable line.

"You don't put limits on me."

"I know better than to try it, Lola."

The front door opened, attracting her attention. Her girls bundled inside.

"I'd be in pieces, you're so strong," Jane was saying.

"What's going on?" Roxie asked.

The guy in her ear was no longer the priority. "Babe?"

Toria stomped into the kitchen and grabbed the Grand Marnier to begin gulping.

Jane tiptoed closer. "She lost her job."

"What?" Roxie said, surging to her feet. "Oh my God, what happened?"

"Roxanna—"

"I've gotta go," she said, blowing him a kiss. "I'll drunk call you for phone sex later." Pressing disconnect, she threw the phone on the couch. "What happened?"

"She punched her boss," Jane whispered, then quickly covered her mouth.

"You punched her? What happened?"

"She swung for me first! She hates me, she always hated me. Ever since her deprived husband grabbed my ass at that Christmas thing a couple of years ago. I gave the bitch what she deserved. She treats everyone like crap." Roxie and

Jane reached the breakfast bar at the same time Toria slammed the bottle down. "How am I gonna make rent?"

"Don't worry about that," Roxie said.

Jane went to stroke Toria's hair. "We'll get through it together. You'll find another job in a snap, you'll see."

After assaulting someone, it wasn't best form to ask for a glowing reference.

"Whatever it takes," Roxie said, handing her glass over to Toria.

"Yeah, and don't forget Roxie's dating a billionaire."

She perked up. "Yes! Uh huh. If you want your job back, Z will fix it. He fixes everything, no problem, he'll make one call."

"I don't want my stupid job back. They can keep it. I don't need them."

"We may need his money though," Jane said from the corner of her mouth.

Toria went to pour the remaining contents of the cocktail shaker into the glass. "We need to get drunk," she said. "Very, very drunk."

THIRTY

TWO HOURS LATER, in her apartment, Roxie leaped up from the floor to answer the front door.

Someone had knocked. Who? No idea. The roommates hadn't ordered anything. Food had come up a few times, but they hadn't got as far as...

Zairn. Okay, so not exactly him. It was Trevor, holding a bottle toward her.

Her lips reacted in a smile. "Thank you."

The bodyguard just nodded. She closed the door and returned to her girls. They were on the floor in front of the couch where she'd left them.

"No," Jane said to Toria. "It doesn't matter. I don't want to talk about it."

"You should! I can't believe you didn't tell us," Toria said, grabbing Jane's arm to give her a shake. Roxie sat on the floor under the TV, putting the bottle on the central coffee table. "What's that?"

"The Cin," she said. Her girls shook their confused heads. "It's red vermouth... For the Gin and It I couldn't make earlier."

"Someone just brought it to our door? You ordered

it?"

"Zairn," Roxie said, which was explanation enough.

"How did you get into Gin and It?" Jane asked. "You never told us."

"Zairn wanted me to try it in Italy." She sucked in some air. "He wanted me to try something new and, apparently, the real Casanova loved this stuff," she said, turning the bottle by its base. Memories of Italy only went so far before sliding down hill. Her buzz was too valuable to send it in that direction. She folded her arms on the coffee table and changed the subject. "What don't you want to talk about?"

"Thank you," Toria said, presenting a hand her way and gesturing at Jane. "Someone's been keeping things from us."

"I didn't keep anything from you," Jane said, focusing on the liquid in her glass. "It's no big deal."

"Fill me in," Roxie said, slapping the table.

Hmm, maybe they should slow it down on the liquor front… or they could go out. Where would be open and secure?

"She…" Toria wiggled a finger Jane's way, "neglected to tell us that London Guy is in New York this weekend."

Roxie's shoulders jerked back. "What? Oh my God!"

"It doesn't matter," Jane said. "Why does it matter?"

"Because you've been talking to him for like ever and have never met him in the flesh."

"She's right," Roxie said, nodding. "This is like the closest he'll ever be. A safe distance too. The flight is only two hours. Manageable, it's not a trek, but it's far enough away that you can come home without worrying he might stalk you. I say go for it."

"It doesn't matter, it's too late," Jane said. "He got into town yesterday."

"When is he leaving?" Roxie said. "Today?"

"Early next week."

"It's not too late," Toria said, grabbing Jane's hand. "You have to do this, honey. You'll always wonder if you don't. What if he's The One?"

Oh, that got Jane's attention. They knew each other so well. Jane's big thing was fate. She really believed there was one person out there for her. A soulmate.

"True," Roxie said, sweeping up her glass to tip it Jane's way. "You have been flitting on and off each other's radar for a while."

"Yes!" Toria said, rising to her knees. "There's a reason for that, right? A reason you keep coming across each other. The universe is telling you something."

"We work for the same company," Jane said, skeptical.

"London. New York. Chicago. There must be ten thousand employees. How many others are popping into your inbox every other week?"

Their friend was so impressionable, it was sort of a travesty they should use their powers of persuasion for evil. Was it evil? Maybe this guy was a prince. How would they know otherwise?

"Ballard has this guy he calls for investigations," Roxie said. "I could call him for the number, get this Graham guy checked out."

"Oh, good idea," Toria said, then frowned. "Is he expensive?"

"Extortionate, I imagine," Roxie said. "It's an international investigation, so, yeah, expensive. Zairn will pay for it. He'll have an account and won't even notice."

Squandering his money on pampering wasn't her thing. But her friend's safety? Yeah, she'd hit him up for that.

"Do it. Call him!"

"No," Jane said, throwing out an arm. "No! You can't investigate him!"

"Why not? It's just smart. Even Roxie Googled her boyfriend."

"I've never Googled Zairn," she said, restraining her urge to declare he wasn't her boyfriend.

"But you knew he wasn't a serial killer before you slept with him." Roxie conceded Toria's point with a half-shrug. "Jane doesn't know that."

"You don't investigate your soulmate," Jane said,

attracting their attentions. "Not that I'm saying Graham is…" On an inhale, she surrendered. "It's not supposed to happen that way."

"How is it supposed to happen?" Toria asked, casting her a subtle eye roll.

"You make a date… Prepare, you know?"

"Get a bikini wax?"

Toria was hilarious.

"Not that, you don't… If he's my soulmate, he'll wait."

"For what? He's in town less than a week."

Probably to divert the conversation, Jane looked across the table. "How long did you make Zairn wait?"

"Uh… like six weeks."

Jane smiled. "See, he waited for Roxie."

She snorted. "Not out of chivalry, he was ready to do me the minute we met," Roxie said. "We knew each other six weeks before we did it… You've known Graham a lot longer than that."

"Are you telling me to sleep with him?" Jane asked.

"I'm not telling you anything," Roxie said. "Did he ask you out? Does he want to meet?"

"He wanted to have dinner tomorrow night."

"So have dinner tomorrow night. Perfect. There's your date. Do it!"

"I can't."

"Uh, I lost my job today," Toria said. "I need this distraction. Give me something to live for."

Laying it on thick was just like Toria. Maybe the push was exactly what Jane needed.

"Yes, you lost your job," Jane said. "And we went on vacation less than a year ago. We need to save our money for rent and utilities."

Woman had a point. Figuring they were done with that conversation, Roxie emptied her glass into her mouth. Toria was looking at her. Why was she…? Oh, those were devious eyes. What was about to happen?

"Roxie can hook us up."

She put down her glass. "Hook you up with what?"

"New York."

"How do you want me to do that?"

Despite asking, she already suspected her friend's implication.

"Where does your boyfriend live again?"

"You want to stay at Zairn's place?" Roxie asked.

"Uh, duh! I'm offended you haven't already invited us to raid his underwear drawer."

That was a joke? It was a joke… right? Why did Jane now appear to be considering it?

"You want to go to New York and stay in Zairn's apartment?"

"Haven't you been itching to party?" Toria asked. "We can do that at Crimson… No way his girlfriend doesn't get into the Ruby Room."

"We're not public. You know we're not public."

Toria groaned. "Okay, well, no way the Talk at Sunset contest winner doesn't get into the Ruby Room. You've been to every other one. Why would they bar you from New York?"

They wouldn't. Whether the press would get wind of it… How would they? Zairn's apartment was in the Rouge building. If they could sneak into his apartment under the radar, getting to and from the club would be easy as pie. Staff discretion shouldn't be a problem. Like Zairn had said about the contractors, if employees squealed, they wouldn't be employees for long.

"We were in a VIP area at New Year," Jane said.

"Yeah, but that's like the Joe Schmo VIP zone. Zairn has the Ruby Room. Bet you could get in there… Maybe we can have it to ourselves!" Having never been to the Ruby Room, she didn't know the setup. "What is the matter with you two? It's an adventure… We have to do it."

Roxie exhaled. "I'll need my ruby."

GETTING TO NEW YORK was as easy as Toria making a phone call while Roxie and Jane packed. She didn't know about the call until the driver delivered them to a waiting private jet. It was her fault, she should've anticipated Toria. Duh! Her girls were Zairn Lomond encyclopedias. Of course they knew the name of his jet company. And, it turned out, Zairn must have made good on his promise to authorize her.

The teeny Gulf Stream did its job, though it was sort of laughable compared to how the CEO traveled... She really should stop sucking his cock if this was the service she received.

Mentally teasing him even when he wasn't around. Man, she had some sort of problem. Hello, my name is Roxie Kyst, and I am addicted to playing with Zairn Lomond. First step, check.

At her instruction, the car that awaited them drove to the secret side entrance of Rouge HQ. Inside, noise around them suggested the quadrants of the building buzzed with activity. The glass corridors, that had been transparent when they arrived in daylight, were now opaque. Protecting the identity of anyone who wanted to party in private. Smart.

Getting upstairs was easy. The lone person at reception noticed them, but didn't say a word when they went to the elevators. Cool. Discretion... Thank God! She'd never been more grateful for the media splashing her face all over the planet.

"Oh my God," Jane whispered as the elevator came to a stop. She covered her eyes with both hands. "I can't look."

"I can't not," Toria said, vibrating with excitement.

Was this a good idea? Taking her friends to Zairn's penthouse? Too late to reconsider. Just three hours ago, they'd been drinking at home. Now they were... it wasn't even midnight.

The doors opened. She grabbed the extended handle of her suitcase to drag it out. When her girls didn't follow, she paused to look back.

"What?" she asked. A couple of lamps flicked on and the recessed lighting warmed. Wow, even the lights did their job without prompting. "What's wrong?"

"This is Zairn Lomond's private apartment?" Toria said, eyes wide as she tiptoed toward the threshold.

"Don't!" Jane exclaimed, grabbing Toria's arm.

"Okay," Roxie said without hiding her amusement. "You two take your time, I'm going to…"

Pointing, she showed which way she was heading and took her suitcase with her.

"Oh my God," Toria said. Suddenly, both women were hot on her heels. "Is his bedroom down here?"

"Last I checked," Roxie said.

The double doors at the end of the hall were closed until she slid them into their secret wall recesses.

"Oh my God," Jane whispered. "We can't go in there."

Going inside, Roxie laughed. "You were the ones who thought this was a great idea!" Leaving her suitcase, she turned around, opening her arms to the space. "This is where the magic happens."

"Have you had sex in here?" Jane asked, blushing at the brazen idea.

Roxie just smiled and nodded.

"Of course she has," Toria said, marching into the room. When she spotted the bed to the right, she stopped. "Oh my God, has he slept in those sheets?"

"I have no idea," Roxie said, laughing when Toria went back to grab Jane to drag her over to the bed. "There are guest rooms."

Toria tore off her shoes. "Yeah, and we'll sleep there, after I lie in his sheets."

Wrinkling her nose, Roxie wasn't sure how Zairn would feel about her girls rolling around in his bed. He wouldn't care… would he? Maybe. Either way, she was definitely keeping them away from his underwear. While her roommates were occupied, she dragged her suitcase into the closet. She'd only thrown in a few essentials… And some things maybe Jane would need if the London Guy meeting was a success.

Music suddenly blasted on, startling her. Backing out of the closet, she found her friends huddled around a touch panel by the bed.

"Are we partying up here now?" she shouted over the

music, but her friends didn't hear her.

No, because they upped the volume. Oh, well, a party was a party. At least they didn't have to worry about being discovered if they didn't venture to the club. Zairn would have liquor around somewhere… wouldn't he?

THIRTY-ONE

WHAT WAS THAT SOUND? She knew that noise, what…
Mmm, the bed was so comfortable. On her front, with her
face buried in the pillow, Roxie didn't want to move. But that
stupid noise…

Stretching toward the nightstand behind her head,
she fumbled the phone from the dock. She switched it to the
other hand and answered the call with only one eye open for
a couple of seconds.

"What?" she mumbled, dropping the phone to the
pillow next to hers.

"What happened to drunk phone sex?"

Her lips curled, though her face stayed in its cloud of
comfort. "Casanova," she purred, real pleasure seeping
through her.

"So you do remember who I am. What happened?
Your girls came back and you bolted."

"We got your present. Thank you."

"You're welcome. Did you drink it?" No, she hadn't.
It was in one state, and she was in another. "Why is it black?
Are you still in bed?"

"Have you even been to bed since we last talked?"

"No," he said. "I was at the club tonight. Just got back."

"You're in Sydney," she said on a sigh, enjoying memories of that hotel.

Despite the continent making her ill, and her streaming scandal, she had fond memories of the city.

"Mm hmm. Now I want drunk phone sex."

Pondering that for a moment, she frowned in her sleep. "Have I seen you drunk? I don't think I have."

As was his right, he swerved the question. "If you passed out before calling, it must have been some night. What happened with your girls?"

"You should get some sleep," she said on an exhale. "I recommend it."

"Really was some night. Are you hungover?"

"Mm mm," she made a sound meant to imply a negative response.

"Babe, I want to see you. What's going on?"

"Nothing's going on," she said, moistening her lips. "It's black because my phone is on your pillow."

He exhaled a laugh. "I like that you're recognizing my place in your apartment."

"No," she said, her fingers curling around the phone. "Your actual pillow."

Raising her arm up, she gave him a view of… something. She didn't know what because her eyes remained shut. Swinging her arm in something of an arc, she hoped he'd recognize his own home.

"You're in New York."

Was that offense or just surprise? Incredulity was a better word.

Her arm flopped to the bed again. "Yeah. You mad?"

"Are you naked?"

Her brow creased. Was she? Concentrate. Concentrate. Without moving a muscle, she registered how much fabric touched her skin. "No."

"Then, yes, I am mad. You should always be naked in that bed."

She smiled. "I'm wearing one of your shirts."

Yes, there was a vague memory of raiding his closet during a restroom stop while her girls grooved in the living room.

"That's something, I guess," he said.

"I like the new tub."

"Claw-foot, roll-top slipper tub. Did I get it right?"

"Perfect."

A new fantasy replaced the other when she saw that tub. A man who could deliver… apparently they did exist.

"You didn't call," he said.

"You said the ruby would work… It sorta happened fast… I should've called."

"Lola, you don't need permission," he said. "I want you to do what you did. Were you downstairs?"

"That was the original plan, but we didn't get that far…" She winced. "We raided your bar."

He laughed. "Scared to tell me that?"

In for a penny… "We played loud music and danced in your living room."

"That's what you're supposed to do. Treat everything that's mine as yours."

Her eyes opened. "This is not me moving in."

"Didn't think it was. You could've shut the club if you were worried about being seen. The staff can be trusted. No one gets near anything personal without a track record. I own the building and no one told me you were there. That should be proof enough to put you at ease. I'd ruin anyone who tried to hurt you. Anyone who thought about hurting you."

"He said after telling me to close his flagship club," she said, wriggling onto her back, taking the phone with her. "Is that under the radar? Isn't there a legion of paparazzi and wannabes always hanging around outside? Don't you think they'd notice everyone being kicked out?"

"I want you to be happy, baby."

Raising the phone from her chest, she blinked at him, rousing herself. "Oh, you look good," she murmured, pushing her crazy hair from her face.

It felt like an age since he'd been above her…

especially in his bed.

"Nothing to how incredible you look."

No doubt her face was a mess. "I didn't even take my makeup off last night."

"I love it," he said, genuine in the swagger of that damn smile. "You're fucking hot, baby."

Pushing the covers from her body, she unbuttoned her shirt… well, his shirt. "My girls are in your guest rooms, I don't know how much time I have." Parting the fabric, she exposed herself, giving him as much of a view as the phone would take in. "You always say you wish I was there with you."

"Mm hmm," he said, his gaze growing heavier. "Now I want you exactly where you are."

Somehow, she'd anticipated that. "I wish you were here."

"It would be tomorrow by the time I got there."

"I know," she said, running a hand over her breast and down her body. "I feel closer to you here. Is that stupid?"

"No," he said, one corner of his mouth tilting higher. "Maybe now you get why I wanted you there full-time."

Uh, quick subject change required. "Toria lost her job."

"Does she want it back?"

A quick laugh escaped her throat. "I already offered your services on that score. I don't think that place was the right fit for her."

"So you decided New York was the best medicine?"

"We decided liquor was the best medicine," she said, still stroking her torso.

"Right down the middle, baby," he murmured. She raised her knees as her hand went between her thighs. "That's it… and go all the way up…" She was learning just how he liked to touch her and how he liked her to touch herself. "I should turn the air con up." That smirking sentence wasn't so subtle. Pinching her nipple, she gave him what he wanted. "Goddamn, you're beautiful."

"You don't want to know how we ended up here?" she asked, fondling her breast.

"Yeah, okay." He cleared his throat. "New York.

Toria. Job. I'm listening."

"You can listen while you get in bed. Why aren't you in bed with me?"

"Okay," he said. The phone moved as he undid the buttons of his shirt. "Tell me."

"Jane has this kind of transatlantic flirtation thing with a guy in her company's London office." He shirked his shirt. "Pants, baby, work faster. Anyway, the guy is in New York this weekend."

He stopped to focus the camera on his frown. "You're in New York to meet some strange guy?"

"I'm not here to meet him. We brought Jane so she could meet him. They've been talking for months… well, they've known each other for years… They've never met and our argument was that he could be her soulmate."

"You don't believe in soulmates."

"Yeah, but…" Her hand stalled. "How do you know that?"

He sat down on the edge of his bed. "Because I know you. And if you did, this wouldn't be taking so long."

"What wouldn't be taking so long?"

"Thank you for proving my point," he said, nothing but gracious. "Go on with your story."

"About London Guy?" He nodded once. "Right, so Jane and London Guy, have been talking, messaging… getting digitally horizontal in the dark… but they've never met."

"And he's in New York."

"Right."

"So you took her to New York."

"It wasn't my idea to stay here," she said. "Just so you know. Jane's argument against was financial. We already blew all our fun money on the LA vacation and Toria lost her job, so we might not make rent. We needed to stay somewhere for free." Her train of thought was so on her friends that her hand no longer did its job. "If you want us to leave, we will."

"Did you hear me say that?"

She continued. "Feels weird being here without you."

"You've been in my place without me before. Fact, that's how you and my place met."

Her ruby and an elevator ride. "I brought my girls this time."

"I trust you, Lola. With everything. Every part of my life. Your security clearance is equal to mine. I like knowing you're in my bed?"

"You said that the day I met Knox."

"Imagine how I feel about you in my apartment."

"Don't get used to it. I won't make a habit of it. Today, my girls and I are going out to find a spa that will pamper Jane. Then we're going to dress her in something sexy you bought me on tour."

"You're welcome. There's a spa in the building, they'll do whatever you need in the apartment. You don't have to go anywhere."

They'd planned for Jane's pampering because they didn't want to waste money they might not have.

A scowl tensed her. "I don't want that."

"What?"

"Strange people in your apartment."

"You're in my apartment, you're pretty strange."

She adjusted the angle of her phone. "You see my breasts? You like my breasts, don't you?"

"Mm, gorgeous, baby."

Grabbing both edges of the shirt, she closed it over her chest before showing him the new view. "I hope you have a good memory."

He laughed and swung his legs onto his bed to lie down. "How do I bribe you onto a plane?"

"I was on one of your planes. Last night."

"Is that the trick? I'll issue a directive. The next pilot who gets you wheels up and brings you to me gets a hundred K bonus in his pay packet."

"Is that all I'm worth to you? A hundred K," she teased, flaunting her smile.

"Lola, I'd give up every cent to have you in this bed with me now."

"Maybe if you were poor, I wouldn't want to be in bed with you."

"So unconvincing, try again, baby."

"I'm going to get in your shower," she said, sitting up. "I'm not making the bed either."

"That's okay, I'll call housekeeping, tell them not to touch the sheets… That's both my apartments you've slept in without me."

"You have a key for mine… or you did. You can sleep there, I'm not home right now."

"To get to yours, I'd have to fly past you. No way I'd pass you by."

Oh, that sound was the door opening. It was amazing that she'd remembered to close it.

"That's my girls."

"Roxie!"

She blew a kiss to the camera. "Sweet dreams, Casanova."

"Be good, Lola Bunny."

She hung up and bounced to her feet just as Jane and Toria appeared.

"The elevator started making this weird sound," Jane said without preamble. "And I just… the button was flashing."

"What?" Roxie asked, buttoning the shirt.

Jane and Toria spun to open their arms at the hallway. "Look!"

Her girls hurried off. She rounded the corner to see what had them so psyched. A room service trolley, at the opposite end of the hall, by the elevators.

"There is like every breakfast food you like," Jane called back.

Toria lifted the French press. "And coffee."

A smile curved her lips. "How does he do that?" she whispered to herself.

He'd been on the phone with her and hadn't known they were in New York. How did he…? Breakfast couldn't be automatic. For staff to know she was there, they'd need to talk to each other. They were chosen for their ability to be discreet, to keep secrets.

No. It was Zairn. She knew it. He continued to amaze her.

THIRTY-TWO

"WE LOVE YOU!" Toria called out.

The elevator doors closed on Jane.

Standing in Zairn's apartment, silence reigned for a couple of seconds.

"She should sleep with him," Roxie said.

"She won't."

Inhaling, Roxie released a slow sigh. "I know."

Looping their arms through each other, Toria navigated them in the bar's direction. "Wanna get drunk up here before we go downstairs?"

"You think we should go to the club?" Roxie asked. "Jane might need us to mobilize fast."

"Hmm, yeah, maybe... We could invite people up here," Toria said, yanking her closer. "Are there any celebrities in the club tonight?"

"How would I know?"

On the coffee table, her phone buzzed. Toria let her go and continued on to the bar.

Expecting Casanova to be on her screen, it was a surprise to read "*Hatfield*" instead. "Hey, stranger," she answered. "Been a long time."

"You are a hard woman to get hold of," he replied. "Ever check your voicemail?"

"Not anymore," she said. A glimmer of a memory tickled her. "You sent me an email."

"Trying to make plans. I figured your email was inundated, calling didn't get me any further."

Flopping onto the couch, she loosened. Toria was behind the bar, doing things with liquor. "What is it you need?"

"I wanna come up to Chicago to talk to you."

"Uh, I'm not doing interviews if this is about the Gambatto thing. These days I make it a rule not to pick up the phone to your kind."

He laughed. "I'm on your side and still under contract. I need to talk to you about the retrospective. Tell me when and where. I can be in Chicago tomorrow… Tonight if you have a window. It will take me a couple of hours to get there, I'm in New York."

"Funny," she said. "Me too."

"You… you're in New York?"

"Yep."

"You wanna meet?"

"Sure! Where?" she asked, already knowing he'd answer with something Crimson.

"There's a basement bar in the Rouge HQ, under the wine bar that—"

"I know it."

It had been a stop on her first tour of Crimson, New York.

"You remember it?"

Why was his tone…? Oh, yeah, he'd taken the tour with her. Whatever familiar thing he was trying to convey was lost on her, but she could fake it.

"Uh huh. Half an hour?"

"See you there."

She hung up and raised her legs to dump her feet on the table. "We're going out."

"Okay," Toria said, popping the cork from a bottle of champagne. "Hope your man wasn't saving this for a special occasion."

"He'd know better than to leave anything valuable lying out in the open."

Tottering over on her tiptoes, Toria held the bottle and two flutes. "Having a rich boyfriend has its advantages."

"You're so lucky," Roxie said, smiling in response to Toria's laugh.

"We should celebrate."

"Celebrate what?" she asked, taking the flutes when Toria sat down. "Don't spill on his couch."

Both scooched to the edge as Toria poured champagne. "Jane is meeting London Guy. She'll be in that fancy car of yours, on the way to a fancy meal with the guy who could be her future husband."

Putting the champagne bottle on the table, Toria raised her glass.

Roxie did the same. "We're drinking to…"

"My two best friends finding their forever guys." Toria's glass tinged on hers and she drank. Roxie wasn't so quick to down the liquid… which her friend noticed. "What? What is it?"

Leaning to the side, she put her flute on the table. "It doesn't suit me."

"What doesn't?"

"This," Roxie said, gesturing up and around the vast space. "This kind of lifestyle, the money—"

"Okay, it's nothing to do with lifestyle or money," Toria said, picking up Roxie's flute to put it back in her hand. "I can't believe I have to spell this out for you. *You*, Rox! You're supposed to be switched on."

"Spell what out?"

Groaning, Toria slanted closer. "It's about the man, genius."

"The man?"

"Zairn," Toria said, drinking more champagne. "We don't get to set their specifics, just like they don't get to set ours. Pick the man. Everything else gets worked out."

How could her friend simplify it so much? Zairn did it too with the whole, "*Are you happy?*" thing. Life wasn't like that. It wasn't easy answers to basic questions.

"There's got to be criteria though, right?"

"Criteria?" Toria asked, screwing up her face. "Can you imagine what we'd think about any guy who said we didn't meet his 'criteria'?"

Good point. Well made. "I never wanted to be one of those women who trailed around after her guy like a lost puppy."

Her champagne bubbles at least gave her something to lose herself in. The trance didn't last long.

Toria hooked a finger under her chin to raise it up. "If you hadn't noticed, he's the one trailing around after you."

Maybe not in a literal sense, but it was a chase. Men were easy, usually. She was into them or she wasn't. That was that. Zairn was different. So many times she'd told herself it would be easier to break away from his orbit. Then he went and asked stupid questions about her happiness.

Shrugging off her moment of melancholy, she widened her smile. "You want to meet Greg Hatfield?"

"The documentary director? That's who was on the phone?" Toria raised her glass again. "Let's do it."

Whatever Hatfield had to say, he could say it in front of Toria. They were in New York, a night on the town was required reading… And maybe it helped a little that Hatfield would unknowingly give her cover for being in Crimson. If anyone saw her or questioned why she was there, she was meeting the documentary director for drinks.

Thank you, CollCom affiliate.

AH, IT WAS A COZY SPACE. The establishment wasn't small. Not until compared to other Crimson sectors. The basement bar consisted of separate rooms, with low lighting, comfortable seating, and a rustic décor.

"Roxie!" Greg exclaimed when she approached him at the bar.

She opened her arms and they did the cheek-to-cheek double kiss thing that media darlings adored. Stepping back, she presented her friend. "This is Toria."

"I've heard a lot about you," Greg said, shaking her hand. They all sat, and Greg nodded in the direction they'd come from. "He yours too?"

She didn't even have to turn around to know what, or rather who, was there. "Security just show up when I'm around," she said, waving a dismissive hand over her shoulder. "I just go with it." The bartender came over to put a drink in front of her. "A champagne cocktail for my lady friend." She gestured toward Greg. "And he'll have a beer, just whatever's on tap."

Toria leaned in close to whisper, "I love how they know your drink."

Bumping her friend's shoulder with hers, Roxie murmured back, "I'd be surprised if Z hasn't added my preferences to the employee handbook."

"I shouldn't drink," Greg said, distracting the women from their whispers. "It's business, you know?"

"I'm business?" Roxie asked, twisting her stool in Greg's direction. "My have we come a long way from Montreal and Miami."

He laughed. "Yeah, well, you're like Crimson royalty now. How is Zairn?"

Her eyes narrowed. "How would I know?"

"Chicago was no coincidence. We both know he has a reason for everything."

"Obviously, you don't watch the news. Didn't you hear about his involvement in the Gambatto trial?"

"I know Trish has disappeared. Everyone on the planet knows that. Yet, the SA's office isn't concerned. Why would that be?"

Roxie squinted. "Didn't you hear me say I don't give interviews?"

"Sorry, habit."

Something she'd heard from him before. "You better come up with a real reason for this meeting or I'll suspect it's a ruse to hit on me... Thank goodness I brought my friend."

His lips curled. "I've missed you, Rox."

Hearing that from anyone connected to Crimson was always a compliment.

She sipped her drink. "Why are we here?"

"The retrospective."

"You said that on the phone. What does that mean? The retrospective?"

"The Retrospective Tour," Greg said. "You didn't read about it?"

As she searched her recollection, her eyes widened a fraction. "I read about it. I also read the word 'optional' in the contract."

"You don't want to do it? It's only a month this time… Six weeks. We travel around, meet up with the Experience winners, take some with us, and end in LA. You have to give your approval to the edit."

"You've done the editing already?"

"It's in the process, almost there," he said. "We will divide the documentary into several parts. The retrospective is important. It's supposed to be 'Nothing to Hide' so we have to get feedback from the Experience winners now they've had time to reflect."

Made sense. On the actual tour, they'd been concerned about getting from one location to the next… and her illness… and the Gambattos… and Zairn fleeing the reservation. Huh. All caused by her. She really had screwed Crimson.

"She'll come," Toria said, hooking an arm around her. "She'll definitely come."

"I will?" Roxie asked toward her shoulder, though she was already leaning that way too.

"Sure, it's still five-star, right?"

Greg laughed. "It'll be on Rouge's dime, as before, but I can't attest to the quality. When Zairn Lomond's in the party, things tend to be more… polished. He's particular and people like to impress him. Us? Not so much. Our production team has been working with an intermediary here at Rouge. I haven't spent a lot of time poring over the details."

Good. That way Greg wouldn't notice when Zairn had them all changed. Assuming he didn't already know about this invitation.

"Do Crimson know you're asking me to come

along?"

"They know it's in your contract," he said. "The 'optional' part was there to cover their asses, not yours, from how I understand it."

"So if she was dull or a lush, Crimson could dump her," Toria said, shimmering with excitement.

Roxie couldn't see her roommate yet could already tell how the idea excited her.

"Yeah, I guess so," Greg said. "We don't have to worry about that because Roxie's a hit everywhere. Come on tour and you could start streaming again… we could get the Experience winners involved."

"Ah," she said, easing back, leaning against Toria. "Maybe not such a great idea."

"You were drunk, I know," Greg said, referencing her last streaming adventure. "But we'll be around… We won't let you do anything embarrassing."

Yeah, right, embarrassing meant greater exposure.

The bartender came over with the drinks. "Miss Kyst?" He got her attention. "Would you like us to close one of the lounges?"

"One of the lounges?" she asked. When he cast an eye around the room, she followed suit. Cellphones. Security. A growing gang of people pushing closer. Damnit. "No…" She sighed and hopped off her stool, holding her drink. "We'll go to the club."

They were out anyway, and couldn't take Greg to Zairn's apartment. If Jane needed them, they'd move fast… they'd just do it with some alcohol in their systems. Dancing into oblivion was something she'd missed. It would upset Ogilvie if she turned the club VIP room into her own mini-nightclub, but what the hell. Wasn't like the guy was her biggest fan. What would one more slight be?

THIRTY-THREE

"I CAN'T TALK RIGHT NOW," Roxie said into the phone, doing her best to forget Greg was in the car beside her.

"Can't talk now. Can't talk last night," Zairn said in her ear. Oh, please say Greg couldn't hear him. "Hatfield still hanging around?"

"Uh huh."

"That guy always had a hard-on for you and now he's got you on his lap."

"Not quite," she said. "Almost, but not quite."

Zairn wasn't amused. "You know it's Valentine's Day, right?"

"Mm hmm. Can I call you later?"

"I got any choice in that?"

"No, not really," she said, hanging up the phone before he could say anything else.

"Don't mind me," Greg said. "You can talk to whoever."

She tucked her phone into her purse. "Yeah, right, says the journalist."

"I'm an independent film-maker."

"Is that what you call it?" she asked, showing him a

smile.

They'd spent a lot of time together before Sydney. With everything that happened with Zairn after, she'd forgotten about the dinners and drinks. The coaching sessions where he'd deconstruct her streams with her. Give her encouragement, offer tips. Okay, so, yeah, she didn't lack confidence and there was some mansplaining involved, but it was sweet of him to at least pretend to listen.

"Your friends enjoyed the flight."

"Yes, they're not so used to the private jet thing."

"Yeah," he said, stretching out. "We're blasé about it now."

What a goof.

The flight from New York had been a slice of déjà vu. The Retrospective Tour started in Boston, just like the actual tour. And, just like the actual tour, they swung a detour to Chicago and dropped off her friends.

"I'm sorry your friend's date was a bust."

"Hey, we don't know unless we try, right?"

"Remember that when I make my move on you sometime."

She laughed, waving his hand away when it came toward her face. "Not a good way to start this tour. You've said it will be a different beast to the last time."

"Close quarters."

"Weren't you sharing with Tevin and Carl the last time?"

"Yeah, and believe me, I'm looking forward to close quarters with you a thousand percent more."

"Close quarters with me comes with a harassment suit if you step out of line."

"Noted," he said with a snicker that suggested he might not believe her. He nodded out of the window. "A lot has changed since we were last here."

The Grand Hotel, Boston. Yes. A lot had changed. More than he knew.

"DIDN'T I SAY I'D CALL YOU," Roxie hissed into the

phone she'd just answered.

Holed up in a shiny hotel bathroom, she kept her back to the door.

"Four hours ago, Roxanna. What's going on?"

"I don't know, you're jealous or bored or losing your mind? Am I getting warm?"

Wandering around the small space, everything was pristine. Like they might have installed it yesterday. How did hotels always make everything look new?

"I'm calling my girlfriend," Zairn said. "Until Hatfield came into the picture, you didn't have a problem with that."

She couldn't figure it out. Was he mad? Teasing her? Whatever it was, he needed to be smarter.

"I can't play with you around him," she whispered, resting her hips on the vanity.

Checking herself out, she slanted into the unflattering light of the ceiling halogens. Ugh, shadows, bags. Man, she needed to get more sleep.

"I'm the other guy now?" he asked.

Ah, relief. That was a smile in his words. A swaggering smile, easily pictured.

"You've been my dirty secret for a while," she said. "You should be used to it."

"What's he got that I don't have?"

"He's present."

"You'll follow him around the world, but you laughed in my face."

"Oh, are you pouting?" she asked, pushing out her lower lip. "Is the big, handsome billionaire feeling all sorry for himself?"

"Got no one over here to stroke my fragile ego."

"Ha!" she exclaimed. "There is nothing fragile about your gargantuan ego, Casanova. And there's a line of women waiting to stroke whatever you ask them to."

"Only woman I ask is you."

"And if you were here, I'd do that for you… not your ego, but anything else that feels neglected."

"Would you?" he asked. "With your documentary buddies down the hall?"

And once again it came to the secrecy.

"Be careful what you wish for. If *we* are leaked to the public, everything will fall apart." Silence stretched. Weight formed the longer it went on. "Baby?"

"Everything will fall apart? You mean us?"

"I mean Crimson's stability. Your board won't appreciate you boning the PR princess. For once, I'm being a good girl. Because it's in your best interest. I listened to your lawyers and your PR people." More silence. "What is going on?" She laughed. "The brooding thing is hotter when I'm there to see it."

"Dunlap. Elson… Salad?"

"What about them?"

"Are they the ones who told you to deny this?"

"I didn't need anyone to tell me it wouldn't be a great idea to scream it from the rooftops. The press would tear you apart, the fans would go nuts—"

"Do I make you happy?"

"This again," she asked, spinning on the spot and boosting herself up to sit on the vanity. "I'm a complex woman, you can't reduce me to—"

"If I'd heard them speak to you that way—"

"I thought Ballard filled you in about the conversation. In the morning. At my place."

"About the debate over pulling out of Chicago. My people should know better than to invade my personal life. They'll be out of a job the minute we hang up."

"Don't you dare," she said. "Just what we need, scorned employees. The press would be right there, ready to roll out the red carpet for them."

"If they're those kind of people, we don't need them. You don't get it. Goddamnit, Lola."

"Goddamnit, what?"

He sighed. "Nothing… Forget it. This Retrospective thing is… a month?"

"Yes… Six weeks Greg says. You should've warned me it was coming."

"You already gave me an earful about this," he said. "Last night when you were hiding in our New Year screw-room."

"Don't call it that."

"I told you to use the Ruby Room."

"It was locked up. No one was in there."

" 'Cause it's usually only open when I'm in residence."

Her laugh came out like a snort. "Like you're the Queen."

"The Empress was in residence, baby. You have that power. How many times have I got to tell you? Your ruby grants you access everywhere."

Hatfield might have noticed if she'd produced a massive gem and swanned into the Emperor's lair.

"You know, I've just figured it out. You like the headlines. You want the world talking about you."

"Baby—"

"You do. You must. Why else would you always be talking like this?"

"I can't think of a reason," he said, like he was humoring her.

"You have too much time on your hands, Skippy. You need a hobby. Something to keep your mind off my caboose."

"Nothing can take my mind off your caboose. It's on my mind all day long."

"Because you have nothing better to do?"

"Than you? That's right. There's nothing better to do than you."

Stroking her thigh, she flattened her skirt. "After this, the tour, we should lay low for a while."

"Logan Lowe is banned for life. No chance of that happening again."

With a tsk, she rolled her eyes up and sank back to lean on the mirror. "Nothing happened. He's not even that cute."

"Yet he got closer to your pussy than I did."

"You'd been in my pussy by then," she said. "Not my fault you ran away from it."

"You've been getting your own back ever since."

"I have."

"You think I love the headlines? I think you love running away from me."

"Okay, well, this is a conversation we can have when, you know, we can actually have it," she said, sliding off the vanity.

"Sex and drama," he said. "We get distracted by sex and drama when we're together."

"Yes, we do. This is just the way it is, baby. It's easier to accept there's nothing we can do about it."

"There's nothing we can do about it?"

"We have no choice," she said, bobbing her head to the side. "Unless we want to call it quits."

"Calling it quits is not an option."

"Okay, then get used to it. If you want me, this is the way you get me. When, where, however we can. You end it or accept it, those are your choices."

"My choices?"

"Yep."

"My only choices?"

"Yeah," she said.

"Rox?" Hatfield's call through the door diverted her attention.

"I have to go, baby," she whispered. "Bye." Hanging up the phone, she went to open the door. Greg was right there on the other side and leaped backwards, spiking her suspicion. "Eavesdropping?"

"No," he said and nodded at her hand. "You always take your phone to the can?"

"Maybe. I don't ask about your personal habits, don't you ask about mine."

"Fair deal," he said, nodding. "We're going for something to eat. You hungry?"

"As long as there's security, I'm there," she said, passing him.

The tour was good for Crimson. This was where she had to be. What she had to do. It would stress her relationship with Zairn. That was understandable. If they couldn't handle being at opposite ends of the world, under the pressure of global scrutiny, what chance would they have to survive?

THIRTY-FOUR

HAIR, MAKEUP, SMILE, check, check, check.

Dinner became drinks. They ended their night in Crimson, VIP area only, of course. It was fun. And thankfully, she didn't have to be up early.

That morning, the only activities on her agenda were sleep and a long soak in the tub. What Greg and his crew got up to was a mystery. One she was happy for them to keep.

The first place she had to be was downstairs in the conference room where the Experience winners would be interviewed. As for the setup, she wasn't entirely sure.

Traipsing out of the elevator, the day was half gone, yet she was only getting started. Greg was at the edge of the lobby. Near the stairs to the conference rooms, not in one as she'd expected.

He noticed her striding toward him halfway across the lobby and ended his call before she reached him.

"What's going on?" she asked. "I was going to grab a coffee, then come up to the conference room. We're meeting, right?"

"Yeah, that was the plan," he said, exasperated. "The fucking hotel gave our room away." Probably when they realized Zairn wasn't sharing the wealth, taking over entire floors and handing out four-figure tips. "They said double-booked, clerical error. Bullshit. We've got the damn Experience winners on their way here and nowhere to put them."

"Okay, don't freak out," she said. "This is fixable. Can't we just take them up to the suite?"

"There are six bodies. All the kit. You. Me. The crew."

"Not big enough."

"Not to light and set in this amount of time."

"There have to be other options. We're in a great big city. There are other places."

"Available? Immediately? Secure? That we can control? We fly out tomorrow, we can't postpone. Everything is planned; we miss one, the dominoes collapse."

Yeah, something she was aware of. The original tour missed entire countries for her.

"We're not canceling. No, we just need to brainstorm. Do you know anyone in Boston?" she asked. "Where did you grow up?"

"Me?" he asked, eyes wide. "I'm from Buffalo."

"Where's Tevin from?"

"Detroit."

"Geez!" She tossed her head back. "My kingdom for a goddamn Patriots fan." That struck a chord. "Oh!" she exclaimed, searching her bag for her phone. "I have an idea."

"What idea? Share it."

"No, give me a minute."

Locating her phone, she scrolled to his name, but waited until she was a distance away before pressing call. It rang and rang. As usual. If he was tied up and couldn't talk, he'd divert her to voicemail. If it rang and rang, or rang and answered to silence, he was getting himself in a position to talk.

After the tenth ring, the line connected. "Perfect timing," Zairn said. "I needed to hear your voice."

She paused, struck by worry. "What's wrong?"

"Nothing, I always need your voice."

"Not my body?" she teased.

"If that's on offer…"

Wandering around the lobby, she kept her volume low. "Maybe we can work something out, but you have to do something for me first."

"What's that?"

"Remember that first night in Boston when I met Kesley?"

"Yeah."

"I met those sports guys too. You remember the tall, brawny one who kept staring at my ass?"

"Myles Gesner."

"Right," she said, though the name didn't ring any bells. "Can you send me his number? You could get his number, right? Do you have his number?"

"You're in Boston?"

"Yeah."

"And you want me to hook you up with a guy who's attracted to you? You know I'm the guy you're seeing, right? Did you mix me up with some other Zairn in your phone?"

His number wasn't saved under his name on her phone. As per his instructions way back when.

"What?" she asked, failing to see the problem. "You do favors for people all the time. Connect one person to another. Does riding your cock exclude women from that privilege? You should've told me that earlier, like, right upfront."

"Ask for the moon and the stars and I'll give them to you, Lola. Other guys? No. I'm on another continent and know how horny you get."

"Please," she scoffed. "One playmate at a time. If you know someone else from Boston who can help me out of a jam, I'm all ears… Do you know anyone from Boston? Of course you do. Who do you know from Boston?"

"Kesley's from Massachusetts."

Hope! Yes, amazing. "Oh, that's good! Does she have a big, empty house lying around somewhere nearby? Is it pretty? Is she with you? Can you ask her? Please."

"She's at a director's meeting. The house has five

bedrooms, seven and a half baths. It's on the water, it's beautiful. Why do you need a house? I'll buy you a house. Pick one. Use your credit card."

Uh, overboard much? "My boyfriend, the go-getter," she said, sidelining for a moment how insane it was that a credit card could be capable of buying an entire building. "I don't need to buy a house, I just need something for the afternoon."

"What for?"

"The hotel messed up our reservation, and the suite's too small for everyone. We need somewhere for the interviews and discussions. Somewhere not cramped. We need like six, eight… ten-ish people all in the same room with a bunch of equipment."

"Use the club."

She paused to process. "Use the… what?"

"The club, before it opens… or after, whatever. Keith's our manager up there. I'll call him. We'll send a car for you. Anything for the Empress."

Using Crimson hadn't occurred to her, but it was… perfect. "Can we do that everywhere? Use the clubs as we go along… while they're empty, not when they're open or reserved or anything."

"Shouldn't be a problem."

"Send me the numbers," she said. "I'll organize it. You won't have to do a thing."

"Okay, babe."

"Next time we're on the same continent, I'll do something special to say thank you."

"Yeah, you will. I'm keeping a list."

The offer would've stood even without her promise.

"You know…" she said, "you're a pretty nice guy."

"Don't tell the press."

"I'll add it to my book. Thank you, baby."

"Mm hmm."

Being with Zairn was a cascade of surprises. It shouldn't be. All of her needs were attended to whenever she asked.

Dropping her phone into her purse, she spun to show

Greg her grin. When he caught sight of her striding toward him, his eyes grew in anticipation.

"Done."

"What?" he asked, shocked at her certainty. "What— how? You got the room here?"

"No," she said, screwing up her face. "We don't want their stupid room. We have somewhere much better, somewhere that will be waiting for us in every city."

He opened his arms. "Tell me."

"Crimson."

It took him a few seconds to respond. "What? You… We get to do it in the club? The interviews, the whole shebang?"

"Yes."

"How?" he asked. "You were on the phone for like three minutes."

Her smile was slow and definitely saucy. "Never ask a lady to reveal her sources," she said, then patted his arm. "We better get moving. Call the Experience drivers, tell them to re-direct."

Being the savior was sweet. It was just a shame she couldn't give credit where it was due. Zairn was amazing. Always on hand to help. He was too good for her. He deserved the world, not a screwed up nobody afraid of losing her independence.

GREG WASN'T THE ONLY one impressed. Roxie didn't even need to call ahead. No number came through to her phone, but when they got there, Keith was waiting to receive them. A whole legion of Crimson staff showed up to provide superstar treatment. They lugged equipment, rearranged furniture, accommodated lighting it was… impressive.

In the transition from interview to club night, everyone was allowed into the VIP area and the music was turned up high. Not typical of a Crimson VIP room. She didn't have to ask who'd approved that.

They got back to the hotel late and slept late. A brunch had been setup for the Experience winners and the docu guys. She wasn't invited, so didn't know about it until Greg called her to come meet them. By then, it was time to bundle into the van and head to the airport. Their numbers would grow as they went along. Not everyone could join them for the whole tour, but the three Boston Experience winners were with them for the duration.

Excitement hit a new high when they got to the airport.

"Oh my God!" one of the Experience winners exclaimed.

Looking up from the text she'd just sent Toria, Roxie discovered why the van was pulsing with elation.

One woman screamed. "Oh my God, is that—"

"The Crimson Craft!" another Experience winner yelled.

Greg leaned in, his shoulder pressing into hers. "Did you know about this?" he murmured.

Her head moved in a loose shake. Why the hell…? The Triple Seven. Damn. Her letting him down gently… ish. Him in that fluffy white towel. His mouth on her breasts… Ah, memories.

The van pulled to a stop. "Wait here," she said, leaping out before Greg could respond. Running up the stairs, the pilots waited inside where she expected them. What she didn't expect was Zairn's personal, private pilot. "Dennis?"

"Miss Kyst."

"Roxie," she said, her jaw tight. It wasn't his fault. This guy was doing a job. "What are you doing here?"

"Roxie?"

The question brought her around. She couldn't have heard…

"Astrid?" Marching away from the pilot, she went to her friend. "What the hell is going on?"

"Experience winners will be expected to remain in the club section, unless you authorize—"

"Astrid," she said, taking her friend's arm to drag her out of the plane's club into the lounge. Once the door was closed, she let go to throw up her arms. "What is going on? I can't authorize anything!"

"Um…" Astrid swallowed. "You have carte blanche."

Clenching her teeth, she blew out a breath. "I'm going to kill him," she hissed and began scrolling through her phone.

"He's, um… Mr. Lomond's unreachable right now."

"I bet he is," Roxie said, gesturing at Astrid with her phone. "He won't be unreachable forever… not if he wants to see me naked any time this century."

"Roxie," Astrid whispered. "Oh my God."

When the young woman peeked around her, Roxie guessed she was checking they were alone. "You think I'm being too loud? Broadcasting our relationship to the world?" Astrid's brows moved as she kind of half sort of side-nodded. "What do you think this is? He sent a goddamn billion dollar plane for us! When did that become the plan?"

"They'll only know it wasn't the original plan if you tell them it wasn't."

The Experience winners wouldn't, the docu guys would.

"And why did he send you here?" Roxie asked. "You don't want to be here. You want to be with him." The assistant's eyes flared. "Not like that." She growled and folded her arms. "Though, right now, if you want him, you can have him."

"Rox," Astrid said, hazarding a weak smile. "I think it's sweet that he wants you to have comfort."

"We're only flying to Canada."

"Then to Miami and Buenos Aires. And Sydney… We'll be flying to Tokyo."

Good point. The larger plane would be better for the long haul portions of the tour.

Holding up a pointed finger, she pondered for a second, then pointed behind Astrid and gestured for her to follow. Striding through the plane was reminiscent of her walk with Zairn in Sydney. Oh so long ago.

They went through one section and another until they reached the boardroom. On the long table, a single martini glass. She swept it up to gulp the Gin and It without losing a step.

"Roxie," Astrid said, taking the empty glass.

Still, Roxie didn't stop. The master suite door was the next thrown out of her way. Damn right she got in there. If he'd cut her diamond off for his bedroom, they'd have more than just media problems.

Bypassing the couch and the bed, she went into the closet and the bathroom. Okay, so he wasn't around. Never hurt to check. Leaving the bathroom, she noticed the post-it on the vanity mirror.

"No one changed the sheets. —Z x"

"Asshole," she whispered, peeling off the paper to raise it to her lips.

Sweet, kind, presumptuous asshole.

Wandering back to the bedroom, she noted the bed didn't look very well made. He wasn't lying. Astrid obviously hadn't followed her for whatever reason, so she went to the boardroom where the assistant was waiting.

"Roxie?"

"Let them on," Roxie said on a nod. "It's okay."

"Are you sure? Because he said whatever made you happy—"

"Yes, I'm sure," she said, noticing the new clock on the wall. The time was set to Central, but the plaque underneath said something else: "*Roxie time.*"

"If you want us to take it down…"

"No," Roxie said, trying not to smile. "No one will be back here. They can use the lounge and dining area for the longer flights. No one gets in here but me and you."

"The boardroom?"

"Yes, and if you want to go back to him—"

"I'm here for whatever you need," Astrid said. "I've arranged for the Crimson clubs to be on standby for our arrival. We can forward specific requirements whenever we have them. Whenever you want."

Going over, Roxie laid a hand on Astrid's shoulder. "You want to be in the thick of it. I won't be the one to take that away from you. It's okay to go back to him. I can handle this."

Astrid shrugged. "I like working with you… I can talk

to you without…" Her cheeks warmed. "And you are in the thick of it Roxie. Deep in the thick of it."

Was she? Whoa, boy. Crimson was sort of taking over her life and… that was okay. After finishing the Retrospective Tour, her link would be severed. Except… if her association with Zairn continued, Crimson would keep being a part of her life. Especially with the new Crimson, Chicago in the cards. Clubbing used to be what she did for fun. To kick back and relax and now… Now. What? What was Crimson to her?

THIRTY-FIVE

"MMM…" Roxie barely managed to mumble after slapping the answered cellphone to her ear. "I'm dreaming about your cock."

"Ha," Zairn said. "How d'you know it was me?"

"If I was more awake, I'd joke about mistaking you for someone else." She groaned in a semi-stretch without opening her eyes. "No one else would call me at this time, Casanova. You're the only one allowed to wake me in the dark…" which led to a relevant question. "What time is it anyway?"

"In Argentina? Around eight a.m."

"It's still dark."

"Not outside. You didn't notice every suite you sleep in has blackout blinds and drapes?"

"They do?" she asked. Despite opening her eyes, hair blocked her view. Not that she'd be able to see anything in the dark anyway. "How do you know that? Did we have blackout before?"

"I say things out loud and they happen."

Ah, another of his genius strategies.

Clearing her throat, she took a second to get her

thoughts together. "How's California? Isn't it the middle of the night? Last we talked, you hadn't even eaten dinner." Like maybe ten hours ago. Evening plus ten hours… ugh, she'd tried that one before. "What happened to the party at what's-his-name's-house? Did you go to the club after?"

"Nope."

Uh-oh, there was something in that casual dismissal.

Rolling onto her back, she swept her hair from her face. "Where are you, Casanova?"

"I don't want you to panic."

Now awake, she frowned. "That statement leads to panic. Straight to panic. Where are you?"

"We're at the police precinct."

She sat up. "What? What happened? Are you alright?"

"Yes."

"Is it Kesley? Did someone get hurt?"

"No."

Frustrated, this wasn't the time for twenty questions. "Z! Tell me!"

"Okay, it's fine," he said. "No one is hurt. No one is under arrest."

"You don't go there just to hang out," she said, piling her pillows behind her to lean against them. "I'm gonna ban you from California, Zairn Lomond. Every time you go there, the law gets involved."

"One of those times was on you."

"It was not on me, it was on your overeager goon." Closing her eyes, she shook her head. "Stop changing the subject, what's going on? Are you reporting a crime?" She squinted. "Doesn't a guy like you have the pull to get a detective to come to him? The paps will love getting shots of you going in and out…" And the early call suddenly made sense. "Which is why you're calling me."

"I'm calling you because I'm pissed," he hissed, his volume dropping. "I lost count of how many times I avoided Noel Clifton's invitations. Tibbs does it by rote. Clifton's a dick, but he invested in Kes's movie and suddenly I have no choice."

"You always have a choice," she said, stroking her

covers. "We talked about it. I thought it was a good idea too, she needs your support." But that wasn't the point. "Draw a line for me between the party and the precinct."

"Clifton's was raided. SWAT, the whole deal. Timed perfectly for maximum impact. Hollywood knows how to put on a show. Cops brought everyone in for questioning."

"Raided? Why?" she asked. "Oh my God, everyone? Kesley too? Being interrogated? How is she handling that?" Silence. Had they lost their connection? "Baby?"

"Why do you never give me shit about it?"

"About what?" she asked. "You're social, you go to parties. I knew that about you pretty early on."

"About Kes," he said. "You never comment on her traveling with us."

"Why would I?"

"You've never asked if we're sleeping together again."

She smiled and wriggled deeper against the pillows. "No, I haven't."

"Because you don't care?"

"Because there's nothing keeping you here," she said, meaning in communication with her. "If you and Kes were on again, you wouldn't keep calling me… or seducing me with your sly, smooth bedroom voice."

"I'm a player. Did you forget?"

It was difficult to contain her laugh. "I've met you, Z. Don't lie to me."

"I can't figure you out, Roxanna," he said with wonder and curiosity. "You said you could never be with another woman's man. You can't be okay with another woman being with yours."

"No one is anyone's unless the whole world knows," she said. "You can't claim something until it's public knowledge. But I'm not worried about you and Kes."

"Because… I was with her prior to being with you? Because if I was with her, I'd stop calling you?"

If he took enough shots, he might hit on her reasoning. Rather than spend the rest of the day listening to his guesses, she helped him out.

"Because every time we're not having sex, you're

telling me about the long list of drama going on in her life. Friends. Family. Career. Some producer making a pass. The stubborn director who won't consider her for a role until you call. The woman has issues. Troubles. She's emotional. She needs you."

"And you don't."

"Not in the way she does," Roxie said. "I don't compare her and me, not when it comes to you anyway. She may be beautiful, demure, elegant in a way I couldn't ever dream of being—"

"You're perfect."

"Far from it," she said, recognizing a line when it came at her. "If I had anything to worry about, you'd tell me. I'm jealous she shares air with you while I'm a million miles away. But I'm jealous of Ballard, Tibbs, and Og for the same reason."

"Providing I get out of here at some point tonight, I have a board meeting later and CollCom tomorrow. I don't think there's anything we can't cancel, if you want us to join—"

"You can't," she said, appreciating the offer. Attempting to talk her into meeting was a feature of almost every call. "This is a growing mass of bodies. Every new city means picking up people. How do we hide us from them? From the docu guys? Everyone knows you being here isn't part of the plan."

"A surprise visit. A perk."

She toyed with the edge of her blanket. "For me or them? You'd have to make a show of being social. If you're being social, we're not doing what we want to be doing."

"Each other."

"So what's the point?" More quiet. Such a shame. She wanted to be alone with him too. It just wasn't in the cards. She sighed. "Have you spoken to Dunlap?"

"Not yet."

"Ballard?"

"Just you."

"Don't do anything stupid," she said. "Don't go off at anyone. Keep your head."

"I already got through the questioning."

"Without firing anyone?" she asked. "Or is that why you haven't talked to Ballard?"

"I could try to fire him, he wouldn't leave, but I could try. You two should switch jobs."

"It's Ballard's job to observe the scene around him. How likely is it I'd do that with you drooling all over me?"

"If you had his job, we'd never go out."

She laughed. "True. Best way to keep you safe would be to keep you in bed."

They appreciated existing together for a few seconds. It couldn't last.

Eventually, he exhaled. "Sex and drama."

"Could do with more of one and less of the other, baby?"

"You said it."

"It's the women in your life. If you were gay, this wouldn't happen."

"Not so sure about that. These past couple of years, I can't seem to get out of the cycle. Drama finds me."

"Because you collect lost sheep," she said, tossing back the covers to get out of bed. "You are a good man, Zairn Lomond. Kind and generous."

"More fool me then, huh?" Apparently, she hadn't reminded him of their first night together. He sounded so... tired and unhappy. "Why the fuck do I do it, Lo?"

Pausing with a hand on the curtain she'd been about to open, Roxie frowned. "Was that a rhetorical question?"

"Hmm? Yeah."

"Because you know why you do it," she said, only to be greeted by silence. Her hand dropped from the fabric. "There's a reason you haven't told Kesley to beat it. A reason I am so understanding about her following you around."

"Because the world doesn't know about us."

Turning her back to the window, she shook her head. "Casanova," she murmured, unable to believe that... "I am not a psychologist. There's a lot about the world and people that I don't get. But I know exactly why you're so driven to help others. Why you can't refuse a woman who needs your help. Why I do my absolute utmost to always remind you I'm okay. There's a reason you helped Trish. Why you help Kesley. A very obvious one."

"I don't—"

"Baby," she said, amazed that he didn't see it. "You're terrified of ever facing Dayah again." No response. "You help these women. Stand up in front of the press over and over again because you think the world judges you for what happened to her. It doesn't matter that the whole world is too fickle to ever care about one person for this long. Every time you stop to answer questions or release a press statement, you're asking for forgiveness." Even without saying the words. "Baby, you're forgiven. A thousand times over. It wasn't your fault."

More quiet. Was her timing off? The guy was up to his eyeballs in stress. And surrounded by cops. The subject had come up. Relevant, right? She could be random, but this wasn't random. It dumbfounded her that he didn't know his motive for trying to be everything to everyone.

"So switched on," he murmured. "You should charge for this."

"I do," she said, whirling around to open the curtains and welcome the day. "In sexual favors, next time we're together." He laughed. Her Casanova. If he lost that spirit she adored, it would be a tragedy for the world. "When Kes was this demanding before, you broke off the relationship."

Post-Dayah, he was bending over backwards for the woman he'd once been unable to satisfy.

"We're not in a relationship now."

"No, but you can't say no to her. Because if anything were to happen to her…"

"Damn, I should be in therapy."

"We'll work it out," she said, taking him into the bathroom. "Whatever it takes, we'll be okay." Slipping the straps of her cotton chemise from her shoulders, she shimmied it from her hips and went to turn on the shower. "I have some time, we don't take off until noon… Wanna watch me play with myself in the shower?"

"More than you know," he said. "But in my current

environment…"

"Okay. Maybe later? I'll be in the air for like twelve hours… with nothing to do."

"Charge your phone."

"Okay, baby. Whatever happens, you have me," she said, a wide smile brightening her words. "I don't care about the media or the cops. No matter what, I'm sticking around."

"You're all I need, Lola Bunny."

Sometimes life got on top of everyone. While she didn't doubt Zairn's ability to deal with anything, it wasn't fair that life kept throwing this kind of crap at him. The relief she could offer wasn't enough and wasn't at all practical. Still, he'd called her. Over everyone else in his life, he'd needed her in that minute. That was worth something to her. Worth a lot.

THIRTY-SIX

"IT'S SCARY," Toria said. "Tell her it's scary."

Her roommate adjusted the tablet to include Jane in the video call. The pair of them sat on the couch in their apartment.

With Argentina in her rearview, Sydney was next on the agenda. Maybe this time she'd get to enjoy Australia.

The docu guys and a bunch of Experience winners were somewhere at the other end of the plane. Roxie lay on the bed in the Triple Seven's master suite.

"It is creepy," Roxie said. "The messages and calls were strange by themselves, but if he comes to Chicago…"

"Right! Exactly," Toria said. "We're buying a gun."

"No!" Jane exclaimed.

"What if he shows up in the middle of the night? What if he breaks in and carves us up into little pieces?"

"You don't have to worry about that because you're going to join Roxie."

"No," both she and Toria said at the same time.

"What?" Jane asked. "You were excited when we talked about it last week."

"Yeah, then I saw the cost of an express passport.

No, thank you. I've gotta eat. There she is languishing in five-star everything, and I'm here living on Froot Loops and Oreos."

Her lips curled. "You always live on Froot Loops and Oreos, Tor."

"Nu-uh… sometimes Jane cooks."

Security concern? There was only one guy to call.

"Hold on a second," Roxie said, sitting up in the middle of the bed to prop her tablet up beside her.

"What are you doing?" Toria asked. "Rox?"

"Solving the problem," she said, stretching to grab her phone from the charging dock on the nightstand to dial.

"Who are you calling?"

"One sec," she said, putting the phone on speaker and repositioning the tablet further down the bed to give a wider view.

"You're a lucky bitch, you know," Toria said. The ringing line did its thing. "Are you calling him?"

After party raids and wee hours interrogations? "No, he has other things on his mind today," Roxie said, barely getting the words out before the ringing stopped.

"Little Rox?" Ballard answered. "What's the trouble?"

"How rude is that?" Toria said. "Like you'd have no other reason to call."

"I wouldn't," Roxie said. "If Ballard and I are talking to each other, either Zairn or I are dealing with drama of some kind."

"What's going on?" Ballard asked. "Who you talking to? Thought you were in the air."

"I am and if you weren't so averse to video calls, you'd know that… Ballard hates video calling," she said as an aside to her friends.

"Yeah, 'cause that's what I need, more of you in my day. I hear enough about you already."

"Aww," Jane swooned. "Zairn talks about you."

"Those your girls?"

"Yes. Jane needs protection."

"Why?"

Roxie sucked in a breath. "She went on a date with a freaky guy in New York."

"London Guy," Ballard said.

"Yeah."

"Uh, how does he know that?" Toria demanded.

"Ballard is the closest thing Zairn has to a boy… like you're my girls."

"Oh-kay," Toria said, unconvinced.

"Give me everything you know about him," Ballard said, nonplussed by Toria's doubt. "Full name, date of birth—"

"Jane will email you that stuff," Roxie said. Her friend was detail oriented. "Call Stone, ask him to look into this guy. And get Trevor's posse off their asses. They should be looking after my girls. They have nothing better to do. Zairn's still paying them."

"How do you know that?"

She refrained from growling at him, but seriously? "Because he wouldn't go to the trouble of telling Tibbs to cut them off. I'll be home in a few weeks. He likes his people on standby, always ready to move."

"Since when did you start giving orders?"

"If I say pretty please, will you help me?"

"I have to help you. It's in the job description… And Zairn would crucify me otherwise… You're taking to this Empress thing."

She groaned. "He needs to stop calling me that in front of people."

"I'll mock you for it later. I've gotta put on—"

"Oh!" Jane yelped. "Zairn's making a statement."

"A statement about what?" she asked. Her roommate flipped the tablet camera to let her see the apartment screen. Watching on the TV in the plane's master suite would be easier. There were two of them after all. Concealed behind wall panels, back to back, one for the bedroom and one for the lounge. But it was nice of her girls to include her. "Is it about last night?"

"You talked about it already?" Ballard asked.

She tossed her hair from her face, doing a terrible job

of hiding her interest in the television on her tablet. Zairn walked over to the bank of cameras and reporters outside the Los Angeles Grand Hotel. They'd met there. In that building. Why was she suddenly so nostalgic?

"He called me from the precinct while they questioned Kesley," she said. "He wasn't happy."

"Would you be? You go to a party at a friend's house, a person who likes to call you a friend, and the party's raided. They found drugs… and not just for personal use."

"That explains the middle of the night interrogation. He did well to keep his cool."

"Shit," Ballard breathed out. "He gets a minute to make a call and he calls you." On screen, Zairn was talking the reporters through events. "Not his lawyer." No connection. Party at a friend's. A private party. "Not his security director. No, his secret girlfriend." Pleasant evening. Misunderstanding. Fully support the cops. "Why would he call you? You don't give a shit when this stuff happens."

"I give a shit," she replied, still half listening to the man on TV. No suspicion. No crime. "It eats into our drunk phone sex time when he gets arrested."

"He was questioned." Yes, he attended the party with Kesley. No, just a friend. "Not arrested."

"Why is California so mean to him?" she asked. No romantic involvement. "Is it because he supports tax hikes for one-percenters?"

"You haven't discussed whether you have a future, but you've talked taxes."

"Sure, we—" was that her name? Her attention swung back to the tablet. "What did he say?"

"No comment," Jane said.

"To what?"

"A reporter asked him to elaborate on his relationship with you," Toria filled in the details. "Probably because you're touring Crimson again."

"And streaming."

"Only sometimes. Why are they asking about me in relation to last night? I wasn't there. I'm on a different continent!"

Between continents, but whatever.

"They asked about Kesley and Trish too. Guess they're trying to keep track of the women in his life."

"Good luck," Ballard muttered.

"Are you going to take care of my friends?" Roxie asked.

"Yes."

The intent was to hang up and switch her focus to Zairn. Except he wrapped up and turned away from the cameras, so… He stopped. Why did he…? A second went by, then he turned back to the reporters.

"Ask me again," Zairn said. Uh-oh, what was happening? "Duane, ask your question again."

"Shit," Ballard exhaled the word that was in her brain.

"Uh, sure," said a voice on the TV. "Can you explain the nature of your relationship with Roxie Kyst?"

"Short answer?" Zairn asked. "No. The long answer is more complicated, but it all comes down to one simple fact…" No. He wasn't… what was he— "I'm in love with her."

"Oh my God," Toria said.

Roxie was sure her own silent lips recited the same words.

The reporters went crazy. Just like on Talk at Sunset, he raised a flat hand. "That's enough." The press wasn't so quick to silence, but he called over the lingering voices. "I don't have a statement. Nothing prepared. This is off the cuff… and no doubt something I'll regret… if she lets me live that long." The crowd quieted. "If I can't claim something until it's public knowledge, my only recourse is getting it out there." What the hell? This was so not what she'd meant! "Roxanna Kyst is a dynamic woman. Beautiful. Smart. Quick. And, yes, we are in a sexual relationship." Her mouth opened. His voice was like a cannon blasting every inauspicious word into her ears. "We have been since New Year. She is the reason I left the reopening party early."

Her family would hear this. Why would he…? How could he…? The car crash happened over and over with every word he uttered. This had to be a nightmare. She'd wake up any minute. She better damn well wake up.

"Were you having sex on the World Tour?" a reporter called.

"Yes," he said and actually had the gall to smile. "Not as quickly as I'd have liked. I wanted her from the moment we met." What was he doing? Frozen in position, she couldn't form a full thought. "Being together was complicated for various reasons. We put a stop to it at the end of the World Tour."

"Is your relationship the reason for her joining the Retrospective Tour?"

"No," Zairn said. "That was an optional part of her original contract." He paused to lick his lips. "We see less of each other now than we would if she was at home."

"Chicago," someone called out. "She's the reason for Crimson—"

"Yes," Zairn confirmed. "Roxie is the reason."

"So with Trish…" someone else said. The whole thing was changing hue. From adversarial to something much friendlier, the honesty led to an openness she definitely did not support. "The Gambatto trial was not—"

"For legal reasons, I shouldn't talk about that while it's still ongoing," Zairn said. "Though it's fair to say I had no discussions with Trish prior to her statement."

God! What was he doing? Her fingers scrunched the hair by her temples.

"Rox?" Ballard said, though she didn't really process it.

"What the hell is he doing?" she gasped.

"Did Roxie influence your—"

"Roxie influences everything I do," he said. "She's my closest friend. My most honest advisor. I trust her completely. She has carte blanche with everything that is mine."

"Are you engaged?"

"No," he said, another flash of a smile. "We're pretty clear on that."

"Do you plan to get married?"

"I don't know, we haven't discussed it fully," he said, pointing at someone else.

The bastard was taking questions! Like he wasn't igniting trouble left, right, and all over the place!

"By seducing her on the tour, you exploited a position of power—"

"You want to accuse me of a crime? Go ahead," Zairn said, ease cocooning him. "Our relationship has been fully consensual at all times. Roxie won't tell you any different. And…" One side of his mouth tipped higher in amusement. "She has more power in our dynamic."

"Fucking hell," she gasped, her dry eyes burning in need of a blink that she couldn't grant them.

"Did you and Roxie discuss this disclosure?" a reporter asked. "Why aren't you doing this together?"

"We did not discuss it. She'll tear me a new one for this… She's somewhere over South America at the moment. Her flight took off from Buenos Aires little more than an hour ago. I didn't discuss it with staff either. This is all me."

"How does Kesley feel about your relationship with Roxie?"

"I don't know," he said. "I've never asked her."

"But she knows you and—"

"I don't discuss Roxie with anyone but Roxie… Though I have a sense that's changing as we speak."

Yeah, because Ogilvie would go nuts. Dunlap would despise legalities being involved in the discussion. Cutting Salad and Fuller out of the loop would piss them off. She could sympathize with all of the above.

"Why keep it a secret?"

Zairn inhaled. "Revealing this has the potential to cause problems, which I'm sure you'll all help with when you get over the shock of my honesty. On tour, secrecy was pertinent given our respective positions and our involvement ended with the tour."

"You didn't want the relationship to continue? To be anything more than physical?"

"I wanted it to continue, but our lives are complicated. Roxie is not… used to this kind of relationship."

"Long distance?"

"Being in the public eye too."

"Didn't the Sydney stream change that?"

He paused, taking the time to consider his words. Shame he hadn't thought to do that earlier. "My life has its pros and cons. For the most part, I remind myself, I chose this path. The contest thrust Roxie onto it. Yes, she could've refused the prize, but neither of us knew we would become what we are. Being with me isn't easy for any woman. Another thing I can thank the media for."

"Does Knox Collier know about the relationship?"

Shaking his head, Zairn, for the first time, became discerning. "I won't get into specifics like that. No one lied for us. This relationship was my choice. I am fully responsible for any fallout that comes from it. If the business suffers, if the stock tanks, I'll take it. I choose Roxie over everything else and I'm sorry if that upsets anyone. She is my absolute priority. Key. Foremost. The sun which my world revolves around."

"Oh my God," Roxie said, her head throbbing. "Oh my God! Ballard, is he drunk? Shut him the hell up!"

"Yeah," he said.

The line went dead.

It couldn't be happening. It couldn't be real.

On screen, a reporter asked, "Are you moving to Chicago full-time?"

"That hasn't been decided."

Behind Zairn, a hotel side door opened. Out came Ogilvie with Tibbs close at his back. She'd never been so pleased to see anyone in her life.

"How can we contact Roxie for comment?"

Ogilvie came striding over. "Thank you, everyone," he said, taking Zairn's arm. "That's all we have today."

"It's okay," Zairn said, removing his arm from Og's grip. "If we answer the questions now, we won't have to do this again."

With a tight jaw, Ogilvie leaned closer to Zairn's ear, though his words were still audible. "You are not this naïve."

Car crash? Is that what she'd dubbed this? More like a meteor strike on course to destroy them all.

"Are you concerned Roxie could be interested in your

money?" one voice from behind the camera asked.

Zairn snickered. "I can't pay the woman to spend my money." Everyone enjoyed the joke. She couldn't breathe. "Any more questions?"

They came in a quick-fire flurry.

"Is Roxie giving up her career?"

"When did you decide to restart the relationship?"

"Was there communication between the tour and the re-opening?"

"Have you discussed last night with Roxie?"

The mass feared its feast was about to be whipped away. They wanted to consume every last available morsel.

"Does she know about last night?"

"Does she support your drug habit?"

There was always one troublemaker. Usually more than one.

Tibbs was just standing there in the background. A deer in the headlights. Ogilvie tried again to take Zairn's arm, but was unsuccessful. Hell! Were they going to brawl right there?

The side door burst open. Hope struck Tibbs a second before Ballard appeared. Thank God! Just like Ogilvie, he went marching over to Zairn and took position at his other side. Rather than speak to the crowd or try to manhandle him, he leaned in, cool as anything. Zairn's head tipped his way to accept the brief whisper.

Whatever he said, she could kiss him for it.

Zairn raised a hand. "That's all we have," he announced to the group and turned in time with his friend.

The gaggle called after them as the Crimson crew retreated to the building.

Blowing out a breath, she blinked about ten times. Had that really just happened? What had just happened? Was that real?

"Rox," Toria said, flipping the camera to her and Jane again. "Honey?"

"I…" The anchor on TV was talking. Roxie couldn't see her, and the words made little sense. "Zairn. Announcement. Revelation. Confession. Global news.

Scandal!" Squeezing her eyes closed, she shook her head. "I…
I can't… I've gotta… I'll call you later."

Pressing the end button, she quieted the tablet just as
her cellphone rang. Ballard. No way was Ballard on the end of
that line. What did she want to say to Zairn? What did she feel
about…? Her head was a mess. Grabbing the phone, she
turned it off and quickly did the same with the tablet. She
could do this. Figure this out. Hours lay ahead. Nothing but
time in the air.

Her attention rose to the central wall between the
master lounge and bedroom. There were other people on the
plane. Astrid. The docu crew… the Experience winners.

She wasn't going out there. No. She had until Sydney
to get herself together. As for answering questions… Closing
her eyes, she breathed out and fell back on the bed. It had to
be a nightmare. Why couldn't she wake up?

THIRTY-SEVEN

EVERY PIECE OF WORK on her computer was complete. She hadn't eaten or slept, but was beyond up to date with her clients. Productivity was the serendipitous side effect of being screwed over. The remedy worked until there was nothing more to do.

She moved on to invoicing her clients, which meant a trip into her email. Even while ignoring the inbox, she was aware of the number next to it rising. Four figures. No, five. Who the hell were all those people? How did she have any hope of ever getting through that many messages?

In an attempt to cure her ails, she went for a long, hot shower. After it, she felt better until the light above the blow-dryer flashed, alerting her to the captain's audio…

They were landing.

Anxiety came rushing back.

Sydney.

They'd shared a suite in Sydney. He'd cared for her in Sydney.

Shaking off her growing aggravation, she buckled herself in and finished her makeup on the descent. After the plane taxied to a stop, she freed herself from the seatbelt and perused her wardrobe.

Was she taking her time? More time than usual? Yes. Transport to and from airports varied. Sometimes they were all in a van or bus together. Other times it was a bunch of cars. The idea of traveling with eight Experience winners and the three docu guys… She didn't know where to begin and didn't trust herself not to say something she shouldn't. But what the hell should she say? What was the right thing in this scenario?

Damn. Forget it. Thinking about it only amped her up again. He had a whole damn team of people geared up to help him with the fallout. A massive machine of moving parts there at his side to support him. Who did she have? Her girls. As much as she loved them, they weren't trained to deal with this kind of thing. They'd want to talk about Zairn and her feelings. Roxie couldn't put either in order.

Jane was too romantic to understand anger and ambivalence. Toria's advice would be to go with the flow or torch the guy. Neither were her style. She hadn't called them. Hadn't turned her phone or tablet on. She'd ignored the knocking on the suite door every time it came. Astrid meant well, on a personal level anyway. Unfortunately, the young assistant was a slave to two masters, one of whom had his own interests to protect.

Clothes. More of her wardrobe hung in the Triple Seven's closet than she took to the hotels with her. Home away from home had been more prophetic than any of them could've predicted. Sheesh, was that really half a year ago?

Lunchtime in Sydney would be warm. Despite knowing that, she went to one of the closet windows to raise the shutter and… dark. Why was it dark? They were supposed to land at like one thirty in the afternoon. It should be day… in Sydney. Straightening up, a possibility occurred to her.

"If this isn't Sydney, where would—" The suite door opened and slammed. "He did not," she murmured, hurrying to the bedroom. As she entered one corner, he appeared in the one diagonally opposite. "You fucking prick!"

"Rox—"

"We're in LA? What the hell gave you the right to—"

"I needed to see you."

Turning on her heels for the closet, she called back. "No, you did not!"

"Roxanna—"

"Don't you dare with Roxanna," she said, glaring at him when he appeared at the other end of the closet. "What you did was so far out of—"

"I know," he said, holding up his hands like he meant to calm her. Asshole. "I know you're mad."

"Like you would accept it if someone... I don't even know where to start, Zairn. You can't just divert someone's life without permission!" she said, grabbing underwear from a drawer. "Who the hell does that?" She put panties on under her silk kimono robe. "Who is so goddamn arrogant that they'd think—no, sorry, I know exactly who's arrogant enough to do that!"

"We couldn't get you on the phone for a consult," he said. "Restricting access to the suite maybe wasn't such a good idea."

"You better not be joking with me, Lomond," she said, untying her kimono to toss it aside. "You can't just..." She didn't know what to say. Despite all the hours that had passed, she was no clearer on her feelings. "I am not a toy or an employee. I don't march to your beat just because you try to finagle it that way."

"I know."

"I am not a zillionaire. I am not a supermodel or a glamorous actress," she said, whirling to gesture at him, bra in hand. "But that doesn't make me less of a person. I have the same rights as every other human being. Just because I don't rake in big bucks or..." His wandering attention suggested he wasn't listening. "What the hell is—" Glancing down to see what... panties were the only thing on her body. That was the distraction? Her head tilted as her renewed glare landed on him. "You are not serious."

His smile was more than a little sly. "It's been weeks."

"You want it?" she asked, pointing down the plane, her arm outstretched. "Go get it. They're lining up for you, Z. Any woman you want."

"There's only one I want," he said, moseying closer, oozing charisma. "And you're hot. Irresistible. What guy wouldn't notice?"

"No," she said, taking a step back, shaking her head. "You can't charm your way out of this, Zairn."

"Sure I can," he said and tried to put his arms around her, but she pushed them away. "What happened to 'only because I'm so good at it'?" That was a lifetime ago. "I love you, Lola."

What a…? "Which I found out on national television. International television!"

If he thought licking his lips would hide his amusement, he was wrong. "Come on, Lo. You knew it. You had to know it. I've been in love with you for months. Since before our eleven days and Rome and… Sydney."

"So everything we ever were is a crock," she said. He frowned. "Either you do love me and let me walk away from the Zee-Jet willing to let us pass you by, or you don't and you think I'll fall for a line."

"It's not a line." Finally, he seemed to at least be taking the situation seriously. "I do love you."

"You can't love someone and do what you did," she said, not sure she recognized him. "You stood up there and announced I was yours like I'm some prized steed or a sports car." It hurt. That's what she felt and probably why she struggled to face it. "Without talking to me, without… my family will be under siege—"

"Everyone's being taken care of."

Which meant they were holed up in hotels, hiding from their lives.

"This isn't my life, Zairn," she said, turning her back. Was she struggling to look at him or fearing her hurt would manifest for him to witness? She couldn't embarrass herself in front of him, wouldn't. "I can't ask everyone in my life to duck for cover whenever I… every time we… This is not my life…" The words made it past her lips, just, though she didn't know how. Suddenly drained, the weight of emotion in her gut became an anchor, holding her in place. "How did I get here?"

A long span of nothing didn't offer answers. With her head full and her heart aching, it wasn't possible to focus or figure anything out.

"We have taxied everyone to the hotel. There's a car waiting for you on the tarmac. You won't have to see a soul," he said, an odd bass in his tone. "The plane will be fueled and ready to leave in the morning. Chicago, Sydney, go wherever you want."

What was he saying? Why was he…? By the time she turned around, he was no longer in the closet. The suite door closed a moment later. No slam, no urgency, just a quiet period punctuating the end of their encounter.

A car. A plane. Whatever she wanted. Always whatever she wanted… maybe it was time to figure that out.

THIRTY-EIGHT

BEING ALONE ON THE PLANE didn't feel strange until she left the master suite. In minimal light, walking through the empty sections was eerie. Like it was haunted. In a way, it was. Each area conjured a different memory. Sitting on Zairn's lap. Eating with the Crimson crew. Chatting with the assistants and letting Zairn down gently. All the way through to the club zone where she'd partied with her girls.

So much had changed. About her life. About who she was. The travel contributed, of course it did. The experience of cities she'd only dreamed about before was a factor. The people. The parties. The details influenced her identity, her goals. Her horizons were broader. Sometimes anything seemed possible; sometimes she was a stranger to herself.

In the back of the car on the way to the hotel, she tried to picture the future. The one she wanted and the one that might be ahead.

Life couldn't be decided on the answer to a single question, no matter how much anyone wanted it to be.

She should call her girls. And her mom. Turning off her phone saved her from admitting a lack of answers, but with time dragging on, she couldn't delay much longer.

The car didn't pull into an alley or to a side door. A security agent granted them access to an internal parking area under the building.

The same security agent opened her door. "Follow me," he said.

Wearing Grand Hotel ID, he wasn't on Zairn's payroll, but he had saved her from the baying mob no doubt at the front of the building. That earned him points. Beaucoup points.

They went up in an elevator. She didn't bother to check what number he'd pressed. When the doors opened and he gestured for her to exit, she did.

Oh.

Right.

The penthouse suite. Of course. What would she face on the other side of that door? Zairn. Ogilvie. Ballard… No hope of comfort.

As the security agent opened the door, a sound carried from inside. A laugh. A female laugh.

Rushing past the security guy without a polite word of gratitude, she had to find out if…

In the living room, she came to a quick stop. "Jane?"

Not just Jane, both of her girls, and no one else in sight.

"Hi, honey," Toria said. Jane got up to come over and give her a hug. "How are you doing?"

"How are you here?" Roxie asked, stunned. "You were in… How did you…?"

"Zairn," Toria said.

Jane led her over to the couch. "Astrid, actually. She called. Zairn wanted you to have whatever you need."

"Yeah, and his people are already working on my passport. I'll be able to go anywhere in the world with you."

"He talked to my boss," Jane said, seating them on a couch. "I'm distance working for as long as you need me."

"He…"

"Yeah," Toria said, shuffling across the thick carpet on her knees, cocktail glass in hand. "Are we hating him or loving him?" The glass was put in her hand. It was… She was… "What he did was super shitty."

"He knows that," Jane said. "Doesn't he?"

"I don't know," Toria said, shrugging. "If he was aware it was shitty, why would he do it?"

"Why did he do it?"

Both women looked at her. "I…" She swallowed. "Made a stupid comment on the phone. It was totally offhand and wasn't meant to be taken… I said you can't claim something until it's public knowledge. I didn't… He should know I don't always think before I speak. I wasn't giving him an instruction or hinting at anything."

"But he thinks you were?"

"I don't know," she said, shaking her head, handing her drink off to Toria for a second while she cast off her jacket. "I don't know what he was thinking."

"He was thinking that he loves you," Jane said and winced when she set eyes on her. "I know you're not a… that you're not into romance, but…" Her wince became a wary smile. "He loves you. That means something… doesn't it?"

"He can't rule her," Toria said. "Super-hot guys always think they're entitled to something. They go through life having everything handed to them. What did he expect would happen? He blew up her life with no consideration for her needs."

"Yeah, there's no going back to normal after this," Jane agreed. "We were out of the apartment like an hour after Zairn did the… thing. The block was mayhem."

Sinking back to sit on her feet, Toria retrieved her glass from the table. "Which is really stupid because you're not even there and the world knows that. They know everything."

The world knew a lot about her and her movements… and her sex life, thanks to Zairn.

"He did go overboard with the details," Jane said and leaned forward to pick up her drink from the table. "I guess he was overwhelmed by what he felt."

"Yeah, or strutting," Toria said. "Boasting that he got the girl. It's arrogance."

"Or true love," Jane said. "He loves her so much that he couldn't keep it in."

"Please," Toria said. "Real life isn't like that. He's an overbearing prick, trying to take over her life. You'd be smart to ditch him, Roxie, honey."

Jane was quick to object. "No! Not when he loves her so much."

The good cop/bad cop was a practiced routine. The trio had it down. Whenever there were guy issues, one roommate took a supportive of the guy position, the other a disparaging one. It gave the woman in crisis permission to do whatever she wanted, love the guy or lose him. This time, it wasn't helping. Maybe because she couldn't make sense of her own feelings.

"I can't believe this," Roxie said, tipping her glass up to gulp down the alcohol. "I need to get out."

"What?" Jane asked.

Roxie was already stepping past Toria and by Jane's crossed legs to head for the bedroom.

In the same suite she'd once shared with Zairn, Roxie knew the drill. As expected, her things were laid out and hanging up in the closet.

Her girls came in as she perused the dresses.

"Out where, honey?" Jane asked.

Toria wasn't so reluctant. "She's totally right. Whenever our Rox is frazzled or messed up about a guy, a night out is what she needs to clean the slate. Start anew. Get her head in order. I say we hit the town hard."

Sounded perfect and a-ha, the perfect dress.

"But the press," Jane said. "They're everywhere."

"Not in Crimson."

Yes. Going to Zairn's club might not be the best idea. But showing up in a competitor's space would be even worse… and likely get her in trouble.

"You really want to do this?"

"I just want to dance and drink and forget about the whole damn world for a while."

"Okay," Jane said. "Let's get changed."

Credit to Toria, it only took about forty-five minutes for her to get ready. That was definitely a record. Roxie was reapplying lip gloss when an unexpected reflection joined hers in the mirror.

"Astrid," she said, turning away from the mirror. "What are you doing here?"

"I… came to check on you."

"You don't have to do that," Roxie said, busying herself by putting the makeup away. "I mean, thanks, but you can tell him I'm fine."

"I wasn't…" Astrid came closer. "He didn't tell me to come here. I wanted to know."

Was that the truth? Maybe.

Roxie pasted on a smile. "I'm great." Despite her protestations, she asked, "How is he?"

The bamboozled Astrid shook her head. "He won't see anyone. Not even Sean."

Zairn Lomond wasn't often alone and didn't give much credence to solitude. "Where is he?"

"In a suite downstairs," Astrid said. "His phone is off, he isn't taking calls. Mr. Collier is very relaxed about the whole thing." Knox was in town too? She hadn't known that. "I don't think his attitude is helping Miss Walsh. She's beside herself."

"I'll bet," Roxie said, checking her friend. "Does that mean you're off the clock?"

Astrid faltered. "I… suppose, maybe. Tibbs is staying close. He doesn't know what to do without Mr. Lomond's instruction."

"We don't have to talk about that," Roxie said, scanning the dresses hung up nearby. "This one…" She went over to pluck one out and held it up to Astrid. "Get changed, we're going out."

"Oh no, I could—"

"You can," Roxie said, grinning. "Who knows when we'll get this chance again." The chilling prospect brought down a more somber mood. She chased it away. Fake it and maybe she'd make it. "Come on. Let's live a little."

OFF THE CLOCK OR NOT, Astrid made calls that got them a car. The line of people outside Crimson called out to their vehicle as it pulled into the alley. People wanted a way in; she didn't blame them for being eager. The tinted windows concealed their identities, so it wasn't like anyone knew who was on the receiving end of their whooping.

Their troupe got out of the car, purses in hand, and went toward the side door, which was being held open by a security guard. She glanced at the guy, ready to acknowledge his help. The moment their eyes met, she stopped. How did she…? It took her another second, but when she hit on how she knew him, her lips curled.

"Riot guy!"

He swallowed. "Miss Kyst."

Toria gasped. "Oh my God, we know him!"

"Yeah, we do," Roxie said, still smiling.

"What's wrong?" Astrid asked, returning to their group.

"We know this guy," Toria said, looping an arm through hers. "He's the guy who got us arrested."

"I didn't call the cops," the guy said.

"Someone did," Toria said, teasing, though it did seem she was in the mood to bust his balls. "You didn't believe us when we said Roxie was our ticket in."

He made eye contact. "Miss Kyst—"

"It's okay," she said. "Groveling is unnecessary."

"I didn't know that—"

"Neither did I," Roxie said. She and Zairn hadn't even met on the night of the riot. "You did the right thing. Protecting those inside is your job." The flash of surprise that came in his blink made her laugh. "What's your name?"

"Stephen… Barrow."

"Well, Stephen Barrow, stop beating yourself up. What's done is done."

"Mr. Lomond—"

"Won't hear anything from me," she said. "I have a habit of getting myself into scrapes. No big deal."

His surprise became suspicion. "Am I gonna get fired later?"

"Not because of me," she said and patted his arm. "Keep doing your job, Stephen Barrow."

Giving her friends a nudge, they went inside. Following Astrid, they went upstairs to the VIP area. One of two they had in LA. A long line of private glass pods separated the zone. Oval-shaped, each had slightly different décor but was designed to look like slick modern living rooms. Nice.

The bar.

That was her focus. Her friends oohed over the VIP zone and the pods, Roxie had seen it all. Before she could get more than half a dozen steps, someone jumped into her path.

"Miss Kyst!" Geez, what was it with the gorgeous blondes all over the place. "Would you care to follow me?"

"Would I care to—no," she said, pointing past the woman. "I would care to go to the bar."

"Your drinks will be brought to you," the blonde said, taking Roxie's purse right out of her hand. "I'm Debbie and—"

"Look, Debbie, I don't want to be rude, but—"

"Will you be joining Mr. Lomond?"

Oh and that… She glanced around.

"He's here?" Astrid asked, astonished.

The blonde's brow twitched in confusion. "Yes, he's in his preferred pod."

"I'm sorry, Roxie," Astrid said. "I really thought—"

"Oh-kay," Toria said, materializing at her side. "No, we won't be joining the Emperor. We're here to dance… a lot."

"Dance, yes," Debbie said, locating her pep. "Come with me."

After dragooning Astrid to join the cause, they'd spent another forty minutes glamming the assistant up. Fun, even for the young Astrid. Anything could've happened in that time. It shouldn't be a surprise that Zairn was at his own club.

Her friends crowded around as Debbie took them across the room. All eyes followed them. Why was she flavor of the week? Oh, yeah, because Zairn told the world they were having sex. Now the world wanted to know why.

Zairn's table. Of course they took her to his table. There was no one around it, but she knew it was his. Not only because it was elevated in the corner, as most of his designated areas were, but because they'd shared that couch before... Eleven days.

Her excited roommates scurried around her. She took both of their hands to stall them, keeping her focus on Debbie. "We'd prefer to sit at the bar."

Shock smacked the deference out of Debbie, but only for a second. "The bar..." She looked around like someone may be nearby to save her. "We've never had... I don't know how to..."

"It's no problem," Roxie said, swinging around to point at the corner between the bar and the glass wall showcasing the view of the dancefloor below. "We'll sit over there. Have Stephen Barrow sent up with a colleague he trusts, they'll keep us safe."

Without waiting for a response, she swung her friends around, letting go of Toria to put an arm around Astrid to draw her into their momentum.

They got halfway there when someone else appeared in front of them. A guy. Goddamn Logan Lowe. Whoa, boy.

"Rocks Out!" he exclaimed, raising his glass to her.

"Rocks Off," she said in response.

"Where have you been? We've missed you."

"Yeah, you know, things to do, places to be."

His perusal went over her and her friends. "Wanna dance?"

"Drunk first," she said, nodding past him.

"Dance later?"

"Maybe," she said to be polite. She was there to dance with her friends, not to make waves. Further waves anyway. "We're going to the bar."

"Wanna join us?"

"No," she said, edging around him. "But thanks."

Toria leaned in to whisper. "That was Logan Lowe."

"Yeah," Roxie said from the corner of her mouth. "And that's as close as we want him to get."

She might be mad about the predicament Zairn put them in, but she had no intention of playing games.

People gawped as space was cleared around them. By

the bar, Roxie and her girls arranged high stools to face each other. Music blared from dedicated speakers, though their position didn't spare others from hearing it.

What more could she do? Demure didn't fit her. It didn't suit her at all. Was it too much? Maybe. But they only took over a little corner. If Zairn wanted them to stop, apparently he was around to say so himself.

Crimson was going to take her mind off her woes… she had to do something and couldn't keep drifting through life without direction. Crimson would save her… wouldn't it?

THIRTY-NINE

LOGAN LOWE DIDN'T STAY AWAY for long. He brought his bandmates and celeb friends over to join them. Her girls, Astrid included, lapped up the attention. Thank God.

The perfect corner turned out to be not so perfect after all. It gave her direct line of sight across the bar to the central private pod, which just so happened to be… Yeah. Zairn's.

Had he noticed her? Yes. More than once she'd glanced over and caught him looking in her direction. It was dark, and he was more than thirty feet away, but, yes, he was looking at her. She just knew it. He'd probably know she was looking too. They didn't acknowledge each other. In fact, any time he was caught, he'd immediately turn. Not just avert his eyes, he'd literally turn his whole self away.

People flitted in and out of the pod. Famous faces. Ogilvie. Dunlap. Knox. Others she didn't know. People moved in and out. The only constants were Zairn, Tibbs, and Kesley. Once again, she was on the outside, looking in. Was it Rome all over again?

A fresh drink was brought over and she thanked the

bartender. The other partiers in her group danced in their exclusive corner. Her heart hadn't put her on her feet yet.

As the bartender returned to his duties, he revealed the view of Zairn's private pod. Tibbs, for the first time, walked out, leaving Zairn alone with Kesley. The couple stood in the middle of the space talking. They were beautiful together. Perfect in so many ways. Appearances could be deceiving.

Zairn said something and stroked Kesley's hair until his hand came to rest on her shoulder. He wasn't a cheater. He wasn't. Trust still existed between them, didn't it?

The two exchanged a few more words, then Kesley passed him to go out the opposite door into the other VIP area.

Alone. Zairn was alone. Phone in hand, his focus intent. Emails? Texts? Either. She could text... No. Zairn's press conference erased the need for discretion.

Hopping off her stool, Roxie said nothing and slipped away without her girls noticing. They were too involved in their fun. She didn't want an audience, but was vaguely aware of security following her. Fine. Whatever.

It wouldn't go unnoticed that she was on a specific course, one that took her to the door of Zairn's pod. Tapping a knuckle on the glass, she held her breath until he looked up. Laying her hand on the glass, she waited for a response. He could tell her to go to hell. Maybe he'd be entitled.

Instead, he tipped his chin up in a nod that granted her entry. Thank God. Now if she could just be sure her diamond would... Yes, the door opened, letting her inside. The moment it swung shut behind her, all other sound was blocked out. Impressive.

"Hi," she said, sensing hostility.

"What do you need?" he asked, more detached than she could ever remember him sounding. His busy thumb moved across the phone screen. "Do you want me to clear the floor? Give you the building?"

Teasing might be their way, but those questions weren't playful, they were almost... resentful.

"Can we just..." She started toward him. "Can we be

us for a minute?"

"What do you need?" he asked again. "Astrid is with you, she has the power to fulfill any of your wishes."

"I don't care about my wishes," she said, stopping in front of him. "Casanova, I just want—"

"Something you can't get from me. I know."

Goddamn him, why did he have to be so sensitive?

Putting a hand on the phone, she pushed it down, forcing him to look at her. "You're sulking."

"Am I? I made a mistake. In front of the entire planet. Allow me some time to lick my wounds."

Was that what he felt? Wounded? How could so much have changed between them in such a short time? They could get back to where they'd been. They could. She just had to remind him.

"Why do it yourself when there are so many others willing to do it for you," she said and reached for his empty hand.

He pulled it away and stepped back. "Don't play with me, Roxie," he said, anger flavoring his words. "It's cruel."

"Cruel?"

What was he saying? That she was cruel? Why? They'd always played with each other. Always teased and flirted.

"You know how I feel about you. I can't believe you claim not to have known it before, but there's no excuse now. I've stated it bluntly."

"You love me," she stated. "That was the mistake you made in front of the entire planet?"

"No," he said. "Misjudging you was the mistake."

"What does that mean?" she asked, at a loss. "I don't know what's wrong. I don't know why everything's different between us. I was mad and hurt… What's done is done; we can't go back and change it."

"No, we can't."

Inching closer, she was nervous to put her hands on his torso in case he pulled away. He didn't, though he did tense. As she nestled closer, he grew rigid, the exact opposite of his usual reaction.

"Last night you called to confide in me, now you can't even put your arms around me."

He breathed out, which loosened his muscles a fraction. "This is not your fault, Roxanna. The only place the fantasy existed was in my head. I let myself down."

Like the white dress and kids women she'd talked about in New York.

"Thank you for bringing my girls here."

"I thought you would need support. I didn't want a repeat of Rome."

"It's not Rome," she said, smoothing her hands across his shirt. "It's different. Worse." She blinked up at him. "This time I can see you, but I still can't reach you."

"I'm here."

"No, you're not," she said, exhaling and stepping away. "You want to be anywhere but here. My Casanova never wants to be separated from me. He never gives up a chance to touch me."

"I'm licking my wounds."

"I didn't mean to wound you. I don't know how I… Can't we just go back to the way things were?" Tipping her chin higher, she moistened her lips. "Forget about who did what and just… Kiss me, Casanova."

Hope pierced her when he came closer. She drew in a breath when he ducked lower, but he hesitated. No, she couldn't have that. Sliding her hands onto his neck, she linked her fingers and pulled him down. His kiss could cure them. It would solve everything.

The initial tentative touch of his lips switched to confident fast. Yes, he could kiss her and everything could go back to how it was. Pulling him closer, she parted her lips, welcoming the invasion of his tongue.

Music. Alcohol. They were just fine and had their place, but nothing was more redeeming than the certainty of his mouth on hers. When he grabbed her waist to yank her to him, the urgency of her need became more than comforting. There they were in a glass room. Surrounded by others. Curious eyes all over them. Wonder and intrigue. It meant nothing. She didn't care; he was all she needed.

Without breaking the kiss, he sat on the couch, guiding her down to straddle his lap. They were together. That was all that mattered. Them. Like this. Reassuring and consoling each other.

He tore his lips from hers. "I can't, Roxanna," he said, his eyes closing as his head fell. "Shit, I'm sorry, I can't do this."

"You can't do what?" she asked, stroking his cheeks, trying to tempt his mouth to hers again. "You're doing just fine."

His focus rose to hers. "Every time we do this, every time we're in each other's space, I fall farther and I can't… I won't get out if I don't jump now."

"Jump?" Concern clenched the need in her belly, altering it from sexual desire to desperation. "What are you saying?" She tried a nervous laugh. "Everything is the same as always. We are the same."

She tried to guide his forehead to hers, but he took her arms to put some space between them. "Nothing is the same, Rox."

Now there was pity in his eyes. A deep hurt, something far superior to her own, shone through in his gaze too.

"You're ending this," she whispered. "Us."

"You said there were two choices, I accept we would always be secret or I end it. I thought there was a third choice. I thought if I got it out there…" He inhaled, held the breath for a second, then let it out. "It doesn't matter. I was wrong. You were right… as always."

"I am not always right," she said, trying to caress his face again, but he caught her wrist to restrain her. "You're dumping me." Suddenly self-conscious, the eyes from beyond the glass heated her skin. "In the middle of the club, in front of everyone."

"It was over on the Triple Seven," he said. In a spot that once held such amazing memories. "Finished when you told me this wasn't your life. You were right. Again. This life is my choice. You never wanted it."

"I didn't mean… I wasn't trying to…" Why couldn't

she get the words out? "I wasn't blaming you, I was asking myself the question."

"It's okay," he said, his hand loosening from hers to stroke her arm. "It's been bonus times since New Year. Ballard told me to stay away; I should've listened."

Offense was pretty hard to mask when it hit so hard. "You regret us? All of us?"

"I should've seen it in Rome. Hell, I did see it. I didn't want to acknowledge it."

"Acknowledge what?" she asked, climbing from his lap to stand up. "That I'm not easy?"

"Babe, sex is—"

"I'm not talking about sex," she said, anger rising. "I'm talking about you bailing because I am not easy to deal with. Because I don't march to your tune. I don't fall in line. You announced to the universe that we're together and thought, what? You'd divert my life to suit yours, literally, and I'd be overjoyed? Can you imagine if the situation was reversed and I tried to pull that shit?"

He jumped to his feet. "We needed to see each other. I thought we'd need to strategize. Didn't work out that way, but this is better. At least I can look you in the eye and know."

"What? That I'm not perfect Kesley or desperate Trish? Because I want to be your equal—"

"My equal? Shit…" He wandered a few steps away. "Our relationship has never been equal, can we at least be honest about that?"

"We've never been equal?"

"I chase you and I chase you… Clement was right."

"Don't bring him into this."

"If you stopped running for just one goddamn second—"

"I wasn't running, I was with you."

"Halfway around the world. You couldn't even stay in Chicago when I showed you I was willing to call it home."

"I'm doing your tour. I'm working for Crimson."

Cool as concrete, he leveled his harsh gaze on her. "Crimson will survive without you."

Another blow. She didn't want to show him her hurt,

but couldn't kid herself that she was disguising it well. "You're firing me?" she asked. "From the Retrospective."

"Do whatever the hell you want," he said, throwing up a hand to run it through his hair as he turned his back. "That's what you're best at anyway."

The publicity would be horrible if she walked away. For both of them. The world thought they were a couple. In love. And then she'd slink back to Chicago and… live in obscurity? Hardly. The block would remain mobbed. Until they realized she'd been dumped.

That couldn't be made public. The media would rip Zairn to shreds. Taking advantage of her on the tour, as they saw it. Seducing her at New Year. Announcing she belonged to him in the press. Then casting her aside as soon as the chase was over.

Her mind stopped. Emotion drained out of her until her whole being was numb. Screaming and shouting wouldn't change anything. Over was over.

Taking her pendant from around her neck, she put the diamond on the couch by his phone and let the chain fall over the screen. "The ruby is on the Triple Seven," she said, trying to hold her composure. "Nothing else is… important."

Walking away this time was different. On the Zee-Jet, she at least had a glimmer of hope she might see him again. There hadn't been bad blood then either. Whatever the cause, the spark that fused their energies was broken. He was right. They should've left it alone after the tour.

Every step felt wrong. Like on the Zee-Jet, she was compelled to say something. But when she paused, hand on the glass door, nothing came to mind. Without turning around, she left the pod.

The music was just a drone. Smiling faces and joy churned her stomach.

"Are you okay?"

Lost, drowning in numbness, her attention drifted to the man who'd asked the question: Stephen Barrow.

"Can we get out of here?"

Everything was left behind. Her purse. Her friends. Her dignity.

Barrow was her saving grace. He got her out of the building without them being spotted by press. His beat-up car was more discreet than the one she'd come in wherever that was.

"You and the boss had a fight?" he asked, still driving.

With the window open, she stayed low so as not to be identified or photographed. The night air hitting her face kept her breathing. Nothing was… nothing felt real. Not even reality.

"You haven't said much…" he said. "If you want to go back to the club—"

"No," she said, shifting in her seat. "Can we drive for a while or go to your place?" Silence. After a few seconds, she dragged her attention around. His focus flitted between her and the road. "I'm not propositioning you." Funny. That was funny. If only she could remember how to laugh. "I can't go back to the hotel, and I don't know anyone in town. I'd go to another hotel, but…"

"The whole world is watching you." She acknowledged that with a nod and shrug. "We can go back to mine… But I… The boss can't think—"

"He won't," she said. "You don't have to worry about your job." Because they were through. It was over. Why didn't it feel real? Maybe because none of her did. "I just need a place to crash for a while. Somewhere to clear my head. Nothing screwy."

"You keep things interesting, Roxanna."

"Roxie," she corrected him and turned back to the window. "Just call me Roxie."

When had she lost control of her life? When did the spiral start? Why hadn't she noticed it? Her girls didn't loop her in either. She was lost. As Roxie or without Zairn? Who knew anymore? Who knew any damn thing?

FORTY

"ROXIE!" Jolted awake, it took her a second to focus. "You've gotta get up, Roxie."

Breathing in, she lifted her head from an unfamiliar pillow. "What?"

What was…? Glancing around the small room, it was only when she registered Barrow throwing open the curtains and striding back toward the bed that she recalled what had happened.

His apartment was comforting. Although not that neat, it was clean. She'd curled up on the couch and closed her eyes before they got to conversation. Talking to anyone was beyond her capability. Last night and in the light of the new day.

"You've gotta get up."

"What's going on?"

"I'm gonna get arrested, that's what's going on. Come see this."

He stomped his way out of the bedroom. The bedroom. Had she fallen asleep in the bedroom? Pushing the covers from her body, she kicked them away, but stayed on her back to rub her face. On the Triple Seven, watching Zairn give his press conference, she'd prayed to wake up from the nightmare. That hadn't been the nightmare. The club… the private pod…

Heaviness slowed her down. She got out of the bed without even the motivation to stretch her tight muscles. Dragging her feet toward the door, she heard the TV before she saw it.

"…Miss Kyst was seen at Crimson in LA last night. After a public argument in a private pod with owner, Zairn Lomond, she vanished. Her friends and relatives are concerned. Police will not step in at this stage as she has only been missing for a number of hours. They have said, however, that anyone with information on her whereabouts or what might have happened to her, should call the tip line."

The tip line? There was a tip line? Stunned, she stopped in the living room.

"You need to call him," Barrow said.

"No, I—my purse is at the club."

A cellphone was thrust into her line of sight. "Call him."

Shaking her head, she tuned out the television's speculation on her argument with Zairn. "I don't have his number."

His chin dropped. "Your boyfriend? You trying to tell me you don't know your boyfriend's phone number?"

"I don't know it by heart. His phone number is in my phone," she said, pushing his phone out of her face. "Which is in my purse." And probably dead. "I don't know anyone's number. Who memorizes phone numbers these days?"

He raised the phone. "Get in touch with him. Somehow. Now."

Trying to hold her temper, she pushed the phone away again. "And how do you think he will react if I call him from some random guy's phone?"

Still holding the phone, he gestured at her. "You said I wouldn't lose my job. Shit…" He groaned as he turned away. "Shit. I should've left you on the street, I'll be out of a job anyway."

"No. It's fine. You won't," she said, reluctant to

admit the end of the relationship. "I'll go back to the hotel for my friends and it'll all be fine."

For Barrow anyway. Not so much for her. Nothing would be fine for her, but for different reasons.

A knock brought his attention swinging back around.

"Who is that?" he asked, striding across the room.

"How do I know? This is your apartment." He checked the peephole and tossed a glare at her. "What?"

She asked, but he didn't answer. Well, he did, when he opened the door to reveal who was on the other side. Ballard. His glare was far darker than Barrow's. Zairn's friend stepped back and opened a hand to the hallway. Fine. She'd go with him. Only because it was easier than calling a cab.

"Crimson would appreciate your discretion," Ballard said to Barrow.

"Sure. Yeah… I didn't touch her. We didn't… you know, we weren't… Do I still have a job?"

"For now," Ballard said.

"Don't threaten him," she said. Ballard grabbed her arm to pull her out of the apartment and down the hall. "I think you enjoy dragging women around. I really do."

Not a word. Down the stairs and out, he tossed her into a Cayenne and backed out of the alley. They got to the end of the block before he smacked the steering wheel.

"Are you fucking kidding me?"

"Am *I* fucking kidding you?" she asked, propping an elbow on the door. "What took you so long? How'd I end up on the damn news?"

"What the fuck do you think? Word got out." As it somehow always did. "Took us time to pull the video. Don't change the fucking subject."

"Stop swearing at me. What did I do?"

"What did you do?" She kept her attention away from his, but in her peripheral vision noted him glancing at her. "I told you to walk away. If you weren't serious about Z—"

"I didn't sleep with Barrow," she said, exhaling her frustration. "Not that it matters."

"No, sure, it doesn't matter. Why would it matter that you left the club without telling anyone…? That you walked out with a stranger?"

"A Crimson employee," she said and half shrugged. "We have history."

"I don't give a shit. Weeks ago, I told you to walk away if this wasn't it for you. All you had to do was quit taking his calls. Quit letting him in."

"Hey!" she snapped. "I am not the dumper here, I am the dumpee. I am not good enough. I didn't jump fast enough or high enough. I wasn't good enough for him and he wasn't willing to wait so…" Her shoulders dropped as she faced the truth. "He should get back with Kesley. He needs a woman to need him. She's perfect for the job."

"He doesn't love Kesley."

"You know, it wasn't all on me," she said, sick of being blamed. "It wasn't like I demanded he declare our relationship to the world then pulled the rug out from under him. Can you imagine, just for one second, what would've happened if I stood in front of a flock of reporters and announced my relationship with him to the world before he was ready?"

"He'd have figured it out. He wouldn't have abandoned you."

"I'd still have been the bad guy. To you and Ogilvie and Knox, all his people, you'd all look at me like you look at me now. So I'm damned either way. And…" She raised a finger. "Again, dumpee, not dumper. I didn't abandon him. He abandoned me." Adjusting her position, she turned more of herself toward the side window. "Just like Rome. He gets in a snit about something and I'm cast out. Yet, somehow, it's still all my fault."

"He brought your girls to California so you'd have your own support network."

"Yeah," she said, nodding. "I thanked him for that." She exhaled before muttering, "Now I've gotta get the three of us home commercial and pay rent… We'll just give up hot water and… you know, food."

With Toria out of a job, things would be tight. Maybe too tight. If she had to, she could always go back to her parents. They'd take Toria and Jane in too, but it would be a helluva squeeze. Her sister still lived at home. Well, she *had* lived at home. Her family wasn't at home, they were in hotels. Or they had been. Hopefully Zairn at least let them spend the rest of the night before kicking them out in the morning. She couldn't afford security or protect the people she loved. Shame she'd torn up the fifty thousand dollar check. Not that she'd cash it even if she hadn't.

Maybe one of those media jobs was still good. Or it would be until they found out she and Zairn were done. After that, the only jobs she'd likely be offered would require trashing her ex. She wouldn't do that. Not ever.

What we are is not their business.

That was no longer true. Zairn blasted that apart in front of the cameras. Was that really just yesterday? Time zones screwed her up every time.

"You're leaving the tour?"

"Hmm?" she asked, half registering Ballard's calmer tone. "Yes. The Retrospective? Yes."

"Rox, do you get the message that will send the world? They were already accusing him of abusing his power. If you walk away, if you *run* away, it'll look like… Like they have a point." So he could only be calm if he was appealing to her humanity? "You can't do it. I'll be the first to admit I don't know everything that went on in your relationship, but I knew more than most. He didn't abuse his power. He didn't force himself on you or take advantage. Is that what you're going to do now? Tear him down? Why? Because he told the truth? *They asked questions and I answered them.* Didn't you once throw that at him? That's what he did, Roxie. He told the truth."

Shifting again, she frowned at his next glimpse. "What the hell are you talking about?"

"Here in LA when you met—"

"Yeah, I get that's what you're… He kicked me off the tour. He dumped me," she said. "Not the other way around. I yelled at him on the Triple Seven about diverting our plane. I didn't get a chance to talk to him about the press thing. Not really. I tried to talk to him about it last night and he couldn't even… He dumped me."

"He said it was mutual, which we figured was just his

way of saving face."

"No," she said, cold prickling her skin. "I guess he was trying to save mine."

"He left you."

"He ended our relationship right there in the middle of Crimson."

"The same place he finished it with Dayah," he muttered. "That explains a lot."

"Glad you're enlightened," she said.

"He's been crazy. Astrid called Tibbs, asked if you were with Z. He was standing right there. I saw it. The second he realized you were missing."

"Shit," she exhaled. Only a couple of nights ago, she was telling him about his Dayah pathology, then he'd practically relived it. "At least this one had a happy ending."

Depending on perspective.

"You think this is a happy ending?"

The words hung in the air. They reminded her of something Zairn had said months ago on the Triple Seven… *"That's not how this ends."*

Could either of them ever have imagined?

For the rest of the drive, neither she nor Ballard said a word. Traffic. Birds. Pedestrians. Anything was a distraction. Facing reality was a daunting prospect.

"You should duck down," Ballard said. "We'll go round the back into the parking garage, but in the drive up…"

"Yeah," she said, doubling herself to stay out of sight.

The media wanted to see her, but she didn't want to see them. Borrowed time or not, she'd take it.

When the vehicle stopped, she sat up again, throwing her hair from her face. Ballard slammed his door and came around to open hers.

"Do you mind if I wait in here?"

"In where?" he asked, scowling at her. "Wait for what?"

"If you tell my girls I'm here, they'll come down with my purse. I'll call a cab and try to get through to Hatfield."

"Oh no, it's not that easy," he said, stepping back to gesture her out. "You're coming upstairs."

"For what?" she asked. "More humiliation? Can you at least give my girls a chance to pack their things? I don't care about mine. I get what I deserve, but money is tight for us. They can't afford whole new wardrobes. I don't know if you remember what it's like to live in the real world—"

"Always with the real world," he said, lunging over to grab her arm and haul her out.

"Ow! Hey!"

"Everything we live is as real as anything you live," he said, marching across the parking garage, pulling her with him. "Tell yourself he's fake all you want. Tell yourself it was a game or a hobby or a flirtation, maybe it was just a fling for you, but it was real for him."

He stopped at the elevator. Her jaw was still tight as he dragged her in and they traveled upward.

"You say it's all real," she said. "He says our relationship was unequal. I wonder if anyone's looked at the damn thing from my perspective."

"What perspective is that? The spoiled princess angle? He gave you everything and it still wasn't enough for you."

She spun to face him. "Dumpee! Not dumper! Damnit!"

The elevator doors opened, and he grabbed her hand to lead her out. The penthouse. Good. She only needed a few minutes with her girls. Ballard opened the door. Thank God. She'd have no way to get in otherwise.

He pulled her over the threshold into the living room, swinging her around to his side. He stepped back, putting her front and center.

What the…?

Her girls were there. Astrid. Tibbs. Ogilvie. Knox. Dunlap. Everyone. Salad. Elson. Kesley… Zairn.

Scanning the faces aimed at her, the sense of expectation was impossible to ignore. What did they want? What did she have to give? What was left? Numb. Hollowness. Nothing. Roxie Kyst was a husk of her former self. Her energy was just… gone.

She couldn't even muster an excuse. Turning away

from the weight of their anticipation, she left them to go into the bedroom and on into the closet. Dropping back against the shelving, she buried her face in her hands.

What was her life? What the hell was she going to do? Everyone knew Roxanna Kyst was strong. Impervious. Invincible. Her knees buckled and down she went. Melting onto the carpet, her face still in her hands, her knuckles sank into the pile. Breathe. Why couldn't she remember how to breathe? Everything hurt. Every inch. Her brain throbbed, her heart heated, her eyes too. Everything was wrong.

"You think it's that easy?"

Zairn. Not what she needed.

"Go away," she mumbled the words against her palms.

A second later, someone took her shoulder to turn her over. She tried to pull back against the insistence, but what was the point? Her hands slid from her face as he brushed her hair from her eyes. Lying there, focused on the man crouched at her side, she breathed just enough to survive. That was her life now, survival.

The image of his frown blurred. All of him was… warmth tracked down her temple. What was…?

"I'll fucking tear him apart," Zairn growled.

What was that? She'd never heard his voice like that. When he tried to stand, she grabbed for his hand, flipping to her side, holding him in his crouch. "No, don't…" Tears. That's why her vision blurred. She was… He'd taken one look at her distress and gone straight to the worst-case scenario. "Nothing happened. He didn't… we didn't…"

He picked her hair from her face, tucking it back into the rest of her locks. "I've never seen you cry," he murmured.

"Take a picture," she said, letting him go to shift onto her knees. "It's a once in a decade experience. Last time I cried, a dog died."

"Dog?"

"Marley and Me."

The slope of his smile seemed more polite than genuine. If the guy didn't have time for Pretty Woman, he definitely didn't have time for fun canine frolics.

"This guy didn't hurt you?"

She shook her head. "You took care of that all by yourself."

"Roxanna—"

"What? You're going to yell at me some more?" she asked. "Go ahead. It doesn't matter."

"What doesn't matter?"

"Nothing," she said, forcing herself to her feet. He rose too. "Do I have time for a shower or are the cops on their way to throw me out?"

"No one's throwing you out," he said. "You can take a shower."

"Thank you."

She intended to do just that.

This time, it was he who caught her hand to stall her. "What's wrong?"

After a deep inhale, she breathed out her words. "Nothing, my life's a peach. Rotten as shit beneath the pleasing skin, but, that's life I guess. Be glad you saw it and got out early."

"No part of you is rotten, Roxanna."

"Mm," she said, taking her hand out of his to go into the bathroom.

Turning on the shower, she let the water run for a second, then went to look at herself in the mirror. Sheesh. Rough. Thank God the press didn't get pictures of her with last night's makeup smeared around her eyes and her knotted hair lying lifeless. Bending over the sink, she washed her face as best she could.

What was the point?

Catching cool water in the cradle of her hands, she submerged her nose and mouth. It was nothing. Everything was nothing. What did that even mean? Nothing. Just like every other part of life.

Dropping the water, her eyes stayed closed as she braced her hands on either side of the sink.

"The Triple Seven's waiting for you."

Shit. Hadn't he gone away? Forcing herself upright, she ran her fingers into her hair. "It's okay. We'll fly commercial."

His single burst of humorless laughter startled her. "Yeah, you won't be doing that. Do you know how dangerous it would be for you right now?"

"One of the best things about being dumped," she said, leaning into the mirror to wipe away a remaining smudge of eyeliner. "I don't have to consider your opinion anymore."

"Did you ever?"

For the first time, it occurred to her that she wasn't wearing shoes. Damn, was she that messed up?

"Consider your opinion?" she asked and shrugged. "Doesn't matter anymore."

"No, I don't suppose it does."

She retrieved a towel from a rail and tossed it over the end of the shower. "Are you staying for the show?"

When her fingers went to the zip under her arm, she expected him to leave. Instead, he semi-shrugged and propped a shoulder on the doorframe. Okay, fine. Unzipping her dress, she shed it and her underwear.

"We need to make some decisions."

"Now he wants to talk," she said, getting into the shower.

There was no heat in the water, but it wasn't cold. Her interpretation of her senses was all off. She squirted some conditioner into her hands and started to work it into her hair. It was so much effort. Too much. It was just… Heavy, her hands dropped to her sides.

How had gravity changed? Why was everything just so… wrong?

Stepping out from beneath the water, she slid open the shower door. There he was. Still standing in the doorway, watching her.

"What do you need?" he asked, a familiar rasp in his words.

"Come over here."

He boosted himself from the doorway and strolled across the room to stop in front of her. Without lifting her head, she swayed closer, shutting her eyes to breathe him in. Nestling nearer, the tears on her cheeks mingled with the water rolling from her slick hair.

"Lo—"

"Put your arms around me," she said, shivering, but not because it was cold. "Please…" The pathetic whimper in her plea didn't bother her. No walls could survive whatever she was feeling. "I can't…" Her voice trembled as fresh tears escaped. "I can't find my balance. I can't…"

Instead of doing as she asked, he stepped away. Wobbling on the spot, she grabbed for the glass to steady herself. His curled finger slid under her chin to raise it up.

Mysterious intent tinged his curious blue eyes. "I'll be damned."

"Is that relief?" she asked, trying to swipe away her tears. "You're relieved? Why?"

Scooping a hand around the back of her head, he guided her hair to his kiss. His lips lingered for a few seconds. "You need your girls." That wasn't an answer. "Get washed, I'll send them through."

He left without explaining his demeanor. Didn't he realize how difficult it was for her to show him weakness? To reveal her vulnerability? He could be harsh, quick to anger, even cold, but he didn't usually have any trouble owning his behavior.

They were over. That was the message. One she got loud and clear.

FORTY-ONE

HER GIRLS WERE SITTING on the bed when she came out of the closet in a fluffy hotel robe.

"What happened?" Jane asked, rushing over to pull her into a hug. "Oh, honey."

"Nothing, it's fine," Roxie said, glancing around. "Do you know where my purse is?"

From behind her, Toria raised it over her head. Roxie left Jane intending to get it, but Toria yanked it away at the last second. "Did you screw him?"

"Who are we talking about now?" Roxie asked, going around Toria to snatch her purse.

"The dude. Whoever you went home with last night."

Wow. Was that the time? The wall clock couldn't be right, could it? How long had she been in the shower?

"I didn't sleep with anyone last night," she said, less surprised to find her phone dead. "No one thought to charge it for me?"

Judging her friends was beyond rude given she never remember to charge it either. Maybe it was her attempt to joke. The spirit just wasn't in it, in her.

"Zairn was so worried," Jane said. "We all were. What

happened?"

"Nothing," Roxie said, going into the closet to seek a charger. "Are you both packed?" She called out to her friends. "We might have to wait on standby, but I'll call the airlines and see what's available for today."

If they didn't get out of California that day, they'd have to pay for another night in a hotel… somewhere. They couldn't afford the suite. No way… One night would be more than their rent for the month. Why weren't her girls responding?

After connecting her phone to the charger, she returned to look into the bedroom. Both of them were wide-eyed, confused? Shocked? What was wrong?

"We're staying in LA," Toria said.

"We're… No, we're not," Roxie said, leaving the closet. "We can't afford this, guys. Me and Z are done. It's time to go back to life as we once knew it."

Toria got up to grab the remote from the nightstand. One button opened the panel at the end of the bed, allowing the television to rise from the frame. The next turned the television on.

"They've showed it like fifty times…"

"Showed what?" Roxie asked Jane while Toria scrolled through the channels and came to a stop.

Zairn. Outside the hotel. Listening to a reporter's question.

"…go missing?"

"Keeps things interesting," Zairn said, smiling.

God, he looked so good. The sunglasses, the tan, he was just so at ease with the world and who he was in it. Did he have to be so charming? He'd dumped her, she should be mad… But anger wasn't what poisoned her.

"Where was she?"

"Who was she with?"

"Is your relationship in trouble?"

Man, the media was hungry.

"I've learned my lesson. You should direct any questions you have about my relationship status to Roxanna Kyst. That's Roxanna with an a, not an e. Pisses me off when people get it wrong, you might have noticed."

The crowd laughed. Funny? Was he making jokes… at her expense? The reporters lapped it up.

"Is she mad at you?"

Wincing, Zairn bobbed his head side to side. "I don't know if she'd want me to answer that."

"Where is she?" someone called from the back. "If you want us to talk to her, why isn't she here?"

"She and her girlfriends haven't seen each other for a while. They're catching up."

"Here in LA?"

"Yes," Zairn replied. "They'll be staying in LA for the foreseeable. Roxie has work to do with the documentary. I'll be taking over on the Retrospective."

"Why the switch?" someone called out.

The din of questions increased again until Zairn raised a hand. "Calm. That's enough. I don't have to stand here and talk to you."

"Call Roxie! Bring her here!"

Zairn's smile grew. "Anyone who knows the beautiful Roxie, knows that her phone is rarely—"

"Charged!"

His attention swung to the left, further than it had gone before. "That's right," he said. "We have some Lola fans in the audience."

"Why do you call her Lola?"

"That's a private story," he said. "Are you guys not getting the drift that I'm keeping my lips sealed?"

"But Roxie isn't?"

"She calls the shots," Zairn said. "Sorry to say."

"She could say anything," a reporter said. "Next time we see her—"

"It'll be up to her what questions she answers and which she doesn't. Dig into the archives, I said in front of a camera once that I'd never censor her. Never have. Never will."

No, he just wouldn't be with her.

"That's trust," a male reporter said. "What if she talks about your sex life?"

"You mean like I did yesterday?" Zairn asked, earning himself another laugh. "Roxie can say what she likes to who she likes, I can't make it plainer than that. She'll be in town, working at CollCom monitoring the progress of the documentary."

"And you'll be...? Roxie should be in Sydney already."

"Again, my fault," he said. His chin rose like he was searching his recollection. "I was presumptuous and arrogant and..."

"Those Roxie's words?"

He scratched the back of his head. "There might have been some expletives in there. I don't want to upset the sponsors."

More laughter.

"What the hell is going on?" Roxie demanded, whirling to land her affronted confusion on her friends, only to witness them swooning. "No." She pointed at them, one after the other. "Do not melt for him. He screwed me over."

"He's being sweet," Jane said. "Self-deprecating. Humble... All for you."

"I never asked him to be humble. I never asked him to change. He dumped me and now he's standing out there like..."

Marching into the closet, she grabbed her phone. It took an age to come on. By the time it asked for her passcode, her friends were in there with her.

"Maybe he wants to make up," Jane said.

"If he wanted to make up, I'd have gotten laid before he left," Roxie said, scrolling to his number to hit call.

Raising the phone to her ear, she wasn't even sure what to say. Other than WTF, that kept rolling around in her brain. Except...

"*The number you have dialed has not been recognized...*" an automated voice spouted at her, "*please hang up and try again.*"

She lowered the phone slowly, stunned into silence.

"What?" Toria asked. "What is it?"

Nothing. She couldn't...

"Honey?" Jane asked.

Toria took the phone to listen to the message. "Oh…" Toria hung it up and answered Jane. "He changed his number."

For a minute, they all just stood there. To the press, Zairn made it seem like they were on good terms. The last time they'd seen each other, she'd been naked, begging him to hold her. Did that sound like good terms? No!

"What about Ballard?" Jane asked.

Calling around in desperation wasn't her style. If Zairn didn't want to talk to her, then he didn't have to. He might have given her some guidance on what the hell she was supposed to say to the press, especially given that he'd directed them to her. But whatever, she'd figure it out.

"Same deal," Toria said.

Only then did she notice Toria scrolling through her phone, calling people.

"What about Tibbs?"

Having access to the Emperor meant there was no need for her to talk to his minion. "I don't have his number."

"Astrid?"

They all looked at each other. They were friends. Beyond Zairn. At least, they were supposed to be.

"We can't put her in the middle," Roxie said, but Toria was already on the hunt. "It isn't fair." Toria put the phone to her ear. "Her job is her life."

Toria's elbow unlocked to let the phone hang between their trio. The drone of the message telling them to hang up and try again was foreboding. In Rome, after they'd… She'd thought that was cut off. This complete and total disconnection was terrifying in its finality.

What should she do? Go home? But…

"What did he say to you?" she asked, but got no answer. Roxie grabbed the nearest friend: Jane. "What did he say to you?"

"Nothing," Jane said, shaking her head, appealing to Toria. "Zairn didn't say one word to us."

"After I got here and… When he came into the living room after talking to me, what did he say?"

"Nothing," Toria said, peeling Roxie's fingers from

Jane's arms. "He went onto the terrace with Ballard and Tibbs. They did a little huddle thing, then Tibbs came for Astrid. I guess she got instructions because she came back a minute later."

"Came back for what?"

"She took us aside and said we should wait in the bedroom for you. That you'd need support. That we should be there for you, you know?"

Yes, she was aware, but that didn't explain why they were staying in LA. "What else?"

Her friends looked at each other. "Nothing just…"

"She said we were to stay here, in the suite, with you. That everything would be paid for, to treat the place as our own."

"And?"

"Your family will continue to be looked after where they are too."

Relief? Yes. Explanatory? Not so much.

"What else?" Roxie asked.

Jane blinked a few times. "That Hatfield will be with them, Zairn and the other Crimson people, on the Retrospective. You have edits to do or approvals or something. Here. In LA. Astrid said a car will pick you up at noon tomorrow. That they'd take you to CollCom… to work on the documentary."

It was in her contract that she could have final approval. The documentary was meant to have several parts, and Hatfield was still filming. Maybe it was about keeping her under control. Or some part of Zairn wanted to protect her while the media was still hyped after his episode. Why else would he keep looking after her family?

Maybe it was guilt. His big mouth had… Okay, so, yeah, maybe hers had too. Damn, they were a pair.

Whatever was going on, she was grateful. Returning to her life would be the best course. With the press so interested in invading their privacy, it just wasn't a viable option. Her family was safe. Her girls were safe. All she had to do was watch a movie. Easy. Oh, and not think about Zairn… Not so easy.

FORTY-TWO

TRUE TO HIS WORD, a car was waiting in the underground parking area the next day. It transported her to the sprawling CollCom complex. At some other time, she'd have made a joke about the Collier's overcompensating. In her current mood, the closest she got to happy was appreciating her sunglasses for shielding her tired eyes.

The car took her to a building tucked behind a bunch of others. Or it would be tucked, except it jutted up into the sky, overseeing all beneath it. It wasn't skyscraper tall, just phallic in an otherwise low-lying world.

Some guy came trotting down the stairs, reaching her position at the same time the driver opened her door.

"Miss Kyst," the guy said.

"Roxie." She stepped away from the car door. "You can call me Roxie."

"Sure," the guy said, gesturing up the stairs. They ascended together. "You have a lot to get through. More than two hundred hours of footage."

He opened the door. Rather than go through, she paused to look at him.

Surprise weighted her jaw. "I thought I was here to

approve an edit."

"Oh, they have started," he said, gesturing at the open door. Okay, so they couldn't stand there all day. She went inside, and they started across the grand lobby. "We were told to make everything available to you."

"Well, yes, but… two hundred hours?"

"That's just the start. We've set you up in an editing suite. It's pretty easy to figure it out, but we can have someone sit with you if—"

"I don't actually have to edit anything, right?"

The chances she'd delete the entire CollCom archives were more likely than her achieving anything productive.

"No," the guy said. "No."

"Just play, fast forward, rewind?"

"Pretty much," he said, bypassing the abandoned reception and opening another door to take them down a corridor.

"Okay, I should be able to handle that."

"The point guy is out sick today."

"Of course he is," she murmured, continuing at his side while putting her sunglasses in her purse.

"From how I understand it, some of the footage is just raw, no adjustments, other parts have been spliced together."

"So what am I doing here if there's no final product to approve?"

"You can be as involved as you want. Anything you want in or out, say the word and it's done. Mr. Collier was clear that you're to be given everything you need."

"Mr. Collier? You mean Knox?"

Confirming the assumption was just smart. The guy could mean any of the male Colliers, father or brothers… maybe the grandfather was still alive. What did she know?

"Yes, he briefed us this morning," he said, taking her through double doors and swinging a right. They bypassed the elevator to ascend stairs. "Whatever you need… but we're not to crowd you."

Maybe Knox lived in LA. Who knew? Plenty of people, obviously, just not her. Whatever his reason, he'd stayed behind when Zairn and the Crimson crew took off for Japan.

"Okay." They went through another set of doors at the top of the stairs. "Get me set up. I don't need a babysitter. Let's just do this."

The quicker they started, the quicker she'd get home. With the press still hungry, it wasn't like she could go anywhere or do anything. Maybe reviewing the footage would be a good way to pass hours she'd otherwise spend under siege. By the time she was done, the media would have moved on to something else.

SITTING IN A DARK ROOM without windows was therapeutic in its own way. Being enclosed gave her a sense of protection. And there was plenty to keep her occupied. Hours and hours of nightclub footage. Most of it she watched on fast forward.

Occasionally, an Experience winner would appear to give an impromptu interview. Various celebrities popped in and out of shot too.

Some of the filming took place in the VIP areas, yet there was little of her and little of Zairn. No, that wasn't true; he was present sometimes. In the distance, ignoring the camera. Even if it was up close, he paid it no attention. Once she'd considered that a sign of his professionalism. Now it seemed prophetic. He could switch off like that. Forget those around him and carry on. Regardless of the carnage left in his wake.

That wasn't fair. She really wasn't mad at him.

Fast forwarding through the footage was as much about saving time as it was about protecting her sanity. Could she relive the tour without wondering where it all went wrong?

At the end of one file, she closed the window to return to the list. The guy who showed her the ropes had opened the first one. There had to be something more interesting than hours and hours of people dancing, drinking, and fawning over Zairn and his celebrity friends.

Lomond. One file with just his name. Why was she

such a masochist? The question popped into her head at the same time she clicked to open the file.

The still frame was set on him. Sheesh. This was a bad idea.

Still, she pressed play.

Hatfield's voice rose. "…we'll get a sense of—"

"Just get on with it," Zairn said, doing something on his phone before returning it to his pocket.

Where was that? With the backdrop, it was difficult to tell. At least it was until she noted the tie. The one she'd tied for him. Boston. They were in Boston.

Hatfield ran through his pre-prepared questions. Much like hers, there was a history lesson. Zairn's answers were short, concise, practiced.

"Boundaries," she murmured, propping her chin on the heel of her hand.

"And Miss Kyst, what are your first impressions?"

First impressions? By then they'd sensed the fire between them and woken up together.

For a flicker of a beat, something crossed Zairn's expression. An odd light that hadn't been there before. He shut it down instantly.

"She's an asset to the team," he said. "We can trust that she'll do what's required of her."

"To report back to the masses about what really goes on behind the scenes?"

"Exactly."

A break in the recording startled her. Suddenly, Zairn was sitting in a different position and sans tie.

"There's an energy about her," Zairn said. "I'm sure you've noticed."

"Yeah," Hatfield said, a laugh in his voice. "How would you sum her up for all those people out there eager to get to know her?"

"Roxanna Kyst doesn't fit into many categories. Getting to know her is a privilege. She's kind and funny and…" His tongue salved his lower lip. "Words like that are her, but they don't fit… They're not enough. You can't know Roxanna Kyst until you're in her orbit. It's not possible to articulate just how… immersive she is. Her power comes from her heart. How she cares… even when she doesn't."

"You sound impressed."

"I am," Zairn said. "Some might consider her life sheltered. Compared to my world, it certainly is. Yet, she adapts. Takes everything in her stride. If something needs to be done, she does it. She doesn't complain or simper, she's strong. Stronger than she gives herself credit for."

Another break in recording. A new light. Different shirt.

"There is no life after Roxanna Kyst," Zairn said, sincere in the depth of his tone. "No one can be the same again. Once you've experienced her light, you're a different person."

"Agreed," Hatfield said.

Zairn continued. "She's impervious to the world. To anything it throws at her. One smile and she… It's like she can read minds. She plays and torments, but her wit comes from a place of joy. Her mouth is sometimes faster than her mind. Every atom of her is racing the others. To say that she's beautiful would be an insulting understatement. To say she snares those around her with her energy does her an injustice. She's captivating. The most enticing temptation. Rare in her determination." His eyes flicked away from the man asking the questions. "Even in her lowest moment, she raises herself up. Roxanna Kyst sees the world, in her own unique way. Her mind captures the heart of everyone who meets her. She's genuine, which is why her streams work so well. Her whole self gives the rest of us something to aspire too."

Snap. The picture changed again. This time, Zairn was laughing, somehow lighter than he'd been in the previous shot.

"It's not sexual voyeurism." That was her voice, somewhere behind the camera.

"Get out of here," Zairn said, his attention tracking around suggesting he was watching her leave.

"She's everywhere, isn't she?" Hatfield asked.

"You have no idea," Zairn muttered, adjusting his position to focus on Hatfield. "Where were we?"

"She fits in well. With your people."

"That's a testament to her," Zairn said. "She's personable."

"She's quite a contrast to your usual style."

"My usual style?"

"The women from your past tend to be less approachable. More distant. Exist on some sort of pedestal."

"Hey, let me tell you…" Zairn said, flashing another smile. "If anyone tried to put Roxanna Kyst on a pedestal, she'd kick that shit down and tell you to eat it… We have to keep our admiration on the down low."

Both men laughed.

"You know, you're right," Hatfield said. "She isn't the type of woman interested in being worshiped."

"If she wanted it, there would be a queue of men ready to accommodate her."

"She's been quite a hit, with those she's met in the clubs. How many guys ask you for her number every night?"

"Plenty," Zairn said. "Don't know any who'd make me part with it. Roxie might be strong in her independence, but she needs to be protected too. Not that she would admit it."

"That why you bundled her up after the Sydney stream?"

"She was sick in Sydney and didn't need to deal with the media."

"But you reached out to her family, her roommates, you protected them while protecting her."

"Roxie has a bigger heart than she realizes. People mean something to her. The invulnerable thing is an act so convincing that even she believes it. She's stubborn too and won't ask for support."

"And that's where you come in?"

"I'd never do anything to hurt her," Zairn said. "But, yes, sometimes she does need others acting in her interest. In my fortunate position, I can provide her with whatever she needs. Whatever she wants."

"You respect her. Care about her."

"I do," Zairn said, his brow sure. "I challenge any

man not to. Roxie needs space to be her own person. Balancing that with a need to defend and shield her is difficult. The idea of figuring out what she wants, committing herself to one path, terrifies her. She wants to be a part of something and to be her own person too. You have to tread carefully. Spook her and she'd disappear in a flash. Her instinct when cornered is to lash out and build her walls higher. The time she spends exuding her indestructible air distracts her from looking within. From realizing what she really wants."

The next break took her to a completely different moment. One she remembered from living it. Them. Dancing. In Rome. From across the room, they were filmed holding each other, moving to music that didn't exist.

Everything had been perfect. Then they went back to the hotel and had sex. Everything went wrong after that. Everything. All because…

Why had it gone wrong?

Because of her stupid mouth. Her stupid inability to relax and let herself live her feelings.

The way she'd shrugged him off in Rome was hurtful. She hadn't intended it to be. When he'd spoken to the press about them, she argued the situation would've been different in reverse. So would Rome. If they'd slept together and he'd shut her down the next day, he'd be a player, a cad, an asshole.

Zairn Lomond was anything but an asshole.

Yes, he could be stubborn and domineering. So could she. They could be as bad as each other. Yet, at New Year, there had only been one thing capable of erasing her fears and doubts. Him. Zairn Lomond.

The same man who'd heard her say there were only two choices: end it or stay secret. He hadn't wanted that. He'd spoken about outing them in New York after just one night together. Whatever they were, it was real to him. He loved her. He'd declared it in front of the world, proud of his feelings.

"—*for when you're ready.*"

She was so switched on, yet tone-deaf to them.

Rising so fast that the chair shot away from behind her, Roxie couldn't believe that she'd…

"*Are you happy? When we're together, you and me, are you*

happy?"

He'd asked in her bed before his Ackley meeting…

What had Toria said in New York?

*"I can't believe I have to spell this out for you. You, Rox!
You're supposed to be switched on."*

Everyone seemed so…

"It's about the man, genius."

"Oh my God," she whispered, forgetting the footage.

He loved her. He'd loved her since before their eleven
days and Rome and… Sydney. Her fingers ran into the hair by
her temples. He loved her, and he'd known it forever. How
had she missed it? He loved her before they had sex and
she'd…

He'd loved her on the Zee-Jet. When he said *anything
you want*, he'd meant it. Even his heart was there for the taking.
Losing him had hurt. That was why she'd been so sluggish and
depressed after leaving the tour. Why she'd been reluctant to
see him in New York…

And in New York… when they'd… and she'd…

No other man featured in her thoughts; she hadn't
looked at one since before him. And Porter… it was so
different. What she felt for… That was why she couldn't find
her balance. Why the only thing that could make her feel
was…

"Shit," she said, grabbing her purse to flee the editing
suite.

She needed a plan. Some way to show him that he…
A phone call wouldn't do it, even if she did have a number
that worked.

No.

That wasn't them.

They were… bigger than mundane realities. He'd
stood up in front of the world to make his declaration.

She had to do the same.

Rushing to the elevator they'd passed on the way in,
she pressed the highest number and waited. Would it go all
the way to the top? It didn't matter. If there was one thing
Roxie was good at, it was being determined… Zairn would
call it being stubborn. She smiled. He loved her anyway.

The elevator doors opened. The moment she stepped out, a beefy guy in a security uniform appeared in front of her.

"Where's your pass?"

"My pass?" she asked, glancing around. Looked like an executive floor, though she didn't see the required man. Hooking the strap of her purse onto her shoulder, she cocked a hip. Life required the ridiculous sometimes. "Do you know who I am?" He faltered. "I'm sure you get a lot of celebrity wannabes trying to sneak past the guard." Damn her sass, but it had its place. "You might have seen my boyfriend on the news declaring his love for me to the entire planet." Right before he'd broken up with her. Thank goodness he hadn't clued the press in on that. "Zairn Lomond."

A flicker of recognition lit his eyes. "You're Roxanne Kyst."

"Roxanna, but whatever," she said, waving a dismissive hand. "How pissed do you think his best friend will be when he finds out you barred my entry?"

"Knox Collier. You're here to see—"

"Yes," she said. "I'd appreciate it if you'd lead the way."

Because there was a chance Knox would take one look and get her ass tossed out anyway. At least this way, the vigilant security guy wouldn't lose his job for listening to her.

The hair on her neck prickled as they passed various rooms behind glass walls and partitions. Everyone was interested. Why was she there? Was she who they thought she was?

Yep. She was.

The security guard took her up some stairs and whispered to a woman at a desk while Roxie waited. It was okay. They could whisper. She spotted her target, Knox Collier in a glass office, on the phone, back to the door.

That was all she needed.

Passing the security guy and the assistant, Roxie went toward the office, ignoring the pleas of those behind her demanding that she wait.

Walking into Knox's office, Roxie wouldn't back down. This was important.

Knox turned and noticed her just as the assistant came in.

"I'm sorry, sir, she—"

"It's okay," Knox said, then spoke into the phone. "I'll call you back." The assistant left. Roxie glanced around to check they were alone as Knox hung up the phone. "Roxanna."

Striding across the room, she dumped her purse on the desk. "I need you to pull some strings." Curiosity lowered his brow. "Please. At the very least, I promise you'll be ensuring my humiliation eclipses your friend's. You know the press conference was bullshit. You know he ended things."

"Yeah," Knox said. "Which makes me wonder why I should help his ex."

"Because if all goes right, I'll be his future. Please, Knox. Asking for help isn't easy for me."

He exhaled. "What do you need?"

One thing, and she knew exactly how to show him that.

FORTY-THREE

"WELCOME OUR NEXT GUEST… Roxanna Kyst!"

The audience went nuts. Maybe not on a Zairn level, but more than she'd have expected. Stepping through the curtain, she waved to the people cheering as Drew Harvey came rushing over to do the LA air kiss thing.

"You've got balls," Drew Harvey whispered in her ear, then leaned back to show his grin.

Her smile stayed in place as he ushered her across to the couch. She waved once more before tucking her skirt against her thighs and seating herself in the spot Zairn had occupied more than once.

"Wow, thank you," she said.

"You're popular," Drew Harvey said. "And we've got to thank you for stepping in last minute."

Because the guest who was supposed to be on the show had canceled? Yeah, that wasn't completely true, and they both knew it.

"Not at all, it's my pleasure."

"You're hot," he said. When her head tilted, he laughed. "You are gorgeous, but I meant you're in the news, at the top of the A-list."

Roxie semi-nodded. "I suppose you could say that."

"I did," he said. "Which was a lot less than your boyfriend said. Did he give you any talk show tips?"

"I can only follow his example."

"Great! That's what I wanted to hear. He's been forthcoming in recent days, especially about your relationship. You're in town to work on the documentary edits?"

"That's right."

"You weren't tempted to finish the Retrospective Tour?"

"I go where I'm needed," she said. "Crimson is important to me. I plan to do whatever I can for the Rouge organization. To promote and extend our hospitality as needed."

"As a sort of Crimson ambassador."

"Yes," she said, thinking that was an excellent way to put it. "A Crimson ambassador. Seems the least I can do after all Crimson has given me."

"You traveled the world with Crimson."

"I did."

"And met Zairn."

Her smile flourished. "Yes."

"Not to be underestimated," Drew Harvey said, edging a little closer. "Now I know he'd be unhappy if I put you on the spot—"

"Didn't you see his last interview in LA? He doesn't censor me. I can say what I like whenever I like."

"And what would you like to say, Roxie?" Drew Harvey asked, genuine in his smile. "Zairn was reluctant to discuss your relationship when he was last here on the couch."

"It wasn't an easy time. We'd just said goodbye to each other. Neither of us knew how we felt at that point…" She took a breath, admitting to herself that wasn't entirely true. "I didn't know how I felt at that point."

"But your physical relationship was over."

"Yes. We had no contact at all between that point and New Year."

"So it was over?"

She nodded. "It was."

His smile rose to something saucier. "But that changed in New York?"

"Yes," she said on a quiet laugh. "I will spare you the details." The audience groaned in disappointment. She laughed. "We… reconnected." Stroking the arm of the couch, she focused on the soft fabric. "Zairn can be overwhelming in his perfection. He doesn't try to be everything I need, he just… is. He says I'm quick…" She side-glanced at the audience. "Which is his way of saying I have a fresh mouth." Everyone laughed. "But he's always one step ahead of me."

"You don't seem to resent that."

"No," she said, making eye contact. "I didn't even realize it. He's so much more… aware than I am. So much more attuned to what's going on inside him. More in touch with his emotions."

"A modern man," Drew Harvey drawled like it was a joke.

To be polite, she laughed. "In some ways, yes. In others…" Pushing her shoulders back, she sassed with her own smile. "He's positively primitive."

"Oh," Drew Harvey drew out the syllable.

"Being with Zairn changed me and my outlook. I just didn't… He gives me carte blanche to say whatever I want… and I know there are questions. I was mad when he spoke to the press about us without consulting me. But I know why he did it now… Sometimes something is so big that it's just impossible to suppress. That's what we are. He is the sun which my world revolves around."

Using his words earned her a kind of collective swoon.

"You love him?" Drew Harvey asked.

Without a drop of uncertainty, she held her head high. "I do. I love Zairn with every ounce of my being. I love him more than I've ever loved anyone else… My life would be nothing without him."

Though Drew Harvey seemed happy to hear that, he cleared his throat. "Some might say it's easy to feel that way about a billionaire."

"Money means nothing in our relationship. If he gave

away every cent, I'd still love him. My future is with him."

"In Chicago?"

"Most likely New York," she said. "Though there will be a lot of travel for both of us. Promoting and protecting Rouge is a full-time job. Maybe I'll be able to take some of that burden from him."

"How do your friends and family feel about—"

"My roommates and I have discussed it. Wherever Z and I end up, my girls will move with me. As for my family? They love Zairn, he's very respectful. Any man who shows respect for his daughter wins points with my father." She laughed. "It's possible my dad's frustrated we haven't got ourselves together faster."

"Getting yourselves together? Does that mean more than living together? Are there wedding bells on the horizon?"

She shrugged. "We'll get married whenever he wants to get married, but we'll put off having kids for a while."

He blew out a breath. "Zairn Lomond, the family man, did anyone think it possible?"

While others in the room enjoyed the joke, her response was more subdued. "A lot of what people think about him is inaccurate. He's caring. Sensitive. He understands women and knows how to listen. He's loyal and thorough. Hosting people may be his job, but that attention to detail doesn't go away the moment he steps out of the club."

"We're learning so much about him tonight," Drew said, slapping the arms of his chair. "I think it's time to bring out the surprise." Surprise? What was he…? She hadn't been told about any surprise. Drew Harvey thrust himself onto his feet. "Ladies and gentlemen, put your hands together and welcome the man himself… Zairn Lomond."

Oh shit. The curtain moved and… yeah, that was him there, greeting the audience. Drew Harvey went over to shake his hand. Damnit. Everything could… Why was he there? Why had no one told her that…?

The men whispered to each other as they crossed to the couch. Zairn shook the hand of the other guest. Someone she'd completely ignored. Then he looked at her. Oh… fuck.

Her heart was racing. Was she sweating? Was he about to slap her down in front of the cameras? They'd play the footage over and over and…

He stepped closer and stroked her hair, his hand sweeping down to her chin to raise it higher.

"Lola," he murmured before leaning in to kiss her.

The room went wild. At least, it probably did. Her ears rang. Her heart pumped so fast that the whoosh of blood surging through her stretched the veins inside. His tongue touched her lip and she opened for him. Shit. He was kissing her, like really kissing her, there in front of the whole world. Grabbing his lapels, she pulled him closer, welcoming and encouraging the very public display of affection.

"Whoa, okay, geez," Drew Harvey said, shattering their moment. "There are kids watching."

The show aired at midnight, so she doubted it. Still, Zairn sat on the couch, doing his usual of taking her hips to pull her down next to him. As she crossed her legs, his arm draped across them. Their natural state. Together. Damn, it felt so much better to be free and public.

"You've been busy, man," Drew Harvey said, leaning over to hit the arm of the couch. "Busy. Busy."

"Yeah, you'd think," Zairn said, glancing at her.

Why was he smiling like that? This felt… What was going on?

"Hear you're getting married soon," Drew Harvey said.

"Apparently," Zairn said, earning a laugh from the room.

The last thing she wanted was to come across as a crazy bunny boiler… or any *more* like a crazy bunny boiler. "I said whenever he wanted."

Zairn leaned in to kiss the side of her head.

"Weren't you supposed to be in Tokyo?"

"I was," Zairn said. "For a few hours, did the bit, met the Experience winners…"

"And then jumped a jet back to sunny California? Just can't stay away."

Stroking her leg, Zairn wasn't shy about pushing her

skirt a little higher. "Not when my woman's around, no."

Tokyo. He couldn't have been there for more than a few hours. That would mean... that he'd come back to California before she even saw the footage. Knox couldn't have told him about her plan. Not to bring him back from Tokyo anyway.

"So you got chewed out for revealing your relationship to the press," Drew Harvey said. "Then she comes on here and declares your future together."

"Yeah," Zairn said. "Whenever she was ready, I was going to be waiting." *Empress—for when you're ready.* Oh, wow, that was what it meant. When she was ready to be his. All the way. To belong to him and Crimson and their whole life together. "Which reminds me..." He slipped a hand into his inside pocket to produce... her ring box. He held it in front of her. "You left this on the plane."

She left it on the plane. She'd told him it was there because she assumed they were done. The hint of vulnerability in his eye wouldn't be visible to the camera, not from that angle. Did he think she'd reject him in front of the world? Why wouldn't he think that? She hadn't exactly been the most selfless.

"What is it?" Drew Harvey asked.

She smiled and put her thumb on the lid. "It's my Empress Ruby."

Instead of taking it out, she opened the lid and then held out her hand... more specifically, her ring finger. When their eyes met and she relaxed her head, he smiled and took the ring out to slip it on. It fit. He'd gotten it resized. Damn, how had he known...? When had he noticed? Details really were where it all happened.

The room went wild. She got it. Her insides were just as elated. Wow, what a ride... Now it was time for their something spectacular.

TO BE CONTINUED...

Thank you for reading this tale!
If you can, please take the time to review.

~

Ask your local library for more Scarlett Finn
novels!

~

For all things Scarlett Finn
check out:

www.scarlettfinn.com

BOOK THREE

SCARLETT FINN

OUT NOW!

Printed in Great Britain
by Amazon